GRIM SOLACE

"The writing was smooth, fluid and beautiful at times. It never failed to create an awesome atmosphere. A solid book with a very interesting premise. 90/100."
—THE WEATHERWAX REPORT

"Galley has created a fascinating world that feels rife with stories that could be mined across multiple series. Its history is rich with detail and there're so many avenues to be explored."
—ADAM WELLER, FANTASY BOOK REVIEW

"*Chasing Graves* is a dark, compelling entry into a trilogy."
—ROCKSTARLIT BOOKASYLUM

"Unique, fantastic worldbuilding, interesting characters, and much more."
—THE FANTASY INN

"A heavy hitter, this follow-up to a gruesome, sometimes funny, and riveting tale, Grim Solace is a runaway winner."
—GRIMMEDIAN

BEN GALLEY

GRIM
SOLACE

THE CHASING GRAVES TRILOGY 2

"This book is a work of fiction, but some works of fiction contain perhaps more truth than first intended, and therein lies the magic."

– Anonymous

GSHB1 First Edition 2022
ISBN: 978-1-8381625-8-0
Published by BenGalley.com

Edited by Andrew Lowe & Laura M. Hughes
Map Design by Ben Galley
Cover Illustration by Chris Cold
Cover Design & Interior Layout by STK·Kreations

For James, Lucy and Ben.

MORE FANTASY FROM
BEN GALLEY

GRIM SOLACE

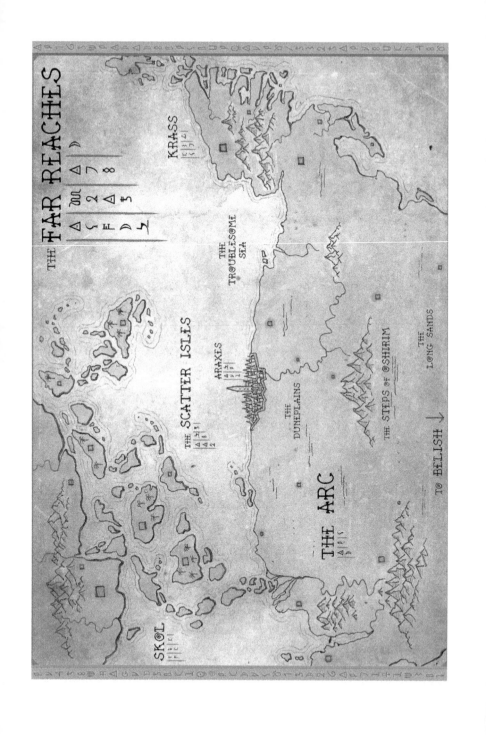

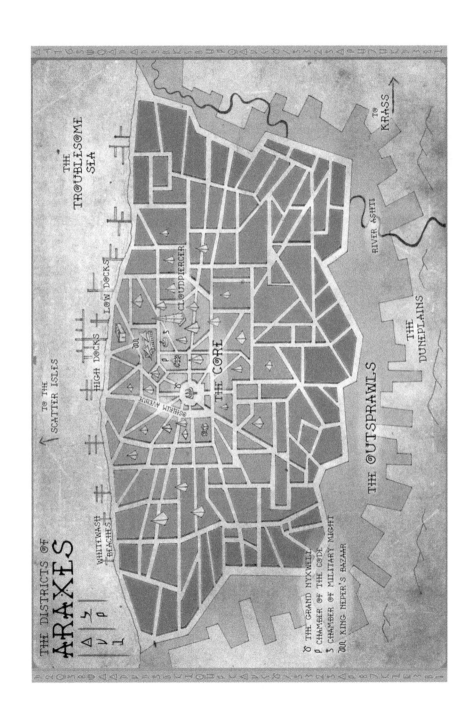

TENETS OF THE BOUND DEAD

They must die in turmoil.

They must be bound with copper half-coin and water of the Nyx.

They must be bound within forty days.

They shall be bound to whomever holds their coin.

They are slaved to their master's bidding.

They must bring their masters no harm.

They shall not express opinions nor own property.

They shall never know freedom unless it is gifted to them.

CHAPTER 1
SAME OLD BEGINNINGS

The first shade ever to be bound was a man
named Asham, stabbed through the heart
by a man who, after founding the Nyxites,
would later come to establish the Cult of Sesh.
Asham survived four hundred years in service
before he was rewarded his half-coin and
immediately sought freedom in the void.

FROM 'A REACH HISTORY' BY GAERVIN JUBB

S TARTING THE DAY WITH A street awash with blood and gore was sure to demolish any good mood. Fortunately for Scrutiniser Heles, it had been five years, maybe more, since her mood could remotely be classed as "good." The best she hoped for these days was "mildly disgruntled."

'This fucking city,' she muttered, poking a dismembered finger with her black boot. It looked like an uncooked sausage, one that even a street dog couldn't stomach more than half of.

A retching sound distracted her, coming from a young man with a face that was swiftly turning green. Milky vomit dribbled from his lips, mixing with the pool of ichor at his feet. Some had made its way onto the lapel of his proctor's livery.

'First day?' she asked the lad.

'Second.'

'If you don't stop vomiting by the tenth day, look for another job.'

'Mhm,' he said, before another heave saw him flying into the mouth a nearby alleyway.

There was no mirth on Heles' lips; just the downward slant the years had carved into them. She began to pick her way through the blood-drenched streets, counting the pools and smears where bodies and pieces had been dragged. Where the blood had dried, she spotted the hoofmarks of donkeys and the sand-smeared ruts of carts. Beside a scrap of skin, complete with long blond hair still attached, she spotted a dirtied handkerchief. Heles reached for it, eyeing the grin of red across its soft white fibres.

'Sloppy job, this,' she said, hearing tentative footsteps behind her. The young man had recovered, and was busy trying to scratch the stain from his black and silver threads with a threadbare handkerchief. Some vomit had made its way onto the Chamber seal. He scrubbed at it furiously.

'Desperate,' Heles added.

'I wouldn't know, Scrutiniser.'

Heles examined him. He only wore one neck tattoo, given his rank. His trews were baggy, his collar askew. The greenish hue clung to his cheeks. 'Now you do. Come then, Proctor...?'

'Jym.'

'What a peculiar name. Come then, Proctor Jym. Impress me.'

Jym took a shaky breath as he forced himself to survey the grisly scene, as if the vomit might pounce again. 'Murder on a mass scale. No bodies, which means soulstealers.'

'Or made to look like soulstealers.'

The man tapped his teeth. 'But the ruts of carts?'

'Good.'

'Perhaps it went wrong? An alarm was raised, and they had to be quick. Hence the... sloppiness.' His eyes were fixed on the piece of skin and hair, and would not be torn away.

'How many taken?'

'Seven?'

'Nine. Look at the smears on the walls. The gutters have taken their blood. Who were the victims?'

'City folk, I'd assume?'

'Then you'd assume wrongly.' She held up the kerchief. 'Scatter Isles cotton.'

'Scatterfolk traders, then?'

'Or...'

Jym sighed. Heles looked to the sapphire sky while she waited. Orange tendrils of sand streaked the air where a sandstorm had blown in from the south. The factory smokestacks leaned under its duress. The wind was rising slowly, making ripples in the glassy pools of blood, still only half dry.

'Or refugees from the wars out in the Isles?'

'Refugees is right. Thread's poorly woven, fraying. A trader is more concerned of his or her appearance. And?' Heles gestured to the lost finger. 'Callouses. Hard labour. Hardest work a trader does is count silvers, and that isn't enough for callouses.'

'I suppose,' mumbled the proctor.

Heles stood over him, using her height to intimidate him. 'Who recruited you?'

'Volunteer, ma'am.'

'Unusual. Why?'

'My brother and sister were taken just like this. In Far District.'

'Outsprawler, then?'

'Yes, ma'am.'

'I see.'

Heles swept to the other side of the street, striding carelessly through blood patches and stains. Several onlookers had gathered in the mouth of an alleyway to look at the mess and tut disapprovingly.

'You gawkers see or hear anything this morning? Or last night?' she challenged them.

One balding man took offence. 'Who you calling gawkers? That's all you lot do. Gawk and rub your chins. Nothing ever comes of it.'

His equally balding wife chimed in. 'Always getting here after it 'appens, you Scruters.'

Heles shooed them away, not caring for their presence any more. In a city drenched in crime, tongues still refused to wag. It was as infuriating now as it had been when she first pledged herself to the Code twelve years ago.

She was about to turn back to the scene when she caught another flash of red in the alley. Not gore this time, but cloth. A glowing face smiled politely.

Heles approached cautiously. It was at least a year since she had seen the crimson garb of a cultist. 'You're taking a risk. I'd wager we're a street away from the Core Districts.'

'Then I assume there is no issue me standing here. One street away.'

'Fine.'

'Quite the mess,' the shade sighed.

'And what would you know about it?'

'No more than you.'

Heles bared her teeth, like a desert wolf would smile. 'Don't your kind excel at gathering information? If so, it's about time you shared some of it with the Chamber of the Code. Maybe the Cult could do some good for once, instead of lurking in dark alleyways, being unnecessarily mysterious.'

The sister took a moment to adjust her hood. Heles could see the shade's eyes examining the tattoos on her hands and bare neck, the dark swirls of her office. 'You are simply jealous we don't admit your kind. And we prefer *Church* these days.'

'I'm happy having a beating heart instead, thank you. Maybe that's what you lot are in dire need of. Now, if your Church isn't going to be of any help, you should move along, Sister—'

'*Enlightened* Sister, Scrutiniser Heles. Enlightened Sister Liria.' The shade smiled as she walked away. 'We'll see each other again soon.'

Heles thumbed her nostrils and scowled, wondering, not for the first time, why the royals hadn't completely eradicated the Cult of Sesh. Only once the shade had disappeared did it dawn on Heles that she hadn't told the sister her name.

'Scrutiniser Heles!' came a shout. A man was waving to her from the other side of the street, where thicker crowds had gathered to gawk, like pigeons around a muddied loaf.

Murder was nothing new for a denizen of the City of Countless Souls, but it was a distraction nonetheless. People could always be relied on to stare at tragedy. It made them feel better about themselves; to still be a breathing bag of skin rather than a pool of blood on a dusty flagstone.

'Well, Jym,' Heles said, turning back to the proctor. 'Shame to hear of your family, but everybody's got their own dead. Bought, butchered or lost to age, we've all got them. You're not special, Jym, and the quicker you learn that, the easier it'll be for you here.'

Heles swept away from him, buttoning her black robes about her. She was halfway to the waving man when Jym called after her.

'Who did you lose?'

Heles didn't break her stride. 'Everybody.'

The waving man wore the blue sash and dotted face tattoos of a clerk. A lower rank than her, and he bowed to prove it. 'Chamberlain Rebene has summoned you.'

'Can't he see I'm busy?'

The clerk flapped his mouth as he followed Heles' gesturing hand to the wash of blood. 'How could he… I… He would like to see you immediately.'

Heles sighed. 'Where?'

'In his offices at the Chamber, naturally.'

'Where else? It would do you dusty fuckers some good to get out onto the streets once in a while, remember what it is you work for.'

The man's cheeks twitched as he cycled through a range of expressions, each more unsure than the last. 'So, is that a yes?'

'He's my superior, is he not?'

'Yes, Scrutiniser.'

'Then lead the way, man. Stop wasting my time.'

'Yes, Scrutiniser.'

Through the strangled streets they strode; scrutiniser in front, clerk struggling to keep up with her long legs and sweeping gait. Heles remembered when the crowds parted for her black Chamber robes. Now, only her height and practiced scowl moved them aside. And her elbows, for good measure.

The Chamber of the Code was a huge building. Not in height, like the Cloudpiercer, but in width and bulk. A giant pyramid capped with gold stood at its core, with twelve wings peeling off from its square base like the teeth of a cog. Each of those must have stretched ten floors into the sky, studded with windows and arrow slits. History had it the Chamber was once the emperor's fortress, until the nobles turned to height to prove their worth and status. Now, it was a warren of overlapping corridors and dead ends, of honeycomb rooms and cavern halls full of files and men sneezing at dust.

Heles circled the building until she reached the main entrance. She lost the clerk in the endless queues, full of people clutching scrolls, and shades trying to shield themselves from the sand kicked up by the growing breeze. He no doubt scurried back to his desk, already scorched by his brief outing in the Arctian sun.

Every day, the unfortunates, the slighted and the outraged came to bleat their claims and file their complaints. Every day they formed their cacophonous winding lines, shuffling forwards maybe a dozen yards, maybe two dozen, before sunset shut the Chamber doors. The next day, they came back to queue again, and so on. A few faces she spied had been coming for almost a year now. Such was the backlog of the mighty Chamber of the Code, sole authority on matters of indenturement.

Inside the wide, arched doors, the vacuous atrium was marble cool and full of clamouring voices. Heles wormed through the lines, full of figures in foreign-cut clothes and a spectrum of skin tones, from milky pale to the darkest charcoal. A few desert nomads stood in a group, taller than the crowds even though their backs were as curved as longbows. They looked miserable despite their vibrant cloth wrappings. The nomads chattered away in an unknown dialect, but all Heles paid attention to were the stubs of short horns poking from their foreheads, and their goatish eyes, the pupils of which looked like slots meant for coins.

At the centre of the atrium was an immense core of marble and steel. Sweeping stairs led up into the Chamber's countless rooms. A seawall of desks parted the crowded marble expanse, dividing the offended from the black-clad officials. Heles caught their broken sentences.

'But I've been waiting for six months!'

'The Code clearly states a three-year wait.'

'Is there nothing you can do?'

'He stole me, curse it! Stole me!'

'Permits for the white feather is the other line, I'm afraid.'

'My children!'

Heles was deaf to it all. She strode past the desks, met the challenges of the guards, and passed into the innards of the grand building. Three flights of stairs took her to a vaulted hall where towering stacks of papyrus rose from every desk. One of several halls within the Chamber, here sat the great pile-up of the city's Code-related crimes. Unfortunately for the Chamber, that was pretty much the city's only brand of crime. Every claim, every complaint, every accusation and petition – all of it entered through these halls and waited years to escape.

To Heles, it looked as if they were recreating the skyline of Araxes in papyrus. A good number of the stacks rose to scratch the marble roof. Here and there, wooden stairs and scaffolding encircled the bigger towers. Clerks and proctors waded through the paper canyons, or wobbled up high, plucking through scrolls piled on lofty, buckled shelves. Others ran wheelbarrows piled high with files through the maze of desks. Their job, like hers, seemed never-ending, and therefore without satisfaction.

At the foot of one tower she passed, a crew of clerks were busy shoring up a desk with bricks. It wasn't unheard of for a desk to crumble under the weight of countless documents, and come crashing down. If there was anything that introduced more clerical work and time to the Chamber's backlog, it was a tower of a thousand files exploding. Not to mention those who had been unfortunate enough to be splattered under their weight.

It took Heles seventeen flights of stairs, a rickety lift and innumerable corridors to reach the offices of the chamberlain. Good silver had been spent on tall doors, drapes and gold leaf, when it could have been spent on scrutinisers, proctors, or perhaps diminishing the soaring piles of claims in the halls below. Heles glowered at the patterned marble as she dug into it with her boot heels.

The ring of guards around Rebene's desk parted to admit her, and she stamped her foot as she halted. Chamberlain Rebene looked up from his papyrus, looking almost surprised. The man was perpetually sweating, even in the cool of the Chamber. His black hair, normally slicked to the side to cover his balding patches, fell in greased curls.

'Scrutiniser Heles, reporting as ordered.'

Rebene placed his writing reed in its inkwell. 'I didn't expect you so soon, Scrutiniser.'

'The clerk did say "immediately," sir.'

'Forgive me. I am not used to such punctuality.'

'This city seems to have forgotten the word, sir. But I have not.'

Rebene leaned back in his grand chair of mahogany and silver palm frond. 'And that is precisely why I summoned you. We have an issue, as I'm sure you're aware.'

'We have many issues, Chamberlain. To which do you refer?'

'The disappearance and possible soulstealing of several nobles. A handful of medium-level tors and tals.'

Heles had no love for noble blood. She couldn't respect those who idly watched the poor and the dead from their lofty windows while drinking from golden goblets. 'Allow me to guess: the Cloud Court have clicked their fingers now it's their kind getting murdered. Funny, that. They don't normally spare a drop of piss when it's commoners or tourists.'

There fell an awkward silence. One of the guards cleared his throat.

'Careful, Heles. I've demoted others for kinder words, but I'll give you leeway considering the recent death of your colleague, Scrutiniser Damses.'

Heles bit off the end of his sentence. 'Murder. The recent *murder* of Scrutiniser Damses. Nobody has a knife shoved through their teeth and down their throat by accident.'

'Fine. Murder.' Rebene sighed. 'In any case, he was a good man.'

'He was a terrible man. A drinker, a cheat, and as faithful to his wife as a vulture is to a corpse. But he was a fine scrutiniser. He believed in the salvation of this city, and that's hard to find these days.'

'As do you, I hear?'

'Passionately, sir.'

'Well, these recent developments may give you a chance to bring such a fable into existence.'

Heles cocked her head, bringing her eyes down from the back wall to his.

'In fact, it's Her Highness the empress-in-waiting who's asked me to solve this matter. To put a stop to these disappearances… or murders. Find out who's behind them and hunt them down. Bring them to justice any way we can: subterfuge, bribes, torture, the lot. Paperwork be damned. I've decided I want you leading this matter.'

'Why?'

Rebene templed his fingers. 'Because, Heles, despite what the rest say about you, nobody has cleared as many claims nor sent as many stealers to the boiling pots as you have in the last ten years.'

'Twelve. And do you expect me to do this on my own?'

'Hardly. I have other scrutinisers across the city tackling this as well as you. The princess and the emperor have provided silver.' He took a moment to wet his lips. 'And shades for districts outside the Core.'

Heles almost laughed. 'Shades? Working for the Chamber?'

'I don't like it either, but these are dire times—'

'You're right about that. I bet Ghoor and the other magistrates jumped at the chance to spend more time on his bloated arses.'

Rebene flushed. 'Mind your tongue, Scrutiniser!' The cracking of his voice withered him, and he pressed his sweaty palms together, prayer-like. 'Do we have an agreement, then? I can leave this important matter in your hands?'

Heles put her fists to his desk and leaned over the sea of papyrus that adorned it. 'I want independence. Autonomy, I think they call it. And first say over resources.'

'No scrutiniser has ever—'

'Autonomy, or you can pass this job onto Scrutiniser Faph and the others and watch the tors and tals disappear one by one. Don't call me the best and then treat me like the rest.'

'This is serious, Heles.'

'Deadly serious, sir.'

Rebene threw up his hands. 'Fine. You have it.'

An ordinary person might have grinned, or at least smiled, but Heles curled her lip. With a squeak of boot leather on mosaicked marble, she left the chamberlain to his scribbling and headed for the bowels of the great Chamber building. To the torture holes with their white plaster-wall corridors filled with screams. They were a good place to glean some rumours from the underbelly of Araxes. Plus, there was nothing like seeing a criminal suffer to make her feel marginally better about the world.

CHAPTER 2
A FRESH HELL

When examining the rise and fall of empires,
one forgets the forces of fashion. I do not
mean threads and silks, but the power of
obsession. Indenturement was a fashion
once, and it dissolved religion. Then came
phantoms, ripping souls from animals. That
led to deadbinding and strangebinding.
Despite those fashions being banned, each
further dehumanised the soul and solidified
the Arc's obsession with death. Now look at
it: the so-called greatest empire ever known.
More dead than alive. More wishing for
breath than taking it. I fear their greed will
one day overtake my borders.

WRITINGS OF KONIN FELUST, PHILOSOPHER
AND CURRENT RULER OF KRASS

THE WARDROBE WAS FANCY. GILDED, carved and solidly made. There was barely a joint to be seen in its construction, and only one thin sliver of a seam between its doors to peek through. Not that I could see much through the rough sacking that covered my head. Just a featureless line of a grey, unlit room. There was just my glow, blue wood, and iron spotted with black rust. Nothing to tell me of my exact whereabouts.

Nowhere good, I know that.

The sacking over my head had convinced me of that rather quickly.

Somewhere I shouldn't be.

That, too, was obvious.

A tower or mansion.

I'd heard the squeak of feet on marble. Felt the ascent up stairs. Many stairs.

But whose?

I was sure I would find out. Hopefully sooner rather than later.

The manner in which I had been seized and attacked pointed to a theft. A ghost-napping, we called it in Krass. It was like stealing cattle, or sheep, but it came with a higher penalty. It was much the same in the Arc, I was sure. In any case, I fumed. I had been robbed twice. Physically and personally. To land myself an opportunity for freedom only to have Vex interfere was infuriating. That eyeless bastard of a ghost would get his, I swore it. Either I or Horix would see to that. I had a sneaky suspicion it was the latter, and felt no disappointment in that. Justice at the hands of others can still be justice well served.

All I could focus on now was not thinking of how much the wardrobe felt like the sarcophagus. Whenever I reminded myself, I was thrown into a cyclical argument of not thinking about it, and therefore thinking it, over and over.

Mercifully, at last I heard a scrape of a key in a lock. I tensed and wondered briefly whether I should come out swinging. Before I made my decision, just as I was leaning away from violence, the door was wrenched open and a bright light stunned me.

Lamplight filled the room, making the stone and furnishings glow yellow and an inordinate amount of metal sparkle. At first I thought I had been stashed in an armoury. I eyed the room between blinks, and found it somewhat lacking compared to Horix's tower. This place was still opulent, but the widow had been classier.

It was no armoury. It was a sitting room disguised as some sort of tasteless gallery. Glass and stone and metal mixed freely. Curves clashed with corners. Naked sculptures had been draped with furs and dressed in silks. Ancient things poked from the walls between gaudy nomad tapestries. Rugs of all colours and threads battled for domination of the floor. Decorative weapons jutted from hooks in the low ceiling. I counted a Krass halberd, a bow of oryx horn, and a black sword on the mantle of a fireplace. In the corner, a full suit of armour had been encrusted with gems.

The man was clearly a collector of some kind. As a thief, I would have cheered; this was the sort of house that deserved to be burgled, even just to jilt its owner for his poor taste. As a fellow appreciator of fine things, I was disturbed.

Four shapes stood against the light. One was wearing a vast coat. The others wore white tunics, dark gloves, and skullcaps of bronze. They held clubs that shone with copper. I was immediately grateful I hadn't chosen the fighting option.

The one in the coat spoke. A dark smudge of a moustache lurked beneath his nose, as if he'd wiped his lip after playing with charcoal. Though the rest of him was balloon-shaped, his pasty northern face was as narrow as an axe-head. I remembered noticing a man of similar description not so long ago, amongst the crowd of a soulmarket.

'Will my men need to instil some manners in you, or are you able to talk like the man you once were?'

I got to my feet, looking at the bronze-capped men standing around me. Their arm muscles bunched, straining against their sleeves. They were clearly eager to use their clubs.

'I'm perfectly able to be civil,' I replied.

With a hand heavy with golden rings, the man gestured to a nearby chair. 'Then if you please?'

I was pushed into it before I could shake a leg. It was a great arm-chair; the kind that swallowed a person in an embrace that was far too comfortable for its own good. The kind that were perfect for pointing towards fireplaces and counting time in the crackling of flames.

I found no comfort in this one, just more uncertainty. The man stayed standing between me and the guards, who looked somewhat disappointed.

This was the first time I'd been ghost-napped, but not the first time a sack had been forced over my head. It was how many dealers in my trade liked to say hello. If word was put out that somebody wanted to talk to somebody, that word had a habit of growing legs and scampering around where it didn't belong. That's why it was normal to forgo the invite and use some strong men and a sack instead. The result was the same, just with less talk scampering around town.

'What is your name?' enquired the man.

'Jerub.'

'Your real name.'

'That is my name.'

'I thought you were able to talk as a man? I order you to tell me your name.'

'I am still bound to Widow Horix. You can't order me to do anything.'

'Very well, shade.' He nodded to a house-guard, who promptly came to batter me across the head. I took four blows before the bastard clicked his fingers.

'Enough!'

The copper stung me, sizzling down my back. I twitched involuntarily. Normally, a summoning by sack ended in a shake of hands, a lucrative offer of shares in some shady deed, and took barely any time at all. With this moustachioed prick, I got the feeling I would be sitting there some time, and eventually end up doing something for the terrible price of yet more strife.

He sat down across from me, keeping a glass table between us. The table looked to have real tiger's legs at each corner. Their claws had been painted a bright red. I had half a mind to smash it.

'What do you want?' I asked him.

'Your real name.'

'And I told you. Jerub.'

He tutted.

'Do the tors of this city make a habit of going about thieving other people's property?' I challenged him.

The guard raised his club. I put up my hands, ready to dampen another beating, but the man had other ideas.

'It's a kind of sport in this city, *Jerub*. Haven't you heard? It's how we stay sane in this strange world the Arctians built. We do it quietly, cleverly, usually taking our time. Unfortunately, in this case, certain elements have forced my hand.'

With a thumb, I prodded the widow's seal on the chest of my

smock. 'Tal Horix won't be pleased. She'll come for me. She'll realise it's you, whoever you are.'

It was a clumsily cast line, and he didn't bite. The moustache shivered as he chuckled. 'A lowly shade like you? Why is that?'

'I'm not lowly. I'm rather important to the tal.'

'Then I take it she has discovered your… *past*, shall we say?'

That stalled me. Clearly this man also knew of my past, otherwise I'd have been swiftly reminded of my place in society. Ghosts didn't have a past unless it was either useful or worth coin.

I played nonchalant. 'I don't know what you mean.'

'If you must have it, my name is Tor Simeon Busk. I collect rich and expensive items, and have made my fortune doing so. I have a knack for seeing the value hidden under smears of dust and decay. An eye for detail, they call it. Looking at your rounder jaw, I know a foreigner to the Arc when I see one. Krassman, I'd guess?'

'Perhaps.'

'I'm a Skolman myself. Arrived in this city aged thirteen. Since then, I've worked myself up to tordom, and made a space for myself amongst the nobles.'

A lowly one at that, I silently wagered.

'A man doesn't manage that without learning to accept the true business of ascension. One must sometimes consort with less savoury characters to accomplish it. I've known many in my years.'

'I'm sure.'

Busk grinned, showing golden caps at the back of his mouth. 'The unscrupulous come in many forms, as you know. Tors, tals, generals, all the way to fences, thugs, even locksmiths.'

Here we have it. Perhaps it wasn't just Widow Horix who needed to recite a soliloquy before circling to a point. Maybe it was how Arctian nobles did their business. Krass lords, on the other hand, liked to spit the truth at you like an apple seed, and I preferred it.

As he spoke, Busk dug into his coat pocket and withdrew something narrow and long, like a reed. I heard the clink of metal as he laid it on the glass table. Leaning closer, there was something familiar about it.

A second piece came down, thin and flat like the other, but with a hooked end. This piece I knew well. I had battered that hook into it with my own hands. And a hammer, of course. I was no wizard.

Another and another came, until there were six. I raised my impassive gaze to his, giving nothing away. His eyes were avid with expectation. I held back a sigh as I plotted where this conversation would lead. 'Go on.'

'I knew of one locksmith in particular. Bright young fellow once, up and coming. Knew his way around all sorts of doors and vaults. Fell off the map until only recently. Bad reputation, or something. Had a peculiar name even for a Krassman.'

'And what might that be, I wonder?'

'Something with a C and a B if I remember rightly.' Busk held up one piece of metal and tapped it with his finger.

'How interesting.'

This time, Busk didn't spare me the club. It struck me across the shoulders, knocking me half out of the chair. The pain clawed at my skull.

The tor leaned down to stare into my face. 'Was it Caltro Basalt?'

I was already nodding before I could stop it.

'Was it Boran Temsa who bound and sold you?'

My eyes rolled.

'I thought it strange how Temsa sold a Krassman only to summon me to inspect the tools of a renowned Krassman locksmith barely a week after.' Busk chuckled. 'I was at the soulmarket that day. I would have paid double had I known who you were. Had they given your old name. You are different from your description, Caltro. They didn't paint you as a large man.'

Somewhat recovered, I let the chair swallow me. 'It's a recent addition.'

'As is the scarf, I imagine?'

A hand moved to my neck and hovered there.

Busk leaned closer. 'So you admit it? You are indeed Caltro Basalt? Second-best locksmith in all the Reaches?'

I scowled. There was no point pretending any more. The man knew his locksmiths. Well, almost. '*The* best, or so I've been told.'

The tor clapped his hands before performing a victory lap of the gaudy room. He grinned to his guards. 'I knew it!'

'Now that you do, what do you want with me?'

'Straight to the point. Krass through and through.'

'You have stolen me from Horix against my will, imprisoned me in a wardrobe and now beaten me. I think it's fair to assume this is all for your own personal gain. So, seeing as you intend to fuck me over, I'd rather skip the foreplay if it's all the same to you.'

Tor Busk stared at me as if I was a sandfly in his wine. 'Very well.'

He gestured to the slivers of metal. 'Your tools. You clearly came here to use them before you ended up on the wrong side of the knife. I want you to put them to good use.'

With his foot, he pushed the tiger-footed table towards me until it trapped my knees.

My fingers went to work instinctively. In truth, I'd missed the familiar feel of my tools; their weight; the cold of the metal. With smart clicks, the slivers came together, forming a long pick and a hooked file. I undid them, and within moments I had them arranged in the shape of the pincers. With these weapons, I could open half the doors in the Reaches. The rest of them would be opened by my mind, but I wasn't about to tell Busk that.

'What a resourceful and effective way of disguising your trade.'

'Just like any assassin wouldn't strut about covered in blades. Where are the rest of them? There should be several more pieces.'

'With another party, currently. I have replacements if needed.'

'What is it, then?' I asked. 'And don't try to test me first. I hate that.'

'Fear not. Your reputation precedes you. I have a chest that refuses to open.'

I tilted my head. 'Lost the key, have you?'

Busk sneered. 'Something like that. I think there is a better chance of it opening for you.'

'Undoubtedly.'

'Do we have an understanding, Mr Basalt?' The tor had the cheek to pretend this was a job I had a choice in accepting. I decided to challenge that, play along.

'Show me the chest first and we'll see.'

With a nod from Busk, I was hauled from the chair and out of the room. The guards' gloves sizzled against my skin, turning my glow white. I couldn't help but wriggle. Busk trailed behind, tutting at my struggles and examining my tools as he walked. I heard the clicks as he tried to figure them out, but only I knew the combinations of how they fit together.

I was right about one thing: the tor was not nearly as high-ranking as Horix. The narrow corridors, the low ceilings, the coil of stairs half as tall as I was used to; they all presented their evidence. The gaudiness also continued in the form of metallic drapes and more animal-furniture hybrids.

Once I had been dragged down to the lowest floor, a door was kicked open into some sort of storeroom. Crates, barrels, and cloth-bound objects hugged the walls. Tables stood guard here and there, strewn with assorted trinkets. It was a scene I knew well from visiting more than my fair share of fences' dens. Seeing it here was as if all the gold and pomp had been ripped away from Busk, showing the scrawny dock-rat that hid beneath.

'Here we have it.' The tor whisked a dust sheet from something large and square, and I found myself staring at my opponent.

The thing was a fortress, not a chest. Skol-made by the looks of it, an ugly mess of black iron and traces of silver. Spikes adorned its edges. Six locks ringed with mossy malachite stared out from the side that faced me. Two great iron straps bound the tented lid shut, each with a bolt and another lock. If I wasn't mistaken, this was the work of Feksi Drood. She was one of the finest and most cunning doorsmiths Skol had ever produced. Even after a hundred years her locks were still puzzling delinquent entrepreneurs like myself.

I made to suck my lip, but my vapours escaped me. 'Must have been heavy to steal.'

'Left to me by my grandfather, actually. A man of great secrecy and wealth. This is his challenge to me from beyond the afterlife.'

'I'm surprised you didn't bind him.'

Busk looked insulted. 'Though I own my fair share of shades, I am no soultrader, Basalt. I am an esteemed collector and—'

I finished that thought for him. 'Fence.'

A club came at my ribs, making me stagger.

Busk pushed me towards the chest. He had gathered up my tools and now he held them in his gloved hands. 'It's a Drood design. I assume you know who and what that is? I've waited decades to find a locksmith who could tackle it.' Here his face cracked into a grin. 'And now I have you.'

With a curled lip, I took the tools from him, along with some spares. 'Aside from the threat of violence and intense boredom, why should I help you? You're not my master.'

'Well, it depends how much of those you can take.'

I decided to measure him against what Horix had offered, partly in cheek, partly in hope. 'I want my freedom.'

Busk laughed heartily. 'And why ever would I give you that? I have the best locksmith in the Reaches in my possession. Besides, I don't have your half-coin, do I? Let's hope Horix is a charitable whore and doesn't have your coin melted too quickly. Now, if you're saying you want to taste the clubs some more before you begin, we can continue.'

I muttered curses under my breath as I settled down before the beast of a chest, and began to poke and prod at the insides of its locks. My eyes were closed; all my concentration poured down my arms and into the metal in my hands. I was grateful I'd chosen steel instead of copper for my tools. The stand-ins Busk had gifted me were crude, but they would do.

Floating cylinder locks to stop me finding the notches.
Two deeplocks, reaching far into the chest's lid to test my picks.
Cast steel bar-bolts that would need a forge to cut through.
And a clever drop-pin cylinder, needing a tube-key to crack it.
Nice try, Feksi Drood.

'It's not going to be a quick job,' I told him.

Busk folded his arms and leaned on a nearby crate. 'Well, why don't you pretend it's one of your usual jobs and imagine you've got until dawn to crack it.'

Surely if the man had waited a few decades, he could wait another day. Drood was a tricksy locksmith, fond of traps that sealed chests and vaults permanently. I needed to go about this cleverly. No doubt these locks had an order to them, and penalties for deviating. I'd tackled several Droods before, and each of them had kicked my ample arse throughout my efforts to break them. I had won, of course. I almost always do in the end. I've only walked away from one vault, and that was because of its deadlock. I had no desire to spend eternity trapped in a door. Some rewards in life are not worth the risk to claim them. Fortunately for me, deadlocks were rarer than rare, and far beyond Feksi fucking Drood.

'This is not your average chest, Busk, you know that. If you want it open, I need to take my time. Otherwise you'll be staring at a hunk of metal for the rest of your life,' I told him.

Tor Busk shook his head, and I heard the scuff of boots coming closer, accompanied by the impatient thwack of clubs against palms. 'Sunrise,' he said, and I shrugged.

'You're the boss.'

In scores of taverns and inns across the Reaches, I'd heard warriors both young and old yapping over their beers, telling stories of bloodlust and battle-rage: the moment when a fighter was consumed by a singular task, blocking out all else. Fear, exhaustion, even pain can vanish, or so I'd been told. I tended to believe it. There are many kinds of battle, and though mine was with tumblers and cogs and clever machines, I knew my own bloodlust. Despite my dulled senses, it had survived the grave with me.

The scuffing of the guards, the impatient humming of Busk, a repetitive dripping in a distant corner... they all fell away to a low murmur. Anything outside my direct line of sight blurred and faded. My tools felt like swords in my hand as I lifted them. All I knew was the chest.

The duel began. I bent closer to the first lock, tapping the metal for signs of mechanisms behind it. My pick explored the first few cylinders, twisting them around to find their pin-holes and notches. I had the measure of it within an hour, and by extension, the measure of half the others. I moved from one to the next, tracing their clicks and whirs to find the order they ran in. Several played bastard, making me work hard to break them, like meeting an equal on the battlefield. In life I would have been streaming with sweat. I always was a sweater. It was not nerves, but more accurately the thrill of treading that thin line between success and failure. The narrower the line, the greater the thrill.

When the fifth lock was done, I moved on to the sixth. It needed a tube-like key with holes cut for the tumblers to fall through when the key was turned. I'd faced only three of these locks before, and they'd taken a night to crack. Breaking from my trance for a moment told me half the guards were nodding off, slumped against barrels and crates. Even Busk watched on with one eye closed, the very definition of half asleep. It must have been early morning already, almost sunrise.

The trick with a drop-pin cylinder was to coax the tumblers out as you turned, testing each one while holding back the others. The rest was repetition until you saw a pattern. Drood must have been having an off-day building this chest, getting predictable in her old age. It took an hour, no more, to smite the lock. It was with a beaming smile that I went on to the final tests.

'How much longer, shade?' Busk grunted, lurching as if he'd shaken himself awake.

'We agreed sunrise, didn't we?'

Busk looked to a nearby hourglass a guard had fetched. He pulled a face. 'Hmph.'

The deeplocks put up a brief fight; one last vain tactic by withdrawing troops. I cracked my file apart and snapped it into a longer position. The same with my pincers, bending the metal out to serve my purposes. Into the keyholes they went, grazing the ridges of the tumblers.

By the time I began to hear the thumps of a household waking up, I had just about broken the final lock. The last tumbler was being stubborn. I had to reset the cylinder several times before I managed to jimmy it into position.

There came an almighty thud as the steel bolts sprang back. The malachite keyholes turned with all the magic of clockwork. With a resounding, mechanical clunking, the lid inched open. The noise wrenched

Busk from his dozing. He came staggering over to the chest, blinking like a pig on its way to the chopping block.

'Out of the way!' he snapped. A few guards did my work for me and threw me back a few paces. I buried my tools in the sleeves of my smock, crossed my arms and watched.

Keys came first; a whole ring of them, all differently-toothed. Busk tucked them into his belt before the thing could lock itself again. I was not needed any more. Next came scrolls, cloth bags with something rattling inside, and pieces of what looked like a shattered sundial, all solid gold.

The more Busk plucked from the chest and the longer he rooted around, the more he smiled. I would have been doing the same; it was a fine haul for any thief. Although I highly doubted his grandfather had ever so much as farted near the chest, in any case the tor had just become considerably richer.

'Fine work, Mr Basalt. The rumours about you are quite true,' he congratulated me.

I lifted my shoulders. 'And what now?'

'Now, Caltro, you'll be going back to that wardrobe until I find something else for you to break into. I could use a half-life like yourself in my trade. Arctian locksmiths don't seem to have your level of...' The word escaped him, but not me.

'Powerlessness? Don't flatter me. You mean to say I'm at your dis-posal, Busk, let's not fool around.'

A club came down on the back of my neck, forcing me to the dust. Another clouted me in the ribs half a dozen times. The copper still hurt through my smock. I endured the beating until they'd had their fun or Busk put his hands up, I couldn't tell. He stooped down to collect the tools that had fallen from my sleeve, and smiled simperingly.

'Take him away.'

That was the sum of my labour. Once again, somebody else got to grasp the prize, not I. It was getting pathetic. I felt not short of pathetic myself as my spectral feet bobbed on the stairs and copper-thread gloves sizzled in my armpits.

It was then that I absently wished for a spear of that metal through my heart. The thought stunned me cold. I had never wished such a thing in thirty-four years of living, and yet a second death abruptly seemed like a good idea. I pushed that notion away from me like a plagued beggar. The cavern of screaming voices scared me more than my current state. Far, far more. Even this fresh hell of mine was preferable.

Into the wardrobe they threw me, not bound but on the wrong side of any locks. By the sounds of it, the thing had four very solid bolts. I found myself once again in the blue wash of my own glow, staring at a wooden door. That was why indenturement irked me so. I had never liked being at the mercy of others' whims. At least this time I didn't have a sack over my head. I sighed.

There was fuck all else to do except listen to the receding boots and the following slam of a door. Silence reigned, apart from the ticking of some strange timepiece I'd seen in the room earlier. It metered out my confinement with its cocky little ticks and taps. I promised to take it apart the quick way whenever I had a moment. Busk could punish me with his clubs all he wanted.

I was just about to begin a thorough session of stewing over my problems and losses when I thought I heard a voice in the room. I stiffened as much as a vaporous form could, and put my face to the thin gap between the doors. The wardrobe might have been well-made and reinforced, but clothes and old things need to breathe.

The guards hadn't thought to snuff out the oil lamps. I scanned the room in slivers, like an invader peering through an arrow-slit. The tasteless room was empty, but I found myself once again distracted by the horrid things Busk had collected for himself. I would have burned all of it just so I wouldn't have to look at it a moment further.

'Hello!'

That time I heard it distinctly. A man's voice. Not beyond the door but inside the room. My palms pressed to the wood, I looked again. Unless the speaker was directly next to the wardrobe, which my ears told me he wasn't, or in the corners behind me, I couldn't see him.

'Hello?' I called.

The voice became high-pitched with excitement. 'Yes! Thank Frit!'

Now there was a deity I'd never heard of. I groaned, forehead against the iron seam. The voice must have been another one of these so-called dead gods, here to chastise me some more. *Why do they always come to me in moments of punishment?* Where were they when I was being slaughtered?

'What is it this time?' I wondered what sort of dead thing they'd chosen for me now. Maybe one of the furry heads adorning the wall, an antelope or an ibis.

'I tried to find these fanatics of yours, but as you can see, other people had different ideas. Unless you can get me out of here, leave me alone,' I told the god.

There was a long pause. 'I'm afraid I don't know what you're talking about.'

'Then who are you?'

A polite cough. 'I'm a fellow captive. Same as you.'

I pulled a face in the darkness. 'Where? I didn't see anyone else in the room. Are you in a wardrobe like me? Are you able to get me out?'

'I, er, haha. Not quite.'

We had traded but a few sentences and I'd already decided I didn't like this person. 'Well…?'

'I am, as they say, "gripp'd by grips of iron unseen".'

'You're shackled, then?'

Some nervous laughter now. 'No, sir. That is to say I am indisposed to help you. It was I who rather fancied the helping.'

I pressed my eye to the seam again. 'Well, I'm locked up,' I mumbled, staring to the fireplace, where it seemed the voice was coming from. Unless the man was sitting in the chair facing away from me, the voice was either that of an apparition, or in my own head.

There was a dull thud as I fell back against the wood. That was it. I'd finally cracked. My inner turmoil had developed a voice and a character.

'Perhaps we could talk? Tell tales. Trade stories.'

I was trying to converse with myself.

'Poetry, even? I actually write some of it myself, you know. Well, less of the writing... more of the thinking up.'

That's when I pushed myself forward again. I despised poetry in all its forms, primarily because I didn't understand it. My unconscious, no matter how depraved and strange the depths of it may be, could never dream up something poetic. I couldn't pen a sonnet if you dangled me over a well full of crocodiles.

'Where are you?' I challenged the voice. 'Tell me.'

'"An edge swung oft in battle, but also drawed in angst, I—"'

'It's "drawn", and tell me where you are!'

'I'm the sword, all right? The sword on the mantelpiece.'

I swung left, looking up to the ghastly painted mirror and the terracotta vases with moulded grinning faces. Between them was a display rack, tilted to show its prize. It was a longsword with an obsidian blade mottled and veined with copper. It was silver in the hilt and forged in the shape of a tree, with a crossguard made of intertwining branches and its trunk the grip. Its roots clutched a black stone pommel, carved like the face of a man.

'The sword?'

'Yes, the sword.'

I groaned. The clubs must have hit me harder than I thought. 'Are you sure you're not an ancient god?'

'Well, I once played a few for the Theatre Guild of Gurra, and in *The Black Scarab*. My performance was reported to be astonis—' He heard my growling. 'But no. Alas. I am not. Just a humble deadbound.'

'A what?'

'Oh, you don't know?' The voice was eager, grateful for the chance to tell its story.

My pause told him no, I hadn't.

'Deadbinding. It was a craze several… What year is it?'

'One thousand and four, by Empire count.'

'In that case, it was a craze several hundred years ago, when the Nyxites decided to experiment with the spell of binding in order to make trinkets for Arctian nobles. You might have heard of strangebinding? Of souls bound in the bodies of animals? They were the lucky ones. We weren't allowed to live as shades or beasts, and instead we were bound to objects. Lifeless things, hence the name deadbound. You know: talking hourglasses, sentient doors, self-playing harps, that sort of thing. But no, I got put into a sword. A soulblade, they called it. Never brandished more than a stage-weapon in my life, now I know more about a blade than anybody else, ha… ha.'

I had heard of talking trinkets before. Even stolen a few. Never once had I imagined they had been souls. I had assumed charms or some old magic.

Once more, the back of my head struck the panel. *So indenturement could be worse.* There was a grim sort of solace in knowing there was somebody in a sorrier state than you, but it chipped away some of the weight that had rested on me since being snatched from the docks.

At very least the sword was something to converse with that wasn't my own thoughts. I was glad for the company. It even helped me ignore the wardrobe until Busk had need of me again. I closed my eyes, and let myself rest against the wardrobe's back.

'Go on.'

CHAPTER 3
WEIGHED & MEASURED

A Weighing is as much a necessity as it is a great and wondrous massage of the egos. Let the other fellows enjoy their baths and visits to cathouses; my pleasure comes from seeing my half-coins counted and measured. They order once a month? I Weigh twice a week. A man knows what he wants for when he knows where he stands on society's ladder.

FROM A MISSIVE MISTAKENLY DELIVERED TO TAL TABATH, WHO LATER MARRIED THE SENDER

L IFT IT.'

Gloved hands laid hold of the ropes. Pulleys squeaked in complaint. Stone grated. Glowing fingers clawed at the dark gap, hungry for light and air and the knowledge that there was a world beyond the close dark press of sandstone.

The lid of the sarcophagus was swivelled aside, meeting the floor with a dull boom. Copper-thread hands grabbed the shade and out he came, quivering like a palm tree in a sandstorm. They had to lift him up so he could face her. Even then his head lolled about as if he had no spine, his empty eyes searching the floor.

Widow Horix stepped forwards, hands clasped, chin high, eyes sharp as butcher's knives.

'Do you feel like talking now?' she asked.

Vex moaned something incoherent. The guards shook him.

'I didn't do it… I don't know anything.'

Horix circled him and his captors as she stared at his naked blue frame.

'The others in the alcoves said Caltro didn't go to the stables with them. One shade by the name of Kon was very helpful. Said Caltro was kept behind. Now he's nowhere to be found. So, for what must be the twelfth time, Master Vex, what explanation do you have for the disappearance of my locksmith?'

'None, Mistress,' he slurred. 'I put him to work in the kitchens later that evening! He must have taken his chance to escape!'

Horix turned to the armoured lump standing next to her. 'String him up, Colonel.'

Kalid rubbed his hands. 'Aye, Mistress.'

'No!'

Vex was thrown against a wall, where his neck was introduced to a thick loop of metallic rope. More pulleys screeched, and Vex was soon hanging like a condemned thief. He did not gurgle, he did not twitch. He simply fell limp, pulling a distorted face at the fizzing sound around his neck.

The widow was handed a pair of elaborate copper shears, decorated with coils of silver. She brandished them at the shade, clacking them together. 'You know as well as I do what these are.'

Vex did. His fresh struggling proved it. Many times Horix had watched him use the very same blades on recalcitrant house-shades.

Horix explained just in case the sarcophagus had addled his mind. 'When a man loses a finger in life, only the body is damaged. The soul remains untouched. But when you're a shade…' The blades parted and took one of Vex's toes into their jaws. The guards held his struggling leg tightly. 'When you're all soul, you've only got your soul to lose. Memories. Personality. They can be snipped away piece by piece.'

Schnick.

There was a puff of light and cobalt smoke as the toe vanished. The stump glowed brightly as Vex howled with pain, thrashing around like a stubborn fish at the end of a line. When he finally resorted to sobbing, the shears snickered in Horix's hands.

'I wonder what I took away. A recollection of a childhood summer's day, perhaps? Or the touch of a lover creeping along your skin? Care to see what else we can trim?'

'I'm telling the truth!'

'His hand, Kalid.'

The colonel and his guards seized Vex's arms, pinning one behind his back and forcing the other outward. He was already howling before the sharp copper touched his wrist. His vapours flared at its touch.

'Final chance.'

'I'm telling the truth!' he wailed.

Schnick.

'Aaaaagh!' His wail became a roar as another piece of him drifted away, never to return. 'Please…'

Horix tutted at him once more. 'I shall keep going until you prove your innocence, Master Vex. A shade can still work without a few fingers and toes. Maybe even an arm or leg.'

He seethed through clamped teeth. No words came. He flickered as if he were a candle in a draught.

'Or his manhood.'

Vex fought the guards back momentarily before they splayed his legs against the wall. Colonel Kalid cleared his throat by Horix's side, and after comparing the size of the shears with Vex's diminutive member, she nodded beneath her cowl.

With a whisper of metal, Kalid's sword slid from its scabbard. It moved as if it were molten, twisting through the air before driving through the shade's crotch. A spark flew as the steel met the stone behind. Blue smoke trailed in the blade's wake.

It took a moment for Vex to realise what had happened. The scream quickly followed.

'Yaaah!'

Horix watched him closely. Once again, he flickered, but this time his glow dimmed permanently.

'Shall we go on, Master Vex?' she asked, staring up at his pain-stricken face.

'I… I…'

'I can't hear you.'

Kalid held the point of his sword to the shade's throat.

'Busk!' The word exploded from him, and as soon as he said it, he sagged, falling limp again. He stared down at his glowing wounds, his hollow eye sockets wide. 'Tor Busk stole Jerub. That Caltro. The Krassman.' His words were malformed.

'Is that so? Why? How?'

'Said he was… dangerous. Said he would take care of him. We made a deal. I let him out… I wanted to keep you safe, Mistress.'

Horix came closer. 'You, Master Vex, have done nothing but contaminate my plans! He was important, curse you! I fucking told you this!'

She lashed at his vapours in a moment of rage, raking her copper-painted nails across his stomach. Four white lines were scratched into him. He gasped, chin bobbing under the rope.

Horix worked her gums before making a decision. She plucked a half-circle of copper from her pocket and thumbed its glyph and seal before handing it to the colonel. 'Take his coin and melt it.'

The shade immediately struggled anew. 'No! Widow Horix! Please! I'll do anything. Anything!'

As the ropes were loosed and Vex crumbled to a heap on the stone, Horix took a moment to stand over him and regard his grief-stricken face.

'Sixth Tenet of the Bound Dead.'

Vex flapped his mouth, misunderstanding at first. He blinked as he inwardly clawed at some memory, now foggier than his skin.

'Oh, did we cut that away already?' Horix scraped her mouth for saliva and spat upon him. '*They must bring their masters no harm.* I will not stomach a shade in my house who thinks himself above the Tenet, the Code, or more importantly, my will. Take him out of my sight, Kalid.'

The colonel had his men haul the screeching Vex out of the room, then hung back alongside Horix, who was busy smoothing her skirts. He flicked the half-coin on his thumb and it chimed as it spun.

'Vex was the last shade I would have expected to do this.'

'Jealousy's not reserved just for the living, Colonel. Such a thing can drive a shade to madness as easily as it can a man. As it did with Vex.'

'Jealousy? Of who?'

'Of *whom*. And of Caltro, the Krass shade,' she growled. 'Now, thanks to Vex's shortcomings, we must go to retrieve our locksmith from the uppity Tor Busk. If he thinks he can simply snatch one of my shades as though I were a lesser tal, he'll regret the day he heard my name.'

Kalid was already walking. 'I'll have a hundred of my men ready in an hour, Mistress.'

She held up a hand, freezing him. 'You forget the nature of this city's game, Colonel. Do not be so rash. Tors and tals besieging each other's towers? That attracts plenty of eyes, and with all this talk of murders and disappearances, we do not want extra attention. We would not want to pique the interest of the Chamber, now, would we? No. We tread softly.'

'And do what?' Kalid looked confused and mildly disappointed.

'Busk must know of Caltro's worth in order to steal him. He must need him for something, therefore we play on his weaknesses, Colonel. Greed, pride, vanity. We make him think I am weak, and that I will eventually forget the matter if he holds out long enough. First, we make a purposefully fumbling effort to play him. We send him a note.'

'Not poisoned?'

Horix tapped her nails together. 'Too old a trick. No, we merely thank him for his warnings and we advise him we are ready to sell the shade known as Jerub. He will not accept, because he already has Caltro. We will pester him until we stoke his pride into anger. He will threaten me, and I will roll over like the old woman I am. We will make him believe he has won, and it's then that we shall send him a gift. And for that, Colonel, we shall need a spook. And a good one at that. The very best.'

'A spook?' Kalid took a moment to process her ploy. He nodded, grinning. 'Clever, Mistress.'

'I have had years of practice. Now, melt that half-coin and then fetch me a scribe. You may deliver the scroll yourself. And find me a spook!'

'Aye, Mistress.'

Horix watched the man stomp from the room, leaving her in the soft glow of lamplight and her own self-satisfaction. It had been many years since her last noble feud. She had played the recluse too well, it seemed. She had almost forgotten the thrill of machination, of guile. *Of winning.*

The widow plucked another half-coin from her pocket and held it up to make it shine. *Caltro's half-coin.* She thumbed the split sigil of the royal crown and the poorly carved glyph and pondered.

Insurance was a wonderful thing.

With a tight smile on her face, she made for the doorway. As her fingers graced the stone to steady herself, she heard Vex's screaming begin. His ghoulish howls followed her all the way to the foot of the stairs, and not once did she flinch or shudder. She only smiled wider.

———◆———

'I'VE GOT THE SHITS ABOUT this.'

'For the last time, shut your trap, Ani,' Temsa hissed, tapping his cane on the ochre marble and making several coincounters look up from their ridiculously tall desks. He nodded to them, and they tugged at their spectacles. The fervent scratching of reeds upon papyrus resumed.

Jexebel fell silent, busying herself with sitting straight and not fidgeting in her new grey uniform. To Temsa's right, Danib wore the same, though his strained more at the seams.

Temsa looked to the end of the grand hall, eyeing the closed door with golden glyphs splayed across it, spelling "Director" in Arctian. It had been closed far too long for his liking. The waiting times at Araxes' banks were almost as famous as the Chamber's, things of legend and song. At least queuing only applied to the poorer side of society; those with maybe half a dozen shades to their name. Temsa could still hear the clamouring from the public desks on the level below them.

At least the banks offered something to gaze at while they made their more important customers wait. Personally, Temsa admired the grim architecture. It celebrated the deaths that filled the vaults of places like Fenec Coinery. The upper halls had vaulted ceilings of gold leaf and white plaster. Whale-oil lanterns hung from skeletal arms cast in silver. They sprouted from six columns of black lava-stone, shaped with hollow ribcages and stretching arms. Skulls hung like bunches of grapes at their heads and feet. They looked down at the rows of desks below them and glowered.

The desks in question belonged to the sigils and the coincounters, and they were so tall they required ladders to reach. Between them stood guards dressed in full battle armour, complete with grilled helms covering their faces and shining halberds. Though they were silent, those they protected were not. The air was filled with the scratching of reeds against papyrus and the clatter of abacuses. Not a single shade manned the lofty desks; no half-lives were allowed to handle or guard half-coins, as per the Code.

The floor was made of a marble so glossy that Temsa could check his reflection in its shine. He had done so frequently since arriving. The new suit was chafing around his good leg. The rich silks were warm, too. Thick folds of it trapped the heat, and though shades stood along the walls, wafting palm fronds, Temsa was beginning to sweat. And his tight collar… well, there was nothing to do about it now besides make a mental note to have the tailor beaten.

A dab of his kerchief saw to the sweat, and he distracted himself with adjusting the multitude of silver rings on his fingers. He had se-lected only his best for the occasion. He had even let one of the tavern girls underline his eyes and blush his cheeks, as was the fashion of the nobles. Ani had scowled murderously when she'd seen him. What she didn't understand was that actors needed costumes, and this was his. His stage? The bank. His role? A successful and thoroughly legal businessman here for his first official Weighing.

Once again, Temsa's gaze slipped to the director's door. The windows either side had been shuttered, but he could see shapes moving behind them, framed by the lamplight within. He narrowed his eyes, willing the figures to come forth, and to his mild surprise, they did just that.

His pet sigil, Russun Fenec, and his father Tor Fenec came forth, along with a retinue of advisors in sequinned robes. As the advisors scattered like rats docking after a long voyage, the Fenecs bustled on-wards. Only one stayed with them: a greying man with an intricately braided beard and gold paint plastered in a line between his nose and his vastly receded hairline.

Temsa rose to greet them. He even wore a smile. 'Tor Fenec, Mr Fenec. Shall we begin?'

Father and son shared a look while the old man just stared at Temsa's leg. Long decades of making people squirm had taught Temsa the language of people's faces. Eyes, foreheads, lips – they were all mouths in their own right, and they could speak volumes. He saw the desperate pleading in Russun's face, the utter displeasure in the tor's.

Fenec the elder cleared his throat. 'Thank you for waiting, Boss Temsa, a—'

'My pleasure.'

'A… thank you. My apologies for the delay and our deliberation.'

'I assume the time was spent wisely.'

'Quite. Well, it is not often we deal with people… with soultraders like yourself, Boss Temsa—'

'And I have explained that is now a tiny portion of my business.

Since I have begun depositing here, I have acquired factories, work-houses, dock-shades, security companies.' *And a great many of them, too.*

'Yes.' Fenec tried hard to swallow his annoyance at being inter-rupted. While he struggled, Russun spoke up.

'And that is why we have decided to allow you to bank in our prestigious vaults on a permanent basis, at a yearly commission of eight percent, as discussed.'

Russun fell silent as his father's hand patted him on the shoulder. Though the sigil bowed his head, his eyes snuck to Temsa's.

'On the basis,' Tor Fenec continued, 'that your Weighing places you within our bracket of clientele. I am pleased to say we were able to acquire a Weigher for you right away. Tallyer Nhun here can assist us.'

Temsa bowed to hide his wolfish grin. 'I am very pleased to hear that. Shall we continue, then?'

'You may signal your men, Mr Temsa.'

'It would be my pleasure. Miss Jexebel?'

Silence. The woman was staring blankly at him. She was getting deafer by the day.

'The barrows, Ani?'

'Aye.'

Temsa watched Ani saunter towards the stairs. With a sharp whistle, she got the attention of the men waiting downstairs amidst a crowd of guards. After a few shouts of, 'Move your arse!' and, 'Get out the fuckin' way!' four large wheelbarrows appeared at the stairs with puffing men behind them. These were not the average farm barrow. These were tall and fat, box-like things, adorned with silver and varnished oak from Skol. *And bought especially for this moment.* Temsa had to concentrate to contain his pleasure.

'If you please.' Tor Fenec gestured to a wider door at the end of the hall. His eyes were already measuring the size of the barrows, and he had yet to look impressed. 'The Weighing Room is at your disposal.'

Temsa and Danib trailed behind the three men. Danib cast him a glance, one that was barely more confident than Ani's scowling eyes. Temsa shook his head. He felt like a hawk, staring down at a carpet of land. They were beasts, bumbling along below. They couldn't see the path he could, and what it consisted of, but they would soon. Temsa hoped so. He could not abide the thought of having to change his guard.

Thick gilded doors, carved with designs of weighing scales and towers of shades and half-coins, swung open with a deep moan. The large room beyond burned with candles and lamplight. A mighty arm of steel protruded from a dark slot in the far wall. It reached deep into the room, and from it hung a burnished pan of copper which was the width of two men laid end to end. It currently hovered at head height. Above it, chutes of dark wood hung from chains in the ceiling. Long, zig-zagging ramps led to high gantries crewed with men in white robes and gloves.

'Quite the operation, gentlemen,' Temsa complimented them.

The tor took a stand on a pedestal in the corner so he could oversee the scene. 'Quite. Though similar to many other banks', our Weighing Room was the first of its design. What you see here is over two hundred years old.'

Russun stepped close to Temsa, his voice low. 'Fenec Coinery has been in business for over four hundred years. My father is its twenty-ninth director. We personally look after one tenth of Araxes' half-coin deposits. The Coinery can't just accept... *anybody*. Tors and tals are regularly turned away.'

Temsa gave the young man a fierce gaze, speaking louder than his meek whisper so that his father could hear. 'Well, Sigil, let's see what Tallyer Nhun here has to say. After my Weighing, I'm sure the Coinery will have no problem having me as a customer.'

Out of the corner of his eye, he could see Tor Fenec shaking his head.

'A problem, Tor?'

'I'm afraid this is only four barrowloads, Mr Temsa, I highly doubt—'

Temsa clicked his fingers at Danib. 'Tell Ani to bring in the rest.'

If the tor's face fell then, it was a landslide of disappointment when the barrows began to pour in. Within minutes, two lines of thirty stood awaiting the men in robes. The gilded doors closed behind them with a deep boom.

'Begin!' Fenec yelled, betraying his mood with his high pitch.

As Ani and Danib unlocked the barrows with two mighty rings of keys, the figures in white came forth. They shuffled Temsa's guards aside and manoeuvred the barrows up the ramps to the gantries. With practice and precision, they were tipped into the chutes.

There was a music in the rattling of coins. A sweet concerto that only the rich knew how to enjoy. Temsa had seen his wealth piled up several times in his cellars, but never all together, and not spilling like a copper river of thunder into a pan. He had also never been this rich before.

Boran Temsa had been busy.

Four names had been crossed off the Cult's list. Four minor nobles fallen to his ambition. Their withdrawals, combined with Temsa's own personal wealth, plus a few debts he had called in, had resulted in his cellars not being used for shades, but for half-coins. It was the only currency that mattered when it came to nobility. Not silver. Not threads and silks. Not adoration, but dominion over the dead. What else was the emperor but a man of mighty wealth? He had no divinity, no prowess in battle and no sway with minds; he was simply rich. The lord of the dead.

The flow of coins continued unabated for some time. Temsa was enraptured by it. The only times he broke away were to watch the slow rise of Tor Fenec's jaw as it set in grim realisation. It was a satisfying moment.

Temsa could not have been so bold without knowing Her Majesty the empress-in-waiting was now his benefactor. His polite note to her had contained only one word: 'Deal.'

Temsa's guards were of course flabbergasted. They had likely never conceived of this amount of half-coin, yet here it was, pouring like twin copper waterfalls. Even Danib and Ani looked wide-eyed, particularly the big shade. Temsa guessed he was busy imagining all the souls that corresponded to these coins. Who they were. What they were… that sort of shit. Temsa didn't care. What mattered was that their coins were here, and they belonged to him alone.

When the flow finally dwindled and the last few coins rattled down the chutes, Temsa clapped his hands. The huge scale was so laden it had dipped into a hollow in the stone floor. His coins were a small hill perched upon it. The slopes of metal were aflame in the light of the lanterns and candles.

The tallyer, his nose now out of his notebook, began to take the measurement. He checked around the pan, walking in lunges before attending to what Temsa saw to be a fine metal needle hovering on a measure on the wall. With a curious humming, Nhun made his checks and scribbled something in his papyrus file.

'And the Weight is?' Tor Fenec called, hands cupped to his mouth.

Nhun approached his pedestal with great ceremony. Temsa didn't hear the number that was whispered, nor did he see the glyphs on the parchment. Fenec simply straightened up and adjusted his silk neckerchief. His tanned face took on a rosy glow.

'Fetch this week's Ledger of Bindings, Sigil Fenec.'

No 'son.' The man was all business.

'Yes, Tor.'

Russun hurried from the room through an adjoining door into his father's office. He returned with a heavy scroll the size of a barrel, clasped in a trolley. Nhun helped him attach it to a bracket in the wall, and together they reeled it out across the marble floor. Temsa eyed the glyphs as it ran past him. Names, numbers, dates, all in the fine, enigmatic scribble of coincounters, sigils and tallyers.

Nhun began to roam the names, hands clasped and silent as stone. With an impatient huff, Fenec came down from his pedestal and joined him. The tor muttered something and then continued towards the wall. He had begun to wring his fingers.

When Nhun stopped to scribble on the blank edge of the ledger, Temsa didn't know whether that was high or low. His heartbeat flickered. It was only when the tallyer rose and nodded to Fenec that he knew.

Tor Fenec's voice was tight, his smile false. 'You have been Weighed. You have been counted. You have been found eligible. Welcome to the nobility, *Tor* Temsa,' he said.

Temsa bowed deeply. 'Thank you, Tor Fenec. And you, Tallyer Nhun. Where do I stand?' He strode forward to meet the man with an open hand. There was a pause before the stiff hand met his. In cheek, Temsa grasped it tightly. A little too tightly for Fenec's liking, and he bent at the knees and gasped.

'Tell me, where am I?'

Still in Temsa's grip, Fenec pointed with his free hand at a spot between a Tal Jiab and a Tor Renin.

'Twenty thousand, four hundred and ninety-six,' Nhun informed him.

Temsa leaned closer, finding a familiar name only a dozen entries above him. 'And where are you, sir?'

Fenec pointed back down the scroll. 'There.'

'How many is that?

The tor held to silence for too long, and Nhun filled it. 'Nineteen thousand and four.'

This time, Temsa didn't hide his wolfish smile. 'I see. Well, I bid you a good day, Director Fenec. My thanks once more for accommodating and protecting my fortune in such prestigious vaults as yours. I assume they are as safe as they are exclusive?'

'Safer than any other bank in Araxes. We have six vaults, each within the other. No other greater vault in the Reaches besides the emperor's Sanctuary,' Fenec asserted.

'Very good,' replied Temsa. Finally, he released the man and swept towards the doors. His barrow-men and guards gathered around him, reverently touching his shoulders or arms as he passed. Temsa let them, shamelessly basking in the celebration. The costume seemed to be fitting rather too well. Then again, as he took a last look at the glittering mound that was his fortune, he felt deserving of his tordom. He had earned it with blood, sweat, and tears. Not his own, mind, but that didn't mean he couldn't fucking enjoy it.

'Guess all you need now is a tower,' Ani muttered by his side.

Temsa grinned at her. 'You know what, m'dear? That's not a bad idea at all. Let's see what Tal Kheyu-Nebra can offer us tonight, shall we? See how Sisine's suggestions compare to the Cult's. Perhaps the tal will be so generous as to lend me her home until such time as I can find a better one. I'm finding the Slab rather cramped these days.'

Ani took a long time to answer. Temsa wondered if she hadn't heard him. 'Like I said, you're taking an awful lot of steps awfully quickly, and it worries me.'

Temsa put some extra effort into his next step, making his foot spark on the marble. The clang echoed through the hall, making the coincounters jump.

'I don't pay you to worry, Ani. That's my job. You just stick to what you're good at. Like removing people's heads.'

CHAPTER 4
OLD GODS & NEW TRICKS

It is said that no gate can stand in the way of
Plenops the Breaker. Some say he had an axe
with the sharpest blade in the Round Land,
that cut through the very fibres of being.
Others say he had a war cry that could shake
apart hinges and locks. But all those who were
there, who stood beside him upon the Plains
of Choke, we knew better. A hundred souls
he'd bound within him, and mastered them
all. Only in battle would he loose them, and
rip the doors asunder in a shape that was not
his own, nor human.

OPENING LINES OF THE EPIC 'BELLS OF
SOLITUDE', BY THE PLAYWRIGHT FRANDI

THE PROBLEM WITH A TALKING sword is getting it to shut up. Dead gods know you can't throttle it.

Our mutual incarceration seemed to have opened some sort of verbal floodgate. For two days the thing had chatted incessantly, telling me his life story and more besides. The issue was that the sword's life spanned about three hundred years, not counting the time before he was deadbound, and he seemed determined to fill me in on every second he'd endured.

By the second day, my head had become permanently affixed to the wardrobe door in a half-sleep of boredom as the blade prattled on about Sir This and General That, or the Battle of Fuck-Knows-Where. I cared little for others' histories unless they could help me crack open a door or claim something shiny and expensive. And yet, despite my polite coughs or interjections, the sword's conversation always circled back to a story.

And bloody poetry. If I thought I despised poetry before, the sword proved me wrong with every half-rhymed, galumphing stanza that he used like punctuation.

'And then I was passed down to his son, Viceroy Reena, who had about as much need for me as a rich man needs a penny. Three years, I dawdled in my case, only to be occasionally gawped at by visitors to his estate. And what a grand estate—'

I thumped my head against the wood in a moment of utter boredom, and the sword fell quiet for a pause.

'Mr Basalt?'

'Mhm.'

'Are you all right?'

'Perfectly fine.'

'Good. Now, where was I...? Ah yes, Reena.'

My forehead met the door again.

I was almost glad when Busk's men came for me, their boots clomping loudly on the plush carpet. The sword fell silent immediately. Through the crack in the door, I watched them line up in front of the wardrobe, clubs in hand.

Busk entered the room, head high and hands clasped in a gesture of eagerness. He was wearing a blue velvet coat adorned with gold chains. He waved a hand at my wooden prison, and I was hauled into the lamplight.

'Need something else opened, do we, Busk?'

A club caught me across the jaw, and somebody reminded me of his station.

'*Tor* Busk,' I muttered through the pain.

'Yes, in fact, Caltro. A fresh haul of Scatter Isle pieces. There's a lockbox I think you'll be interested in.'

Interested was a strong word, but if it got me a moment of peace and passed the time, I was game. I had faith in the widow's need of me, and with every hour that trudged by, the more I expected to hear the clash of guards in the hall below and her crackly voice demanding me back. *Might as well get some practice in while I'm here.*

'Show me the box, then.'

'Good half-life.'

Up and out I was dragged, and this time taken up the stairs rather than down. I had the chance to survey Busk's home. This was no grand spire like Horix's, but more of a glorified mansion. Turrets and rooms had expanded like warty growths on the original structure. The darker nature of the old stone betrayed the extensions.

The gaudy decor followed us all the way to a stubby tower near the roof, as did the stares of the house-ghosts we passed. It seemed Busk was not in the habit of clothing his shades. They threw me and my dusty smock sad glances as they cleaned and polished, completely naked.

The doors Busk attacked with a hoop of keys were of stout construction, thick mahogany banded with steel. Four locks clicked in sequence and the guards saw to opening them. Inside the room, shelves lined the walls and a cornucopia of objects lined them. Each had a small papyrus tag on a string. Numbers had been scratched onto them.

'Here we are,' announced Busk.

A cube of grey metal perched on a pedestal, about a handspan thick in each direction. Between the glyph designs, one solitary keyhole stared at me like an eye.

'This is it?' I asked.

'Don't let its simplicity fool you, Caltro. I expect more from an expert such as yourself.' Busk turned to one of the nearest guards, taking his club from him. 'Leave us!'

I watched the guards file out. None of them looked particularly happy leaving their tor with a stolen shade, but they followed his orders all the same. I suspected it was due to him being their employer, not any kind of fervent loyalty.

'The box, Caltro.'

I grumbled something profane as he handed me my tools. I tried my best not to snatch them.

The box was simple, just as I'd suspected. It took me mere moments to test its tumblers, find its notches, and start picking. Within a few minutes, the lid popped open with a hiss of stale air.

'Told you,' I sighed as I stepped back. Busk stood still, ignoring his prize and staring only at me. I got the sense there was an ulterior motive to this situation. 'What is it?'

'Why are you so important to Horix? Does she know?'

Playing dumb was an art. The trick to it was a mixture of well-timed shrugs, half-lies, and a straight face. I shrugged.

'Surely she does,' said Busk. She holds your half-coin and yet she hasn't punished you yet for leaving her home. I was expecting her to, hence I had you open my most prized possession first. Yet here we are, days later and not a twitch.'

'Maybe she hasn't noticed I'm gone.' That was ridiculous. The old bat had me on a leash so short a living thing would have choked.

'The thought crossed my mind also, and I believed the same, until *this* came to my door.' Busk produced a small scroll from his velvet pocket. I could tell by its wrinkles it had been unrolled, rerolled, crumpled in anger at one point, then flattened out again. 'This,' he said, 'is from your previous mistress. Offering to sell you.'

'I see.' It was all I gave him. In truth, I was confused as to how Horix intended to sell a ghost she didn't have and for some reason needed.

'She had it delivered by the colonel of her guard, no less. Straight into my hands.'

'I'm as clueless as you are.'

Busk scowled. 'I am not clueless, shade. In fact, I am very clueful.' He circled me and the pedestal. 'She was unwilling to part with you when I first broached the subject. And now that I have you, she immediately wants to sell you. It is a ploy. A test.'

I saw the widow's game now: a change of Busk's mind would look suspicious, but agreeing to a sale would mean following the path Horix was laying for him.

'One does not play such games in this city unless it is for something important. Tors and tals do not dally with trivialities. Shades get stolen all the time, constantly shifting from house to house. A hundred here, another hundred there. What does one shade matter to a noble with thousands under her control?'

I sensed a rhetorical question and kept my trap shut.

'Do you know what we nobles do when a shade is taken from us illegally? We melt your half-coin. Send you to the void. You, however, are whole and sound. That tells me you are important to her in some way, and I wish to know why.'

I shrugged.

Busk raised the club menacingly.

'Perhaps for the same reason you were keen to steal me,' I offered, not too eager to get another hit. My jaw was still throbbing. White spots lingered in my vision.

'My thoughts exactly!' Busk exclaimed. 'The question is *why*, Caltro? Tal Horix might be an enigma, a hermit, and an old bag with no manners, but those few who have dealt with her respect her. Fear her, even. Yet she is never seen at balls or the theatre. Horix rarely leaves her tower except for the soulmarket. She has not Weighed in a year. What I do know is that she is no fence. No soulstealer. Why, then, would she have need of you?'

Another shrug, and this time the club did strike home, right across my shoulders. I pitched onto the pedestal, my head striking the box will a dull *whump*.

'Let's try again. Why does she need a locksmith like you?'

'I cook a fucking good rabbit stew. Maybe that's why.'

The club came at me again, mercilessly so. Busk beat me like a dusty carpet until I was on my knees. Pain shot through my body with every hit, contorting me. When Busk tired, breathing hard, he stepped back to rearrange his coat and comb his thinning hair back into place.

'I cannot abide shades who forget their place in the world. I find that reminding them with a club works wonders.'

'Mmmf,' I mumbled, fighting pain.

'What does she want you for?'

'I don't know!' The club cracked against my skull. My face met the floor. 'I'm telling the truth!'

Busk yelled in my ear. 'Tell me everything! Does she want you for a heist?'

'No!' A strange allegiance kept me from spilling what little truth I knew. Perhaps it was the future she had offered me; the promise of freedom that Busk could never make.

'All right! All right.' I held up my hands, cowering more than I would have liked. Pain is a wonderful test of the calibre of a man's soul. Mine had always leaned towards the cowardly side of the spectrum. Flight over fight, I say. It was a trait that might have hurt the pride of another man, but it had kept me alive more times than I could count. I knew the worth of cowardice. And lies.

'She had me open boxes, just like you. Heirlooms, nothing more.'

Busk looked unconvinced. 'Heirlooms.'

'Jewelled boxes and the like. Old things from her collection.'

'I don't believe you.'

'I don't care what you fucking believe.' I glared. 'Horix will come for me. Not because I am important, but because I am hers. She will not abide your thievery.'

Busk's narrow face grew as wide as I'd ever seen it. His grin beamed, unnaturally white. 'She is an old hermit, rusty and stubborn. She wants to play games? Fine! I will entertain her. And all the while I will have you here, opening everything that crosses my path with a lock on it, doing my bidding. Understand, Caltro?'

I lunged for him. I don't quite know what I expected to achieve, but before I knew it I was reaching towards him with hands like pincers, searching for his throat. It was an act of anger and frustration, and in that moment I understood what a crime of passion meant. It seemed that even without my mortal form, the animal in me lived on as I did. The savagery of our distant ancestors survives just beneath the surface of our civility, and I had remembered mine.

Busk fended me off with the club, too shocked to call for his guards. I felt the copper smack against my wrists but the pain was forgotten in my drive to strangle the bastard. I made little sound, no threat but the straining growl of rage.

He found his voice. 'Back! Back, I say!'

I kept at him, reaching and reaching.

'Guards!'

Busk stumbled over his own feet and his fancy shoes, falling onto his arse with his club outstretched. With the back of my fist, I batted the weapon aside and sent it skittering across the marble. Pain lanced up my arm. Busk's flailing legs tangled my own and I landed atop him, fighting to encircle his throat.

I was so fixated on seizing the white flesh between his velvet collar, I didn't even notice my hands piercing his skin. No, not piercing. *Entering.* My glowing fingers reached deep into his throat, so far I could feel the rubbery ridges of his windpipe, feel the blood inside his veins pulsing over my vapour.

It was enough to halt my attack just for a moment; long enough to feel icy fingers at my own throat, and feel the beat of a terrified heart in my chest. I gasped for air against the cold trying to envelop me. My vision was overlaid with blue. I saw a livid face etched into that swirling cloud of vapour.

My own.

I barely noticed when the guards ripped me from the tor. My form lit up where their copper-thread hands touched me, but I felt none of the pain. Instead, I felt the life drain from me with every yard they put between me and Busk, who was still thrashing on the floor. My arms twitched with his movements, mimicking him.

'Get him out. Get him out!' he yelled. I could feel his hot breath escaping my mouth.

Whatever sorcery had bound us was cut with the slam of the door. I was thrown down the stairs, landing next to two ghosts carrying a bucket of mop-water. They spilled it in their surprise, dousing my smock.

I let the guards lift and drag me back to my wardrobe. In truth, I was too stunned to do much else. I did not fight them when they shoved me into the dark and locked the door on me. I simply stood, mouth agape, eyes staring but not seeing. I was too busy wrestling my mind into something that resembled sense.

A voice called out to me. It might have been calling for some time, but this was the first of it I'd heard.

'I said, are you okay, Caltro?'

The bloody sword.

'What happened?'

'I—' I paused, realising I had no answer to give. My own conclusion still seemed too ridiculous in its impossibility, and yet…

'Did they hurt you? Busk tried that with me once. Showed me a forge and held me in the fire—'

I had little patience for any more stories. 'Shut up. Just shut up for one moment.'

Even then, the sword had to say his piece. 'Well I never.'

'Look… *you.*' I realised that in all his blabbering, I'd never gleaned a name. 'What is your name, anyway?'

'I've gone by many names. The Black Death. Absia. Yer'a Ankou. Once I was called Bonespli—'

My hands waved impatiently in the dark. 'Whatever. I'll call you Pointy until you settle on one.'

'Pointy…?'

'You're a deadbound, right? Bound into something lifeless. Inanimate.'

'I hardly need reminding, but yes. I am a soulblade, to be precise.'

'And in all your years, have you ever heard of a ghost, a shade, being bound into someone that's already alive?'

'Well, there have been animals. Horses. Hawks. Dogs. They call it strangebound, remember?'

'Yes, I know that. Not animals. People. *Living* people.'

Pointy paused in thought. 'I know a few tales.' He sounded cautious. 'What happened?'

'It never worked too well. The Chamber of the Code banned the Nyxites from doing it several hundred years before I was bound, if not more. In fact, there's an epic poem about why they—'

I gritted my teeth as hard as vapour can be gritted. 'No! No poems. Just tell me.'

'Well, it was something to do with religion. Something no Arctian has worried about in the years since the gods were proclaimed dead and gone. Apparently, the gods used to walk among us, inhabiting bodies, testing those they met. The Nyxites and the Chamber both thought this practice too similar. Too religious for their liking. Men trying to be gods.'

'What happened to the people?'

'For a shade, you really don't know much about binding, do you?'

'I'm still new to it.'

'Well, a body's only built for one soul, not two. It seems only the gods are capable of that. The tales tell of men and women driven mad. Of their bodies giving up after rotting from the inside out in a matter of days. Some ripped themselves apart with their bare hands, trying to fight with the foreign soul. Almost always, they both died. Permanently.'

I instinctively held myself, checking I was still there and not rotting. As for madness, well, I was talking to a sword. I didn't dwell on it. 'And what do they call that? Livebound, I guess?'

'*Haunting*, Caltro. They called it a haunting.'

A haunting. I turned the strange word over and over in my mind until, like a clockwork toy, I had teased it apart and put it back together again.

Pointy was unusually silent. Perhaps he could hear the cogs of my brain clanking. When the silence had dragged out beyond all reason, he spoke, sounding almost afraid.

'Why do you ask?'

I sighed, hardly believing it myself. *Fuck.* I hated it when others were right. *Especially gods.*

'Because, Mr Sword – Pointy – I think I just haunted Tor Busk.'

CHAPTER 5
MURDER MOST LUCRATIVE

Vaults and doors became big business in the
centuries after binding was discovered. As trust
eroded and each noble became more insular,
they trusted to vaultsmiths and doorsmiths
to keep them and their half-coins safe.
Guards and mercenaries also became highly
lucrative positions, with many Skol, Krass and
Scatterfolk sellswords flooding into Araxes,
ready to protect the highest bidder.

FROM 'THE CITY OF COUNTLESS SOULS –
A KEEN-EYED GUIDE'

THE SANDSTORM CONQUERED THE OUTSPRAWLS within hours, swallowing the shacks and piled buildings with its ochre jaws.

As its hunger stretched towards the city heights, the sun slunk into the sea, leaving Araxes to fend for itself in the half-light.

The mighty towers became channels for the wind, squeezing more ferocity from the storm. Shutters rattled against the howl and roar of biting sand. The streets were emptied save for shades forced on late errands by callous masters, or unfortunates with no towers to hide in, no doors to bolt behind them. Abandoned carts and stalls tumbled down the streets, adding deep booms to the merciless rush of air.

Against the cold ocean gusts, the storm reared higher, claiming the staggering heights of the tallest towers. Even the pinnacle of the Cloudpiercer was devoured. In their upper reaches, yellow lightning forked and crackled through the clouds.

In the orange darkness of the streets of Quara District, a lone figure struggled towards a tower built like a stretched-out conch shell. The figure staggered left, right, paused to fight the wind, and battled on. Hands outstretched, it found a wall and paced with its palms until an archway was found.

The courtyard beyond was a gyre of sand, obscuring all but the lights of two hooded lamps guarding a door. A fist reached out to strike the iron panels. The wind drove the shape from the doorstep twice, but each time it fought back to hammer on the pitted metal.

'Please!' A female voice, muffled by cloth and storm-roar. 'Help!'

Iron rasped and a hatch opened. A shaft of lamplight speared the roil. A man's face appeared behind the grille, immediately recoiling with a mouthful of sand. After the coughing had abated, a harsh voice called, 'What?!'

The woman pressed her cheeks to the grille. 'Shelter, please!'

'Go away, beggar!'

'I am no beggar!'

She pulled aside her cloth mask, showing lips and eyes painted with crushed purple quartz. 'I'm Tal Patra's daughter! Give me sanctuary! Noble to noble!'

The hatch closed with a snap. Her fists drummed on the iron in angry desperation.

'Sanctuary! My father will owe a debt to you!'

A heavy clanking rose over the din as cogs turned inside the door. At its centre, a strip of light ignited, blinding against the darkness.

Hooded, masked figures appeared and beckoned to her. 'Enter, Taless Patra!'

The woman held the doorstep, unmoving, cloak crackling around her in the flurries.

All formalities eroded. 'Quickly, woman! In!'

The smaller of the two figures braved the rush and came to guide her by the hand. 'What are you waiting f—*urch!*'

The dagger withdrew from the man's throat, drawing an arc of dark blood in its wake. The man clapped a hand to the wound, confusion carved into his face. He dropped to one knee in front of the woman, blinking at the shadows as he gargled and drowned from within.

From the inside of the tower, it might have looked like an impromptu romantic moment had it not been for the blood spurting rhythmically with his failing heartbeat.

'Shit!' yelled the other guard, pressing hands to the great doors.

A dull boom echoed as a fist wrapped in steel met the iron. The guard fell to his arse and skidded across the marble. A hulking figure followed the woman into the lamplight, one clad in steel plates and wearing a spiked helmet. Blue light glowed through the seams of the armour, fading to green where the sand rushed in. A huge spear was balanced in the shade's hand, and with a single thrust it pierced the guard's stomach and burst from his back. He toppled with a scream, taking the weapon with him.

In poured more shapes, sweeping past the woman standing on the doorstep. They were a wall of black leather and chainmail, bristling with sharp things.

'Very well done, m'dear!' called a voice between the repetitive clang of metal. White sparks scattered as a figure emerged from the haze. Lamplight played on copper talons.

Boran Temsa withdrew his mask and laid a congratulatory hand on the woman's shoulder, a serving girl borrowed from his tavern. She was tall and he had to reach. 'Very well done indeed, Balia. I knew you had more talents than merely squeezing silver out of drunkards.'

'Many more, Boss Temsa. *Tor* Temsa.' Balia performed a curtsey, and let him shepherd her inside by taking his elbow.

The wall of leather and armour parted, showing them a wide atrium of red-veined marble. Sand was already spreading over it like yellow mould. Alabaster figures stared down from alcoves, their pale faces frozen in severe disapproval of the new arrivals. Taut bands of crimson silk separated them, reaching from floor to domed ceiling. Painted hieroglyphs adorned the smooth plaster, telling stories Temsa didn't care to know.

'How fancy,' he mused, craning his stiff neck.

A blue glow bathed him and somebody grunted at his shoulder. Danib had recovered his spear from the corpse by the door. Blood dripped from its point and pattered on the floor. The doorman's scream had alerted the household; the echoes of rushing boots could be heard descending the stairs in the rooms above. Danib cast his master a sidelong glance.

Temsa waved his hand as if shooing a sandfly. 'Of course you may, old friend. Go ahead. We're not here to admire the drapes, now, are we?'

The shade tramped over the marble, steel clanking. Temsa's men spread out behind him, masks torn aside to reveal eager grins. It seemed they enjoyed this almost as much as Temsa did. *Almost.*

Temsa stayed put, arms resting on his cane as he idly watched his men go to work against the house-guards streaming down the stairs. Balia's grip on his arm tightened with every clang of steel and dying cry.

There was a downside to trained men. Once a man is taught to cut and slash in certain ways, his actions are confined to those rules. He is caged by rote and technique. Fighting, to that manner of man, is a formal dance one might find in noble halls.

It was why Temsa preferred his throat-cutters raw. They didn't cling doggedly to form. They didn't posture. Their dance was far from noble, more like the cavorting of desert tribes or island savages. A trained man was no match for such barbarity.

Leaping, bounding, playing dirty tricks with their steel, Temsa's men cut the guards to ribbons. Even when their opponents were lying trembling on the floor, they hacked until limbs were hewn free, armour and all. The pieces spilled down the stairs in a slippery river of blood and shit.

With Ani and Balia by his side, Temsa picked his way over the detritus and corpses. If any of them still moved, they met his golden talons. When their shades arose naturally in several days' time, he would send them south to the desert mines, where nobody would hear this story.

Up they wound, conquering the tower level by level, house-guard by house-guard. Balia soon lost her stomach and had to return to the atrium. Her retching echoed up the stairwell.

Shades prostrated themselves on the carpets and in their alcoves, not wishing to die again. Temsa left them be. Stock was not to be damaged.

They found her in the highest reaches of the tower, where the conch shell thinned into a coiled spire. Tal Kheyu-Nebra was a wizened and crooked woman at the best of times. Here, at her worst, she looked like a leprous beggar: hands clasped and waving above her head, legs folded beneath her, back as curved as a bucket-handle. Had she not been wrapped in silk sheets, Temsa might have flicked her a gem for charity. He wondered what she had done to irritate the empress-in-waiting enough to be on her list.

'Tal! How kind of you to accommodate us at this late hour.'

Kheyu was not begging, as it seemed, but praying. Her muttering was no answer, but a stream of platitudes for the old gods.

'Stuck in the ancient ways, I see. Didn't anybody tell you the gods are dead?'

With a sigh, Kheyu straightened to look up at the men spread about her bedchamber. 'Audacity is the hobby of fools, sir.'

Temsa rubbed his beard. 'Or the pleasure of the daring. In any case, I am here, and we have business to conduct.'

Kheyu snorted. 'Business? You mean murder.'

'You know as well as I do that the royals and nobles blurred that line centuries ago. They are one and the same in this city. I simply follow your lead.'

The old tal shuffled from her bed. Temsa reached for her cane, leaning nearby, and handed it to her. Kheyu fixed him with a rheumy stare, a calm look of damnation in those glassy eyes. There was no fear.

'Get it over with, if you must,' she said. 'I will not beg a criminal.'

Temsa wagged a finger. 'Not so fast, my dear Tal. There are questions, signatures needed. Do not take me for some dockside soulstealer.

That is far behind me now. As I said, this is business. Now, I have it on good authority that you have a vault. I imagine one who clings to the old ways would reject our city's fine banks, am I right?'

For the first time, Kheyu's confidence crumbled. Temsa saw it in the wobble of her lips: her faith in justice was wavering. She lifted her chin, defiant. Perhaps she believed in *ma'at* as well as the dead gods. *The halfwit.*

'Do your worst.'

Temsa came so close their noses almost touched. 'Madam, I plan to.'

With a snap of his fingers, his men carried Kheyu from her chambers, Danib loomed once more, spear still dripping with ruby gore.

'She'll be tough, that one,' Temsa mused. 'The sun tans these old bats harder than leather.'

Silence from the shade's mouth. A world of meaning in his cobalt eyes.

'Good practice indeed, my old friend. Horix will have her turn soon enough. Come, let's begin.'

Outside the quivering windows, the sandstorm roared on, unabated and uncaring.

CHAPTER 6
MURDER MOST FOUL

Farazar married as a prince before he killed
his father. His princess? Nilith Rikehar, Lady
of Saraka, second daughter of the Krass king
Konin. It was a promise as well as a marriage;
old Emperor Milizan's way of letting Konin
keep his lands and the peace between them.
His son Farazar has held that promise since,
waging wars in the Scatter Isles instead.

FROM 'A REACH HISTORY' BY GAERVIN JUBB

'I ALWAYS THOUGHT AN EMPEROR WOULD be prettier-looking. You look better on your silver coins.'

'Fuck you, bird.'

Farazar swept back to the bulwark, a word Ghyrab had taught them. Nilith stifled a chuckle. Bezel's foul mouth – or beak – was a welcome addition to her tired and grumble-sore ears. Though they hadn't spoken much, and his loyalty still hung in question, she was undoubtedly warming to him.

The falcon preened in thought. 'It's true, though. And you married that face, Empress. I can see why you killed him.'

River water filled the pause. Nilith had grown used to the river as the days dragged by, her fear of it slipping away with the scenery. Nevertheless, she had made camp in the centre of the barge. The furthest place away from the water on a square boat was always the centre. It was simple geometry.

The canyon walls reared above them, taller now the Ashti had thinned, ember red and worn smooth from centuries of eager river water. The overhanging ledge that had given them cover had all but diminished. Already, half the barge baked in the hot sunlight that poured down into the gully.

Ghyrab had not moved from the tiller. Night and day he had stood, mahogany eyes affixed to his waters, keeping the rock close by. Every so often, his gaze scanned the lip of the cliff above, watching for black figures and black horses. Few words had escaped his mouth, and he had taken no interest in his passengers, even though one of them was the dead and unclaimed body of the Arctian emperor. Trusting people was a dangerous pastime in the Arc, but Nilith took a chance with the bargeman.

Her luck had held so far. There had been no glimpse of Krona or her Ghouls. Just a faint echo of hoofbeats the night before. The full moon had brought Nilith and Ghyrab into the light, jaws set and wary, wincing at the notion of arrows. Safety was a strong word, but the barge was as close as she'd come since the desert tavern.

Since bursting into their lives, Bezel had been largely absent. He stuck to the sky, keeping them abreast of their progress between circling the barge for hours on end, putting his dagger-sharp eyes to work. According to the bird, the Duneplains were as blank as papyrus. Salt flats for miles. When asked of the city, he had merely shrugged his wings and said, 'You're getting there.'

Nilith had met a strangebound only once before. A duke in her father's retinue had brought a wolfhound to court when she was nine. It was a bitter, sarcastic thing, spending its short moments in the longhall complaining about the smell of barbarians before the duke had been asked to leave. She never saw the hound or its owner again.

Bitterness seemed to be a trait of the falcon, too. Perhaps it was the nature of a human soul trapped in a lesser body. Despite her jealousy of his ability to fly – deep-set in every being since the first eyes had glimpsed the first birds – Nilith could understand his frustration. No fingers, toes, lips, or arms. His voice and thoughts were all of him that remained. The lack of himself had clearly bred resentment in his feathery breast. She hardly blamed him. No doubt her daughter's treatment of him hadn't helped. She decided to take his short rest as a chance to get some answers.

'Bezel,' Nilith said, drawing a stare from the bird. 'How long has Sisine been your master?'

'Seven years, I've belonged to your daughter.' His reply was a mutter.

'You didn't mention how she came by you.' Nilith's conversations with the falcon had been scant. The threat of the Ghouls meant they hadn't even got down to bargaining.

'That northern tit, Prince Phylar. He was my master before Sisine. The idiot never figured out how to use the silver bell I'm bound to. Instead he gave it as a gift when he came to court your daughter. Remember that?'

Nilith did. She also remembered not having any choice in the matter. Farazar's idea, as usual.

'Sisine figured it out fucking quick-like. Summoned me up and put me to work spying on you two, or sereks and tals, paying me with whatever joys are left to a strangebound. Food. Wine. Fucking. Freedom to roam. She never told a soul about me.'

'That doesn't surprise me one bit. She's always been secretive. She barely talks to me, and whenever she does her words are full of spite, contempt, blame, or all bloody three. You know, in the last year I've perhaps traded a dozen sentences with her. She's avoided me ever since Farazar locked his vault.'

Twenty-two years, and the closest they'd ever been was the day Nilith birthed her. Farazar, the tutors, and – before their banishment and death – Farazar's parents had all tried their hardest to turn Sisine into the perfect Arctian princess. It had worked, and now she had come of age she was scheming like the best of the family line, hungry for her father's throne.

'Does it worry you, leaving her behind? Alone?' asked the falcon, shuffling his wings.

'It should,' hissed Farazar, eavesdropping as always.

Nilith nodded. She had spent more than a few sleepless nights worrying about what her absence and her daughter's ambition could mean. The Ghouls had distracted her, but with the arrival of the falcon, those worries had slid back into her mind like smoke seeping under a bedroom door. At the very least, as long as Nilith held the body of Farazar, Sisine was limited in her ability to wreak havoc.

Bezel clacked his beak. 'Seeing as it's fucking question time, here's one I've been itching to ask.'

'What's that?'

Bezel cast a look at the ghost. 'How'd you catch him? How'd you track him down?'

Nilith chuckled softly. 'Well, falcon, I'll tell you. But first, tell me what you want in return for your help. Why are you here?'

The bird cleared his throat haughtily. 'Not yet,' he said, and the conversation was shattered as he launched himself into the sky with a throbbing of wingbeats. A keening wail chased his path to the strip of blue above them.

Nilith watched him, feeling that jealousy once more. She wished he was a gryphon, strong enough to carry her and Farazar's corpse all the way to the Grand Nyxwell before it was too late. Without the thud of hooves beneath her and reins to control, she was at the mercy of the Ashti's flow. She could not control it any more than she could the tangible passing of time, and together they conspired to make her continually anxious. It felt as if she stood in a gigantic hourglass, with the minutes hammering down on her head.

Fortunately for her, the Ashti no longer languished as it had. The river was starting to gather speed. Their path was becoming narrower in places, pinching the river and making it run faster.

Nilith shuffled to Anoish, who had taken to sleeping through the pain of his deep arrow wound. The shaft had been snapped and the arrowhead dug out of his back leg with much thrashing and whinnying. Nilith had been kicked halfway across the barge more than once, almost cracking several ribs, but the grisly business had been completed.

A heavy poultice of herbs and oil, fashioned from food scraps Ghyrab kept on his vessel, was now tied about the leg. It looked like a crest of stuffing perched on an undercooked haunch of meat. She wished she had a spare ghost and some Nyxwater instead, like in Abatwe. Her own wounds were now almost healed, and somehow that made her feel guilty.

The horse was in a blue mood. His tongue poked out between his grey lips from the heat. His eyes were two dark orbs of sadness that followed Nilith as she pottered about him. She poked, she checked, she whispered nothings in his flat and dejected ears. He thumped a hoof in reply, but that was all she got from him besides the staring. Nilith sighed and found a spot on the deck near his head, where the flat hull nosed the water.

When she could bring herself to watch the flow, she saw a shadowy brown bottom beneath the diamond-clear waters, strewn with boulders the size of carriages and slick with opportunistic algae. The rocks looked uncomfortably close, but Nilith knew water could play tricks with light. She scooped up a handful to wash her face, and found it cold enough to make her gasp.

The sky and sun gave the water the colour and sparkle of lapis lazuli. The further ahead she looked, the more of the sky's colour the river stole. Where the canyon walls overshadowed the waters, they were a mirror to the red rock.

An hour, maybe more, Nilith sat there, growing attuned to the bobbing of the barge. It took time to reason with fear, especially the irrational kind. Logic was of little use. It took real proof: the sort that eyes could witness, not the sort the mind could conjure. The longer the barge stayed afloat and proved itself to her, the weaker the knot in her stomach became, the calmer the throb of her heart.

It was short-lived.

'Rapids!' Bezel screeched, swooping between two knuckles of rock that almost touched overhead. The word stabbed Nilith in the gut.

'*What?*'

Farazar chuckled snidely. 'Afraid of the water, wife?'

'Shut your face, ghost.'

Ghyrab scoffed at their wide eyes, like a father to a bothersome child. 'Ain't rapids, bird. Just eddies.'

'Who's Eddy?' Farazar asked.

'Are you sure?' Nilith asked of Ghyrab.

The bargeman snorted back some phlegm as a response, but he still wrapped his arm around the tiller. That was cause enough for Nilith to squat down in her usual spot at the centre of the barge. She just wished the craft wasn't so flat. She could feel the ripples slapping at the wood beneath her fingers. The river felt as though it was speeding up, and the approaching rumble of rushing water filled her ears. Once more, she envied Bezel, soaring above like an ambivalent balloon.

'Eddies.' The word was too soft for the way the water churned against the rocks, or gathered in spinning whirlpools in the hollows of the canyon walls. Nilith eyed their watery mouths, funnelling down into darker waters. She found a new and chilling fear in them. She didn't want to imagine what it was like to tumble into such a thing. Ahead of them, she saw a faint curtain of spray obscuring tall, dark shadows. Rainbows filled the air, but their beauty did nothing to assuage her fear.

'Ghyrab?' she cried.

'Trust me!' he yelled over the hiss and roil.

Nilith pressed her cheek to the jittering deck as if it was another hand she could hold on with. Through half-closed eyes, she watched a tall spur of rock sail past the barge. Its cold shadow fell across her.

'Ghyrab!'

'They're just the Fangs. Don't worry!'

A morbid curiosity betrayed her. Before burying her head, Nilith glimpsed three more ugly spines of rock in the barge's path. 'Don't worry? *Really?*' she yelled into the deck.

Under Ghyrab's expert tutelage, their craft twisted this way and that through the whirlpools and eddies. Nilith finally understood why they called these craft "barges". Using his oar-like tiller, he threw his vessel into every bank and swell of water, shoving them aside with enough momentum to weave around the sharp rocks.

Nilith felt the turmoil beneath the deck calm as soon as the last shadow passed over. The fear faded quickly. She had managed to hold her breath for the entire duration of the rapids, and only now did she exhale. A peek showed her the canyon walls were retreating, like the sound of the churning water. Instead, she heard the hiss and snap of reeds meeting the bow. She saw them poking over the bulwarks, dappled green and yellow in the slanted sun.

A polite cough from Ghyrab brought her to her feet. He held her eyes, his chin high and confident, and she gave him a curtsey. 'I was wrong to doubt you.'

The bargeman hummed. 'Many are. You aren't the first. Won't be the last.'

Nilith's gaze followed the edge of a skinny teardrop lake. It was like the bulge of a swallowed rat making its way through this snake of a river. Fields of reeds hugged the lake's edges, pink-edged lily and lotus flowers blossoming amongst their stalks. They were giant, and spun like wagon wheels in the barge's wake. The stickled backs of small albino crocodiles lurked between their green, platter-like pads. Ibises stood guard in the shallows on legs as long as broom handles. They moved so infrequently Nilith fancied them sculptures until she saw one bend and stab the water in a blur of white feathers and catch a wriggling fish.

Nilith raised her face and arms to the last of the day's sun, breathing in the perfume of the lake flowers. It was a rare moment of bliss, despite Farazar's insistence on pacing about the barge.

'No sign of your friend Krona,' called the falcon, his voice a whistle on the wind. He circled the lake once to make sure there were no marauders in sight before landing on the barge. 'Just a herd of goats, a village, some more salt flats, and maybe a wild camel or two.'

Nilith didn't doubt him. Bezel's golden orbs could probably spy a mouse at fifty miles.

'I don't like being in the open,' Farazar was mumbling.

'We'll be out of it soon enough. Then we'll pass through Kal Duat,' said Ghyrab.

'Where?'

'Hell... Majesty.' Ghyrab cleared his throat, probably unused to his passengers having such titles. The concept of royalty seemed somewhat loose out here on the fringes. The reach of the emperor extended into the wilderness only so far. His name counted for little outside the Sprawls. 'The White Hell. I would've thought you types would be aware of such a place. Isn't this your country?'

Nilith had never heard of it. Her gut wrenched. 'More rapids?'

The bargeman smiled. 'No, madam. You'll see.'

'Bezel...' she began to say, but stopped at seeing the bargeman's smile die, quickly and ruthlessly.

'Still don't trust me?' Ghyrab challenged her.

'I... Fine. Bezel, stay on the barge.'

The falcon shrugged his wings. 'All right. But if this ugly bunch of planks starts going under, I'm fucking off sharpish.'

Even though Nilith's breeding afforded her little respect, Bezel spoke to her as if she were a chamber-shade. It had caused her hackles to rise at first, but it was refreshing and welcome. There was no ceremony in him, no fawning, no senseless drivel courtiers were so fond of. Just truth and sense.

She gave him a mock scowl. 'See? We trust you, Ghyrab.'

'Hmph.'

The bargeman said no more. Nilith moved to his side, sharing the job of the tiller with him as he guided the barge back into narrower waters, scattering the white crocodiles. Her teeth pulled at her bottom lip. Her heart still hadn't calmed from the slalom through the Fangs.

Back in a corridor of red rock, the sun had fallen too far to give them much light. After the lake, the shadows fell heavy and cold. Anoish whinnied ominously. Animals had a sense for danger, be it storms or approaching swords.

Even with the lack of sun, Nilith found that same old sweat creeping down her brow. She looked to Ghyrab and found him lazy and slouched, eyes half closed. Not a bother in the world. She found a scrap of comfort in the old man's posture and tried to adopt something similar. Leaning against the bulwark, she focused on her heart, trying to drown its hurried beats in the burble of water. Despite its capacity to drown, flood, and otherwise inconvenience her, Nilith had to admit there was something calming about a river's song. It even put a stop to the ghost's infernal pacing. Farazar took up a stand in the centre of the barge instead.

This stretch of the Ashti had a deeper tone. At first Nilith thought it an echo of the rock, but with every twist in the route, the louder it became. Even when the strip of sky widened and the canyon walls became stunted, the noise overpowered the river.

Nilith shot a look at the bargeman beside her, all sorts of words for crushing amounts of water running through her mind. He just sucked his teeth.

'You said no more rapids,' she ventured.

'That's right. I did.'

Farazar turned. 'A waterfall, then?'

The question gave Ghyrab cause to snort. 'Oh, no. Not a waterfall. That sound you're hearing is hammers of a big ole limestone mine, almost a hundred years old and still churning. They say the place has eaten more souls than it has hours and stone. That's the Kal Duat. The White Hell. You royals really ain't heard of it?' He looked between the ghost and Nilith, apparently surprised.

'The Arctian Empire is a vast domain, my good man,' Farazar explained through a sigh. 'The largest in the Reaches.'

'And don't you ever wonder where all the white stone for your fancy towers comes from?'

'From the Chamber of the Grand Builder or the Chamber of Trade, of course.'

The bargeman had an imperious look on his face. 'And where do they get it from, hmm? Tsk.'

Farazar blustered. 'Did you just tut at me, peasa—'

Nilith silenced both of them with a stamp of her foot. 'What Farazar means to say is that's what the Grand Builder is for. Royals are not directly involved with the dealings of the traders and architects. *Especially* the emperor.'

'More important things to do,' muttered the ghost.

Ghyrab nodded. 'Like making merry in your famous vault and making war? Well, Majesty, you'll soon see what happens when you don't pay attention to a kingdom.' His words made Farazar seek out a corner of the barge, and Nilith grin rather widely. She couldn't have put it better if she tried.

For an hour, the hammering grew from a hum to a roar. It could almost be classed as thunder by the time she saw a fat gatehouse stretching over the river. She reached for the trident that leaned next to the tiller and held it like a staff.

Armoured planks and bars formed a heavy gate that blocked their way. A swathe of green slime besieged the sun-bleached wood. It had already conquered half the wall and looked intent on claiming the rest sometime over the next decade. Twisted black spikes adorned the jagged battlements. Between them, black shapes stood against the dimming sky, flat, wide-brimmed hats on their heads and triggerbows in their hands.

Bezel clacked his beak at the sight of their bows. 'Yeah… I'll see you folks on the other side of this place. You can tell me the story later.' With that, he burst into the sky, becoming nothing but a wheeling fleck.

'Leave this to me.' Ghyrab thrust the tiller into Nilith's spare hand. He strode for the bow and used a pole to stop the barge from butting the gates.

'Stop there!' yelled one of the figures.

Nilith peered upwards, just about understanding his thick desert dialect. On the flat barge, under shrewd eyes, she felt like a delicacy on a platter being served up for dinner.

The voice hollered again, this time accompanied by a dark face with big ears and a sprout of hair. Nilith heard the cautionary creak of bowstrings and wished once more for a vessel with a roof.

'Announce yourself! Business, passage or bandit?'

Ghyrab banged the pole against the gate. 'It's *me*, Thaph! You know it's me. Twice a year I come through, and every time you ask! And why would a bandit tell you he's a bandit?'

'Bandits are stupid. Might trick 'em,' suggested another voice from behind the parapet. It was barely audible over the hammering of the quarry. Nilith could smell acrid tar and rot on the air.

'Orders is orders.' Thaph banged a palm against the wood. 'Business or passage, Ghyrab?'

'Passage, curse it!'

'Your name?'

'You've just—'

Thaph cleared his throat loudly. 'How many passengers?'

'You've got eyes, haven't you? Two living. One shade. And a horse, if that counts.' Ghyrab struck the gate again. 'Just hurry up.'

After much muffled discussion, the gates split in half to the clamour of chains. They moved at an aching pace, revealing their precious secrets so gradually that Nilith had soaked in most of the horror by the time the barge passed under the wall.

Once more, the river reached an open clearing, though this one was far deeper, wider, longer, and infinitely more sinister than the last. Nilith craned her neck to take in the breadth of milk-white rock walls. They had been cut into mighty steps, fit for the feet of titans. Machinery and scaffolding sprawled like a city across their angular slopes. A tangle of ladders and ramps stitched it all together, like sutures trying to stop a vast, gaping wound in the earth from bursting open.

The thunder emanated from this foul sprawl. It was not just comprised of hammers, but of countless feet and barrows and voices as well. Both the scaffolding and the surfaces of the bare rock writhed with activity. Even as the day turned to evening, hordes of miners toiled on fervently. They dug, they chipped, they cut, they drilled; ghosts toiling alongside the living. The former gave the limestone a cold glow, while the latter might as well have been corpses for the amount of dust and blood that caked them. More than a few shapes lay prone amongst the piles of stone chips and rubble. Whether dead or dying, nobody tended them. Beasts toiled alongside the miners. Horses, beetles, spiders and ponies hauled blocks or heaved on rope. They looked in no better shape than the humans who worked them; shaky, emaciated creatures.

Unable to witness their plight any longer, Nilith's eyes followed the huge blocks of limestone as they were hauled down the ramps. Lesser blocks swung from ropes as teams yelled and sweated to keep them airborne. Down went the blocks, always down, progressing like picnic items along a column of thieving ants. Down, until she realised the quarry dipped below the river's level. She looked ahead, and found the river had an edge to it, and shit all else beyond it.

A moment of panic struck her, along with that word again. *Waterfall.*

'Steady now,' Ghyrab said, feeling her twitch on the tiller. She had yet to let go. 'Watch.'

Nilith could do nothing but watch as the edge crept closer and the repugnant bowels of the quarry were laid bare. The clanking of machinery and sloshing of water rose above the roar of labour, but all she heard was her heart, louder still in her ears.

As her screech was poised to leave her throat, the lurch of the barge interrupted her. Wide-eyed, Nilith looked to Ghyrab. She found him smiling once more.

They were falling, but not in the traditional way one tumbles over a waterfall. They glided downwards with all the speed and grace of a feather. The water had come with them, not rushing in a deluge, but instead hugging the barge, sloshing about in the confines of some unseen platform. Behind them, the river poured down in a sheet, hiding all but the edges of huge girders and cogs grinding away. The rhythmic pounding of some clockwork machine battered Nilith's eardrums.

The barge lurched as the platform sank into the river below and sent it washing forwards to the next precipice. Level after level, they descended in this fashion. Each mighty step was conquered effortlessly. For a brief time, Nilith saw a beauty in the stubborn ingenuity of human minds; minds that could bend rivers or build towers to top mountains. These were feats that lifted her heart, and restored some faith in her kind. And then she gazed down into the hell that the same minds had dug into the earth, and that faith withered. There was no valour in greed, and Kal Duat looked like the birthplace of greed.

'They call these the Nine Levels,' Ghyrab told her, motioning up at the huge steps now towering over them. 'One for every decade the White Hell's been churning. The tenth's being dug now, down into the earth.'

They splashed onto the ninth as he spoke, where what remained of the river had been confined to a wide gutter of stone that ran along the bottom of the quarry. Either side of it, beyond the sprawling stone docksides, Nilith could see channels where the first cuts were being made into the dirt, like flesh scraped away from a shin bone. She nodded, mouth agape. 'There must be thousands. Tens of thousands.'

Ghyrab's stance of draping over the tiller had not changed, but his lazy eyes had taken on a sharper slant. His forehead had found some more wrinkles. 'Hundreds of thousands.'

'And not all ghosts? *Ba'at?*'

'No,' he grunted. 'In some places in the Arc, skin is now worth less than shade. Slaves. Prisoners. Wanderers. Outcasts. The White Hell accepts all. The rest are shades. Between the living and the dead, there's not a day or night they don't work.'

'I guess that's what's causing the smell.' The air carried the tang of old sweat, the rotting of dead things and overflowing latrines.

'Aye.'

Nilith knew the Arc was a step away from barbarism on any day of the week, but this quarry seemed one very large step indeed, and one that crossed a line. 'Surely if the owners of this place seek to make a profit, they should take better care of their workers?'

'These are rich men, Majesty.' Ghyrab raised a finger to a bank of glowing lights at the high rim of the pit. Nilith had to crane her neck to see the dark building, like a tower on its side. 'Richer in silver than some of your sereks are in half-coin. Food, medicine, even water; all take a cut out of the profits. If a worker dies, he gets to work again in death. If they can't keep him bound, they sell him on, swap him for a live one, or melt his coin to reuse the metal. There's plenty of chained flesh coming from the south, and your city and the Sprawls bring shades here by the carriage-load. What goes into Kal Duat don't matter; just what comes out of it. Stone and silver.'

As if to illustrate the bargeman's point, they heard a cry over the racket of the quarry. Nilith looked up to see a living worker on the level above, struggling in vain to stop a block the size of their barge from sliding down a ramp. His legs slid through the sand and mud as he fought to stay upright, back pressed to the white stone.

Nilith had already guessed his trajectory. The slope was steep and led down to the river's edge. A hundred blocks had already been stacked at the bottom, waiting for barges to take them away. She winced as she saw the man had realised too. He flailed, trying to escape, but the block's weight was against him. He roared as it slid down the ramp with him tumbling at its head.

The clash of stone might have drowned out the sound of a grown man being flattened, but it did nothing to hinder the carnage that spurted in all directions for a dozen feet. Nor did it soften the wretchedness of the grasping hand, still poking from the gap between the bloodied white stone. Still clasping for air amidst the stone-dust.

Not a word came from any of the nearby workers. Whips cracked, orders were hollered, and backs bent to labour once more. Nilith watched on, fighting the rising bile in her throat. She was a fighter, accustomed to death, but this twisted her stomach.

As they slowly drifted along the wide channel, made for barges far mightier than Ghyrab's craft, Nilith watched the waters turn foul and milky from the limestone and the filth of industry, streaked with rainbows of leaked oil. The Ashti was barely flowing now.

'Why aren't we moving?' she asked.

Ghyrab wiped his nose with the back of his hand. 'Blockage o' some sort.'

Nilith had been too busy staring at the bloody stone. Now she turned to the lump of slimy wood and stone sitting in their path. It was a huge barge, half-loaded with limestone blocks and already sitting low in the murky water. Seeing that it was on the cusp of sinking, a sailor had the sense to call a halt to the sweating teams working the ramps and pulleys by the dockside. They conversed in a rapid patois Nilith didn't recognise: some pidgin Arctian.

'Can you understand them?'

'Not really,' Ghyrab said. 'Bits, at least. It's Hellish.'

When Nilith remained silent, he shrugged, making the tiller squeak.

'Don't look at me. I didn't name it. It's the tongue of the White Hell. Hellish. Means they can give orders quicker. You don't learn it swift-like? Well...' His finger angled toward the crushed worker. Nobody had made a move to clean him up.

It took an age for the stone-barge to cast off and for the weak momentum of the sick river to claim it. In the meantime, they were paid a visit by half a dozen men clad in colourful, puffy silks. Bustling down the stone dockside with smiles and waves, they looked completely at odds with the miserable surroundings. These were not desert-folk but city dwellers. Several had the audacity to wear turbans with jewels and gold medallions dangling from their folds. They clutched the hems of their silks in front of them as they negotiated the puddles and detritus.

'Travellers! Welcome!' called the closest of them, a pudgy man so red in the cheeks he matched his scarlet trappings. His hands were held to his face as if he were eating an invisible pie of some kind. Nilith assumed it was a greeting until she saw he was twirling a dark and waxy moustache.

'Business? Business?' the others clamoured, grinning like beggars stumbling across an untended banquet. Nilith watched their eyes measuring her clothing, the horse, and Farazar, standing as far away as possible beside his body.

'No. Just passage,' Ghyrab answered for them. 'And we're late, so if—'

The scarlet man took his hands from his moustache. 'Have you no wish to barter? Nothing to sell?'

Nilith crossed her arms, a sign of a firm no in Krass. In Araxes, it was a sign for merchants to try harder. 'None, thank you.'

'Horse-flesh, perhaps?'

'No.'

Chests were puffed. The scarlet man climbed a few steps to stand on the brick lip of the riverbank. 'Then in that case, you must pay us a toll.'

Ghyrab swept from the tiller. 'Toll? What damn toll?'

'The toll.' It looked as if it wounded the man to repeat himself.

'First you build a gate and start taking names. Now a toll?' The bargeman put one foot on the bulwark, his hands clutching his hips. 'There's never been no toll on this river and there never will be. You folks should know that just as well as I do. Not in a hundred years has that changed!'

Scarlet tittered. 'You would know, sir, but times eventually do change. The Consortium has decided to start charging a toll on those who pass through Kal Duat. We can't have your kind interfering with our operations.'

Nilith piped up. 'The who?'

'The Consortium! You have not heard of us, peasant? Shame on you. We have run this mine for a hundred years. This and countless other businesses. Half of Araxes is built from Consortium stone, I'll have you know.' Scarlet paused his tirade to pout at the ghost. 'Is the shade for sale?' he asked of Nilith. 'He has a familiar face—'

'Absolutely not,' Nilith and Farazar chorused. She fought not to glance at him, silently thanking him for keeping his gods-damned mouth shut.

Scarlet threw up his hands. 'Shame! We like a half-life with a mouth, don't we?' Another titter. This time his gang of friends joined in, sniggering. 'The toll it is!'

'What is this toll?' Ghyrab growled.

'Silvers or gems.'

'We have neither. Bandits waylaid us.'

Scarlet smiled. 'Then it would appear the ghost and the horse are indeed for sale, wouldn't it?'

Nilith replaced Ghyrab at the edge of the barge, leaving him to work his way back to the tiller. She calmly dug the points of her trident into the wood, hackles bristling. She leaned on the weapon as she slowly looked between the multicoloured buffoons. 'I find it very strange they didn't mention this at the gate. And, as you haven't provided any proof of your authority, your ownership, or even your identity, I can only assume that this is some kind of elaborate swindle, and so I'm unfortunately going to decline to pay you anything at all,' she said. Behind her, Ghyrab put his weight into the tiller, using it like an oar to put some distance between them and the dockside.

Scarlet's ruddy complexion grew darker. 'You're educated, for a desert yokel, aren't you?'

'I read a lot of scrolls.'

'It matters not! Nobody dares question the Nyxites when they ask silvers for their Nyxwater, claiming Nyxwell after Nyxwell. The Consortium have kept this empire in trade, grain, and stone for centuries, not that you would know it. Why shouldn't we charge a toll for our land?' Scarlet leaned closer, compensating for Nilith drifting away. 'As far as we're concerned, peasant, we have more authority here than the emperor. Now—'

'That's treachery,' Farazar hissed.

Scarlet was now leading his gang down the dockside in an effort to keep up with Ghyrab's subtle paddling. He was set on having the last word, refusing to be out-argued by a peasant. 'Is it, half-life? My, you do have a tongue! The emperor cares only for himself and his wars in the Scatter. Why else does he hide in his precious Sanctuary atop his mighty tower?'

Farazar began to stride forwards, but Nilith blocked his path with the trident.

'Explain yourself,' she challenged the man, baiting him some more.

'Oh, I'll tell you why! He barely rules over the city, never mind the Duneplains or the Long Sands. Instead he leaves it to his empress-in-waiting to rule in his stead, and deal with the empire's problems. Yet they have no power out here, in the wild! The Consortium, however—'

Nilith gritted her teeth. 'What problems?'

'Ignorant as usual, you desert-folk! The Nyxwater shortage, of course, soldiers on the streets, and murder... Wait!' Scarlet realised his error as he found his way blocked by a limestone boulder, and Nilith and the barge slipping beyond it. 'Enough talking! Pay the toll!' he yelled.

A horn blew along the river. The stone-barge finally cast off, ambling ahead under the power of half a dozen oars. Ghyrab threw himself at his tiller, sloshing water behind them in great arcs. One managed to spray a few of the gaudy swindlers.

'We're very late!' Nilith yelled at them.

Scarlet flapped his manicured hands. 'Halt, I say! The toll!' The nearby workers and rowers gawped cluelessly at their masters. Whether they were playing dumb or just dead in the brain, Nilith didn't know, but she thanked them anyway.

Ghyrab used the width of the river to put the stone-barge between them and the dockside. With a few more strokes, they were ahead of it, beating it to the bottleneck in the river. 'We'll pay on the way back,' he called out.

Scarlet was trying to climb through the mess of limestone and ropes, but was quickly running out of path. His silks were now ripped and dusty, his face the very picture of outrage. 'You'll pay double, peasants! You hear me? Triple!'

'Whatever you say!' Ghyrab shouted, just as they lost sight of Scarlet and his gang behind the stone-barge once more. Another threat came, but the words were lost to the wash of water. Nilith joined Ghyrab at the tiller as he paddled, silent and still wary. They listened out for more shouts or ringing bells, but none came.

Night was falling quickly. Though torches blazed like the campfires of a vast army, the darkness masked some of the ugliness of the White Hell. Even then, they were still drowned by the noise of the place. The hammering, the yelled orders, the whinnying of beasts, the frequent screams...

Nilith was glad when they reached the first of the nine steps, and the sloshing of water and machinery drowned it out. She could see the mechanism better now there wasn't a waterfall in the way. A huge cog was embedded in the cliff, red with rust and slick with water and torchlight. On both sides of the cog, under cotton tents and awnings, two armies of glowing shades toiled on cranks. There must have been several hundred of them, shoulders bare and arched in labour. Their thin strands of cobalt muscle stood out like whipcords. White scars crisscrossed their backs.

As their barge approached, something hooked their section of river and lifted it into the air with a deep groan. It squealed like a murder victim under the weight but it held fast. Steel plates snapped shut to hem the water in, and with much juddering and sloshing, they began their ascent. Any water that escaped was caught in pools, and through the magic of pumps and bellows manned by more ghostly crews, it was forced up through a knotted network of brass and wooden pipes to keep the river flowing. Shades crawled across the trembling pipes like spiders, or hung from ropes like odd lanterns. They ignored the barge, seeing to their repairs of rusty junctions instead, where murky river water escaped in jets of fine spray.

The pull of the earth was always kinder to falling, not lifting, and as such it took an age to climb out of Kal Duat. It was a miracle any of the Ashti managed to make it out of the White Hell at all. By some chance of design, it did, but it was a dirty, murky flow. Nilith spent the journey in silence, waiting for the mechanisms to come to a crunching halt and guards to appear with lanterns and triggerbows. She was surprised all the way to the first step, where the canyon walls reappeared.

Just as Nilith thought they had escaped without repercussion, she spotted a gatehouse. A few shouts at the gate tried to stall them, but at the sight of the stone-barge behind them, the guards were idle about cocking their triggerbows. It seemed stone and timely deliveries were more important than tolls, and the gates were cranked open without further complaint. Ghyrab's barge slid out into the dark, slow river.

The only thing that chased them was the insistent hammering, which gradually faded over a stretch of several miles. The quieter it became, the more the river recovered its flow, fed by springs, or so Ghyrab said. He had finally gone back to steering instead of paddling, and by the look of his slumped posture, the old bargeman was grateful for it.

Nilith cleared her throat. 'This Consortium. Who the fuck are they?'

'Traders. Businessmen. Though not like your tors and tals. They only care for silver,' growled Ghyrab. 'Own a whole bunch of trade routes and quarries across the deserts. Jumped-up bastards, is what they is.'

Nilith looked to Farazar. The ghost had taken up his usual brooding spot in the corner of the prow. He liked to sit hunched, his back turned, like a spurned gargoyle.

'You see now what hiding in your Sanctuary has done to the empire, dear husband? A Consortium. Problems, they said. A Nyxwater shortage. Murders. Soldiers on the streets.'

'I have done nothing. If this is anyone's fault, it is yours.'

'I kept that city from tearing itself apart for five years while you played drunken exile in the south! It is our daughter. Funny how I never had to use your army when I was the one delivering your decrees. She's scheming, just like you taught her. She's most likely trying to pry open the Sanctuary door as we speak.'

Farazar had been silently bubbling for some time, and she had just removed the lid. His anger turned on her. 'And whose fault is that, *wife*? I told you leaving her unattended was a colossal stroke of idiocy on your part! Clearly I was right!'

Nilith crackled her knuckles. She had dearly hoped that sending Bezel to look for her was the summation of Sisine's interference. Bezel knew nothing more of her plans. Nilith had also hoped leaving her house-ghost Etane behind would have curbed some of her daughter's scheming. Now it appeared she was playing empress in her absence. Her hopes were dashed like a vase against a boulder.

'As if you care a damn for anything but your throne,' she hissed, moving closer to him. 'You hadn't even mentioned her name until the falcon turned up. I doubt she's even crossed your mind, even though it's your fault she is as devious as she is! If you remember, Farazar, I wasn't trusted to raise her. And just like your father, you raised a royal monster. Your own successor.'

Farazar stood up, fists raised and shaking. 'That is why you should have curbed your greed and stayed there to watch her, to maintain control as you're supposed to! Now she's making decrees as if I was already dead. That's bold, wife. Against the Code. Treasonous! Only you could have taught her that. I see that now. I'll be surprised if there is an Araxes left to drag me back to!'

From her pocket, Nilith took the copper arrowhead she had dug out of Anoish and made a fist around it. It was large enough for its charm to work on the ghost. She pushed him, making his hands fly out to the bulwark. 'As I'm *supposed* to? Is that what you think my life amounts to? Collecting notes from a door? Reading them for a surly court? Doing your job? No more, Farazar. I grew tired of not being the dutiful and silent wife you expected long ago. You married the wrong woman for that. I am stronger than you know.'

'Your duty, Nilith, was to bear a child for this family and do what I tell you! You managed the first; why is the second so interminably difficult for you?'

Another shove. More flailing.

'I could only be ignored and despised for so long. Only read so many scrolls. Only deliver so many idiotic decrees. And each morning, I would wake up to see the streets awash with fresh blood. No more, I say!'

Farazar's foot dipped into the water. He did not like that one bit.

'Away from me, Krass peasant!'

Nilith heard the thump of a falcon as Bezel landed somewhere behind her, felt Ghyrab's wide eyes on her back.

'What did I miss?' whispered the bird, but nobody answered him.

Nilith had no fear of water now. Though it rushed beneath them, she leaned over Farazar, their noses almost touching. She felt his cold spreading across her cheeks. 'Haven't you realised yet, you ignorant fuck? It's that arrogance that brought my knife to your neck in the first place; this pride and skewed sense of entitlement you Arctians are born with. I slit the throat of the empire because you do not deserve to rule it. Not you. Not Sisine. None of you do. Not over life and especially not over death. You think yourself better than those stone-mongers? Those masters of hell? Twiddling moustaches while men die around you? You are the same wretched, soulless breed, and you'll realise it by the time I'm done.'

'I knew it! I knew my murder was some grand lesson! You are nothing but a venomous, shrewish, greedy—'

Nilith was not finished. She jutted out her neck, boring into Farazar's eyes. '*You* are nothing but the wine-blotched leftovers of a feckless king. You are weak. Deluded. Your only claim to the throne is you murdered your father. You and your kind are the reason the Reaches are rotting, and if I don't do something about it, there'll be nothing left of it.'

Shove.

Splash.

It was no more complicated than that. So rewarding was the ease of it, and the ferocity with which he thrashed against the water, that it brought a wide smile to her face. Her anger faded away as she watched him trail in their wake, bound to the decomposing corpse that was firmly lashed to the deck.

Bezel cocked his head and began to chuckle, a crackling sound like leaves crushed under a shoe.

Ghyrab cleared his throat. 'Erm… ain't he still the emperor?'

'No dead emperor or empress has ever sat on Araxes' throne,' said the falcon. 'At least not for more than five minutes. Some family member always binds them or casts their bodies into the Nyx coinless and sharpish-like. But until his body's bound or given up, Farazar's still *technically* emperor.'

Nilith drew herself up. 'And I am still the empress by right of marriage if not by half-coins. And we know who rules a marriage, now, don't we, gentlemen?

The bargeman nodded sagely, eyes distant and occupied with some old memory. 'The wife.'

'Well done, sir.' Nilith beamed at the bargeman. Bezel just laughed his strange laugh, tiny tongue poking from his beak.

'And on that note, I have some brooding of my own to do,' she said. 'Does the river start to flow faster, Ghyrab?'

'Aye.' It was all he gave her, but it was enough.

Although she addressed the bird, she looked at Anoish. The horse was fast asleep, ribcage rising and falling in slow succession. 'Bezel?'

The falcon knew her mind. 'Five hundred miles, maybe more. Give it a clear day and get out of this canyon. You'll see the city gleam.'

Ghyrab coughed, and it thankfully covered her own hitch of breath. She had expected the river route to be faster than this, with fewer interruptions. It was no horse. She counted the days. Just over two weeks. That was all she had left in her hourglass before Farazar was lost to the void. And all the while, her daughter was plotting away in the Cloudpiercer, following precisely in her father's footsteps. She thanked the dead gods that Sisine – and the rest of the Arc for that matter – still believed the emperor was locked up tight in his Sanctuary. It was a mercy while it lasted. At least Farazar had done something right during his reign: he had built a solid vault.

'Do you still want your answers, falcon?'

Bezel waggled his head back and forth. 'Fine.'

Nilith couldn't help but flinch as he launched himself at her, alighting on the railing next to her hand.

'You first, Empress.'

Nilith turned back to watch Farazar still floundering a dozen feet behind them. She guessed the decades-old fear of drowning was a hard one to shake. 'It took me two years to realise he'd left. He stopped using the words "I want" in his decrees. Tiny difference, but I knew something had changed. I spent another three years proving it and tracking him down. I read every scroll in the Cloudpiercer's libraries, followed rumours, scoured maps, and toured the streets. Finally, I found a trace. He had tried his best to hide his escape south, had the guards who escorted him out of the Piercer slain and buried in the dunes. Disguise, different name, the lot. Clever for him, really. Misdirection, the Krass conjurers call it, but not clever enough to fool me. He switched wagons many times going south. Used questionable sellswords, too. I found a diary reporting a man of Farazar's description south of the Steps of Oshirim. A drunk, he called him, boasting about the greatest escape in all the ages. Means nothing until you match up the dates with his decrees changing. A month or two in between, perhaps. Spies in Belish found a lord living on the outskirts of the city. A lord with a healthy obsession for wine, concubines and lavish parties. I had to go see it myself, and lo and behold, at the far end of a dining table, I saw him. I had come to kill him, but I almost took my knife out and gutted him right there and then. I climbed back into his mansion that very night and cut his throat while his cock was still in a duke's daughter.' Nilith found herself breathing hard. 'That enough of an answer for you?'

Bezel shrugged his wings. 'A fine fucking story. For a person who prides himself on his ability to find elusive bastards, I'm impressed.'

'Then name your price. Your turn, bird.'

He took a moment to stare up at the star-spattered sky. 'Death.'

'Whose?'

'My own,' said Bezel with a sigh. It was not a sad sound, but a tired one. His golden eyes turned back to her. 'Apparently, the Nyxites bound me a little too well. What thirst and hunger the body gives me, my soul gives it the inability to die. Trust me, I've tried. I am tired of life. Tired of immortality. Tired of this body, and yet I can't escape. Old age can't kill me. I'm two hundred years old. Blades don't work. Not even copper. Poison only makes me sick. Flew into more walls than I can count. Froze for two weeks atop a mountain. Can't tell you how many times I've tried to die, and every time this fucking body heals. Slowly, painfully, but every time. It refuses to die unless somebody destroys my half-coin: the silver bell. And I've always been too useful, too much of a prize, to let go. I thought Sisine had forgotten me, that I had freedom, but now I know she will never give me up, and I will never be free. That's why I came to you. I was hoping a woman who traipses several thousand miles across a desert to kill her husband then drags his dead body back just so she can teach him a lesson would either be mad or desperate enough to accept my offer.'

'Maybe I'm both,' she whispered.

'Once you accomplish whatever it is you're fighting to accomplish, I want you to take my fucking bell from your daughter and melt it. Throw me into the void. Finish what the Nyxites started.'

Nilith took a moment to think. Murder, however merciful, should never be taken lightly.

'What would you do if I said no?'

The falcon shrugged. 'I had considered killing her.'

The underlying ferocity of his tone took her aback. 'You'd do that?'

'I've done it before,' he said, pointing a curved talon at his neck. 'It's all about the throat.'

Nilith winced. 'I meant my daughter, Bezel. I had hoped to save her, when all of... *this* was done.'

'What's your answer?'

The bird was smart, and Nilith bowed her head in agreement. 'Fine. Help me get to the Grand Nyxwell and I'll give you anything you want. Your death. Your freedom. No killing required.'

Bezel whistled. 'Deal,' he said, and they spoke no more on the subject. 'Well, I don't know about you, but I'm fucking starving. The downside of a living body, right? I'm going to gut a mouse. Want one?'

'I'll pass.'

'Suit yourself.'

With that, Bezel took flight once more, and being left alone was all the excuse Nilith needed to tumble into the hole that was a fine old brooding session. Meaningless internal rambling, helpful and yet paradoxically aggravating. Like being tortured by a feather.

At least she had Farazar's cursing and splashing to entertain her.

CHAPTER 7
A HERO

As the first to master binding and author the
Tenets, the Nyxites were swift to proclaim
themselves the sole guardians of the Nyx.
And so they have remained. The Nyxites were
mere sages before, pagan masters of funeral
ceremonies, simply there to make sure the
boatman received his copper and the gods got
their souls. And yet, almost ten centuries later,
they are still the only ones allowed to harvest,
hoard or sell Nyxwater, even outside the Arc.
They no longer usher the dead to the afterlife,
but imprison them here instead.

FROM AN ANONYMOUS SCROLL SENT TO
CHAMBERLAIN REBENE IN 987

THEY SAY MISERY LIKES COMPANY, but what they don't say is how much curiosity likes company. Especially strange company. It loves it. Adores it.

I had become aware that my opinion of Pointy was based on how useful he was. At that moment, he was as good for research as any library, and as fine for tales as any beer-sodden bard. Every question that popped onto my tongue, the sword had an answer for. At the very least, he offered some anecdotal tangent I could follow. For the first time, my head was pressed to the door not in boredom, but so I could hear the blade more clearly.

Pointy was waxing lyrical. 'And that's when the mighty Horush pulled the sun closer to scorch his enemies. As the burning soldiers ran for the sea to douse the flames, his undead army caught them on the shore. Sesh was defeated before the sun broke its bonds. In punishment for altering the flow of the Nyx, slaying the boatman, and giving humanity the secret of binding the dead, Horush imprisoned Sesh for the rest of time.'

'And I thought the dead gods of the east were strange.'

'Strange is the only fruit that grows in the desert, so the poets say. In any case, some say that Sesh was the protagonist of that story, as the world now revolves around his gift of binding. In some ways, Sesh won. The gods' power faded and so we threw them aside, forgot them. Even Sesh. Or for the most part. There are some who worship him for his deeds. Guess who?'

'Those Cult people. Cult of Sesh.'

'You're getting good at this.'

I shrugged, despite the wardrobe's darkness. 'I've a thirst for information, when it's the useful sort.' My head was full of old combinations, names of important figures, and a comprehensive list of Taymar brothels. Epic tales of treasure were for adventurers and the fanciful to listen to, not I. No, I preferred solid tips over stolen maps. Such stories had a habit of floating in one ear and straight out the other, like a breeze through a fence. That was until now.

'You still haven't told me why you're asking all these questions about binding. In fact, I feel like I've been talking for two days straight.' In truth, he had. I had barely said a word.

'Why, you ask?' It was a good question, one with many answers. Was it because I had a thirst to know more, like any soul who uncovers a new skill? Was it for the purposes of escape, or revenge? Could I have branded it as a thirst for justice? Or lie and say it was for the honour of those old, dead gods? I could have bleated any of those answers at the sword, but in the end they would have all pointed towards one path: getting my half-coin and getting as far away from this maniacal land as ghostly possible.

Every reason is a little story we tell ourselves to dress up our desires. We offer reasons to explain or excuse ourselves, to fit in. We do it every day. But these stories are dangerous. Cyclical and devious. We tell them over and over so many times we start to believe they're true, when instead all along it is all just justification to hide what drives us: to have what we desire.

I told him what I wanted. 'Because I don't want this.'

'This?'

'*This*! This wardrobe. This indenturement. This… half-life!' I yelled. 'I want my freedom, and I'll do anything to get it. If understanding the dead gods, the Cult, or haunting helps me, then so be it.'

Pointy took a pause. 'Well, you might be able to do something about the wardrobe and indenturement. Being dead—'

'I've made my peace with that.' I hadn't, but I'd heard positive reinforcement worked wonders. I had almost forgotten the beat of my heart until I felt Busk's in my chest. Since then, I had thirsted to feel that again.

'It took me a long time to grow used to this form. That's all the dead have: time.'

'No offence, sword, but I've got hands, feet, and something gods-given I intend to use.'

'Gods-given?'

I pursed my lips. I had told him of my vocation, how I had come to Araxes, and how Busk had claimed me. I hadn't yet told him of my 'visitors,' as I'd taken to calling them. I was certain it would have sounded like madness, even to a deadbound soulblade. All the reason I'd given him for my haunting was the age-old excuse of, 'It was an accident.'

'It's an old Krass phrase.' It wasn't. 'It means a kind of magic.' It didn't.

The sword hummed, sounding like the fading drone of a bell. 'Never heard that one before.'

I decided to distract him with the bait of a story. 'So, if Sesh was so glorious and beneficial to us mortals, why don't more worship him? Why's the Cult not more accepted in a city of the dead?'

'Because most believe Sesh died, just like the other gods. There are some who still follow the old ways, but they are like single grains of sand on a beach compared to the rest of the Arc and the Reaches.'

'Making half-coins the only religion.'

'Convenient, when you're the one who owns the most shades, hmm? And yet we still believe an afterlife awaits us. Such gall, we humans have.'

I knew what afterlife truly waited for us: a cold and screaming place beneath the earth. I held my tongue. 'And the Cult?'

'Ever heard the word "extremist"?'

I had not.

'Well, that's them. They've been around since the Nyx changed and binding was discovered. But they are fanatical about Sesh, and known for their delusions of grandeur. Never mind their treachery.'

'We had a god like Sesh in the east. But in our old religions we called binding a curse, so not a soul dared worship him.'

'Lopt, if I'm not mistaken.'

'You know your Krass mythology.'

'This world has been telling the same myths for thousands upon thousands of years, Caltro. Our gods are just regurgitated from the gods of the ancients. Krass. Arctian. They're all the same if you look deep enough. You should try reading Master Falafef's series of epic poe—'

'No.'

'All very derivative, anyway,' Pointy muttered.

I buoyed him with another question. 'I know the Nyxites wrote the Tenets, but who wrote the first Code? The Cult or the Nyxites?'

'It was the first emperor of the Arc, Emperor Phaera. The Tenets set down the rules of binding, but he needed laws that made him, and kept him, emperor. Thus the Code was born, and it has been rewritten and amended with every single successor. I think it's been updated more times than Frandi's *Weeping Sky*,' he added with a smug chuckle.

His joke – if that's what it was – fell on dead ears. 'And where are the Cult these days, if one wanted to find them?'

'They keep to themselves these days, but I wager you could probably still find them outside the Core Districts. Anyone wearing red robes is a cultist. Secretive bunch, though. Plenty of free shade tors and tals are members, and donate to their cause, according to talk I've overheard. The Cult even used to have a church, but when the royalty banned them it was burned to the ground.'

'Emperor Milizan.'

'You've heard this one.'

'Widow Horix told me he was murdered by his son.'

'The story goes that Milizan fell in with the Cult, and the deeper he fell, the more they wormed their way into the Cloudpiercer. When he began to talk of killing himself to join the Cult and be closer to Sesh, Farazar the emperor-in-waiting took a stand. And rightly so, if you ask me. By then the Cult had their fingers in the Chamber of the Code, the Court, even the Chamber of Military Might.'

He was waiting for me to ask, I knew it. Normally I would have played silent and out-waited him, but I was too impatient. 'Then what?'

'Milizan's son murdered him in true Arctian style. Farazar hid in his father's private latrine for near on a day before skewering him with a sword. They say the blade went in his arse and out his mouth. After he bound his father in the Grand Nyxwell, as per royal tradition, Farazar claimed his father's half-coins and became ruler. Then he banished his mother, the Empress Hirana, to the north of the Reaches and appointed his Krass wife to the throne instead. That was just shy of twenty years ago. Nobody has seen her since, nor received so much as a note from her. She just disappeared. Or died.'

'That sort of thing seems to happen far too often in this city.'

'The royals are the only nobles who dare to murder so openly. The rest are content to play their little games.'

Pointy got no further. It seemed Busk had grown bored of imprisoning me. Either that, or he had some more strongboxes for me to open. I went limp as soon as they opened the wardrobe doors, eager to make the men work for their living.

I hit the floor with a soft thud, and rolled my eyes.

Not one of them touched me. Busk's orders, no doubt. I sighed and hauled myself up, giving Pointy a roll of my eyes as I passed him.

All he could do in response was catch the lamplight.

'Remember what I told you,' came a faint whisper. The guards flinched, but nothing was said.

Clubs poked me down the stairwell and into another dusty room, where an array of boxes had been arranged in a circle, like a downtrodden fight-pit beneath a Krass tavern. In its centre stood a shirtless, toad-like man, swollen with muscle and inked with geometric Scatter Isle tattoos. He was sweating in drips. His shaved, dented dome of a head glistened in the lamplight. Bruises darkened both his eyes, as if he hadn't slept for a year. He had rings of greenish metal around his fingers and bare toes, and he wore the blankest expression I had ever seen on a human being. Or a toad, for that matter.

'What now?' I asked my guards. They poked me into the circle as the man began to shrug and roll his head around his shoulders. I'd seen enough of the pits in Taymar to know a fighter when I saw one.

'Have you lost your mind, Busk?' I had no idea if the tor was in the room, but I called to him anyway. 'I'm a locksmith, not a prize fighter!'

A whisper came from the shadows of an adjoining corridor, where two figures waited. A hand ventured into the lamplight and waved. The guards shoved me to the dust.

A punishment. It had to be. For daring to touch the tor, no doubt. I had no clue whether he realised what I'd done to him, or whether he even knew of haunting. I knew next to fuck all beyond what Pointy had told me: that the practice was a rumour, neither acknowledged by the Code nor remembered by half the Arc since the Nyx had started to spit the dead back out. Time has an awful habit of eating away at knowledge.

The man raised his fists and began to dance around me, feigning strikes. I shook my head. 'I'm not a fighter.' Though I said no more, he must have assumed I added, 'So please, feel free to hit me.'

He eagerly obliged me. His fist, copper-ringed on every finger, drove into my ribs. I slumped to the dust, curling up around the waves of pain that spanned my body.

He nudged me with a foot. As I levelled a glare at him, I noticed his bruise-framed eyes kept sneaking to the edges of the room, paying too much attention to the guards. I felt nothing but cold in the room and yet his sweat continued to pour.

I knew the many expressions of fear. Some wore it openly in quivers and chill sweats. Others preferred to bury it behind grins or stoicism. This toad of a man was the latter. If there was anything to be gleaned from his expression, he looked almost apologetic. *Not too apologetic*, I thought, as he flexed and dug a toe into my side.

I challenged the invisible man again. 'What's your goal here, Busk?' No answer.

I hauled myself up and decided to play along as best I could. My answers were more important than a bit of pain. Our fists rotated between us, one set grimy, the other glowing. I threw the first swing, a wild and useless one at that. The fighter's knuckles connected with my chin like a mallet, then came a strike to my nose. Over and over, back and forth. My face was a mask of pain.

Outrage pushed me up from the dust. I clawed for the man but he brought me close, hooking arms around my head to drive his knee into my gut. It had little effect without copper, but it was still deeply unsettling having somebody else's limbs thrust into you over and over.

I twisted away. My neck would have broken had I been made of bone and flesh. For a moment I was free, but in came the fists again, more desperate this time. I fended off blow after blow until I found my arse on the floor again, eyes blurry.

As I fought through the pain, I saw the guards rush in. I was on the cusp of insulting the parentage of everybody in the room when I realised they weren't after me. They were after the fighter. He was pushed against the boxes amid curses and muffled warnings.

It was a challenge. A test, not a punishment. Busk wanted to recreate our incident, though this time with him far out of reach. Whether he knew I'd haunted him or not, he knew *something* had happened, and he wanted to see it again. I decided it must have been his thirst for profit; he was following the reek of a new opportunity. That brought a smile to my blue cheeks.

Pointy had told me a playwright once opined that theatre was the only universal joy of the people. I had scoffed at first, but now I realised it was true. The fight-pits of Taymar and Saraka may have been designed for the scrapings of society, but they were still grand theatre at their core. The curtain opening? The first punch. The sharp dialogue? The parries and blocks. The crescendo? The crack of a skull splitting, the puff of blue smoke, the wet suck of a face collapsing inwards. All theatre, very much like this situation. I was the hero of my own squalid play. I saw it now: Busk wasn't about to risk me, just goad me into action.

As they pushed the fighter back into the ring, I saw in his face that he also knew his role: *expendable.* The word hung between us in the clammy, sweat-filled air.

I let him hit me over and over, getting in the odd punch here and there to make it worth his while. They barely grazed him, let alone stopped him, and yet I could feel him pulling back after every barrage. I dreaded to think how many pints of blood I would have lost by now in a real fight. I was thankful I was already dead.

The farce continued for almost an hour, until the man's shoulders had sloped past the point of no return, until he had not a drop of sweat left to exude. I stood with hands on knees, panting through habit. I glowed white in two-score places; everywhere his fists had punished me.

'Happy?' I looked around the boxes at the frowns of the confused guards and the shadows of the corridor. 'Or do you need to see somebody die to get your cock hard, Busk?'

This whisper was short and angry. I didn't catch it, but the guards did. Their fears now proven unfounded, they seized me at last. I saw the exhausted fighter being thrown some gemstones. Before I was escorted away, I saw Busk's furrowed face pass through an arc of lamplight. He refused to meet my eyes.

As I was manhandled up into the tower, I gazed up at the dust-filled shafts of light that speared the atrium. It was afternoon by my reckoning, and a cloudy one at that. A storm had moaned around the tower several days ago; perhaps its wake still covered the city. Although I hadn't seen it, I'd heard its roar and felt the heavy pressure in the air. Changes in the weather were a lot easier to feel now that I was practically all air.

We had almost climbed the stairs when the knock sounded: the deep pounding of a spear-butt striking metal. The guards grumbled to each other, casting looks down the stairwell. As I was pushed back to my gaudy prison cell, several of them peeled away to see to the visitors. I was locked away in the wardrobe, along with my burning curiosity.

'What did they do?' Pointy spoke up once our room was empty.

I smiled in the darkness. 'Failed, is what they did. Busk suspects something after our last encounter. Tried to goad me into action.'

'And… did you?'

'No.'

The sword sighed, almost sounding relieved. 'So it was a mistake, then. You were wrong about the haunting.'

I laughed. 'Oh, I don't know about that. I just didn't try. But tonight I will. And you're going to help me.'

'Er… how?'

'Fear not, my dear Pointy. You won't have to do much.'

'What, then?'

'Not a clue yet, but I'll come up with something. Don't worry. I always do. And I'll take you with me.'

'As wondrous as that sounds, you worry me, Caltro.'

I sighed dramatically. 'I've spent too much of this half-life worrying. A man with nothing has nothing to lose except himself. I've lost that already. What's there to fear now?'

'Pain. Punishment. Another hundred years on a shelf. Complete death…'

Perhaps it was all the theatre that had puffed me up. Perhaps it was playing the untouchable hero, but despite thinking of that crowded, endless cavern of ghosts, or the black void, I felt the smile on my face and refused to let it fall. Busk had shown his hand today. He was afraid of me.

'I told you I wanted my freedom.'

'Yes…?'

'Well, I intend to have it, and by any means necessary. The widow. The haunting. Even the fucking Cult. I don't care who or what gets me there, but I will be free.' *This is my desire.* It was selfish, maybe, but in a world that extended few helping hands, you needed to be selfish to survive. 'If you want the same, then feel free to come along.'

Pointy pondered that for some time, and at last he sighed. It sounded like a gale howling over a flute. 'All right. Better to have tried and failed than never to have tried at all, eh? Or so Desami said.'

'Another fucking poet?'

'Sonneteer, actually.'

'Then those are the first words of sense a poet's ever uttered.'

———◆———

GLOWING WHITE EYES PEERED THROUGH the grille. An unseen mouth voiced a challenge. 'State your business.'

'Colonel Kalid to see Tor Busk. Again.'

'He's busy.'

'Aren't we all?'

'Just give me the scroll.' A metal shutter below the grille opened with a seagull's shriek. A gloved hand poked forth, palm up and open.

'I have a personal message from Tal Horix. It must be delivered to him only.'

'Ugh. Wait here.'

Both the grille and the shutter closed with a snap, and Kalid retreated to the edge of the steps to wait. He spent the minutes looking up at Busk's poor excuse for a tower, standing barely fifteen stories tall at the most. The colonel counted by the grubby, pinhole windows. Gargoyles, more Skol in design than Arctian, glared down at him from between oriels and balconies. Pointless creatures. Their open mouths probably tasted rain once a decade.

Kalid heard the shouting behind the reinforced iron of the huge doors, which were also smaller than Horix's. This continued for several minutes, with the colonel gleaning such random snippets as, 'Who does that crow...' and, 'Damnable bitch!'

When the doors finally cracked open, they swung outwards at speed. If they'd hoped to catch him unawares, they were disappointed; Kalid was already out of reach. Arctian doors taught that lesson early in life.

Tor Busk stood in the dark of his atrium, squinting at the afternoon light. He already wore a scowl for the colonel. Eight guards surrounded him, short spears out and ready.

'Speak, messenger.'

Kalid flexed his shoulder muscles, making the plates of his armour knock together. 'The lady Tal Horix wishes to know your decision.'

'My decision on *what*, precisely? Don't you know I'm a very busy man?'

The colonel could see that. Busk's hair, normally slicked back with grease, was in strands and pestering his forehead. Most tors and tals didn't like to exert themselves unless it was at a ball or in the bedchamber.

'On whether you still wish for the Krass shade you came to purchase not so long ago? One scroll has already been sent, but we received no reply. My mistress would like an answer.'

Busk smiled, but his lips were white and tightly drawn.

Kalid tried to play patient and insouciant, as Horix had instructed. He'd never heard that word before, and now his mind kept repeating it, over and over, whenever it had a spare moment.

Busk played for time. 'Which shade is this, exactly? I deal with so many, you see.'

'Don't you recall? A Krassman sold by Boran Temsa. A shade who is apparently dangerous and a risk to Tal Horix's life.'

'Ah, yes.'

'And so?'

'Well.' More chin rubbing.

Kalid stepped forward, causing the tor's guards to bristle. 'The widow wishes you to understand that this is the last time she will extend her offer.'

Busk puffed himself up, understanding Kalid's meaning: this was his last chance to right his wrong and return the ghost. 'Oh, is it, now?'

'Indeed.'

'Well, you can tell her that I rescind my offer. Considering her rudeness, I am not interested. I've got enough Krassmen half-lives in my tower. I don't need another, especially a dangerous trouble-maker.'

'So the charity and care you spoke of—?'

Busk was already signalling for his guards to close the doors. 'Withdrawn! I extended my help, and all you and that widow have done since is badger me.'

There was another word Kalid had never heard before. Perhaps it was Skol.

Busk waved his hands as if shaking off an errant wasp. 'I don't expect to see you here again, Colonel. Good afternoon!'

Kalid was shut out with a bang. He turned, chuckling to himself. He didn't pretend to understand the game of words and veiled intentions that the nobles played; Horix had given him his lines and he had spoken them. What he did understand was that his mistress was a skilled player of the game, and Busk had just made a losing move. That was fine by Kalid. What benefitted Horix usually benefitted him.

When he returned to Horix's tower, the widow was waiting for him in the doorway. A swift march through several districts of bustle and commotion, in hot sun and full armour, would send even a hardened Arctian running to a water trough when he saw one. Kalid hastily washed away the dust and sweat before he approached Horix.

'Mistress.'

Without a word, she led him across the patterned atrium floor as the door was sealed behind them. Her hands were ensleeved as usual, but her cowl had been thrown back. Her thin hair shone like silver thread. Her eyes were hungrily affixed to the colonel's lips, as if she could read his words before he spoke them. This jabbing and parrying with Busk had lit an old flame in her; he could see it plainly.

Kalid bowed low. 'My apologies, Mistress. The city is busy in the aftermath of the sandstorm.'

She tutted impatiently. 'I don't care about sand, Colonel, only our good Tor Busk. What did he have to say?'

'He said he withdraws his offer, and that you are to leave him be. Apparently we've done nothing but "badger" him since he tried to help.'

'Have we now? How bold of him to say.'

'Seemed quite put out by the whole thing,' he added. 'I take it that was the answer you wanted, Mistress?'

A wicked smile spread across the cracks in her cheeks. 'Indeed. As I predicted, our prideful Tor Busk has just thrown down a gauntlet. He thinks I am bluffing, that I am toothless and weak. He thinks I will give up Caltro and just let the matter lie.'

'And what will you do?'

'I will crush him, Colonel. Even if Caltro wasn't one of the best locksmiths in the Reaches, nobody steals from me.' Horix stepped away. 'If Busk wants a shade, we will deliver him a shade. We'll call it a gift to dust our hands of the matter. He'll believe I have my restitutions for Caltro and think it settled.' She made a cat's arsehole of her grey lips. 'Have you found me a good enough spook?'

Kalid smiled. 'Aye, Madam. I have. Comes highly recommended.'

'Good. Never cease to please me, Colonel. For your sake.' She left him alone on the patterns of marble, and swept up the stairs to her rooms. The stubborn woman always liked to walk, despite her clock-work lifts.

The colonel shook his head. Not at her, but at Tor Busk. Nobody had ever got the best of Widow Horix, not in all the years he'd served her, and that was before she had something to protect besides her own pride.

Kalid glanced at the door at the end of the atrium, locked and chained in the daylight. Now she had a reason to fight even fiercer.

CHAPTER 8
A VILLAIN

Before the discovery of binding, every dead body was sent to the Nyx or buried with a coin in their mouth. Now, only those who die in peace do that, as we cannot bind them. According to the Tenets, those who die in turmoil are the dutiful ones. They are the ones who dedicate their half-lives to bettering the Arc.

FROM A WORK-SCROLL FOUND IN MOST
ARAXES SCHOOLS

IF THERE WAS ONE WORD Boran Temsa detested above all others, it was 'problem'. It was fouler than any curse. More damning than any accusation. Disembowelment with a spoon was almost preferable to hearing it.

So it was that the look he levelled on Tooth was a razor-sharp and damning one.

'What do you mean, "problem"?'

'The vault ith an old dethign, Both…'

'It's *Tor* now. Tor Temsa.'

Tooth was too busy scratching her head to notice her error. 'I never tackled anythin' like it. Jutht cogth an' thpring-work like I ain't ever theen. No keyth, jutht a dothen bloody combinathonth.'

'And so?'

'I…' Her lip went white as her tooth pulled at it. 'I can't open it, Both.'

Temsa stamped his claws.

'TOR!'

Tooth withered away, shrinking back to the sturdy iron vault that had defeated her. Temsa took a look for himself. The circular door had the look of an enormous drain cover, crisscrossed with thick iron bars and bolts. At its centre was a fine seam, and spaced along it were swollen boxes with half a dozen bronze cogs sticking out from each one. He poked the locks with his cane, kicked the metal with his foot, but, unsurprisingly, nothing happened. When the clanging died away, he bowed his head.

'Danib,' he said to the figure standing nearby.

With speed belying his monstrous size, the shade surged forwards, seized Tooth, and lifted her from the floor. Her throat was clamped between his bicep and forearm. The locksmith gargled as she clawed at his armour.

'You dare tell me you can't do your job?' Temsa yelled.

'Give me another day!' she wheezed. 'Maybe two!'

'*Days?* I'd baulk at giving you hours! It has already been several days. Every moment we linger here arouses more suspicion. An empty tower tells no tales, Tooth. The corpses downstairs? They will! Their shades will begin to rise soon, and they may have families. Friends. No doubt their absence has raised questions already! Soon enough, enquirers will start appearing in the courtyard. And where will I be? Still standing here, watching you tinker away at a door, instead of counting my new half-coins! What does that make me, Tooth?'

Either she was conserving air or as clueless as a hog. In any case, she had no answer.

'Guilty! Guilty is what that makes me! So guilty the Chamber won't have to wait months to process our cases. They'll have us boiling in oil by next week. Now, I don't know about you,' he said, pausing to address the circle of men who stood around the vault room, 'but I'm not too keen on that idea!'

Grunts of agreement followed his words. Tooth had stopped clawing now, falling limp instead.

'Give me an hour,' she croaked. 'Pleath, Tor.'

Temsa signalled for the shade to drop her. 'One hour. Not one grain of sand more.'

Tooth knelt before the vault's door, shaky fingers reaching for her tools. Temsa shrugged. An hour he could afford. It gave him time to offer Tal Kheyu one last chance. He bent a finger at Danib, and the shade followed him to the corridor.

'Don't look at me like that.' Temsa could feel the measure of his gaze without turning. 'It's about time we got a better locksmith.'

Danib huffed between his steps.

'I don't care if she's nice to you. She's holding us back, and I won't have it. And speaking of things that are holding us back...'

He threw the palm-wood door wide open to find his makeshift torture chamber just as he'd left it. Fenec was still in the corner, looking a shade whiter than before. His shoes were splattered with his own vomit.

Tal Kheyu-Nebra lay on the table, her face impassive. So blank, in fact, that for a moment Temsa thought she had finally given up and died. Then her glassy eyes shifted to look at him, and he cracked a smile.

'How are we feeling, Tal? Ready to sign my sigil's documents yet?' he asked.

Her voice was like gravel on a tin roof. 'I won't be party to soul-stealing and forgery.'

'Oh, but you're wrong, Kheyu. Very wrong. You see, I haven't even started yet.' It was a lie. Temsa had started, finished, then started again. The old leather bag still refused to speak. His eyes roamed over the wounds he had already given her; the rough bandages where things had been removed.

Twenty-five years he'd been carving obedience into people, and not once had he failed to glean the truth, even when it had been just a hobby. Now it was an art form, and Kheyu was in danger of breaking his winning streak. A part of him felt like a child, refused a sweet treat at a bazaar.

'You think dying will be a victory? Take it from a soulstealer, Tal. It won't be.'

'Yes, it will,' Kheyu wheezed. 'As long as you don't get what you want.'

What irritated him was that she was right. Short of bringing in stonemasons to hack the vault door from its fixings, without her combinations or signature on Fenec's scrolls, her half-coins, whether in the banks or her vault, would be lost to him. He could only claim whatever treasures lay about her tower. They amounted to an inordinate number of decorative candlesticks and a range of tapestries so ugly Temsa wouldn't have used them as rags for his arsehole.

His quick mind sorted through his options. Taking such a hoard of coins by force without a signature or record would create a glaring inconsistency, even for a bank he was blackmailing. Fenec was already at his wits' end keeping his father's questions answered. Temsa could get by with a pinch of forgery at the soulmarkets. With a bank, he trod a dangerous line, even with a princess as a benefactor. Sisine could control the Chamber only so much. Then there were the rumours. Trial by public was always much swifter than the Chamber's justice.

Kheyu's seal had already been cut from her finger. That was half the problem. Should Temsa fake her signature to claim the estate, well… that was still an option, but all tors and tals were required to register their autographs with the banks several times a year to avoid forgery. Temsa would be taking a very dangerous guess. Should the Chamber start sniffing, the incongruity would sink him. This needed to be done properly or not at all.

Temsa moved to his case of sharp things and took his time choosing. He could hear Fenec groaning in the corner. Danib took his usual stand at the tal's shoulders, ready to hold her down.

'I'm still waiting for your worst, *Tor* Temsa,' Kheyu goaded him.

He showed it to her. Unabashedly and without hesitation.

His hand found the handle of a sickle blade. With a hiss, he plunged it into her wrinkled stomach and wrenched it towards him, baring her bloody insides to the lamplight. To her credit, Kheyu did not scream. The leathery wench just bared her teeth and groaned deep in her throat.

Temsa stepped back, knife in hand, and let the shock and blood loss take her. As blood dripped on the floor like a finger tapping a drum skin, he shared a look with Danib, who seemed mildly surprised.

'Why? Because she was a stubborn old fuck, that's why. She would not have given us anything. Better to put her out of her misery—' Temsa halted, hearing them as well: the uncharacteristic words spilling out of him without the thoughts to back it up. Did he somehow respect the tal's fortitude? Was he going *soft*? Temsa dismissed the foolish thoughts. 'Better to punish her for it, and not waste any more of my time!'

Temsa watched the blood pooling around his talons. 'Burn it,' he said. 'Set a fire in her bedroom. Make it look like her addled mind set the place ablaze. Put a few of the guards around as if they died in the fire, then take her and the rest so I can bind them. Cut their tongues. I'll be damned if I don't get some shades out of this. And speaking of...'

Danib pointed downstairs, indicating the gathered shades on the level below.

'Deal with them. Copper blades. Can't afford to raise suspicion by selling them. If I can't get their coins, they're not rightfully bound to me. I can't bank or Weigh them.' Temsa pondered as he wiped the knife. As he moved to replace it in its designated hollow in his case, he paused, and kept hold of it instead. 'Set a fire near the vault too. Put some furniture against the door. The half-coins will melt, and there'll be fewer tongues for wagging.'

Danib just shrugged. Temsa suspected if Ani were there, she'd have something to say about the matter. She never liked to see a shade go to waste. It made sense: the more shades Temsa took, the bigger her coin-purse. That was all Ani cared about. Though she had the tongue to complain about them, she didn't have the mind for these sorts of games. That was why Temsa had left her in charge of the Slab for the night.

'See it done, old friend!' he ordered. 'Ah, Fenec! Forgot you were there, man. You are relieved.'

The sigil immediately ran from the room. Temsa stamped after him, leaving Danib to manhandle the old body from the table.

Tooth was still scrabbling at the vault's cogs. Tears had drawn clean lines down her mucky cheeks. She couldn't seem to shake the tremor from her hands. She was concentrating so hard, she only heard Temsa once he was right behind her. The sickle knife hooked around her throat, and she froze.

'I thtill have half an hour,' she whimpered, fighting not to gulp in case she cut herself.

He spoke quietly in her ear. 'I've changed my mind.'

The silence was long and painful. In the end, she managed to stutter a word. 'And?'

'You're done. I have need of you no more.' Temsa paused to let her whimper. 'However, you've been party to certain criminal acts, privy to important information. In short, you know too much, Tooth, and I can't have that.'

Tooth began to shake so violently she came close to slicing her own throat.

'Stick out your tongue, Tooth.'

'No.'

'Would you rather the alternative?'

It took her a few quivering moments, but in the end she made the right decision. With his heavily-ringed fingers, Temsa grasped her slimy tongue, pulled it hard, and showed it the blade. Tooth collapsed to the floor, hands clamped over her lips, streams of blood running down her forearms. Temsa looked up at the grim and impassive faces of his thugs.

'I suggest you make yourselves scarce, before you find yourselves on the wrong side of a fire.'

They needed no encouragement to file from the room, and did so in relative silence. Temsa was left alone with the locksmith, who was now ripping strips from her sleeves to bandage her tongue.

'That means you too, Tooth,' said Temsa, nudging her with his golden foot. 'Don't you dare forget this mercy.'

Tooth garbled something as she scrabbled for the stairs, leaving a trail of blood behind her. Temsa imagined it was a 'thank you.'

As he listened to the sound of clomping boots receding, he ground his teeth. Twice now, mercy had interfered. Temsa cursed himself, blaming tiredness. His nights had been sleepless since stepping foot into this infernal tower, and the days had culminated in his first failure. *Problems.* They hounded him tonight. Now he had another: he was short one locksmith.

'Danib!' he bellowed.

The shade came lumbering out of the corridor, the old woman's body folded over one steel forearm.

'I want you to find out whether Tor Busk has had any luck finding me a locksmith.' Danib started towards the door, and Temsa knuckled his temples. '*After* the fire, of course. Priorities, old friend.'

The look Danib shot him was as damning as any one of Ani's doubts, and Temsa did not like it.

'Don't you give me that. I have my priorities straight.'

Danib had no reply. He stood as motionless as a statue, the only movement the natural crawl of his vapours between the plates of his armour.

Temsa sighed, unable to avoid the stare. 'I am simply... vexed, for fuck's sake! I thought our empress-in-waiting would provide some easier cats to skin than this one. Than *her.*' He motioned towards the dead Kheyu-Nebra. Her eyes were still wide and reproachful. 'You know how I despise failure.'

The shade broke his mimicry of a statue and nodded.

Temsa scratched at his beard. 'I think I'll go see her. I think an explanation is due if we are to keep the princess on our good side.'

Danib dropped the body with a crunch.

'No, old friend. Alone. You are rather noticeable, and I wish to be discreet. You concentrate on finding that stuck-up fence of mine. Tell Busk that *Tor* Temsa wants to see him. That'll put a hot poker up his arsehole.'

Temsa felt the shade's eyes follow him all the way to the door. The weight of their judgement pressed down on him. He put a bit more stamp in his stride, making his foot spark on the worn stone.

'Burn it well, Danib. Burn it fucking well.'

He snorted bitterly on the stairwell when he saw Kheyu's shades gathered in droves in the atrium, hemmed in by soldiers with copper spears. They all watched him with wide eyes and silence.

'Doubt be damned!' Temsa yelled at them, and screams rose to the vaulted ceiling as his soldiers went to work, hacking and slashing until blue mist covered the marble.

He would show his doubters their error in time, if they had the stomach to follow him. If they didn't... well. Temsa looked down at the blood streaking his fingers, testament to the kind of judgement he passed.

TEMSA WALKED WITH A CLANGING purposefulness. Alone, save for his black-clad guards trailing a few paces behind, he could enjoy the dying of the day.

The living had a scurry in their steps, unnoticeable to the untrained eye, and to one who didn't know how dangerous evening in the City of Countless Souls can be. The dead shared no such fear, wearing their black feathers beneath dull eyes; fixed on carrying, or working, or fetching, or whatever menial task they had been laboured with. Temsa's gaze bored into the few who dared to lounge on their masters' time, clicking his fingers to goad them back into work. His smart clothes spoke for him, and they sprang back into action.

As Temsa stalked through the congestion of King Neper's Bazaar, he watched the stalls dissolve around him, packed away in time with the sinking of the sun. It already lingered between the jagged spines of the western districts. The great towers and pyramids were carving up the city with their vast shadows. The Cloudpiercer cast a penumbra so wide and long that several districts to the east must have already thought it was nighttime. Temsa walked along the blurry edges of its shadow, enjoying the escape from the heat that emanated from the sand and stone around him.

When the blue above had faded to a dusty pink, he reached the base of the mighty Cloudpiercer. He craned his old neck to gauge the reach of its spire, as he always did. Its top was beyond view, lost to haze and sheer distance. Instead, Temsa looked to the high-roads that spread out from the tower's sides like branches reaching out into a forest of towers. There must have been a dozen on this side of the Piercer alone. Carriages clattered high above as they entered the tower under soaring, skull-carved arches.

The desire to build had burned within the human breast since the first rock was piled atop another. It was an addiction, an all-consuming impulse. It was why Araxes spread for a hundred miles east, west and south, and why here, at its core, the Cloudpiercer challenged the sky. Creation meant domination: bending the rock and earth to one's whims in the effort to create something more. Temsa thought it prudent to respect those who had the same vision of conquest as he had.

His soldiers held back to loiter by the grand entrance as Temsa stepped between the queues and marble columns into the cool of the Piercer's vast atrium, one of four that quartered its vast pyramidal base. Sandstone pillars – some as tall as a noble's tower – held up a domed marble roof that was as white as bleached papyrus. Balconies clung to the stone and spiralled upwards in a mesmerising pattern. They were the shape of a halved seashell, and each had whale-oil lanterns hanging from their balustrades.

A dull roar of voices filled the atrium. It seemed everybody wanted to get into the tower, but hardly anybody was allowed. Security was at its utmost. Core Guards lined every available space of wall. Cullis gates hung in banks over the archways. Ballistae and triggerbows sat in mounts on every other balcony. Soldiers ringed the podiums where the Piercer's clerks wore tall pointy hats and sat in marble chairs.

The clerks were responsible for hearing pleas for entry to the tower's levels. The Piercer held many ministries and official centres, but it was also home to a very large number of sereks and richer nobles, those who could afford space in the tower. As such, there was always plenty of business to be done here. It was a mile-high bazaar for the richest of the rich.

Temsa joined a short line and adopted a bored expression. The trick to looking rich, he'd recently discovered, was to constantly appear as if everything was beneath him. Queues easily fell into that category. *Leave queuing to the Skol*, he thought. Those buggers seemed to have a passion for it.

Half an hour must have passed before a shriek pulled Temsa from his reverie.

'NEXT!'

He stepped forwards under the watchful eye of four soldiers. As usual, their attention immediately shifted to his foot.

'Name?' asked the clerk.

'Tor Temsa, here to consult with Her Majesty the empress-in-waiting.'

'Your papers?'

'I have none.'

'Have you been formally invited?'

'I have not.'

The woman's face, which had previously been puckered up tighter than a fish's arsehole, cracked into an enormous grin. She even went so far as to nudge the guard standing atop her podium and chuckle.

'New, are we?'

Temsa jutted out his chin.

'Right.' She crooked a finger and a young messenger in a turquoise tunic came sprinting over. Barely a whisper later, he was on his way again, leaving the podium so immediately it look as if he had been fired from it. Temsa watched him thread his way through the diminished crowds to the central column: the colossal root of the building above. There, the clockwork and shade-pulled lifts led to the skies.

'He'll return momentarily. Move aside,' the old woman instructed. 'NEXT!'

Temsa spent those moments watching the crowds mill over the patterned marble or loiter between the pedestals holding obsidian statues of dead gods. Each of the deities' heads had been removed, but their bodies allowed to stay, frozen in proud or demure or nimble shapes. Personally, Temsa would have removed the whole lot of them and sold them for scrap. There was a lot of silver to be made in the obsidian trade.

The messenger burst from the crowds and scaled the podium to the clerk. He whispered breathlessly in her ear before sprinting back the way he had come. Temsa waited patiently near the podium for the woman to beckon him forwards with her dried twig of a finger.

'No,' announced the old gatekeeper. 'It appears you have no appointment.'

Temsa's hands moved to his hips. 'It is very important.'

The clerk showed the whites of her eyes. 'It always is, Tor. A thousand times a day I'm told how important this or that matter is. Do you know how many important people there are in this city? Do you? Because to me, it seems the entire population of Araxes deems itself important enough to swagger in here and demand an audience with a noble, or a serek, or a royal. Know your place! Step aside now, if you please. You have been asked to wait outside.'

'What? By who?'

'Did I mumble? The reply ordered you to wait outside. Nothing more. Now step aside, Tor.'

Temsa did as he was told, but with as much scowling and scraping of his claws as possible. The screeching of metal on marble made his spine crawl, but it was worth it to see the clerk and three whole queues wince. He had them all cowering by the time he made his exit. Petty, yes, but he was known for pettiness when he was insulted.

With the hollering of, 'NEXT!' echoing in his ears, he made his way back to the thin plaza that surrounded the base of the Cloudpiercer. He found his guards slouching up against a marble column, picking their noses and scratching other choice areas. They made a fine target for his anger.

'Stand up! Look sharp, damn it! And put that fucking flask away!' he barked.

'Aye, Boss!' they chorused.

At his glare, the corrections came stuttering.

'Tor!'

'*Tor* Temsa.'

'Aye, Tor!'

Temsa sighed. 'Useless drab pricks, the lot of you! I should have
you all fired or given to Ani as toys for her axes. You don't see other
nobles' guards acting this way, do you? Look, there!' He pointed out a
formation of guards marching smartly around their master, some woman
with fiery hair. There wasn't a single scratch or dent in their suits of
fire-blackened steel. Their boots met the flagstones in perfect time, and
they moved with the synchronicity of a flock of starlings.

'See?' Temsa hissed.

'Please, Tor Temsa. We can shape up,' one man had the cheek to
whine. After seeing how lightly Tooth had been treated, Temsa didn't
blame him.

Another had too much cheek: a man with a split lip and scruffy
yellow locks. 'Just need the silver for it, see?'

Temsa stepped up to him, forced to look up at his height. 'Are you
saying I don't pay you handsomely enough for lounging about, scratching each other's arseholes?'

'No, Tor, I—'

'Because that's all I see you doing! You're lucky you're getting any
silver at all.' Temsa rested one of his claws on the man's boot. The others
shuffled away, not wishing to have blood spray them. But Temsa was
more civilised than that, especially in the great shadow of the Cloudpiercer. 'Want more coin? Be *worth* more coin.'

A polite cough intervened. Temsa whirled to find Sisine's house-
shade standing behind him, dressed in a silk suit cut off at the shins.
Velvet slippers clad his glowing feet. The golden feather on his chest
caught the light of the sunset. Beside it was a seal that caught Temsa's
eye: a black circle, crossed daggers and a desert rose within it. Just like
a seal Temsa had taken off a corpse not too long ago.

'Interrupting something, am I?' Etane asked. 'What is it?'

Temsa shut his gaping mouth. 'Nothing. Just you, is it? Well.' He adjusted his coat and smirked. 'A little training, house-shade, nothing more. The living need it too. Shall we?'

Etane followed his gesture and led him along the wall until they were between entrances, where it was quieter. Temsa didn't give him chance to speak.

'I came to see Her Highness, and yet I find myself turned away like a commoner. I am an Arctian tor now, and considering our deal—'

Had Etane been alive and in possession of spittle, Temsa's face would no doubt have been decorated in it as the manservant launched into a tirade.

'You cannot simply turn up asking for Her Majesty whenever the mood strikes, Temsa! It is improper, and arouses suspicion, and the empress-in-waiting will not have it. You are not so high and mighty yet that you have that right. You may be a tor, Temsa, but you are one of thousands in this city!'

'I am more than that. You and her best remember it.'

'Giving orders to a royal now, are we? What's it been, four days? Already your head is outgrowing the rest of you.'

'You mind your tongue, shade.' Temsa had never had a half-life speak to him so.

Etane bared two rows of perfectly ordered blue teeth. 'You do not hold sway over me, Temsa. I am not some fresh shade you've scraped off the docks and bound for market. I was a lord of this empire decades before you were even a tingle in your father's mouldy balls.'

'And look at you now, with a gold feather on your breast.'

'Shall we continue bickering, or would you prefer to tell me why you came here?'

Temsa matched Etane's scowl for a moment, testing which one would break first. In the end it was Temsa, but only out of lack of patience. He hissed. 'It's the calibre of the opportunities Her Highness has given me. So far, they are proving… unrewarding. Time-consuming.'

Etane tutted, a strange sound through ghostly lips. 'I highly doubt that. I helped compile the list. Distant from the Core. Alone. High-ranked. Wealthy. Prize targets, some might say.'

'Kheyu-Nebra was alone and a wealthy old bag, sure enough. But the vault she had was damn near impregnable. She refused to play nice. She left me no option.'

'No option? What did you do?'

'Oh, she's been removed, don't you worry. But the haul was barely worth my time.'

Etane scoffed. 'Excuses! Are you sure you don't mean to say these opportunities are proving too difficult for you?'

Temsa ground his claws against the flagstones, sending a spark fly-ing. 'Do you have any real purpose, shade, or do you just insult people on the empress-in-waiting's behalf?'

'What the fuck is it you want, Temsa? You said you could deliver what Sisine needs, but on the very first try, you fail. Did you just come here to make excuses and grovel?'

The notion of failure was like a needle in Temsa's throat. 'If these are the kind of bounties the empress-in-waiting wishes to have taken care of…' He paused, unused to asking favours. He normally just de-manded them. 'Then I need a new locksmith.'

Etane raised an eyebrow. 'And what do you expect myself or the heir to the throne of the Arc to know of locksmiths? You're the criminal. That's why we hired you.'

'Keep talking, half-life…' Temsa growled.

The shade looked around as a group of pale-faced traders came to touch the sandstone flanks of the Piercer in reverence. In recent decades, the mighty spire had become a place of pilgrimage for many parts of the Reaches, and these men had reached their journey's end.

Once they'd had their moment and wandered on, the damnable shade made a show of thinking. The years had clearly taught Etane many things, but acting didn't seem to be one of them. His whispered tone brought Temsa closer.

'I might know of one man who could help you. A rather good locksmith, in fact. He was due to come to the Piercer for some business a few weeks ago, but he never turned up. Fallen foul of some soulstealers, or so I hear.'

'Is that so?' Etane didn't fool him. It appeared the empress-in-waiting was in the market for a locksmith.

'It's the only explanation.' Etane wagged a blue finger in his face. 'You're a soultrader, aren't you? Maybe you can track him down.'

'I can't do anything without a name or description, can I? And even then—'

'Basalt. Caltro Basalt.'

Temsa vaguely remembered the name, but he played dumb. 'Caltro…'

'Basalt. Heard of him?'

'Perhaps. Famous, is he? Sounds Krass.'

'That he is. Surprised a man like you hasn't heard of him. He's one of the best in all the Reaches. Maybe *the* best, or so they say. However, if you find him, you must inform us.'

'Caltro Basalt…' Temsa repeated the name as he backed away, too busy thinking to bid the shade farewell.

'You think too much of yourself, Temsa. Ambition is a wild horse. Ride it too hard and it'll turn around to bite you. We can only protect you so much,' hissed Etane.

Temsa couldn't have cared less for the shade's advice. Nor could he care for his guards' oafish looks, or stomach their presence any longer. He shooed them away and strode out into the sunset-orange streets alone, eyes downwards and contemplative.

'But Tor...' the guards called to him.

Another wave and more threatening gestures saw them gone. Temsa needed silence for his mulling. That was all the mind ever needed: silence and the slow march of steps to knead out an answer.

Temsa's answer took just over a mile to come to him.

Basalt. He had read that name somewhere, inked into papyrus. He could almost see the face that came with it: a pudgy face constantly in a petulant scowl.

'Caltro Basalt.' He spoke it aloud. 'A "C" and a "B."'

If Temsa wasn't mistaken, they had been Busk's own words. He set his jaw as he looked up at the horizon and saw the first wisps of smoke rising several districts away.

CHAPTER 9
TROUBLESOME SEAS

Emperor Farazar has been a war-maker from
the moment he bound his father and took
his throne. No other emperor has assigned so
many of his half-life stock to military usage. No
emperor has built so many troop-ships, or spent
so much silver on arms. But, in fairness, nor has
any emperor claimed as much territory in as
little time as he, not for several centuries.

AN INTERNAL NOTE FROM THE CHAMBER OF
MILITARY MIGHT

T HE MORNING HELD A FIERCE heat, as if the sun was exceptionally eager to get on with its business of roasting the earth, and those forced to crawl upon it.

The chill breeze washing off the Troublesome Sea did nothing to ease it. The glitter of the waves exacerbated the glare, making fleeting, miniature suns on every swell. It blinded the eye even under the shade of an umbrella.

Sisine held no love for the sea, as she knew many of her subjects did. It held some men's attentions like the promise of a witch, but for her, it was a wetter kind of desert. Merely something for her gaze to sweep over as she looked out from her balconies.

This morning, however, she knew a little of the wonder the sea held. Not because of its shining blue, its power, or its unknown edges, but because of what was travelling across it. That was why she stood on the very edge of the stone quay with her entourage spread behind her, her eyes fixed on the warships.

They were taking their sweet and merry time getting into the harbour. Something to do with tacking against a cross-shore wind, or so a serek by Sisine's side informed her. He was mistaken if he thought her impatience was down to lack of knowledge. A ship was either at sea or tucked into a harbour. Whatever happened in between was unimportant to her.

Oars were put to work as golden sails were taken in. As the warships turned, great painted eyes on their sleek bows leered at the gathering on the quayside. They were old eyes, chipped and salt-gnawed, but defiant in their glowers. Scars of countless battles could be seen across the warships' hulls; scorch marks from naphtha, arrow-cuts, and deep dents from disagreements with other vessels. The once-sharp points to their prows looked like tree-stumps used for practicing swinging an axe.

It took an age for them to sidle up to the quay. The warships rose high above the small crowd, and not just in their thick, slanted masts. Weapons, armour and cargo were the only weight an Arctian warship carried; one of the benefits of crewing ships with the dead. The only living souls aboard were the captain, the soldier-general and a cook to keep them fed. It was what made the Arctian navy the most dangerous in the Far Reaches.

The soldier-general was leaning over the bulwark. He hollered down to the hands on the quayside waiting to catch and tie off heavy lines. There was a squeak as the bundles of reeds positioned between the water and the stone caught the ships' weight, and saved their sides a few more scratches.

Boards were lowered and leaned at sharp angles. Orders were issued, and Sisine heard the responding clank of armour. Shades began to flow down the gangplanks in single file, each of them a facsimile of the soldier behind. They wore identical helms, tall and ridged with spikes. Simple steel plate armour covered them, and beneath that, smocks of royal turquoise, bleached to a pastel shade by sun and salt. Round shields – embossed with a crossed feather and spear – hung in one hand, tridents in the other. Curved short-swords were strapped to their hips.

The beat of their march carried them to dry land. Not a word was uttered. Training, not orders, ushered them into smart lines. Once several hundred shades had flooded the quayside, colouring the white stone a light blue, the captain and soldier-general disembarked.

The captain was a rotund man, but he walked in a way that suggested a lot of muscle hid beneath his fat. He had a face like a wineskin left in the heat, adding years that he didn't own. The soldier-general was a skinnier man, wearing finer armour than his soldiers and more of it, too, as those who gave orders were wont to do. He wore a skirt of mail and a giant, plumed helm with a small window for his red and sweaty face. The tight-fitting steel gave him the look of a pig being squeezed through two fenceposts.

Both of them prostrated themselves on the warm stone before the empress-in-waiting. One of her guards took the sword the general was proffering. It was customary for every officer to surrender their weapon when standing before royalty; an old rule born out of a history that featured far too many military coups.

'Rise,' she said to them.

'Thank you, Majesty.'

'Thank you.'

Sisine waved to the leather-faced captain. 'You may attend to whatever nautical duties need your attention, Captain. I only need the general.'

The man in question bowed again. 'Soldier-General Hasheti, Majesty.'

She couldn't care less. 'Mm.'

'Care to view your soldiers, Highness?'

Sisine vacated the shadow of her umbrella and followed the officer towards his soldiers. As she began to tour their glowing ranks, Hasheti hovered nervously. She could almost hear the words fighting to get out of his mouth. Her eyes roved lazily across each of the soldiers, counting the dents in their steel, or the white scars punctuating the vapours on their necks and forearms. Their white eyes were glazed, fixed on the horizon.

There was one aspect of shade armies she did enjoy, and that was the lack of stink. Living soldiers tended to carry an odour with them: sweat, fear and trench dirt. These shades carried only the smell of sea salt and blade oil.

Another benefit was that most of these shades were mute. Their tongues had been cut out with a copper knife to make sure they could only follow orders, not give them. Spreading dissent was hard without a tongue.

'How many have you brought me, General?'

'Three hundred and fifty-two. Eleven phalanxes. The rest are still fighting in the Scatter Isles under Lord-General Mardok.'

'And what battles have you fought in the name of my father's ambition?'

'Nine successful bouts in Phylan territory. One defeat. Battled shade-pirates in the northern Scatter for the last year.'

'What about law-keeping? In a city or town?'

'We held the fortress of Zantae for several weeks, both against siege from the outside and revolt from the inside.'

'How did you manage it?'

'Executed every last traitor. Bound them to replenish your army and the emperor's cause.'

'Traitors? In my army?'

Hasheti's window of a face puckered even tighter. 'A shade soon forgets his or her past under my command, Your Highness.' He rapped his gauntlet against his breastplate, and every phalanx knocked swords and tridents together in almost perfect unison.

'Hmm.' Sisine was quickly tiring of the heat. She could feel her eye-paint melting. She clicked a finger at Etane, who ran forwards with her umbrella. 'That is what we need in this city, General: order and obedience. There is a war raging here, Soldier-General Hasheti, make no mistake. Just look there, on the horizon, where a tal's tower burned long into the night. Set ablaze by criminals or carelessness – who can tell?' She pointed at the blackened stub of a circular tower, still haloed in smoke. She knew it to be the former, but she wasn't about to reveal that. 'In any case, it is a sign that this city is slipping into chaos.'

Hasheti hummed in the pause. 'Majesty, allow me to assure you, I—'

'I will tell you when you may speak. This may be a war, General, but it is a war unlike those you've fought before. This is a war not fought in lines and ranks on a field, but on the streets of our own grand capital. The battlefield is all around us, and the enemy could be any of your fellow Arctians. This is a war against injustice and greed. A war for the protection of the Tenets and the Code. I need to know: do you think you and your shades are fit to fight such chaos?'

The general bobbed his head, unsure if he was allowed to speak. She waved a hand and he blurted his reply as if he had been holding his breath. 'Of course, Your Majesty. We will do whatever is needed.'

Another click of her fingers brought a sweaty, pink-faced Chamberlain Rebene scuttling from her retinue. He looked like the very definition of sweltering. His tar-black hair glistened with sweat. Sisine half expected the tattoos on his neck and face to start running.

'Chamberlain Rebene is now your direct superior, General. His orders, and those of his magistrates, are my orders. Understand? Together, you will do whatever it takes to purge this city of its injustice,' Sisine ordered.

Rebene didn't look as if he liked the sound of that, but it may have just been the heat getting to him. He wasn't a man who saw a great deal of the outdoors. Hasheti looked no more pleased to be twinned with a bureaucrat. Sisine caught his eyes measuring the chamberlain's silk robes and manicured hands and inwardly sighed. It was the stubborn right of men who had seen and lived through war to reserve their respect for others who had done the same. It was why every royal who had ever sat on the empire's throne spent at least a year in a courtyard, training with the sword. It earned some respect from the lord-generals and the Chamber of Military Might, and made it harder for a royal to be murdered. Sisine had insisted on her own three years of training for that exact reason.

'Do you understand, Hasheti?' she said.

Once more, he prostrated himself. 'Completely, Majesty.'

'Rebene? You look unsure.'

'I…' His mouth flapped around an answer. 'This is still just… so unusual. So irregular. Soldiers have not patrolled the streets for hundreds of years. Surely Emperor F—'

Sisine skewered him with a practiced look, sharp and cold. 'My father the emperor is a wise man. He knows better than anyone that these are irregular days, Chamberlain Rebene, and that such days call for irregular steps. Do not be so naive to think that the world can stay the same forever. Change is survival. Refusal to change is the mark of ruin. If you do not believe me, I would suggest asking the empires that came before the Arc, but alas, they are no more than dust.' She let her point sink in like the tip of a dagger. 'Have these soldiers marked as officers of the Chamber, and have your man Heles put them to good use.'

'*Woman*, Majesty. Scrutiniser Heles is a woman.' At the empress-in-waiting's uninterested stare, Rebene added, 'And yes, right away.' He bowed along with Hasheti, and Sisine swept away, leaving them there between the glowing ranks.

Etane matched her long-legged stride, keeping the umbrella over her all the way to her litter, which was waiting behind a small army of Royal Guards. Silk-draped shades in masks waited beneath stout poles, ready to carry the construction of mahogany and silver filigree. Etane gifted another servant with the umbrella and then perched on the edge of the litter as it was hoisted up.

Sisine didn't say a word to him. Not during the sweltering canter through the alleyways of the High Docks, and not during the shaded walk beneath the awnings of the crowded Spoke Avenues, some of the oldest streets in Araxes, palm-lined and thick with gawping tourists. Musicians stood in worn alcoves, plying pipes or arghuls. The hot air was thick with spices; the catch of chillies at the back of the throat, and the silkiness of cinnamon and cumin to tickle the nose. They wafted from tavern doors and stands where oil-drenched and skewered things roasted over coals. Between the drip and hiss of fat, merchant stalls sold scarves that floated on the sea breezes and pawed at passersby.

Every now and again, one scarf would grow too bold and touch a nearby coal. It would vanish in a burst of smoke, and an argument would ensue between merchants in thick Arctian tradese. Clapping abounded from swathes of oafish tourists too used to a bucolic homeland, too foreign to recognise a fight when they saw one. Half of them were already pink with sun-scorch. The other half would likely be dead by dawn.

Sisine watched it all, holding a finger to part the litter's chainmail curtains. Anything to endure Etane's silence. His punishment for blabbing to Temsa about Basalt had been hers to dole out, and yet somehow it felt as if she were the one being penalised for his loose tongue.

It was the staring, like the rapt eyeballing of a pitiful hound. Everpresent and practised for decades. She had bid him be silent and chosen to ignore his presence, and yet Etane repaid her with *that* look. It was infuriating, and more so because she was wise to his game. After a hundred and twenty years dead, he knew exactly how to deal with his masters and their punishments, and that was to be either as vital or as annoying as possible depending on the situation. It was why he was the freest indentured shade she had ever known.

"Patient" was a word not usually found near her name, spoken, written or otherwise. Yet today it was Sisine's new mantra. The weapon of silence was a difficult one to wield for those unused to it, but she was set on victory.

She had gone an hour, maybe more, when Etane loudly cleared his throat and caused her to flinch. Even in that minuscule way, she had acknowledged his existence. It was a cheap trick, and it made her roll onto her shoulder and poke her head through the chainmail. At least there she could drown in the noise of the avenues.

As they entered the finer districts, the buildings reached higher, as if in praise of the Cloudpiercer. The tourists and traders faded, replaced by those of a richer kind. Tors and tals. Wealthy business owners. Bankers. Veterans, once lord-generals or admirals. Celebrities of music or art. They took their turn to clog the streets.

Like Sisine, each was encircled in their own rings of guards. Though clothes and face-paint could lie when it came to status, the cut of a person's guards were a better measure for how many half-coins they had banked. Guards were pure fashion in Araxes. The first purchase anyone with coin made was either a guard or a lockbox. Those who went without soon found out why security was so popular, and usually they found out too late to do anything about it. The City of Countless Souls devoured the weak and foolish.

Though Sisine's litter lacked any royal glyphs or seals, the turquoise plumes and fine gold armour of the Royal Guard drew plenty of stares. As soon as one bystander had the smarts to bow, the rest followed suit. A wave of respect followed her like a wake behind a keel. It was for this reason Sisine refused her guards' suggestion to take the high-roads back to the Piercer, as any royal would. The adoration was worth the danger.

The empress-in-waiting sat straighter to smile, and left a hand in the sun to wave casually. A royal should never spurn her subjects, even in a world that demanded only wealth as the right to rule, rather than royal bloodlines.

Her sharp mind found names for the faces she recognised behind the wall of golden shields.

Tal Resalp. *Up and coming, so they say.*

Tal Sheput. *Down and drowning.*

Arak-Nor. *So-called finest voice in the Arc.*

Serek Warast. *Useless sack of whining shit.*

Tor Farut. *Gotten fat in his old age.*

Admiral Nilo, the Champion of Twaraza. *Looking very good for his age.*

And Serek Boon...

The shade was standing on the balcony of a building wedged between two towers. He was leaning on the balustrade, overlooking the street by a single floor. His glow was pale in the hot morning light, but Sisine could see his white eyes returning her stare.

It was not his impertinence that infuriated her, or that he had made no attempt at a bow. It was that he did not stand alone. Two shades stood behind him. They wore white feathers on their breasts as Boon did. Their long robes were a deep scarlet, knotted with silver rope, and their hoods were drawn back to show bald heads.

There was a fourth shade beside them, and it was a rare sight. The dead hound sat at heel, leashed by leather cored with copper. The animal glowed a deep, dark blue, and its eyes were piercing white. Sharp, upright ears made a right angle of its long snout. Its vapours outlined the curve of thick muscle. Cobalt fangs poked from its lips. This was no strangebound, locked into a living body, but a phantom. A pure-bound shade of an animal.

Sisine hadn't seen a phantom in more than a decade, not since her childhood, when the emperor had bought her a blue jay that glowed white when it sang. Her father had sent it away for singing too loudly and too constantly. If she remembered rightly, that had made her cry, and *that* had made father even madder.

It took immense effort to bind the shade of an animal, never mind binding it in a stable state. It only worked with smarter or larger animals, already accustomed to humans. It had never worked with wild animals, though many had apparently tried. Five hundred years ago, phantoms had been the fashion of the day, but it only took so many stories of phantoms turning on their owners to erode their popularity. They were unpredictable, largely because they struggled to reconcile their minds with their ghostly forms. Spooked dead things could be just as dangerous as spooked living things, if not more. Since then, the Nyxites had lost the art, as they had with deadbinding and strangebinding.

As fascinating as the phantom was, it was not what held Sisine's attention. The two shades were the subject of her interest.

Sisine needed no more reasons to despise the Cult, but it was the habit of a hate-filled mind to seek out more reasons to affirm the hatred, however banal. That was why many prejudices refused to erode, no matter how many years passed. She refused to let her hate die. It was as steadfast as the Cloudpiercer.

She watched the figures until her litter turned around a corner. Staring straight ahead, Sisine waved mechanically as her mind churned over possibilities for why Boon would be with two of the Cult, and so close to the Core Districts as well. Since the Cult's banishment, she had occasionally spotted a scarlet robe between the tight gaps of the mighty towers, or preaching the glory of Sesh on a street corner, feet on a crate. Sisine always made a point of having her guards move them on.

Twenty years had done nothing to blunt her abhorrence of the Cult. She had watched with her own eyes how they had weaselled their way into the Piercer, then the Cloud Court, and then her grandfather's ears, all the while having the gall to call themselves a 'church'. Milizan's foolishness and greed had cost him his life, and at the hands of his own son. Her father. Sisine had learnt a valuable lesson the day her father had taken to the turquoise throne, leaving smears of blood across the crystal. *Trust nobody, not even family.*

Part of her yearned to turn her litter around, to have her guards take the building and muscle the cultists into the street. Make an example of them. She would spit on them, and show the crowds how fiercely the royals' dislike of the Cult still burned, and how little the city cared for their talk of dead gods. The order hovered on her tongue, but some better judgement kept it from creeping further. Perhaps it was Etane's eyes, still gazing at her, but now with a different glint to them. *No*, they seemed to plead.

Sisine felt the angling of the litter as the carriers began to climb the slight mound the Cloudpiercer was built on. Etane chose that moment to leave her side, and walked on ahead. He didn't join her again until an hour later, once she emerged from the jagged doors of the shade-lifts, high at the top of the Piercer.

Sisine found him loitering in the corridor outside her chambers, head bowed.

'Hmph,' was all she gave him, sweeping past and heading for her balcony. She needed to gaze down on the city instead of crawling through its dusty streets full of morons and traitors. A petty assertion of dominance, perhaps, but what else were towers built for?

The breeze was fierce and tugged at her braided black locks. She felt Etane standing behind her. His cold washed over her in the rushing air.

'Why?' she asked.

'Why what, Your Radiance?'

'Why would Boon be standing with two shades from the Cult? Enlightened Sisters, no less! I was only a child, but I still remember them: the heads of their foul order. They are easy enough to make out.' *Silver rope around scarlet cloth. Heads as bald as eggs. A haughty look that only centuries dead can teach.* 'Tell me I'm wrong!'

Etane came to stand at her side, hands resting on the railing. 'I can't. But how should I know what business Boon has with them?' His voice was not argumentative, but rather low, ponderous. It infuriated her more.

Sisine didn't speak with Etane's level of calm. 'Because you were a cultist, once. You know their minds. Their wily, fetid little minds!'

'I did once, perhaps. But no longer. I have not had contact with the Cult since your grandfather died. Unless you count that hulk of a shade that belongs to Temsa?'

'Don't you dare speak that name so lightly! I still haven't forgiven you for setting our new tor onto our missing locksmith. I gave you no such order.'

Etane bowed his head. 'As I said, Your Grandioseness, I thought Temsa would have the best chance of finding our locksmith. Then, when the time is right, we procure him from Temsa, and continue with the original—'

Sisine screeched in his face, 'Forget the locksmith! Nobody can open the Sanctuary but the emperor! Haven't you realised that yet? The plan was a gamble from the start, and I will not waste any more time on Caltro Basalt while Boon and the Cult plot away behind my back!' She took a breath, feeling more than the sun heating her cheeks. 'You forget yourself, half-life. You make decisions you have no right to make, believing you have a say over my plans! You dare to treat me like you treated my mother. You overstep the mark, and I won't have it!'

The shade did not look at her. He spoke to the floor. 'More silent treatment, Princess?'

'Duties!' Sisine cried. 'Duties aplenty! For a start, you can see to the cleaning of the Cloud Court before session tomorrow. And by cleaning, Etane, I mean the entire hall. By yourself. Not a single house-shade at your bidding.'

Etane kept his mouth shut, and wisely so. The dark glow about him suggested any words he uttered now would be regretted. Sisine cocked her head as a question, and that broke him, sending him packing into the corridor with a low growl. Sisine couldn't resist smiling at his back. She could play her own games, and hers didn't stop at forlorn staring.

Now that Sisine was alone, she took deep breaths, steadying her heart. Her gaze wandered east and north, between the Outsprawls and the faraway smudges of islands. Her mother had crept back into her mind of late. Usually at dawn, when dreams faded into dust motes and shafts of sunlight. Sisine would wonder where she was, whether she was actually in Krass, or a beach in the Scatter, or if it was all some elaborate hoax and she was simply hiding in the emperor's Sanctuary with him. Sisine snorted. If that were the case, then one or both of them would be dead by now. There had never been any love between them to lose. Not that she could remember, anyway.

Outwardly, they were a noble, regal couple. In private, they were as incendiary as oil and flame. Sisine could count a thousand nights they had spent spitting and hissing like cats stuck in a barrel. She had spent most of her twenty-two years waiting for one of them to move from words to a dagger, but it had never happened.

What irritated Sisine was not knowing. If her plans were a neatly woven cloth, her mother was a frayed end she longed to snip off.

Bezel. His name flitted through her mind. She swept from the railing and marched towards her bedchamber.

Using the keys around her neck, she prised the padlocks from her steel chest. Inside, the mahogany-and-iron box was already lying open. Sisine took the silver bell from its velvet cradle and, holding it with both hands, returned to the balcony. She held it aloft to make its feather and storm cloud patterns shine in the sun.

Clang.

The note was piercingly high and clear.

Clang.

Six bells, the falcon had instructed.

Clang.

Six bells, and he would return at his own speed.

Clang. Clang...

Sisine wondered where he had got to, and how far a falcon could fly in two weeks. He could have been in Skol by now, or Belish. It could take another week for him to wing his way back. The bell hovered high once more, teetering. *It must have been long enough.*

Clang! Clang! Clang! Clang!

Patience had never been one of her virtues.

———————◆———————

'I DON'T GIVE A SHIT if you're hungry. You heard what the man said. Poi-so-nous.' Nilith sounded it out for emphasis. Her finger was so close to the falcon's face she was almost tickling his chin. Bezel just stared back at her, golden eyes narrow and defiant.

The bargeman repeated himself once more, shouting from the tiller. 'Blacktooth'll rot you from the inside out, I say. Only fish that eats you after it's dead.'

'You know it won't kill me,' Bezel replied, loud enough so that only Nilith could hear.

Nilith nodded. 'True, but I've already got a sick horse. I don't want a sick bird. We need your eyes to tell us what's coming. Or what's behind. So, please. Don't eat the fish.'

Bezel squawked deep in his throat, the bird version of a growl. 'Fine. But I swear to the dead gods, the next fucking sparrow or dune-pigeon that rears its head, I'm catching it, and you ain't getting any...' His muttering became inaudible as he hopped away down the barge's rail and flapped into the sky.

'Bloody recalcitrant bastard,' Nilith sighed.

She chose an infinitely more pliant beast instead, and settled down by Anoish's side. The horse lifted his head, sprightlier than he had been in days, but still weepy-eyed and stiff. She patted his ribs, feeling the rise and fall of his breath, and the rumble of his stomach. It was calming, and she half-closed her eyes.

At the tiller, Ghyrab cleared his throat with an inordinate amount of noise. 'That horse ain't ready to run yet.'

'I know, I know. A few days yet,' replied Nilith, helping Anoish to stretch out his injured leg then roll to his front. Twice he tried to stand, but the wallowing of the barge made it harder, and twice the leg crumpled to the knee. *Perhaps it's just numb*, Nilith quietly prayed. 'Maybe fewer. He's a tough bastard.'

Anoish snuffled at that. She wished she had something to feed him besides a bowl of poisonous fish. Why Ghyrab let her catch the spiny little beasts before telling her, Nilith wasn't sure. Perhaps he wanted to alleviate some of her boredom, and it had worked for a time, but it hadn't changed the fact they were starving.

They'd pushed the barge day and night since their escape from the Ghouls. They'd had no rations besides those they had run with and the scraps Ghyrab kept aboard, and they were long gone. They had fresh river water, which was always a pleasure in the desert, and if she grew even hungrier, plenty of splinters to gnaw on. At least they weren't being chased. Nilith felt the horse take an extra deep breath, and exhaled with him.

Bezel had seen nothing of Krona and her Ghouls. Perhaps the river led too far north for their interest. Maybe their crater on the Firespar called to them, or Krona had succumbed to rot and pain. Whatever the reason, Nilith was glad for it.

Since leaving Kal Duat, the Ashti had become steadily busier. Before, Nilith and the others had gone half a day without seeing another person on the water. Now, a boat or a barge passed them every hour. It was fortunate the river had also widened in recent miles. The Ashti was no longer a quiet, secluded rift cutting through the desert like mould through cheese. All manner of craft now filled its waterway: wizened old fellows on flat rafts like Ghyrab's; empty stone-barges, heading back to the White Hell; patchwork dinghies filled with laughing children; fishermen on reed coracles, lines on their bare toes and cotton hats tipped over their faces.

At intervals along the Ashti's gutter-like cliffs, desert-folk had built their strange homes. Flimsy ladders and balconies criss-crossed the stone, while dwellings of woven reed and frond bulged outwards, like molluscs left high and dry. In one case, the house was actually an old beetle carapace, hollowed out and suspended from the cliff on ropes.

Older residents had gone so far as to mine holes in the sandstone, like swallows building nests in a river bank. Long poles hung overhead, bound with twine and hooks and patchwork nets. Buckets hung on ropes from their makeshift homes. They moved in constant rotation as water was hoisted up to the desert, presumably for sale or for farming. Nilith attempted to barter with a few for food, but with only a rusty trident to offer, she was ignored by every tiny settlement.

'This is impossible. How do you survive, Ghyrab?'

'South of my hut, there was a village spread over the Ashti, where the river gets so narrow that two barges can't pass. Safe from raiders and soulstealers there. Not like these folk.' Ghyrab nodded towards another web of ladders and ropes spilling over the cliff edge.

Nilith looked up at them, watching a woman trying to bath two naked babes with much difficulty and howling. 'They seem pretty settled.'

'For now,' the bargeman grunted. 'They hide here until the next band of soulstealers come along. Those who survive move on. So it goes.'

As he spoke, Nilith noticed there wasn't a single nail or dab of mortar in the handful of mollusc-like dwellings. Everything was reed or woven palm frond, equally easy to pack up and take or leave behind.

'Lions don't come to watering holes to drink, Majesty. They come to eat the beasts that do.'

Nilith caught the eye of a man above, possibly the babes' father. His gaze was unblinking, and followed her until the river had taken them downstream. Only then did he take his hands from the axe he'd been holding.

'Why don't they leave?'

'And go where? Nowhere's safe in the empire, just bits of it are less dangerous. Isn't any law out here, no more than there is in your city. That is their home for now. Let them enjoy what little peace they can afford.'

Nilith pursed her lips, watching the family disappear behind a spur of rock. 'It's not fair,' she said, gripping her trident.

'The world ain't been right since binding entered it, Majesty.'

Her answer was just a whisper. 'Precisely.'

'Where are we, anyway?' called a voice. It had been so long since Farazar had spoken, Nilith had almost forgotten the ghost was there. They must have been his first words since Nilith had fished him out of the river, trembling with anger. He was now ensconced in a corner with his knees drawn into his chest and his arms wrapped around his legs, glowing darkly and moodier than ever.

Ghyrab took a measure of the sun and the curve of the river.

'We can't be nearing Silok's Springs already...' he said. For the first time since he'd taken them on as passengers, the bargeman looked unsure. 'But we are. Must be flowing quicker than I thought.'

'You lost, old peasant?' Farazar challenged him.

'Truth be told, you're the first passengers I've had in two summers, and they all wanted to go south. Haven't been this far north in... Well, I can't remember.'

The ghost huffed. 'And how exactly does one tell when it's summer in this despicable fire-pit?'

Ghyrab was unimpressed. 'Maybe *you* can't, Emperor, from your ivory tower, but we desert-folk can.' He turned back to Nilith. 'In a few miles, there's another jetty and a hut. Silok's a bargeman like me. Or at least he was. Could be long dead now.' He wiggled a finger in his ear. 'If we're lucky, some of Silok's sons will still tend the barge. They might have vittles. If not, the Springs are named after a nearby patch of palms and grass. Could be some fruits or leaves.'

'Let's hope so.'

'We'd better. Last place before the river starts curving back east.'

Nilith chuckled drily. 'I'll take an empty stomach over one full of sharp steel any day, Ghyrab. It's good to be clear of—'

'TROUBLE!' came a screech from above. Bezel came crashing back to the deck like a meteor. Nilith jumped in fright.

'Dead gods, bird!'

Bezel winked. 'Just imagine if you were a hare or a mouse.'

Nilith crossed her arms, secretly digging her nails into her palms. 'Perhaps when I have the time for such luxuries as daydreaming, I will. For now, I'm more interested in what you mean by trouble!'

He held up a pinion feather. 'Don't get too fucking excited, now. Could be nothing. Could be just a bunch of fast-moving nomads.'

'What did you see?'

'I saw a dust cloud to the south. Thin, but coming this way. I wanted to warn you first before…' But Bezel trailed off, golden eyes fading out of focus, beak hanging agape. 'Oh, for fuck's sake! Not now!'

Nilith felt a twinge in her gut at his urgent tone. 'What is it? What did you see?'

The falcon whacked his head with his wings. 'Please just six. Please! I fucking swear!'

'Bezel! What did you see, damn it?'

He seemed to be fighting something, straining to speak. 'Dust cloud. Riders, maybe. Twenty or so, dressed in black and grey. Only f—NO! That bitch rang nine—'

Bezel cracked. That was the only word for it. A dark rift appeared in his chest and he folded into it with a wretched shriek. The rift disappeared with the crack of a whip, leaving the air to wobble in the spot where the falcon had been perched not a moment ago. Feathers and down fell like fat snowflakes.

It took some time for the barge's passengers to tear their eyes away from the empty space.

'Did he...?' Ghyrab stuttered. 'Does he... do that often?'

Nilith dug her teeth out of her bottom lip. 'I think it's something to do with his bond. His half-coin.'

'What does that mean?' Farazar yelled at her.

'It means Sisine's summoned him! Dragged him all the way to Araxes, damn it!' Nilith ignored the fresh worry knotting her stomach and attended to other matters. 'What's more important is what Bezel was about to say. A dust cloud, but "only" what? Did he mean four? Five? Fifty? Did he mean to say miles or minutes?' She clutched her sandy, matted hair.

Anoish whinnied, turning his snout to the river and staring forlornly at the canyon walls, as though they were prison bars. The bargeman had no answer for Nilith, just a scowl. Only Farazar spoke up.

'I was on the cusp of believing you were a warrior, afraid of nothing. Yet here you are whining about a little dust cloud like a coward,' he hissed.

Nilith moved so her shadow fell over him. 'I ought to make you go ashore first, then. You can play scout, and you'd better pray that dust cloud is not the Ghouls heading us off.'

The ghost's face spread into a broad smile, like that of a street clown. 'Praying is for the foolish. Look at you, after all, and everything praying's brought you.'

'Intolerable man.' Nilith swept away, leaving him blinking in the sunlight. 'How far to the Springs, Ghyrab?'

'Hour, maybe less.'

Nilith retreated to the bulwark to watch the water slip by. Gone was the foul sewage of the Kal Duat quarry, and it was a blurry crystal once again; summer blue streaked black by fish riding the currents.

'Damn that meddling daughter of mine,' she whispered, low so only the horse could hear. Even out here, still hundreds of miles from the Cloudpiercer, Sisine was still making her life painfully difficult.

———◆———

'WHAT? WHAT COULD YOU POSSIBLY fucking want to—'

A finger flicked him square in the beak, which to the falcon was like a soft punch. Bezel flapped his dishevelled wings, almost slipping from the railing. The magic of his summoning always somehow found him a perch. It was considerate like that, considering how cruel it was in most other areas.

'We had a deal!' he complained nasally.

Sisine's face was puckered with displeasure. Her arms crossed over a smart gown of blue and black. Powdered crystal covered her lips. Her raven hair streamed freely in the wind. Despite the golden paint that swirled around her emerald eyes, she looked weary, lacking sleep.

'I refuse to wait any longer for news. For all I know, you've been sunning yourself on the beaches of Ede, or island-hopping across the Scatter.'

'For your information, Princess, I've been very bloody busy indeed.

In fact, before you rudely summoned me, I had just picked up your mother's trail. Now I have lost it. It'll take me a—'

'Where is she?'

Bezel loathed being interrupted. After two hundred years strange-bound, he had learned that the living never truly listened; they merely waited for their turn to speak. Sisine clearly wasn't fond of waiting.

Bezel also knew the trick to lying was not replacing the truth, but bending it. 'She's in the south.'

The questions spewed from Sisine. 'South? What is she doing in the south and not in Krass? Where in the south?'

He sighed, speaking slowly as if trying to talk sense into a drunk-ard. 'I don't know. Like I said, I've only recently tracked her down—'

'Where?'

'Outside of Kemza.' At Sisine's blank look, he sighed. 'Where in the fuck is that, you ask? As I was saying, six hundred miles south. East of Belish. At a crossing of a river called Ran.'

'And what is that lying swine of a woman doing there?'

The falcon had to pause here. There were two answers, and the choice was a difficult one. He could either rattle the princess or pacify her, and every moment he spent weighing them, Sisine became more suspicious. The other trick to lying was not taking too long to answer.

Bezel decided to keep her guessing. *Let the bitch stew and wring her fingers*, he thought. She deserved it. 'Heading back north, by the looks of it. Or east up the coast to Krass.'

Her eyes narrowed. 'Not so certain, are we?'

The falcon shrugged. 'Not certain at all. There are many roads through the Long Sands.'

'How did you find her?'

Bezel rattled off a few faraway places for good measure. 'Heard about a woman travelling with many guards in a souk south of Far

District. They said south, not east. Then in the Steps, in Abatwe, saw a caravan trading with shiny Araxes silver. I had just found the river crossing outside of Kemza, and the tracks of a small group heading north. I followed them and saw her eyes, green just like yours. Unmistakeable. Now I might have lost her for good. And whose fault is that?'

Sisine moved away from him, teeth and fists clenched. 'You had better not. Otherwise there'll be no reward for you at the end of this.'

Bezel was glad it was hard for birds to smile. Nonetheless, the corner of his beak still curved. 'I guess I'd better go all the way back out there, then.'

'You guess correctly, bird. I must know what that woman is doing in the Long Sands. It makes no sense to me, and it makes me all the more suspicious. Now go! And be quick about it! I don't want to have to summon you again!'

'That makes two of us, Princess.'

With that, just as the back of Sisine's hand was swinging towards him, Bezel dove from the railing with his wings folded, and dropped like a spear towards the distant flagstones.

CHAPTER 10
OLD WOUNDS & BROKEN BONDS

Never turn your back on an Arctian, even
when he's dead.

OLD KRASS PROVERB

THE JETTY LOOKED TOTALLY ABANDONED. No barge waited patiently against it. Sand eddied across its warped planks. The discarded ropes hanging from its sides were rotten or frayed, and the whole thing exhibited a distinct leftward lean.

Nilith looked back to Ghyrab, who gave his trademark shrug. The trident she held in her fists did nothing to steady her heart. It thudded so hard she could feel it in her eyes, making her vision pulse. She dearly wished Sisine had not taken Bezel away.

'Doesn't look like Silok or his sons stuck around,' she called over her shoulder to the bargeman. Her stomach growled at the announcement.

Ghyrab sniffed. 'We better hope the spring's not barren.'

With great washes of the oar-like tiller, he slowed the barge and turned it into the calmer shallows. They collided with the jetty with a thud, and the impact shook them all. A loop rope saw to keeping the barge in place. Ghyrab kept his hand on the tail of the knot, ready to yank it loose at any moment.

'I'll be here,' he said. 'Waiting.'

Nilith bowed her head in thanks. 'You don't have to do this, you know. To come this far. To help this much.'

The bargeman cackled. 'Oh, I'm not doing it out the goodness of my own heart, Majesty. I'm doing it because I know what a fat purse o' gems I'll get for all these miles under the keel. Keeping you alive protects my investment. Now you hurry up.' He added a wink, and Nilith smiled.

Anoish was fixed on getting to dry land, beating both her and Farazar to the rough wood of the jetty even though his legs were stiff as fenceposts. He tottered on, and by the time plank turned to dust, he had some of his usual gait back. His injured haunch still dropped slightly, and Nilith wondered if it would ever be right again.

'Farazar, tend to Anoish. Ghyrab, I'll be back shortly. And watch that ghost.'

Trident bobbing, Nilith jogged up the slope, stumbling awkwardly. The steep ground felt entirely too solid for her liking; it had no sway to it at all.

The shaded passage hadn't been cut into the canyon rock by hands and picks, but by water, long since dried up or diverted. She trod on whorls where waterfalls had poured and splashed, or whirlpools had spun.

Nilith was out of breath by the time she broke into sunlight and hot desert. There was a fragrance of palms and water on the hot breeze, and it stirred her empty stomach. A bowshot away, the small oasis called to her thirst, but her practicality pulled her instead towards the thimble-shaped hut perched on the lip of the canyon wall.

Before she moved, she looked south. There was a dust cloud indeed, just as the falcon said, but it had trailed west, and was already fading into a haze. Hooves and riders, sure enough, but who they belonged to, she could not say for sure. Plenty of nomads and soultrains crossed the carpet of dunes that sat between the city and the Steps.

Nilith turned north and felt her breath catch in her throat as she saw the vast smudge of Araxes, sitting like a mountain range on the horizon. At its middle, it reached for the sky in one sharp thrust. *The Cloudpiercer.* Ghyrab had brought them much closer than she had thought, but the city's size belied the distance. There were still many miles left.

The hut. She loped towards the mound of plaster and river stones. It looked out over the Ashti and had a squat door in its backside. Its white plaster was flaking away, revealing the brown pebbles and dried reeds beneath. As with Ghyrab's hut, it seemed dead to the world, but

Nilith was now wise to the silence of bargemen, and how they liked to pounce with tridents.

'Is there anybody there? I mean no harm. Just here to barter for supplies! We've come north with Ghyrab.'

Only the breeze answered her, stirring sand around her feet. Her heart thudded in the silence. Nilith decided to poke around, trident held out and ready to jab. Her mouth was infernally dry.

The door opened easily. It was unlocked and only held in place by rust. The air that wafted out was musty and breathtakingly hot. The plaster was failing to do its job of reflecting the sun.

The hut appeared to have been ransacked long ago, and whatever couldn't be killed, eaten, melted down or sold had been cast on the floor and stamped on. A few fist-sized beetles tussled over a bone on the floor. Silok's sons were either long dead or long gone. In their absence, sand had crept under the door and through the palm frond shutters, decorating everything in a fine coat of yellow.

As Nilith escaped into the relative cool of the day, she heard the clop of Anoish's hooves on the rock. His skewbald snout emerged into the light, a happy gleam in his eye at being a horse again rather than a lump of cargo.

Nilith looked south once more and saw the dust trail had all but vanished now, nothing except wavering heat lines. 'What was that bird on about?' she asked aloud. Anoish snuffled.

She beckoned the horse towards the oasis, jogging to get him to trot alongside her. There was a limp in his stride, but she did her best to ignore it, as he did. His head was high and proud, black mane waving, and that was all that mattered.

The breeze blew harder under the shade of the palms. The scent of grass filled Nilith's nostrils, and pollen scratched her throat. Her feet swished through grass that grew taller the closer it was to the scrap of water. There was no pool or spring; just a shallow puddle over dark mud, edged with yellow, knife-shaped reeds. Wary of her last encounter with a puddle of water in the mountains, she sniffed deeply, but found no poisonous odour. Kneeling, she cupped a hand and sipped. This was cool, heavy with minerals, but entirely drinkable. Nilith dug around in the silt for the tuberous roots of the reeds. She yanked one free, washed it clean, and eagerly bit down on its cotton-white flesh. It was cold, crunchy, and had a bitter mustard taste, but to a starving stomach it was delicious

Nilith looked around as she chewed. Anoish lapped up the water from the far side, caring little for the mud. Tubers were scattered around his hooves, and dotting the grass were fallen nuts from the palms. She gathered up all the tubers and nuts she could carry, making a pocket of the hem of her shirt.

As she straightened up, she looked south, just once more, through the reeds and waving grasses. The winds had changed, and now she saw a streak of orange heading east, and her eyes followed it.

The coconuts fell into the muddy puddle, splashing her legs.

A darker cloud hung in one spot, moving neither north nor south. Nilith saw dark shapes beneath it, distant still but gaining fast on her patch of green. Whether they were Ghouls or some other pack of thirsty wanderers, she had no clue. What Nilith did know was that she wasn't about to stand around waiting to find out.

Her whistle was piercing. 'Come, Anoish!'

The horse grumbled, looking around at the fresh tubers and muddy water with bright eyes.

Nilith was already halfway out of the oasis. 'Now, damn it!'

Hearing the tension in her voice, Anoish obeyed and trotted after her. She placed a hand on his mane and swung her leg up and over his bowed spine. He burst into a limping canter, grunting whenever that fourth hoof touched the ground. Nilith made herself small against his back, as if it would help.

They made the hut in time to hear the distant rumble of hooves bearing down on them. Harsh shouts echoed across the shrinking stretch of desert. Nilith only heard voices, not words, but they were familiar enough to make her skin prickle.

'Down the ramp, Anoish, carefully,' she hissed, praying he wouldn't follow in the poorly chosen footsteps of her previous steed.

The horse had heard the shouts, felt the vibrations in the sand, and was having no qualms at all about hurrying. He clip-clopped down the uneven slope, skidding here and there but staying steady. Nilith was preoccupied watching his hooves, but when she heard the yell, she looked up so fast her neck crunched.

'Agaaah!'

Nilith saw Ghyrab falling, like an old tree submitting to a storm. His face was scrunched up, hand clasped to the back of his head. Farazar stood behind him, holding a rock in his shaking hand. His blue hair wavered in the breeze. He hit the bargeman once more before reaching to loose the rope from about its wooden bollard.

'No!' Nilith cried, sending Anoish galloping down what was left of the slope. She pushed and she pushed him, but it was all in vain. The horse skidded to a halt on the lopsided boards, a dozen feet short of the barge's sides. Farazar stood holding the tail of the rope, wearing that infuriating smile of his.

'You bastard, Farazar!' Nilith screeched. 'You come back here!'

He blew her a kiss. 'I am the emperor, aren't I, wife? I'll do as I please!'

Leaping from Anoish's back, Nilith threw herself into the water, trident still slung across her shoulders. The cold of the river stole her breath away, but she thrashed for all her worth, making great strokes through the water. She could feel the blacktooths sliding past her kicking feet, and it spurred her to grab the back of the barge.

Farazar came running, bloody rock held high.

'Time to part ways, dear!' The rock crashed down on the wood, brushing her hand as she switched grips. She grappled for the trident at her back, but the infernal thing refused to swing around. Nilith tried to catch the ghost's next blow, but the sharp sandstone cut a ribbon of skin from her palm. Blood dripped in her face as she lashed at him with her nails. It was useless. Farazar had the height, and on the next swing she was forced to let go. The current took hold of the barge and pulled it out of reach.

'See you in Araxes!' Farazar cackled.

Panting hard, every other breath one of water instead of air, Nilith had no answer. Not even a threat or an insult. Instead, she paddled to the canyon wall, finding boulders and crannies to cling to while she gained her breath. A sharp whinny reminded her where she was.

The Ghouls!

On the jetty, now a stone's throw upriver, the horse had been nuzzling at Ghyrab. Anoish had got the old man onto his knees, but no further. Nilith was elated he wasn't dead.

'Ghouls, Ghyrab! They're coming!' Nilith hollered, cupping a bloody hand to her lips. She stumbled back into the water, making slimy fish scatter. Something sharp grazed her ankle, and she hauled herself as far out of the water as her shaking hands could manage.

'Hide!' he roared in reply, as hoarse as steel dragged over stone.

Nilith did her best, wedging her forearm into a small nook in the cliff face and standing tiptoe on a boulder that had evaded being eroded. If she pressed herself close enough to the warm sandstone, the jetty disappeared out of sight. All Nilith had to do was stay in that position, and already she was shaking with the effort.

A crimson rivulet coursed from her clenched fist and down the rock face, making the water squirm with the thrashing of skinny charcoal fish. A few snapped at the air with their tiny barbed teeth. They were no longer than her forearm, but there were enough of them to make her curse.

Nilith gasped as her toe slipped. 'Well, fuck today already.'

She poked her head out to see Ghyrab trying to shove Anoish into the water. The horse could see the blacktooths, and wasn't budging an inch. Nilith whistled sharply, and the horse relented, splashing heavily into the river. The fish around her were briefly distracted, swimming off to investigate a bigger meal, and she allowed herself to relax slightly.

Ghyrab, blood streaming down his ear and neck, lowered himself into the water with a gasp, and then pushed the horse under the jetty's planks. Nilith lost sight of them in its shadow.

She waited there, legs trembling with the effort of hugging the cliff, listening to the vibrations in the rock as the pounding hooves grew closer. Shouts now filled the air: orders of, 'Over there!' and 'Down to the river!'

Figures wrapped in ashen mail and black leather emerged from the rift in the rock and strode for the jetty. Half wore faces painted like skulls, the rest white masks with dark slits for eyes. They were unmistakably Ghouls. Nilith sucked in her stomach as she forced herself closer to the stone. The fish were trying to wriggle out of the water, blood-crazed now she'd painted the river red. She tried to shift her foot higher.

'Nobody here, Boss!' yelled one of the figures.

There came a hawking sound above her, beyond an overhang. A glob of phlegm came sailing down to splash in the river. Nilith held her breath.

'Bah! We'll follow the river! They can't be far along now, eh!' called a voice Nilith was very familiar with. One that made her skin prickle. There was a difference to it, however, as if somebody had burned away half her lips.

Krona's orders were taken up and passed on by her captains. 'Back on your horses, you bastards!' came the shouts.

Nilith's foot chose that moment to slip from the cliff face, unceremoniously dumping her in the water between the boulders. She splashed and flailed, trident clanging against the sandstone. It took all her nerve to stay still, fighting off the eager fish with weak punches.

One of the Ghouls on the jetty hung back, curious at the noise. He stood at its end, peering down the canyon through his mask of charcoal face-paint. Nilith submerged herself up to her eyes, pretending to be just another boulder at the edge of the river, her black hair just a mass of weeds. Beneath the rippling waterline, she was a fighter full of rage. Every moment the Ghoul lingered, the more the little teeth snagged at Nilith's clothing, pulled at her hair, and nibbled at her limbs. She thrashed and she kicked, and though she longed to roar, only bubbles escaped her mouth.

Finally, the man grew bored and lumbered back to the rift, no doubt disappointed not to have bloodied the sword hanging limply in his hand.

Nilith dragged herself from the water, streaming red from a score of cuts on her thighs and shoulders. Still the fish writhed beneath her shaking heels. *Insatiable fuckers.*

It felt an age before the rumble of hooves moved far enough downriver. Finally, Anoish scrambled his way back to shore, letting all his enraged neighs out at once. He too was speckled with bites, adding a crimson tinge to his brown and cream.

Ghyrab was also painted red. The fish had feasted on him like beggars attacking a buffet. Too weak to hoist himself onto the jetty, he followed the horse's path out of the shallows. He crumpled to a heap in the sand, and lay there for some time.

Nilith spent some of her own deciding whether to swim or wait for rescue. Given her 'rescue' was in the form of a half-conscious man and a beast with no hands to speak of, she resigned herself to a frenzied and draining swim.

She made it onto the jetty with twice as many cuts as before, and with lungs that burned as if she'd swallowed a coal. She lay in the sunlight, letting the day's fire dry the mud and cake her wounds, and turn some of her panic to relief. Only then could she drag herself up to check on the others.

Anoish was fine. Curled up and in a foul mood, but fine. The bargeman was gasping for water with lips that looked like the edge of a barren well. It took her several trips, but with cupped hands Nilith managed to bring him enough water to rouse him to a state in which he could speak. Or better yet, rant.

'Fuckin' shade. Stealing my fuckin' barge! I'll beat him bloody sense—'

'You can do whatever you want to him, but first we need to get him back.'

'And my fuckin' barge!'

Nilith cringed at the sight of Ghyrab's head wound; deep and ugly, and showing a sliver of skull. No brain, though, which was always a good sign. Fortunately, Farazar's ghostly arms were still weaker than flesh. 'And your fucking barge.'

She ripped up parts of their tunics to make a bandage for his head wound, then for a few of the deeper fish bites.

'Fuckin' blacktooths. Can't even eat them to teach 'em a lesson.'

Nilith patted her trident. 'Then we'll just kill them for sport, when we have the time.'

Ghyrab nodded, eyes half-closed, though for once not in laziness. The sand was red around him. 'Triple.'

'What?'

'I want triple for my barge. Even if we get it back, I want triple whatever you were going to pay me. That's twice you've almost killed me now.'

Nilith smiled as she got him to his feet. Anoish stayed where he was.

'Come. Let's get you in the shade, you old thief. You're worth your three silvers.'

The man flinched in her grasp as if he'd been struck by another rock. 'Three silvers?!'

'Well, you did say triple what I was going to pay you.' She chuckled, trying to lighten the mood. It sounded hollow. There was nothing to laugh at. The Ghouls were back and Farazar was gone. All she could think of was her accursed husband, probably laughing his blue head off somewhere downriver. Whether she caught him or Krona did, he would not be laughing for long. Nilith prayed it would be the former.

'Come on. We need to move.'

It took a great deal of stumbling and precious moments wasted to get Ghyrab up the ramp, and many more to the tiny oasis. Nilith crouched low, wary of the dust still clogging the air, and stared about like a chick left alone in a nest.

The cool of the palms was welcome, and Ghyrab sank into the long emerald grass with a sigh. Nilith almost did the same as exhaustion pounced on her. She shrugged it off, seeking a palm to lean against instead. Before she found one, she remembered the tubers in the shallow puddle, and she tottered in its direction.

'Bloody ghost,' Nilith muttered to herself as she waded through the foliage, cold against her sweaty fingers.

The flasks were gone. They had not floated off, and there was barely any depth for them to sink. Nilith crouched to check anyway, and heard the whoosh of a blade sail over her head.

She rolled through the puddle, spraying water as she jumped upright. The skull-faced Ghoul came at her, a scimitar clasped in both hands swinging madly back and forth. Nilith dragged her trident from her shoulders and held it level and spinning.

The scimitar met the trident's points, shearing one away completely before Nilith could lock his blade and drag him closer: close enough to punch him in his painted face, right in the jagged grin. Fierce, red and sleepless eyes stared at her from between the smears of paint and charcoal.

The Ghoul came at her again, and this time she blocked the blade with the trident's shaft. It was a mistake. The heavy scimitar cleaved it in two and cut a scarlet line in her tunic. Nilith staggered away, throwing the splintered lower half at the Ghoul. He batted it away and kept coming.

Nilith floundered. She waved the trident's head in wild arcs to keep the man at bay. A few he fended. The others he dodged. She kept pressing until they were standing in the puddle again. Dark mud sprayed as they danced.

The scimitar's point caught her in the shoulder blade, and as she hesitated, a fist connected with her temple. Orbs of light filled her vision. Nilith tottered away from him, trident falling out of her grasp.

When anybody without a sword faced somebody with a sword, the usual answer was to run with great intensity in the opposite direction. In that panting, dripping pause, the thought crossed her mind, but the runner in Nilith had been beaten out of her long ago by a wizened old fight-meister named Hock. It was he who'd taught her other answers to such one-sided situations.

Nilith grabbed a thick handful of reeds and ripped them from their shallow roots. She held them out like a length of rope. The Ghoul laughed through his mask of paint, thrusting at her. Dodging aside, Nilith wrapped the reeds around the scimitar's blade until she had a handle. With a twist, she wrenched the weapon out of his grasp, but a fist found her ribs before she could wield it. Nilith fell with the sword still wrapped in her hand. With a splash and a foul-breathed roar, the Ghoul landed atop her. His forearms pressed into the blade's blunt side. Nilith turned her cheek as the sword crept downwards. She could feel her opponent shaking with the strain; the buckling of the reeds before the razor-edge; the heat of the blood starting to pool in her palms.

'She'll want me alive!' Nilith croaked through the effort. The Ghoul didn't seem to care. He only pressed harder, driving his head against his forearms. They traded spit in their ragged grunts, eyes duelling.

With a last reserve of strength, Nilith screeched as she pushed upwards, switching her grip to free her fingers. The Ghoul responded with a cry of his own. The blade sliced into Nilith's cheek, but she had already grasped its wielder's cloth-wrapped ears. Her sharp nails dug into them, drawing his head in as her thumbs plunged into his dark eyes. She felt his eyeballs split as she drove past the bone and deep into his face. The scream that ripped from his throat was blood-curdling. All thoughts of murder crumbled in the face of pain. The sword was forgotten as he began to flail blindly.

The beating was ferocious. Nilith's head swung back and forth between punches, unable to fight back with her thumbs still locked in his eye sockets. Charcoal-stained fingers groped her face, eager to repay the favour. Instead they found her throat, and began to squeeze. Nilith gasped for breath. It was only when shadows started to cloud her vision that the Ghoul stopped dead.

Very dead, it appeared. A barbed trident point was poking from the side of his head. With a wheeze, he toppled to the mud beside her. Behind him knelt Ghyrab, ashen-faced and half alive. He nodded to her.

'That's three times now...' he whispered before crumpling back to the green earth alongside the Ghoul.

Nilith staggered upright, and her legs bowed like sickle moons. Her entire body shook violently. All she tasted in her mouth was blood, and not all of it was hers. Bile threatened to wash it away.

'Farazar...' she gasped, groping eastwards. 'Got to—'

Down she went, demolishing a clump of flowering plants before striking the ground. The blow knocked out what little sense she had left in her, and she fell into darkness. Nilith struggled with it, fought it, but in the end it won. At least it was a sweeter darkness than death.

———◆———

THE UGLINESS OF NIGHTMARES WOKE her: visions of trickling water over black stone, of slipping in it over and over as she climbed and endless slope, dragged against her will by some force. She had looked behind her to see five burning points in a coal-black sky, settled around a sixth, and a glowing blue figure with a crown being lowered onto his head. Before it touched his brow, the rock beneath her fell away, and she plummeted into wakefulness.

Nilith placed a hand to her heart to steady it, but her unfamiliar surroundings weren't helpful. No barge and strip of blue between red rocks, just shade and reaching palms. Grass and dirt filled her mouth, crunching against her teeth.

She pushed herself up before remembering the wounds on her hands and forearms. They stung, and she vowed to wash them before they festered. Other wounds spoke up as she got to sitting, then a low crouch. Standing could come later.

Farazar.

Nilith looked up through the palm fronds to eye the position of the sun. It was in the west, and at such an angle that it made her stomach clench. Though that may have been the early stink of the Ghoul.

Her eyes found the corpse, bloody and blind. The trident's forks were still lodged in his brain. She trembled to look at him. He was not a victory; he was a sore reminder of how close she'd come to failure. One man hiding in some grass had almost ended her great toil. In truth, the narrow miss choked her, but on hearing a snore, she swallowed it and scowled liberally about the oasis. There were more pressing matters.

Anoish was grazing greedily on the grass, attempting to demolish the oasis before they departed. Nilith left him to it, glad he could finally recover his strength. She scooped up some of the smashed tubers and a coconut and went to find Ghyrab. The bargeman was curled up and snuffling. Makeshift bandages had stopped the bleeding, but his head wound needed stitching if it wasn't to rot. In the desert, festering wounds claimed more souls than the heat.

'Farazar,' she said, shaking the bargeman. 'We need to find him before Krona does. With his body, they can claim him, or worse.'

'Mmmf.'

She hooked an arm under his and lifted Ghyrab's dead weight. 'Move yourself, you old bastard! I can't leave you here.'

'River spreads. Fucker'll slow.'

'I don't know what that means.'

'Marshes… before the turn.'

The bargeman's head lolled onto his chest, baring his ghastly wound to her between the bandages. For a moment Nilith thought he had passed, but the beat her fingers felt in his throat told her otherwise. She tied his dressings tighter, then stole some more strips from the Ghoul's shirt to bind her own arms.

It took plenty of attempts and some water from the puddle to be able to whistle. The horse hadn't heard the clang of blades, but he heard that. Moments later he came trotting, looking grumpy, as though he had been disturbed from a nap. His sides had scabbed in the sun.

'Time to run, Anoish,' she said, patting him gingerly on the rump.

'You carried the corpse, so I guess a grey bargeman won't be too dif-ficult. And I'm wasting away as it is.' Nilith plucked at her loose shirt. There was a high chance the Cloud Court may not recognise her on her return to Araxes.

With much heaving, hauling and stumbling, she managed to get the old man over Anoish's back. Once she had retrieved the scimitar from under the Ghoul's corpse, she followed suit, though it took her about five tries. In the end, Anoish had to kneel.

Nilith pointed a finger past the horse's ear, along the dark curve of the river, towards the wavering silver patches on the horizon. Heat or water, it was hard to tell, but they would find out soon enough. 'North, boy,' she hissed. 'And easy.'

Anoish had no wish to be hasty. He started out at a stiff trot, then a tentative canter, until finally the wind under his chin coaxed a gal-lop out of him. Although slower than he usually was, the sand flew by beneath them much faster than the river had. Nilith flattened herself, trying to reduce the painful jolting. The barge had softened her riding callouses, and now she had to grow them back.

Perhaps the horse felt her unease, or maybe he too had noticed the faint cloud of dust ahead, but he piled on the pace until spit streamed from his lips. If it hurt him, she couldn't tell, but she didn't dare com-plain. Farazar and Krona had hours on her, five or six at most, and that was plenty of time to spot a bumbling barge in a canyon that was gradually shrinking away.

Between the beat of the gallop, and between half-formed plans for retrieving her ghost, Nilith's mind slipped back to the corpse they'd left unburied in the oasis. The blood still stained her hands, and they still shook at the memory of the precipice she'd danced along, and almost fallen from.

'Almost' was a powerful word. It signified an escape, and yet instead of a joyous word, it could be just as horrifying as a detrimental outcome. As damning as a strike from a spade. *Almost fell. Almost slipped. Almost killed...* The narrowness of the escape still managed to inject fear and shame into a soul.

Just as a person standing at the top of a tower always imagined the fall, Nilith tortured herself with flashbacks of the fight; every blow, every parry, imagining a hundred different outcomes for each. In every one she came off worse. It proved how close she had come to ruining everything she had fought for.

It was the dust cloud that broke her abusive reverie, growing darker and more pronounced now that the sun had aged to a warm scarlet. She had gained on the Ghouls, busy as they were crawling along the river's edge. They clearly hadn't found her bastard of a husband yet. She wondered what tricks the ghost had resorted to in avoiding them. Five hours was almost... impressive.

Nilith tugged at Anoish's mane, slowing him down so they weren't spotted, and turned to the cargo bumping her in the back. Ghyrab had woken once to murmur something foul about horses, but other than that, his only utterances had been deep snores.

She led the horse closer to the Ashti's curve. As if nature itself was now against her, the waters were faster, rippling along at an eager pace. There was nothing in the water besides the occasional protruding rock and shadows of blacktooths facing into the current. Nilith scowled at them, wishing she had a bow and a sunny afternoon to spend shooting them.

Sunset threw their shadows far across the sand-scattered rock, so far they tumbled over the edge of the river canyon. Nilith made sure to hug every dip and bank in the sand, hiding as much of her and the horse as she could. No doubt the Ghouls would be getting bored now. The few she'd seen looked travel weary. The man she'd fought had stunk of riding, and was far weaker than he should have been.

Krona must have driven them hard across the sands, cutting off the curves in the river. It was a good sign that Nilith had managed to keep pace with the bandits. The afternoon had felt like an endless slog. Going south, she'd been fresh. Eager for change. Now, she was running wounded and exhausted. Her bones felt like porcelain, her skin like stretched leather, and her head pounded harder than Anoish's hooves.

As night stole in from the east, Krona's Ghouls headed west to follow another corner. Nilith trailed in their dusty wake, so far unseen. She was glad for the lack of moon. Her exhaustion began to creep into delirium, and she found herself chuckling as they slowly plodded through the sand.

The hunter had become the hunted. As weak as she was, as unarmed, lost, and running out of time as she was, it was still funny. Having the upper hand often was.

Her grin prevailed long into the darkness.

CHAPTER 11
A HAUNTING

All things that are built can be broken. It is
the very nature of existence. Whether through
time or turmoil, everything has an end.

OLD SKOL PROVERB

'OME ON, POINTY. IT'S BEEN an hour now.'

'And I've told you, Caltro, I haven't the limbs!' The sword's voice was tense with strain. What in the Reaches he was straining, I had no idea.

It was one of the stupider plans I'd come up with in my thirty-four years. I wasn't quite sure it could even be classed as a plan, seeing as it consisted of 'get some oaf into the room, attack him, then escape.' The plan had more holes than a beggar's breeches. We hadn't even figured out escaping the room, never mind Busk's tower.

Currently, our efforts were confined to helping the sword fall off the mantelpiece. A good clang would surely bring somebody running. Nobody paid attention to the ghost in the wardrobe any more; that, we'd established. As Pointy had rightly put it, he lacked the dexterity of an animate object. Sheer will was his only hope.

'Come on! I believe in you!'

'Hnnnnng!'

I recalled the somewhat similar noises I had made while bent over the crone's lockbox on the ship. That seemed like far too long ago now.

There came a rattle as something shook. I pressed myself to the crack in the door. 'Yes!'

Moments later, something flashed as it tumbled, making a solid bang on the fireplace. Pointy made a noise as though he'd been winded, but I knew it was just for show.

He had done his job. After a rattle of keys, a burly man with a bald head and beard the colour of autumn came ambling through the door.

'What's goin' on?' he cried, making a great show of scanning the room. A small croak from me got his attention. 'Who's in here?'

The burly fish nipped at the bait, and came to stand near my wardrobe, hand cocked behind his ear. 'You up to something in there, shade?'

Something whispered by the fireplace, and he spun around. Any sensible person might have called for a fellow guard. This man was so delightfully confused, the sword and I managed to make him wander back and forth between the fireplace and the wardrobe several more times before he grappled with the locks of my prison.

'You'd best be in there, or Busk'll flay you to dust!'

I grinned, removed my scarf and smock, pressed a foot against the back of the wardrobe, and braced myself to jump.

Lamplight streamed in around the guard's dark frame. His face turned from anger to horror as I dove for him, arms outstretched. Something about my wild, naked appearance touched on some ancient nerve and he recoiled with a squeal.

My vaporous frame collided with his, but with no weight behind me I simply sagged against him like a sack against a barn wall. As he batted at me with his club, I desperately tried to hold his gaze, but his eyes were too busy rolling around their sockets as he fought to be free of my cloying.

I had no idea what I was doing wrong, and so I flung myself at him again, tensing my vapours as hard as I could manage. This time, I nudged him hard enough to cause a stumble over the foot of some ugly flamingo stool. In his tumble, the guard somehow trapped his club between the floor and his head. I heard the crack as he landed.

'Bloody bollocks,' I said, immediately shutting the door.

'No, this could be good. He won't put up a fight.'

I went to pick up the sword, gently scooping him up and holding him aloft to the dim lamps. The obsidian blade looked liquid in the light, like molten black glass. The only dullness in it came from the copper veins and patches that mottled its surface. The silver branches of Pointy's crossguard and hilt clutched a face carved from polished black stone: the youthful, lean face of a man, and it held a big smile for me.

'How do you see or speak? I mean—' I was lost for words. Strange-binding was a hard enough concept to grasp, never mind deadbinding. If I'd expected the stone to move as it talked, I was disappointed. The expression was frozen in that clown's grin, though I felt a slight thrumming through the blade. The vibrations spread down my forearm.

'Please, be careful. It's been a while since I was moved around so fast, and a while since I had a master. I suppose this is our first handshake.'

'As long as it isn't anything else,' I said, propping him up on the couch and then clenching my fist to rid myself of the tingling. 'And I'm not your master.'

'You are now you've claimed me. I am my own half-coin. It also means I can speak to you and you alone whenever we are near.'

I shrugged, ignoring his nonsense. I didn't care for whatever spells the Nyxites or smiths had wrought into him.

As I stood over the guard's comatose body, I rubbed my hands, making no sound. I analysed the man like I would an unpicked lock. Red curly hairs stood out on the back of his neck, like weeds growing on a salt flat. There was a pool of blood leaking into the carpet, spreading with all the hurry of spilt jam.

'I have no idea what I'm doing.'

'Sit on him. Or better yet, lie on him.'

I grimaced, gingerly lowering myself down onto the man's spread-eagled frame. Aside from turning his slumbering breaths to mist with my cold, nothing happened. Perturbed at being so close to his sweaty neck, I closed my eyes to concentrate and imagined seeing myself through foreign eyes. There was a brief moment of dizziness, but nothing like haunting. It was more likely my own straining.

'It's no use!'

'Stop thinking so hard about it. A sword-master used to say that to an old owner of mine. Let your mind flow where it wants. Tensing only makes you slower.'

I glared at the blade. 'I'd like to see you try this.'

The reply was flat. 'I'd give anything to try, Caltro. Trust me.'

I bit my cold lip and tried again, this time kneeling by the man's head. Rolling his shoulders so I could see his chubby face, I slapped my hands to his cheeks. I stared at the man's eyelids. One was smeared with blood from the deep dent in his forehead. The other was half closed and showing the milk of a rolled-up eye. I dug my fingers into his skin, and tried very hard not to think.

My eyes grew leaden, so I let them close. Some innate desire told me to rock forward, and so I let myself. I felt the weight beneath me, and the roughness of his clothes holding me back. I ignored them, and let my thoughts become a roar rolling across a scorched plain. Something twitched beneath me and the firm flesh gave way, spinning me over and around so fast I felt my eyes attempt to fly from my skull. A warmth enveloped my vapours.

My eyes snapped open. The world was on its side. A landscape of yellow and orange carpet stretched out before me, turning to chequered marble under a distant lavish couch. The bejewelled eyes of a snake wrapped around a table leg stared at me. For a brief moment, all was silent save for the gentle fizzing of the lamps.

'You did it,' spoke a metallic voice.

I immediately retched, but found nothing in my stomach to hack up. As I hawked and coughed, curled in a ball on the bloody carpet, something flailed at me from within. It was trying to cast me out. I pushed back, hard, and felt something crumble before me, like an old brick wall before a sledgehammer. I was haunting.

If I'd expected a glorious flooding of human sensation – of feelings, emotions, and a wonderful sense of wholeness – then I was cheated of it. The first feelings were of heaviness and pain. I felt like I wore a cumbersome costume made of meat, and one too tight for comfort. The warmth grew like a dawn furnace working itself into fury. My extremities felt numb. My head was throbbing. My eye was sticky. Something itched in my lower back, and yet somehow, these were glorious sensations in themselves.

'I—' My voice felt deeper, hoarser.

'Am apparently fond of the pipe.'

'That's what that taste is.' I smacked my lips, biting them to feel my rubbery, chapped skin.

'Is it a struggle?'

It was. I constantly strained to keep hold of this sack of flesh. The man's soul fought against me still, though weakly. As I tested my muscles and got to kneeling, I would occasionally feel a kick, or a lurch. Vapours would rise from one limb or another before I wrangled it back into place.

It was like one of those magic Skol paintings of corridors and stairwells that defied reality; where if you stared hard and long enough, you saw the mess from another perspective, one you couldn't believe you missed before. And the more you stared, the easier it became to transform the painting. This haunting business was the same: the longer I spent in this body and the more it struggled, the more I understood how to control it.

I made slow circles of the room, stepping like a newborn deer for the first lap or two. Despite my difficulty and the strangeness of wearing another's skin, I had a body once again, and I felt elation swell up in a stomach that wasn't mine. I flexed my gloved fingers, and spoke without thinking. 'Though I feel like I'm wearing a man as a suit, I've missed this.'

'Hmm. I can imagine.' Pointy sounded wistful.

I decided to distract him from my thoughtless words with action, and keep myself focused. 'Have you a scabbard?'

'Behind that chair. Nothing grand. My old scabbard was lost a hundred years ago.'

I fetched the bland black and silver scabbard without hesitation. 'Perfect. Don't want any unnecessary attention where I'm going.'

'And where is that?'

'To see Busk, of course.'

The sword groaned as I stashed him in his scabbard. At least there he was silent.

I ripped a section of silk from a curtain and wrapped it around my head as a scarf to hide the wound. I grazed it with a knuckle and felt a wash of pain so intense I felt dizzy. The rest of the blood I scraped away.

With much fumbling of unfamiliar fingers, I left both the wardrobe and room locked and made my way to the stairwell. Busk had been keeping me halfway up his modest tower, and like any noble, I knew he enjoyed the prospect of height. I set my feet to the stairs, wobbly and drunken. Every step was a challenge at first, and a tough one at that. The body resisted me anew, and it took several flights to subdue it and wrestle my limbs under control. Even then, I tottered, and found myself twitching when nodding to other guards.

Nobody challenged me, even when I arrived at the door to Busk's study. I was ready to gossip with the guard and blag my entry, as we say in Krass, but all he did was tell me sternly that I was late, and promptly open the door for me. I strode inwards, ensuring Pointy was tucked at the back of my hip, away from any gaze.

The bright light momentarily dazzled me, but I saw the shadow of Busk sitting behind a marble desk. He was staring at me, massaging his poor excuse for a moustache. I fought the urge to glower at him, or better yet, march over there and wallop him in the face with my ham of a fist.

'Foor, glad you could join us at last. Did you fetch another to replace you at your post? I want that shade guarded at all times.'

'Yes, Tor Busk,' I replied, stammering with my rubber lips. I noticed a gaggle of other guards and hastily joined them.

It was then Pointy spoke in my mind, making me flinch violently. At first I thought it the soul of the man I inhabited, but I recognised the sword's voice, echoing around my mind.

'*We should have just gone downstairs.*'

Despite the looks from those nearby, nobody seemed to have heard him. Just me.

'Mhm,' I replied, pretending to clear my throat.

Busk continued. 'Before I was interrupted, I was saying I want double the guard on the front door at all times, and an extra man on every other level. Make a good show of it. That stubborn old bag Horix thinks she can threaten me into giving up the shade, but I'll show her what stubborn is. Let her play her little games. More time for us to use the locksmith. More silvers for you lot.'

My ears – or rather, this fellow Foor's ears – pricked up.

The men and women around me grumbled their agreement, clearly bought and paid for. I imagined true loyalty was hard to find in this city. Better to buy willing hands than spend years earning them.

'I want the shade checked on regularly, and nobody in the room but me. Speaking of, give me the registers for guard duty. I want—'

The door burst open, stubbing me in the toe. The handle struck me in the groin. I growled behind my teeth, and hopped to a safer area.

'*Bet you don't miss that,*' Pointy told me from my hip.

A guard, sweat adorning his brow, hurriedly bowed. 'My apologies, Tor.'

'What is the meaning of this?'

'Tor Temsa is here.'

'I told you before, the man is not a tor!'

The man hovered, bouncing on his feet as if his bladder were fit to burst. 'So… should I bring him up?'

'You admitted him already?'

'I, er—'

Busk thwacked the desk with his palm. 'Fuck! Fine! You lot get down there and ensure Temsa doesn't go anywhere near Caltro's sitting room. Take him up the other stairwell. Watch his guards. Both of the big fuckers.'

Busk stood and straightened a puke-yellow waistcoat. 'Well, get on with it!'

We bustled out of the doorway one by one. I was first, along with the sweaty guard. The hurrying made my legs slip more than once on the stairs, but somehow I held onto my body, though my ankles felt like butter.

'You know this Temsa?' the guard asked of me.

'No,' I lied.

'Me neither. Says he's a tor. But Busk says he isn't. Madness.'

'Scintillating,' I slurred. Even amongst a nobility as corrupt as Araxes', surely that weasel of a man couldn't have made tordom.

Sweaty gave me and my silk headscarf a squint-eyed look. 'You don't normally wear a scarf. You ain't been on the sauce again, 'ave you, Foor?'

'Not since this morning.' I grinned, and he gave me a jovial nudge with his elbow.

'You dog. Well, you got some blood on your cheek. I'd wipe that off afore you go down. There he is.'

I saw him over the balcony first, before we descended the steps to the atrium floor. Temsa stood below, gargoyle-like as before, golden-footed and wrapped in a fine velvet medley of cream and blue. Golden

chains were draped around his neck and his fingers were so encrusted
with rings that for a moment I thought he was wearing jewelled gloves.
His thinning dark hair had a fresh shine to it. Even his golden teeth
seemed to have a fresh polish. An armoured and cross-armed Ani Jexebel
stood at his side, looking as ominous and as displeased with life as ever.

Temsa certainly looked like a tor, and I hated him as much in that
moment as when he had left me standing in the soulmarket. Perhaps
even more. I felt my fingers curl into fists, and I contemplated risking
everything on a mad dash for his throat. A question crossed my mind
then: would this body die around me, and I snap back into my ghostly
form? Or would I die again with it?

In the end, I didn't take the risk. Call it cowardice if you like, but I
called it discipline and smarts. Instead, I stood behind the sweaty guard
as he told 'Tor' Temsa he could see Busk.

'Well, I'm delighted. Lead the way,' he said, waving his cane towards the stairs.

I paused, staring at the open door behind the man, where the last
rays of the day beckoned to me. I felt myself pulled in their direction.
The other soul inside me fought to keep me in the shadows. Flashes of
foreign memories crossed my vision, showing me a gap-toothed little
girl with fiery hair, and a wife being claimed by black water.

'Foor?' Sweaty asked me. I realised all eyes were upon me.

'Yes. Sorry.' Inside, I cursed myself for haunting a man of authority, and for my own damn curiosity. I took up the lead alongside him,
just ahead of Jexebel. I heard her snuffling behind me, taller than me
even though I was always several steps ahead on the stairs. Whenever I
stumbled, she snorted. Sweat dripped down my cheek. I wiped it away
and found a smear of blood on my dark wrist.

With so much concentration, it seemed like a day's climb to reach
the peak of the tower, and once there, I was dismissed. I left grudgingly,

my eyes lingering on Temsa as he took up a stance before Busk's desk. I longed to be part of that conversation, but it felt like it would end with blood, and I needed none of that.

I practically tumbled down the stairs, bypassing my sitting room and hurtling straight back down to the atrium.

'Careful, Caltro. You need those legs,' came Pointy's warning, whispered from the scabbard now.

Looking down, I saw glowing fibres escaping from my borrowed legs. I slowed my pace across the marble, nodded to the house-guards who had been left there, and gestured to the door, which was now sealed.

'What is it?' asked the nearest of them.

'Busk needs me to send a message.'

'You playin' messenger now, Foor? Dead gods, you'll do anything to avoid duty, won't you?'

I shrugged, playing the defeatist. 'You know me.'

'Fine, but don't you go wandering too close to any taverns now. Something tells me Busk won't be in a good mood later.' The guard grunted as he tackled a thick lever embedded in the wall. A series of cogs went into action, sliding half a dozen bolts back. I saw sunlight again, and felt its warmth on my skin. It was evening, and the shadows were stretching across the city.

'I'd say you were right,' I breathed.

I flinched as a hand clapped me across the chest, almost making me lose my grip on the body. I found the guard fixing me with a heavy stare.

'I mean it, Foor,' he said. 'Don't want to lose another job now, do you? Think of little Mazi, eh?'

I nodded, inadvertently coughing as the real Foor thrashed inside my chest at the mention of his wife, or daughter. They needn't have worried; they could have him back when I was done.

Slapping the guard's gloved palm with my own, I strode out into the evening, a grin spreading across my face before my feet even touched the street.

I decided west was the right way to go, towards the great pillar of the Cloudpiercer and hopefully Widow Horix's tower. She was the safest, smartest bet right now. The thought of Horix's expression when I strode into her courtyard kept me grinning as I tried to find my bearings in the knots of streets. I'd only had two excursions into this humongous warren, and one of those I'd spent senseless with a bag over my head.

With Pointy clutched tight and my jaw set with the effort of the haunting, I strutted off across the dusty flagstones.

———◆———

BUSK SEETHED QUIETLY AS TEMSA lounged against his desk. *His* desk, as if the stunted little man was a factory manager swinging by to check on production. It set Busk's hackles high, and he spread his hands across the marble, broad as he could reach.

'And to what do I owe the pleasure of a visit so late in the day?'

'Late? This is early for our kind of business, Busk.' Temsa looked around the room. 'A lot of company here, for the talk I'd like to have.'

'My house-guards are staying, thank you. I can trust them.'

Temsa shrugged. 'Your loose tongues to cut.'

One of the guards stifled a cough, and for a moment all the tension in the room piled on him. The guard wilted into a nook like a flower before a sandstorm.

Busk got his questions in first. 'My men say you announce yourself as Tor Temsa now.'

The man's wrinkled and scowling face broke into a grin, flashing a gold tooth. 'And why not, when I have been Weighed and found to be amongst the nobility of this fine city?'

'How noble?' It was all that mattered in Araxes. Who sat above who? Busk didn't want to ask for fear of being poorer, but his mouth spoke for him.

'Far above you, Busk. Naturally. What did you expect? You're a mere fence, living off old money.'

Busk forced a congratulatory smile. 'Soulst—trading has served you well, I see. Perhaps I should jump on the cart.'

'Soultrading has served me well, indeed, but I have grander business to attend to these days. And speaking of…'

Here it comes. The reason for his visit. The introductory prattle had been dispensed with.

Temsa peeled himself from the desk and began to circle Jexebel, who stood like a mail- and leather-clad golem in the middle of the study. Her arms were crossed, but that didn't mean Busk's gaze could stop focusing on the axes surrounding her person. He counted four before Temsa spoke.

'It's been some time since I asked you about a new locksmith, and yet I am still without one. You mentioned plenty last time we met: a Skolwoman, some Scatterfolk, a duo from Belish, even a Krassman or two, if I remember rightly,' Temsa said, keeping his grin.

Busk raised his shoulders. 'You do indeed.'

'What's wrong, then, Busk? Why the delay?'

'It's not just a simple case of sending a scroll—'

Temsa looked puzzled. 'No? Well, let's make it simpler. I heard the name of a good locksmith the other day. Supposedly one of the best. Perhaps you can track him down for me.'

Busk felt sweat begin to gather at his temples, behind his ears. 'Oh yes?'

'A man named Caltro. Heard of him?'

'I can't say I have.' Tor Busk's voice wavered.

'No? Never heard of a Caltro Basalt? A fence like you? I'm shocked.' Temsa clicked his fingers. 'Well, at least that explains why you didn't recognise his initials on the tools I gave you. C and a B, correct? Krass letters. Not Skol runes.'

Temsa pulled a handkerchief from his pocket and dabbed his forehead while Busk produced an answer.

'I... I...' he stuttered. 'I will admit, I haven't yet had them appraised. But now you've said it, I do recognise the name. That would make a lot of sense.'

Temsa sighed. 'I have to say, you've rather disappointed me this time.'

Busk chuckled to cover up the chattering of his teeth. 'I think you've misjudged me for somebody with dishonest purposes, Boss Temsa—'

'*Tor* Temsa.'

'Tor Temsa. It was a simple slip of the mind, is all.'

Temsa came to rest at his desk once more. 'Tell me, then: do you know where I can find Caltro Basalt?'

'I wouldn't know. Saraka, maybe?'

'Wrong again, Busk. Luckily for you, I know exactly where he is.'

Busk sat straighter. 'You do?'

'Of course.' Temsa chuckled. 'Because I killed him, bound him, and sold him to Widow Horix. Turns out he was right under my nose this entire time.'

'Ah yes. Of course.' Busk's laugh came out as a shrill giggle, and it made the guards wince. He saw the yellows of their teeth in the lamplight.

Temsa pressed his fists to the desk's white marble, popping several knuckles. 'But you already knew that, didn't you?'

Busk felt the metaphorical rug being firmly and rapidly whisked from under his feet. His throat bobbed as he repeatedly swallowed, trying to dislodge the lump of fear. 'And what is it to you, Temsa? I am playing the game, just as you aim to do, and I have been a tor a lot longer than you. I have every right to seek out my own gain, wherever it may be found.'

Temsa and Busk locked eyes for some time, Busk's sweat-burned ones against the olive pig-eyes of his visitor. When finally the silence ended, Temsa said but one word.

'Ani.'

The stillness of the room shattered as two axes appeared in the throats of the men either side of the desk. Blood splattered in Busk's face. All he could do was wipe his brow as Jexebel became a blur of steel, followed by arcs of crimson. Two battle-axes, long in the handle, spun in figures of eight as she tore about the study, hacking at throats, skulls and spines with merciless accuracy. Her ferocity redecorated the room within ten panicked breaths, painting the walls with wet scarlet and shit-brown hues. Pieces of guards and unknown body parts were scattered over Busk's furniture and the floor. A few here and there continued to twitch after all else was still again.

Through it all, Temsa hadn't moved. He remained unblinking, staring at Busk with a calm smile. Temsa spoke to the patter of dripping.

'You're right. You have every right to play your games. You're simply not very good at them. If it helps, Busk, this was always going to happen. Betrayal or not, you were bound to slip up at some point.' He leaned closer, so Busk could smell the spiced tobacco on his breath. 'Shall we?'

House-guard Vher burst in through the door, sweaty as always from sprinting upstairs. Apologies were about to spill from his mouth when he found a scarlet fist around his throat. His eyes boggled from the lack of air. They nearly popped free of his skull at the sight of the carnage. Jexebel hissed in his face, scaring him silent.

'Speak,' Temsa ordered.

'T...T...Tor Busk has a visitor.'

'Who?'

'Colonel Kalid.'

Temsa turned to Busk, tapping his quivering chin with his cane. 'I wonder what the captain of Widow Horix's guard could want with you? Been negotiating with Horix for a certain shade, have we?'

Ani Jexebel piped up. 'Shall I kill this guard, Boss?'

Busk noticed a flicker of irritation pass across Temsa's face.

'No, leave him. We'll need somebody to open the door. You clean yourself up quickly, m'dear.'

Jexebel dropped Vher on his arse, and he spent some time gawping at a split skull near the door. The gargantuan woman ripped down a drape and used it as a towel. She then threw it at Busk.

'You too,' she said, almost shouting.

He was aghast. 'You're not seriously suggesting I go down there, are you?'

Temsa opened the door, and made the house-guard scramble to his feet by showing the man his talons. 'My, you're a stupid one. I'm looking forward to finding out what games you've been playing, Tor Busk. Come, now. Not a word about myself and Ani, and if you're lucky, you may just live through this. If you're very lucky, Kalid is here to deliver a new house-shade by the name of Caltro.'

'I...' He said no more. Busk didn't want to give Temsa any more reasons to knife him.

They wound down the stairs, and all the while, Jexebel held the edge of an axe against Busk's spine. Temsa had his cane resting on the guard's shoulder, as if he were knighting him with a sword.

Busk spent the journey hating Temsa for his boldness – or, more precisely, hating himself for how much he was lacking in it. The man had stridden into his tower, taken control, and was now marching Busk down his own stairs. Dead gods knew what was coming later.

The remaining house-guards were threatened into position with waves of Jexebel's axes: two to face Kalid, and two to hide behind the door, pointy things ready and ears pricked. At Temsa's signal, the door was cranked open. A faint rosy glow framed thick steel shoulders and a plumed helmet. Behind the colonel, in the street, a dozen guards escorted a sullen-looking shade, bound in copper-wire shackles and chains.

'What's this?' Busk asked mechanically, desperately adhering to Temsa's rules.

'And a good evening to you too, Tor Busk.'

'I have told you I don't want to be bothered.' Jexebel's blade glinted behind the door.

'Be that as it may, Tal Horix seeks to put recent disagreements to rest. She wishes for no ill will or further actions, and to let the matter of the Krassman lie. As such, she offers you his half-coin and a gift of a fine house-shade.'

'She does? I mean… I don't know what you're talking about.' Busk's flustered words were quick and muddled. To have such fortune as this on the day of Temsa's visit was nothing short of cruel. The old bitch had indeed backed down.

Kalid blinked several times. 'The matter of the stolen shade Jerub, or Caltro as he calls himself. My mistress wishes to put it behind her.'

Busk could have slapped the man for his words, had his insides not been wrenched downwards into his bowels. He caught Temsa's gold smile in his peripheries, and a finger pressed over thin lips.

'Ah yes, of course. Forgive me, it has been a long day.'

The colonel beckoned two of his men forwards, holding a shade between them. The half-life was a willowy character, bearded, narrow-eyed and blank of expression. He wore a simple smock bearing Horix's seal and showed no signs of struggling against his bonds. It was suspicious for a tal to be so apologetic, especially one as crotchety as Horix. It would have made Busk feel powerful had Jexebel and her axe not hovered four inches from his elbow.

'I accept Horix's apology, but I have no need for the shade.' The aforementioned axe waggled. Temsa made a foul gesture and Busk cleared his throat. 'However… I suppose I could find room for him.'

Colonel Kalid held out a hand. In his palm lay two half-coins. One for Caltro, one for the other shade. He pointed to show the difference.

Busk hesitated, patting himself like a hungover man finding himself alive on the street corner come morning. It stung him deeply to take the coins and not truly win; to be so powerless in this moment of triumph. It was frustrating to the point of maddening. It was then that Busk contemplated fleeing between Kalid's men and making for the street.

He realised he had been silent for some time, and the colonel was now staring intently at Busk's neck and shoulder, where he could only assume he'd missed some patches of blood.

'Tell your mistress this is the end of it. You understand? No more games,' he asserted, selfishly clinging to his victory.

'Perfectly, Tor Busk,' Kalid replied, passing him a short papyrus scroll and an inked reed. He kept hold of the shade's shackles until Busk had signed both copies. When he was done, he snatched back the scroll and threw Busk the chains. 'Just perfectly.'

When the door slammed, it could have been the lid of Busk's own sarcophagus closing. With the alluring light of sunset behind two feet of steel, his hall seemed dark, cold, and full of evil things. He groaned as he stared abjectly at the copper links in his grip.

Jexebel chased his remaining guards into a corner, presumably to be dealt with later. Temsa began to walk wide, swaggering circles around Busk. His tone was on the cusp of laughter, as if he had just spent an evening at a theatre, lapping up comedy.

'My, my, Ani. Our good friend here has been quite industrious, hasn't he? Bartering for shades like the best of them, and with that crusty old Horix too. How did you do it, Busk? Was it blackmail? Force? Who cares! I'm almost impressed. Caltro Basalt, delivered straight into my hands with hardly any effort, would you imagine—' Temsa's jovial face sobered instantly. He jabbed an accusatory finger at the new house-shade. 'This is not Caltro Basalt.'

At first, Busk went with it, realising with immediate glee that Temsa had misunderstood the conversation. He fought not to stammer as he clenched his fingers around the two half-coins. 'Yes, it is. Why wouldn't it be?'

In the corner, Vher had started to slip away, but Jexebel caught him in the crook of her arm and squeezed until there came a crack. He fell to the marble like a straw doll.

'Because it is not. I know my stock. I always remember a face, especially one that complained as much as he did. Isn't that right, Ani?'

The woman was too busy kicking at the guard's corpse to hear. 'Hm?'

'Never mind.' Temsa waved a hand.

Busk felt the sweat begin afresh. 'Well… why would Kalid lie?'

Temsa stepped close so that a talon hovered over Busk's sandalled foot. He could almost see the cogs whirring behind those olive eyes.

The shade had been staring at Busk. Studying him, to be more precise. Now he spoke, and fuck it if he wasn't trying to see a knife between the tor's ribs like everybody else this afternoon.

'Busk already has Caltro. Stole him, in fact.'

Temsa cackled triumphantly. 'Straight from the shade's mouth!'

Busk instinctively backed away, but felt the armoured bulk of Ani Jexebel behind him. How she had got there so fast was the least of his concerns. 'I…'

'Horix wants no part of it,' continued the shade.

'Silence!' Temsa ordered. He'd heard all he needed. 'Now I am impressed, Busk. Not just by your soulstealing antics, but that you had the coconuts to lie to me. Several fucking times by my count. Ani.'

The cold handle of an axe tucked under Busk's chin, finding the soft space between jawbone and the lump in his windpipe. Temsa brought his face so close they brushed noses.

'Tell me where Caltro is.'

The urge to survive overpowered his urge to keep the locksmith, and Busk blurted the answer before the gold spike had even pierced his foot. 'In a sitting room, fifth floor,' he croaked. 'Wardrobe.'

Temsa dabbed his face with a handkerchief and sighed. Busk gargled and spat as the axe handle pressed harder.

'What shitty luck you've had tonight,' Temsa said. 'And all because you tried to cross me. To think, I'd probably have shared Caltro with you, once I'd finished with him. But no, you were greedy. Foolish. You know what has to come next.'

He did. Busk thrashed against the woman's grip, but to no avail. Temsa stepped back as she wrapped her forearms around the axe and yanked hard. With the back of Busk's skull against her breastplate, the metal handle had nowhere to go but through his neck. There was a wet crunch as she wrenched again, making shards of his spine. The last thing he saw was Temsa thumbing his goatee, a satisfied look on his face.

BUSK MET THE MARBLE, HIS head attached by skin only. A crimson pool began to spread, and Temsa took steps to avoid it.

Ani wiped her hands on her leather breeches. 'What about his signature? His banked coins? Didn't we need him?'

Temsa bent down to retrieve the scroll and the two half-coins from

Busk's limp hands. One was emblazoned with an older year of minting, and so he stored them in separate pockets to save confusion. 'This was not about shades, Ani. This was about teaching a lesson. Besides, m'dear, Busk has plenty in this stump of a tower to satisfy me. Not to mention a locksmith I'm just dying to meet.'

'And the shade?' Ani was already reaching for her copper-edged hatchet.

Temsa turned to face the indentured in question, but before he could make up his mind, the shade had done it for him. He was already spinning cogs and skipping out of the door with chains flying around his ankles before Ani could make a start after him.

'Leave him, Ani.'

'You mad, Boss? He'll spout all of this to Horix!'

'I have asked you repeatedly to call me "Tor", m'dear.' He levelled his cane at her. 'And don't ever call me mad, unless you want to see me so. And he will do no such thing. I have his half-coin.' He produced the shade's half-coin and trickled it over his knuckles and rings. 'He ran without thinking, and as such, Horix will stay clueless. Until we pay her a visit, that is, at the behest of our friends the Cult. Care to ensure his silence?'

Ani nodded appreciatively, the way she did whenever his genius dawned on her.

Before the coin had stopped spinning on the marble, her axe had cut it in two. Temsa imagined the blue puff of smoke that would decorate the street for just a moment before vanishing. He wondered how far the shade had got.

'Right! To this sitting room! Signal the lads, m'dear. On with the show.'

CHAPTER 12
"OUR WORST"

The scrutinisers and proctors do not enforce
the Code through a show of force. That would
be impossible. Instead, they are gatherers of
proof. Experts in information. Like leopards
watching for lame prey, they lie in wait,
disguised amongst the grasses, choosing their
moment to pounce with all their strength and
energy. That is today's Chamber, enforcing the
emperor's Code, one lawbreaker at a time.

FROM A SPEECH MADE BY CHAMBERLAIN
MENEM AT THE EXECUTION OF ANARCHIST
WILSON DANK IN 870

SENSATION DROWNED ME. I STUMBLED like a drunkard, inebriated by light and sound, taste and smell. The copper and tobacco on my tongue; the rainbow lanterns hanging between washing lines; calls of night-vendors mixed with the sizzle of their spits; the fearsome stench of heavily-used gutters. They all dizzied me.

Frequent stops were made at crossroads or the mouths of alleys. I crouched there, eyes closed and nose to forearm to dampen some of the sensation. I had been dead so long I'd forgotten what life had been like. Our formative years often deaden us to the wonder of the world. I was experiencing it raw, as if for the very first time.

At every pause, Pointy was there to offer me wisdom. Something about his voice floating in my swirling head reminded me of my true state, and illuminated the edges of what I was struggling to grasp.

Street by street, as the neighbourhoods became direr, not richer, I mastered my stolen body. Either I strengthened or Foor weakened. The throbbing in my head refused to go away, and perhaps that was affecting him more than me; slowly sapping away at his resistance. Persistence had once again held me true. I sniffed deep and tasted the city in all its rot and madness.

There was a fork in the road, and with crossed eyes I sized it up. Unsure of exactly where I was in the city – or in other words, lost – I deliberated over which was the better to take. I swore if I fell foul of more soulstealers, I would curse it all and throw my coin in the Nyx.

The notion stopped me dead. For a moment, I had forgotten my half-coin still lay in the hands of Horix, and imagined myself free. The reality was sobering, and I instantly set about denouncing it.

Damn it if I wasn't the freest I'd been in weeks. There was no feather on my breast, and not a single scowl from the living as I clung to busy bazaars and busier thoroughfares. For all they knew, I was one of them. A drunk or mad one of them, but still with a beating heart in my chest.

As I was jostled back and forth, feeling an old knot in my host's shoulder protest, an idea struck me. If I could feel some old injury I had no memory of, why could I not feel more? Regrets. Longings. Every missing piece of me could be sated, at least for the short span of this borrowed freedom.

Why not enjoy it? There it was: the inklings of a bad idea.

A bad idea is a clever parasite whose poison is a lie. It disguises itself as a good idea while it devours you at your own expense,. Like a maggot burrowing into flesh, the more you let it gorge itself, the more convinced you become of the lie, even when everything around you is a flaming mess.

I felt the numb lips spread in a tentative smile. I tensed, squinted, and looked for the lights of a tavern or the blare of some whorehouse. Neither road held such a thing, but it didn't deter my temptation.

'What's in your mind, Caltro? Where is this Horix's tower?' whispered the soulblade by my side. I'd almost forgotten him.

'That way,' I said, turning my head to a few bright spears of light above, stark against the darkness of night. It was for show; my eyes remained on the street, watching the flow of chattering people, and the steady gazes of house-guards and sellswords standing atop their doorsteps and plinths. I caught sight of a brawl spewing out of an alley mouth. A door opened somewhere unseen, and I caught a blare of music and voices. 'There are a few things I want to do first.'

'What do you mean *first?* Like what?'

I gave him no answer besides the jostle of my steps, leading us further into the lively-looking district. It was part-warehouse, part-residential. Shacks clustered like barnacles on every upright surface of stone. A few stunted towers belonging to traders or storage lenders rose above the press here and there. One in particular was a sharp pyramid with a poorly-carved sphinx roaring atop it, braying something about a bank in Arctian glyphs. In between the sprawling warehouses, stables and cobblers had hollowed out their shops. Blacksmiths, too. A few more taverns shone with lamplight and noise, but they looked too crowded for my liking.

Pointy had noticed my wistful staring. 'You can't be serious.'

'As steel, my friend.'

'You discover a power and the first thing you do with it is go to the pub? You really are Krass.'

I looked down at the pommel stone at my hip, and found the carved face different from before, this time with a downward slant to its mouth. I abruptly saw Pointy in the same light as I saw my conscience, and that was a dim light indeed. He certainly sounded like my conscience, only much, much louder. 'Don't admonish me, sword. As long as I can hold it, I can do what I please, surely?'

'As long as you hold it…'

'Why is it your problem, hm?' I challenged him. 'What does it bother you?'

He had no reply to that. He stayed quiet as I strode on, putting my big frame into action.

Around the next corner, I found my haven: a tavern of ample proportions, built into a pyramid that stood on the junction of several streets. It had glyphs splayed across the pediment of its box-like entrance, and they read 'The Rusty Slab.'

My foot hovered in mid-air. I knew that name. 'What are the fucking chances…'

'What?'

'That's Tor Temsa's tavern. We've traipsed all the way back to him, not Horix.' I looked behind me, but a fiendish idea crept into my head. 'We're going in.'

'I say again: you can't be serious. Has this haunting twisted your mind, Caltro?'

'I'm not mad. To sit in his tavern and swill a beer under his nose? That is just too perfect.' *And if I have the scantest opportunity, I'll find a chest of his to shit in.* Now I had bowels again, it seemed a fitting punishment to begin with.

Foor's body wrenched against me then. I felt a tension in my chest, but I gritted my teeth against it and forced the man forwards. I felt something snap and my borrowed flesh grow limp. He'd given in at last, I thought. Finally learned who was in control. I would give him his body back when I was done with it.

'This is a mistake, Caltro,' Pointy warned me one last time before I crossed the dusty expanse of road and squared up to the yawning entrance of the tavern. I could hear the roar of its patrons within. Zithers and arghuls duelled, turning out hectic tunes. Glass smashed so regularly it could have been percussion. During my short pause I witnessed three different troublemakers tossed out into the dust by black-clad guards.

Habit guided me. My legs took to the ramp as they had done in a thousand establishments before this one. This activity was not new, just the flesh I did it with. I wondered absently whether Foor's insides had the same taste for imbibing as mine used to.

I strode into a wall of pipe-smoke and noise. The stink of whale-oil, old beer and an antipathy for showering almost put me on my arse. So long had my nose been without use that so many smells in one place, and such pungency, squeezed a tear from my eye. I fought through, and scoured the expansive tavern. Dockworkers, sailors, soldiers, traders, street folk, guards like me, and others of various unimportant echelons in Araxes formed the vast crowd. The ceiling followed the rough shape of the pyramid, but rafters and upper rooms kept the seedy atmosphere hovering low over the tables. In two corners, minstrels and players cavorted. I spotted at least two fights in progress, and had I been in the mood to gamble, the gloomy far end of the Slab had the reek of a card den.

It was common knowledge in the Far Reaches that the Krass could drink their own weight in wine. But we paled compared to Arctians. When Arctians drank it was as if they were set on suicide by drowning. Even in my brief scan of the smoky insides of the tavern, I saw various examples of binging that would have impressed a Krass alcoholic.

I muscled my way to the bar, careful not to offend but enjoying the ability to push others aside with a form that wasn't vapour. Furthermore, I'd managed to find a body several inches taller and thinner than my old one. Muscular, too, despite its increased age. Although it felt and smelled strange, and though every movement required a practiced effort, it was confessedly more useful.

The barman spent a while staring at my forehead with a toothless grimace before hearing my order of 'Beer!' I was using my fingers to feel where the dent in my skull had bled through the makeshift headscarf when I realised I hadn't checked for coin. I patted myself down, and besides a small vial of a dubious dark liquid, I found several small silver coins. The barman took one from me, and I relaxed in knowing I had time.

The dark froth might as well have been the gates of the afterlife. I dove for it, and supped the thick liquid down. Before I knew it, I'd finished half the tankard, dizzy over the taste of grains and cold, sour alcohol.

I gasped at the taste, forgetting to breathe once more. I kept having to remind myself to ensure I didn't kill the body I'd stolen. Even after just a few weeks dead, the habit of three decades had been swiftly forgotten. They say hogs do the same; even the pinkest, most domesticated pig, finding himself loose and wild, will sprout tusks and dark hair within a week. We humans are the same in that way. Treat us wildly and we become wild.

It wasn't just breathing I'd forgotten, but other habits of the flesh. A waft of pipe-smoke covered me, and I breathed it in deep to feel its sting. I caught the eyes of a woman draped around a man dressed in hyena fur. Her opal eyeshadow transfixed me for a moment before she turned away, but it was enough to stir me. I saw a man passing papyrus packets under tables in return for coin, silver or copper. The packets were held to buyers' noses, breathed deeply, and seemed to induce an instant, doe-eyed stupor. Silver well spent, or so I'd heard; I'd never tried peaksnort, or whatever they called it in the Arc.

Even in the brightest corners of the world, you can find it: the human addiction, nay, *devotion* to destroying ourselves in the tiniest of increments. Both flesh and mind pay the toll. Day after day we kid the truth from our worries; drinking, whoring, preaching, belching smoke or spilling blood, and all the while we excuse ourselves for our iniquities. And why? To feel different from the fibres we were born with. The true hilarity is that we do it to feel alive.

I willingly succumbed to the human condition. *And why not, after all I've been through?* All the toil and trouble and treachery that had been delivered on me since arriving on that accursed ship. At Pointy's sighing, I thumped my half-empty tankard down on the bar and demanded another, sliding a small silver across the dirty, beer-washed wood.

Somehow, I'd drawn the stare of a fellow douser a stool away from me. She was a knife of a woman, hunched over her drink, eyes hooded and bored.

I raised my vessel to her and quaffed the remaining half, much to Pointy's private groaning in my head. I thumped my side as I choked the thick beer down and belched. It tasted vile, but I got a cheer from a fellow on my right, and a dull stare from the woman.

'Charming,' she said.

'I'm not here to be charming, madam,' I said. 'I am here to drink and be merry.'

'I assume you're the sort who uses coin to attract women, then. Not manners.'

I turned my eyes to the rafters and walkways above the bar, where a gang of long-legged temptresses stood, commanding the room with their powdered eyes and pointing fingers. 'If I must.'

'Well, good luck to you. They say the man who runs this place only employs the best, but that makes them the most expensive for four districts.'

'Temsa.' I spat the name into my new tankard.

A single eyebrow crept up. 'You know him?'

'Somewhat.'

The woman looked me up and down, and I her. She had beaklike features, and quick dark eyes. Her dark skin, though lighter than Krass colouring, belied her local heritage. Even under the hood I could tell her fiery hair was shorn. It was done smartly, not hacked at in some display of shame, like they do Saraka. Her clothes were nothing but simple robes and a purple smock. I saw the dark tendrils of tattoos curling up her neck and creeping from her cuffs. Something about their design was familiar.

She skipped stools to sit beside me. Had my mind been in another place – in other words, my own skull – I'd have thought myself fancied.

Yet this woman gave off such a blithe air, I assumed she'd been at the drink a while.

She spoke first. 'You wear the livery of Tor Busk, but you don't drink anywhere near his tower. You seem to have some dire wound on your head that makes me wonder how you're still standing, yet you have a fervent way about you that says you're more alive than half the people in this room. I pride myself on reading people, and yet you, guard, are a mystery.'

A fresh tankard arrived at my elbow and I raised it to her. 'Caltro,' I said quietly, daring my own name. I wondered if she would use hers.

'Heles. Dead gods be with you.'

'And you.'

'So what do you know about this illustrious Temsa? He runs quite the tavern,' she said.

'That he does, and I know a little. Not the sort of thing to be speaking out loud and to anyone, mind,' I said, playing careful. I had no wish to go about drawing suspicion.

'Some think he's more soulstealer than soultrader.'

I coughed into the foam of my beer. 'Some? I wager many.' Already the tingle of alcohol was climbing into my borrowed brain. Strange how its potency increased with time.

'Why would you say that?' Heles asked me.

I wanted to yell in her face and tell her exactly what he'd done to me, but I held myself still, partly due to the body becoming slightly stiff around me. Perhaps I had worn the bastard out. 'I would imagine he's wronged many, building what he has. Doesn't everybody have to step on somebody to climb the ladder of society? I hear he's a tor now.'

'Yes. Interesting, that. Quite recent, too, truth be told.' Heles looked around at the inhabitants of the tavern. 'It's one of the reasons I'm here. Curious to see how a tavern owner and average soultrader buys tordom.'

'At a guess, lying, thieving and unscrupulous murder of the in-nocent.' I twitched as I said it, my elbow seizing up. I had forgotten the aches and pains the years marked a body with. With every blossom that came from being alive, there was a weed waiting to suck it dry. 'But that's just a guess.'

'You all right?'

'I…' I raised my tankard and slopped some more beer into my mouth. I decided to speak my mind once the barkeep had wandered further away. I'd imagined my justice coming in the form of royal or official retribution against Temsa, but tonight I could settle for spreading tavern gossip and rumours. Petty, but I had been known for it.

'I think he needs looking into. By that Chamber of the Code, or the emperor, or somebody.' *Failing that, a knife while he sleeps.*

Heles leaned close, winking slowly. She was sauced as well, I knew it. 'I had the exact same suspicion. A Chamber Scrutiniser… friend of mine… he was killed recently, and not too far from here.'

I became bolder with every swig, alcohol blurring my vision as well as my lies. 'I wish I could get into this Chamber. Or knew somebody there. I need to tell people what he did to m…my friend.'

'Is that why you're drinking? For him? You seem pale. How'd you get that wound on your head?'

I raised a finger to probe it. The throbbing had ceased, and the blood gone sticky. The whole area felt numb. 'You ask a lot of questions,' I said, distracting her as I wondered at the stillness within me, and the inflexibility in my borrowed joints.

'I, er, write about goings on. You know, keep people informed of what's going on in this city.'

'So you… report on things. You're a reporter.'

Dear dead gods. I heard Pointy speak in my head. I ignored him.

'I suppose you could call it that,' she said, wrinkling her nose. 'I spread scrolls around to share important news. Like the Nyxwater shortage. Or these murders, for instance.'

'Murders?'

'Tors and tals disappearing. You haven't heard? Araxes is abuzz. Six nobles gone now; vaults cleared, towers empty, everything gone. Claims have been made on their banks but nobody knows by who. Tal Kheyu-Nebra is the most recent to vanish. Her tower burned through the night. You can still see the smoke rising from Quara District.'

I blamed my lack of knowledge of current events largely on being stuck inside a wardrobe for the past few days. 'Who's behind it all?'

Heles tapped her beak of a nose. 'That's the question, ain't it?' She sipped from her glass. 'I'll find out. I always do.'

Sniffing at my beer, I savoured its nutty aroma before I polished off the second tankard. At the same time, I noticed a slight reek. I blamed the chipped and beaten bar before me. I put a hand on it, keeping it from swaying. 'That's all this city seems to do besides murder: talk. Talk means nothing without actions to follow it. Justice. Freedom.'

Heles cackled. 'You sound like a shade. But you're right. Damn fucking right.' She sighed, drumming her fingers irritably. 'My job means I run into certain people from time to time. Powerful people. You seem like a knowledgeable fellow. If you know anything, you should tell me. Help me find out the truth. Maybe I could help you, or your friend.'

I became aware of her eyes sliding from the bar to mine, no trace of drunken sparkle in them now. 'Well,' I hummed, unwilling to reveal what I was, but drunk enough to consider it. She was no member of the Chamber, just a writer. A 'reporter' with 'friends.' *When have writers ever helped anybody?* I would help myself instead. 'Perhaps you should go see what's going on at Tor Busk's tonight. See if your so-called important friends are interested in that.'

Heles leaned closer, and seemed to catch the same whiff I had. 'What's going on at Tor Busk's? Which one is he?'

I was emboldened further by my sudden urge to leave. The more I used my nose, the more suspicious I was the foul smell was me. 'Minor lord. Bit of a prick. Poor choice in business partners. You should go look yourself, and maybe you'll see what kind of man Temsa truly is. Perhaps it'll give you some insight on these murders, too.' As I took a turn to tap my bulbous Arctian nose, I heard the clearing of a throat in my head. 'And be careful. He's more dangerous than you know.'

Heles caught me by the wrist before I left. 'Is that why you're here drinking and shaking like you are? What happened to your friend? Is that where the wound came from?'

Whether she cared or simply needed information, it didn't matter to me. I stared at the grip of her oddly strong hand on my wrist. I missed the touch of another; of skin against skin, no matter how brief or innocuous. I missed it dearly. I cast one last look up at the balconies above me, then shrugged away, abruptly angered. I was so close to being alive, and yet so far. What pained me more was that eventually, I had to go back to being dead. I had no idea how long I could keep the haunting up.

'You ask a lot of questions,' I slurred. 'Go look for yourself.'

With a hand clamped to my silk-wrapped and dented forehead, I left. The more I thought about it, the more I wondered what the blow had done to the man, and why he'd fought against me so.

'*You know what's happened, don't you?*' Pointy asked as I moved for the exit. His voice was clear over the hubbub of the tavern.

I caught my reflection in the finger-smudged mirror above a private booth. For a brief moment, it was a blessed thing to *have* a reflection again, despite it not being mine. Then I saw the grey pallor of my pilfered skin, and the dark veins of purple spreading out from under the headscarf. There was no life beneath it. I heard the cartilage click in my elbows as I reached to paw at my face.

I was riding a dead body.

'You've murdered him.'

Pointy's words clanged around my head like the dawn bell sounding execution day to a condemned man. I almost lost my grip on the haunting right there and then.

I was no murderer. Selfish, yes. A thief, yes, but to me there was a sliding scale of criminality. Murder was high up there, somewhere below soulstealers and molesters of children. Thievery – especially the skilful and masterful kind I employed – was far down the list, near those types who managed to cheat the card dens of Saraka and keep hold of their tongues.

I wrestled my thoughts back to the point.

It was an accident. A plain and simple accident. I had not known the soldier would headbutt his own club, nor that I had been walking around the city in his dying body. Accidents were not the same as murder. Murders were for the jilted lovers, the jealous, the insane, and the plain, downright *murderous*. Not thieves like me.

'Shut up,' I told the sword as I manhandled my limbs into action. I refused to let them seize up. I made for the door that had brought me into this sordid place. Before I ducked under the archway, I saw a gigantic armoured shade standing with his arms crossed against the edge of the sweeping bar. He had eyes only for me, and a furrow of the forehead that made me wonder if he'd heard my warning to Heles. Mercifully, he stayed still, and I was free to stumble to the streets in peace, looking like any other sozzled tavern-goer peaking too early.

My lifeless body and the two beers had almost sunk me. One was making it difficult to move, the other to think. All I had was the conundrum of how a soul could get drunk, and the grim determination to shut one eye at a time and keep moving for some of the larger towers toward Araxes' core. Annoyingly, night hid their edges, showing only their lamps, which meant I had a hard time distinguishing which building was which. I stumbled for the highest concentration of lights, hoping for the best chance of Horix's tower.

Pointy kept silent. Perhaps he disapproved of me so much he had nothing to offer besides insults and admonishment. It occurred to me then that it might have been his jealousy of my ability to mimic life again; to quaff beer and occupy a barstool, to feel the wind on my cheek and the touch of a hand on my arm. Before I could dwell any more on it, I bit my tongue as I stumbled down a thoroughfare, and damn near bit the thing off.

I thought about finding an alleyway and gambling a night waiting for the sun to come up while my body rotted away. Then again, all I needed to do was make it to Horix's tower. I could have ditched the body and travelled as a shade, but I couldn't bring myself to give it up.

'Or do I?' The thought was so revolutionary it raced from my mind to my lips before I could stop it.

'What?' asked the soulblade.

'What if I run?'

'Where?'

'Home. Away from here.'

'In a dead body?'

I spilled my ideas as I wobbled from flagstone to flagstone. My tone was not too far from the realm of panic. 'I'll find a new body. A live one this time. Horix won't touch my half-coin as long as she thinks I'm in Araxes. I have a few weeks maybe. That's enough to enjoy myself. Maybe hit one last grand mark. I could show you Krass and my home in Taymar, see if I can get you some enjoyment too. Perhaps I'll find you a tasty little deadbound dagger or dish to talk to.'

'Can you actually hear yourself with those dead ears, Caltro?' Pointy was less agreeable to the idea than my addled mind had expected him to be.

'Fuck you.'

'No, fuck you! You've gone mad with this ability. Do what you planned. Trust the widow. Do whatever she requires of you, and you'll get your half-coin.'

I pointed myself to where the moon shone through the chasms between the warehouses, showing me ripples of black waves far beyond. My legs shuffled towards them.

'Fuck the widow! Why should I squander this gift?'

Gift. The thought of the gods and the Cult hadn't crossed my mind until then, but it did now, crashing in like a corpse through a window.

I was running out of excuses for ignoring the dead gods. They had given me a gift, just as they'd said. There was also a Cult, just like Basht warned me. All that remained was apparently saving the known world, and at that moment, I wanted nothing to do with it. I felt like a greedy child, cupping the largest slice of cake in my hands and refusing to share.

Pointy was not giving up yet. I wondered if the gods had sent him to me, to act as my surrogate conscience. 'This *is* squandering the gift! Don't you see? What happened to freedom and justice?'

I grabbed my fiery beard and pulled it hard, feeling outmatched by responsibility. *The right thing can be an evil thing when it doesn't align with what you want.* I scrabbled for something I could justify myself with, searching for a reason good enough to erode the sword's annoyingly accurate argument. 'This looks like freedom to me.'

'You're a self-indulgent coward, Caltro!'

I knew that already. 'And why shouldn't I be? I'm fucking dead, aren't I? I've been passed about like a piece of furniture. I've been kidnapped, beaten, forced to do things against my will, and had to haunt a man to escape this madness! I think I'm justified in wanting a less turbulent existence, even if it's for a moment! Why can't I enjoy this brief respite from the curse of indenturement, hmm? Don't I deserve that? Wouldn't you, if you found yourself in my position?'

Pointy had only muttered curses for me. For a weapon, he didn't put up much of a fight. I kept on towards the docks, hugging walls and chain-wrapped cargo when silhouettes or shades came ambling past. It must have been a kinder night than when I arrived, or a kinder part of the waterfront, if there was such a thing in Araxes. Perhaps it was the higher number of guards standing in warehouse and mansion doorways. Recognising a kindred, although sodden, soul, they pushed me away whenever I stumbled near. No fists or kicks for me.

For what I guessed to be an hour, I trod a path that gradually slipped from flagstone to dust to wooden decking. I soon saw the glitter of water through the gaps, black as oil, marred only by the wavering streak of moonlight.

By now my joints wanted to lock in place whenever I gave them a moment. If I paused too long, my grip on them would falter as they clicked and groaned. What a sight I must have made to any onlookers; I would have turned around to look if there wasn't a chance my neck would stick that way. All I wanted was a ship, and as my vision sloshed about, I saw one, dallying at the end of a long and empty jetty.

Sssclomp. Sssclomp. My boots dragged along the worn and sea-bleached wood. Despite my skin being dead already, I felt as if I was dying all over again. At least this time I got a better ending. No soul-stealer standing over me with a wolf's grin and a wicked knife with my blood on it.

My eyes had started to mist over, and in the dark it made a blur of the ship's backside. Two lamps watched me like eyes. Some runes were stretched between them across a white-painted board.

Faraganthar. I mouthed the name automatically. A Krass name, though I could have been wrong; there seemed to be some distance still between us. It was why finding the edge of the jetty at my toes confused me deeply. I stared down at the churned stretch of monochrome water between the departing ship and me, and cursed my misted eyes and shambling feet. I reached for it with a crippled arm, fingers bent in odd directions. Cranking my head right, then left, I saw a stretch of empty jetties and wharfs. No ship for me.

I hung my head. As the body pitched forwards, I stayed standing on the deck. My blue vapours peeled from his crooked back, and I felt the skin and bone rippling over me as I exited. Despite an overwhelming numbness settling upon me, I made sure to seize the sword as Foor fell, and save Pointy from the depths. I heard the exhale of gratitude in my head as I held him firm.

The smell of rot and sewage had gone. The sound of the heavy splash was muffled. The irksome tang of beer was nonexistent, and although I was naked, my limbs were numb but not cold in the sea breeze. I was colder than they. My mists swirled about me, and I put a glowing hand to my neck to feel the barely tangible edges of a gaping throat.

'Dead again,' I said.

'Oi!' came a holler from along the dock. 'Is that a body?'

Without the muddied head, I was immediately sharper. I quickly began to retrace my steps along the jetty. I was sure scores of bodies found their way into the Troublesome Sea every night, and yet this hero seemed particularly offended. I remembered I was a shade once more, and realised that might have irked him. Maybe he was some vulturous opportunist, and wanted the body for himself.

He was faster than me, and we met at the root of the jetty. He shimmied about, kicking up dust as he eyed the sword in my hand. It turned out it was the latter option: the man dashed past me and hurtled down the jetty for the body. I caught the promise of, 'See you shortly!' as he ran. Perhaps he believed I had tossed my own body into the sea in an attempt not to be bound. Perhaps he wagered I'd rise from whatever Nyxwell he managed to drag the body to. I imagined he would get quite the surprise when an angry Foor breached the black waters like an enraged porpoise.

I drifted into the nearest and smallest alleyway, daubing its stonework blue with my glow. At its dead end, past several doors and suspicious shutters, there was barely any space for a living person to stand, never mind lie down. For a ghost, it was perfect. I tucked myself into the alcove and tried to dim my light as much as possible by tensing myself. The sword I tucked behind me. He and I had no words left to trade that night. The morning would bring more, no doubt, and hopefully some clarity to pierce my apparent madness. I shut out all the shame and guilt and anger, and closed my eyes.

As I huddled there, listening to the clank and clatter of dock districts, and later in the evening, screams and yells, I pondered why we always had our best intentions when we were at our worst.

———◆———

'YOU'RE BACK SOONER THAN I thought, spook. I didn't expect you for several days,' croaked Horix, eyeing the shade as he lounged before her on an armchair. He had rid himself of the loaned smock, replacing it with a smart tunic of silk and the sort of pantaloons Scatter pirates wore. His paler glow painted him a northerner, maybe Skol, as did his heavy brow and the wisps of the bushy beard he'd worn in life.

Meleber Crale was one of the best of his kind in the city. What made him insufferable was that he knew it.

'I have quite the story to tell you, Tal,' he announced with a confident smirk.

'I wanted a shade, and I only see you before me. Stories are worth pittance to me.'

Crale absently stirred the vapours of his beard. 'Depends on the story, does it not? Try this one: a Tor Temsa has murdered Tor Busk in his own tower this afternoon. The man was after your precious Caltro Basalt. He let me go, thinking he had my half-coin. Unfortunately for him, it's safely stored in the bank.'

Horix propped herself up in her chair, holding a hand over her mouth to hide her smile. 'Dead gods bless you spooks and your sneaking ways. Temsa murdered him? And did you say "Tor"?'

'I did. He had his big guard take Busk's head off, almost on his doorstep. You know him?'

The widow was not listening. 'My, my. That paunchy, thieving pissbag finally met his end, has he? And at the hands of an even worse one. And Temsa is a tor now, no less.'

'I'll take that as a yes.'

The smile faded. 'Where is Caltro now?'

'Last I heard, locked up in a sitting room in Busk's tower.'

'And you made no effort to retrieve him? That is what I paid you for, spook.'

'Your lump of a colonel here delivered me after Temsa had already arrived. There was nothing—'

'Then you must go back, and find out what has become of Caltro. I'll be damned if I'll let that soulstealer take my locksmith!'

Crale got to his feet, arms crossed again. 'I—'

'Out!'

Crale stood his ground, prodding the white feather dangling around his neck from copper-cored twine. 'I am a free shade. I'm not one of your house-shades to be ordered about so. You don't own me.'

'I have given you the emperor's silvers for Caltro Basalt. Until he stands before me, I do own you, through contract and coin. Now, get out and do your job, half-life!'

Spittle chased him towards the door, where Kalid promptly shut him out. The colonel ambled towards her, mulling over words. When he finally thought of something to say, Horix cut across him immediately.

'Temsa—'

'Has come a long way from hawking dubious shades at the soul-markets. Already a tor, and now attacking another noble in daylight. He must be mad, brave, or favoured by somebody. And now he is after Caltro.'

Kalid cleared his throat. 'Do you trust the spook to fetch Caltro?'

Although the widow did not trust in anybody or anything except herself, silver could buy the closest thing to it. Meleber Crale was worth every silver, or so Kalid's contacts had said. A good spook was hard to come by in this city. Illegal according to the Code but employed by many, a spook was a tool for getting into places flesh couldn't – or wouldn't – go. Needed to eavesdrop? Sneak into a rival's tower? Poison a stew? Hire a spook. It was dangerous work, but well-paid. As such, plenty of free shades across the Arc offered similar services, but only the good ones survived more than one job. Crale had been working Araxes for years. That made him a master.

Horix sighed irritably. 'I know you are eager for a scrap, Colonel, but aside from hoping Caltro somehow returns by himself, that spook is currently our only hand to play.'

'What do you want me to do?'

She swept to her shelves to prod at scrolls and trinkets. 'We bide our time for now. Tell Yamak to double the workforce in the cellars. Buy more shades if you have to. Double the guard, and no visitors. Leave me to think about our new foe.'

Kalid said the only words Horix wanted to hear. 'Aye, Widow.'

CHAPTER 13
SHIFTING SANDS

Greed cannot be blamed on a poor
foundation, but on the man that continues to
build atop it.

ARCTIAN PROVERB

ND NOW A *FIRE*, OF all things. I cannot remember the last time I saw a tal's tower blaze so, and I am fifty years dead!'

Sisine knuckled her forehead. Boon had been incessant during this session of the Cloud Court, discussing Sisine openly with his neighbours, offering a remark for every one of hers, going on tirades for far longer than necessary. She had wanted chaos in the city, but not the kind that gave windbags like him more excuse to exercise their jaws.

'Serek Boon!' she bellowed. 'Will you please let somebody else speak!'

'Fine!' He threw up his hands and looked to the benches around him, urging others to pipe up. It took an age for somebody to do so. Finally, another half-life serek stood. His shoulder-length blue hair wafted languidly around his face as if he was underwater.

'I agree with Serek Boon, Majesty. Something more needs to be done about this lawlessness.' The Court sighed in concurrence.

The empress-in-waiting made sure to look as offended as possible at the ignorance of her efforts. 'Not two days ago, for the first time in centuries, I welcomed eleven phalanxes of battle-hardened soldier shades into this city. Two days, and already you expect miracles, Sereks!' In actuality, she had made sure General Hasheti's shades were spread so thinly across Araxes, they may as well have still been fighting in the Scatter Isles.

Boon could not stay quiet for long. 'Not miracles, Majesty. Order.'

'And you will have it, Boon, you and the rest of you!' Sisine argued. 'And perhaps then you can stop quaking in your golden shoes.'

Sisine met the muttering discontent with her practised glare, daring them to press her further. Once again, Boon took up the challenge.

'But when, Empress-in-Waiting? The murders are getting worse, more violent. The Nyxwater still dwindles. The Chamber continues to be overwhelmed. If the army cannot help us, then perhaps Chamberlain Rebene needs further aid from those willing and eager to wipe evil from our streets. From those with the knowledge and resources to do so! And considering that shades are already being used by the Chamber—'

'Spit it out, Boon. This court is not a stage for your oratory.'

'The Cult of Sesh have expressed their desire to help by setting up patrols—'

Sisine wished she had a wineglass in her hand to hurl at him. The session had taken a sharp turn towards absurdity. She needed to rein them in. 'Absolutely not!'

'You would refuse their help so quickly?' Boon tried to click his fingers, momentarily forgetting he was made of vapour.

'No, Serek, I would deny them based on their treachery against my family and this empire. There is a reason they were – and still are – banished from the Core Districts. I highly doubt their aspirations have changed much in two decades.'

'You let fear cloud you, Empress-in-Waiting,' Boon accused.

Sisine laughed, brashly and openly. 'If I had any fear, Serek, I'd be hiding in my own Sanctuary like my father.'

There was a pause in their muttering. Not once had she spoken ill of the emperor. Now, with barely an insult, they looked at her in shock. Sisine realised then that, despite all her efforts, her father's authority still hung over her head. She bared her teeth.

'I will pass the matter to our wise emperor for consideration. Since it was he who removed the Cult from this tower, he will have his say.'

She waved her scroll, indicating the subject was done with and the session over. The sereks obeyed, and filed out along their rows, many of them conveniently forgetting to bow on their exit. Too busy muttering and complaining. Only Boon stayed, sitting on his bench, hands upon knees and head tilted down at her.

Sisine crossed her arms. 'When you warned me of ambition not so long ago, Boon, you didn't warn me of your own.' She looked to the gleaming throne behind her. The light shining through the crystal stained the marble around it blue. 'You want it, shade? Try to take it. No shade has ever sat on the throne of Araxes. You won't be the first.'

Boon said nothing as he rose and walked for the doors. They held each other's gaze until he disappeared into an archway.

'That man,' Sisine hissed to herself. 'That *half-life*.'

Royal Guards in tow, she left the Cloud Court and ascended the stairs to her father's Sanctuary at the very peak of the Piercer. The stained-glass windows showed her heights that would have dizzied a bird. Sisine didn't care. She had been born in this tower; her stomach had long since hardened.

For the second time that day, she walked the long corridor to the Sanctuary. Her father's Royal Guards had come to attention and were already tending to the grand door. Sisine bustled past them into the lamplight of the antechamber, and they closed the doors behind her. She hovered near the sandalwood bench, still clutching the scroll in her hand as she glowered at the vault door. The more she stared at the complex loops of gold and copper and the engraved scenes, the more she throttled the papyrus as if it were an enemy's neck.

When Sisine felt the pop of the scroll's wooden spine in her palm, she launched the scroll at the Sanctuary door with a banshee's shriek. Papyrus tumbled like an unravelling ribbon as pieces of varnished wood flew to opposite sides of the small chamber.

Before they settled, Sisine was already pounding her hands on the vault. Over and over, her fists met the cold, immovable metal. Though the blows made something inside the door ring, there was not a sound from the other side. No murmur of apology. No questions of care. No answers for her.

She cursed the empress then, too. Not in words, but with more frantic pummelling. Spit flew from her bared teeth. Her mother had abandoned her, proving herself as cowardly as her father. Though Sisine was closer to the throne than ever, she hated them for being so weak; for leaving her such a farce of a court and country.

Spent, Sisine retreated to the bench. Her hands and chest shook, but there was not a tear in her eyes. She had none to spare for her emperor and empress; just a host of promises. In truth, she somewhat enjoyed the resentment; like putting coals in her shoes, it spurred her to keep going.

'You'll see, Father. You'll see,' Sisine snarled. She turned away from the complexities of the Sanctuary door and burst out into the corridor, sending the guards scattering. She would have liked to replace them with her own, but the Sanctuary guards would not move for any order but the emperor's. That was something else she could not wait to change.

Winding down the tower to her own chambers, she threw the door aside to find Etane practising his sword-dances with his sword Pereceph. The big blade gave off a faint white mist, as if it were freezing cold. Caring not, Sisine bustled past him.

'You tell that dog Temsa to stop making messes and start making progress instead,' she ordered without breaking her stride. 'Else he'll find himself dangling by his toes from the top of the Piercer, food for the crows.'

Etane put the point of his sword on the stone, making the metal chime. 'I'll tell him exactly that. Anything else, Your Gloriousness?'

'Yes, actually. Why don't you throw yourself from the roof while you're at it?'

The balcony door slammed shut behind her with a bang, and she soaked herself in the buffeting of the wind and roar of the city far below. Even then, emptying her mind, her eyes snapped to every scrap of red they spotted.

———◆———

TEMSA WAS ENJOYING THE MUSICAL clank of his guards' new armour. He'd chosen his favourite colours: black and rusty brown. Leather and russet scale covered the guards from chin to toe, and on each of their heads was a classic copper skullcap. His men had protested at having their heads shaved, but Temsa had threatened them all with a beating as well as indenturement. After that, they'd fought to line up for the razor.

Temsa's new armoured litter, carried by mute shades, was also pleasing. He'd spared no expense for the cushions, and through the fine chainmail curtains, he could stretch out and watch the streets slide by him like the scenes of some grand theatre.

The day was hot, and most on foot clung to the street-side awnings and the shade of palms. On wider streets, umbrellas were hawked by young shades. Those with a silver or gem to spare found respite. Those without continued to bake in the onslaught of the noonday sun.

Temsa watched Ani and Danib marching alongside the litter. Both their brows were furrowed in the heat, Ani's flesh sweating and the shade's steel plate glittering. Both wore their new armour: cuirasses of mirror-like metal, chainmail kilts, spiked pauldrons detailed with scarlet copper. It was a gift that hadn't been well received. Both had preferred their own armour, they'd said, or in Danib's case, grunted. All worn in, apparently. But Temsa had insisted on it.

As he went back to his idle staring, he noticed a hooded figure tracing them through the crowds. A young Arctian man, sprightly and long of stride, with no colours about him but black cloth and sand. He was on the opposite side of the street, but had plenty of glances for Temsa.

For a time, Temsa watched him trail the litter, until the man was lost in the shadow of a tower and the press of the crowd. The litter ran on with the carts and the carriages.

Temsa had decided to have Ani fall back and follow the man when he heard the voice: shrill, and full of stress and passion. The words were muddled, but it was enough to cut through the roar of the bustle.

Temsa moved aside his chainmail curtain to find a small crowd had gathered in the shadow of a thick spire. They were huddled around a shade in a blood-red cloak. The shade held some sort of picture splayed across a board, tapping it repeatedly with his glowing fingers as he gave his speech.

'Ani, I want to go over,' Temsa ordered, making Danib look up.

Miss Jexebel tapped the carrying-shades with a stick and had them approach the crowd. Temsa propped himself up from his cushions to listen to the preacher.

'It is he who gave the gift of binding, stolen from jealous gods who would seek to keep man and woman slave to their promise of afterlife! To keep us dutifully praying! It is nothing compared to the second chance we owe to Sesh today. Mine is no half-life, but a second life. That is why we praise him—'

A voice interrupted, sounding so close Temsa thought its owner's lips were in his ear. 'I did not take you for a man who has the time to listen to speakers on the street.'

He wrenched himself up, finding one of the Enlightened Sisters, Yaridin, standing amongst his guards. They flinched away from her, surprised.

Yaridin gently moved their spears from her face, their copper edges sizzling against her fingers. 'I intended to speak with you at your establishment. Alas, you were not at home.'

'So you tracked me down.' Temsa's gaze slipped to Danib, whose face was more impassive than usual.

The sister smiled. 'A happy coincidence.'

Temsa wasn't sure their definitions of happy matched up, but he beckoned her forwards anyway, half-listening to the preacher as he squawked on about Sesh.

'...the lies that he is a wrathful god, a trickster god, or even a vengeful god; these are but rumours spread by other religions throughout the last thousand years. And yet only ours has endured...'

'You have more names for me?' he asked, once she had floated around the litter to face him.

'You have yet to take care of the ones you were given. And those you have not followed in order.'

'There was no order to them.'

'Of course there was. The order we gave them to you in, what else? There is always order. See?' Yaridin gestured to the preacher, as if she knew the sermon better than he did.

'...because we believe in order in all things, and we believe in the order of this great city. It is an order we want to uphold, as Sesh wanted. And so we have, brothers and sisters of Araxes...'

Temsa snorted. 'A blatant lie if ever I've heard one. Is this what you wanted new shades for? So you could prop them up on street corners and have them spew nonsense at crowds? Neither the Chamber nor the royals will stand for it.'

Yaridin waved her arm in a wide arc, showing him the small crowd that had gathered around the preacher. 'These people do. Who knows how many more are listening at this very moment around the city.'

Temsa dreaded to think.

'The list must be executed in order, first to last,' said Yaridin. 'Tal Kheyu-Nebra wasn't even on our list. We trust you are not getting tips from other interested parties, or taking initiative?'

He scoffed at her. 'I will do what I like, Sister, but if you must know, the tal was nothing to do with me. Silly old bat left her lamps burning, or so I heard.' He saw Yaridin's gaze slip over his shoulder and affix itself to Danib.

'Perhaps a clumsy shade, dropping a taper,' she replied softly.

'Perhaps,' Temsa grunted. 'Is that all? Is my unwarranted scolding over?'

'It is, but the betterment of your soul remains. Perhaps you should stay awhile, listen to my brother's words.'

Temsa prodded his gut. 'I would, but I'm no half-life. I can't join your little club.'

'Can't you? Perhaps that will change.' Yaridin slipped backwards into the crowd, one hand raised to the blue sky and burning sun.

'…and we have realised a great and terrible error, friends. A misunderstanding that has gone on far too long!'

The cultist preacher paused for effect. Temsa wished he had a triggerbow to pause him indefinitely.

'And so, we recognise that Sesh's wisdom and love are not just for the dead, but for the living also. And so, we announce that we open the Church not just to shades, but to any who wish to join. The Church of Sesh welcomes you all as brothers and sisters, and together, we can restore this city to the glory Sesh foresaw.'

As a small cheer erupted, Temsa hawked and spat, accidentally catching the chainmail curtains. He curled his lip. *Church*. He saw then what the cultists wanted: respect. A fresh foundation on which to rebuild themselves. Temsa chuckled. *Let them play their games*, he thought. He didn't give a sideways shit as long as it meant more half-coins for him.

Ani poked her head between the chainlink. 'Where now, Boss?'

'The Slab,' he snapped at her. 'And it's fucking *Tor*!'

———————◆———————

'WHAT DID YOU SEE?' HELES asked as the proctor came to a breathless, skidding halt.

Jym took a moment to find some air. 'Nothing but some new armour for his men, a fancy litter, and his two big guards.'

'And their names?'

He scrunched up his eyes. 'Miss Ani Jexebel, and the shade Danib... Danib Ironjaw,' he recited.

Heles pulled her hood forwards; she could feel the sun on her nose. 'Good boy.'

She could tell he had been dying to ask all morning, so it was no wonder the question finally popped out now.

'So... what did you see at Tor Busk's?' he breathed.

Heles wished she had a grander answer to give him besides two locked doors and a lot of clattering around within. Half the night she had spent playing the part of a slouched drunkard, lying in a gutter near a busy corner. One by one, she had watched the lamps of Busk's tower fizzle out. Only a single figure had emerged early in the morning, and that had been Ani Jexebel. By that time, dawn was starting to burn away the night, and Heles' eyes had drooped. Pretending to be drunk always had the strange effect of making one feel drunk. She'd had to fight like a mad hyena to stay awake long enough to return to her modest lodgings and straw bed.

'Enough to make me suspicious of the man,' came her answer.

'So you think he's the one behind the murders and the fire? This Temsa?'

'Right now, he is one suspect of many, Proctor. This whole city is full of suspects. They're all guilty of something.' Masking a yawn, Heles stared out over the huge square, with its churn of living and dead and armoured vehicles. She distracted herself by watching a giraffe being carted through the crowds on the back of a wagon.

A crate enveloped most of its body, leaving its neck and head to tower above. The beast was humming irascibly to itself, swinging its head and table-leg horns in low arcs at its captors. Heles watched a man get batted into a stall of pottery with a crash. She waited for the roar of laughter to subside before she spoke.

'Besides, who said there was only one? Temsa might have partners. He might be a pawn. Never accept anything as certain, Proctor Jym. Never in Araxes.'

'Yes, Scrutiniser.'

'Come, there are more questions to be asked before we are certain.'

Jym fell in tow and Heles led them across the district, back to the streets surrounding Busk's tower. She looked above the rooftops to see its stubby point, and saw the windows had been shuttered against the daylight. That was new.

Today their disguise was of Outsprawl peasants: clad in cheap tarred linen, caked in sand, shuffling here and there and gawping at every building taller than three levels. Sprawlers and desert-folk were only a fraction higher than shades in the food chain of Araxes. It meant eyes spent more time avoiding their dishevelled appearance than examining it. Jym seemed used to the garb.

They circled Busk's tower twice over the course of an hour. Heles' eyes were constantly in motion, watching stalls and windows, comers and goers.

A local would always have a pattern. They would walk the way they'd walked a hundred times before. They would know which traders they trusted and which beggars managed to survive the night. Above all, a local did not dawdle. Heles watched out for these types. Every time she encountered one, she or Proctor Jym would ask their subtle questions. It was hard reaping. Most refused to answer on principle. For a city where everybody constantly watched their backs, an awful lot seemed to go unnoticed.

That was unless it seemed trivial. Heles had discovered this years ago; ask enough people the same banal question, and there was always one dullard who didn't notice anything suspicious about even the most suspicious of events.

Heles found her dullard in the form of a merchant with dark rings under his eyes. Jym hovered nearby as she scrutinised his rainbow collection of dried fruits.

'Six gritapples for half a silver!' he brayed.

'Hmm, not my taste,' she replied. 'Say, you here a lot?'

The man was pleased for a chance to boast. 'Every day and night for a decade, madam!'

It always amused Heles how traders were quick to bray how long they had been in business, as if time was the measure of quality. A merchant could sell shit for ten years and still be selling shit. Experience was the real measure of quality, and that came through learning, not just doing.

'You must know all the gossip around here, then,' she coaxed him.

The trader scrunched his face, growing cautious. 'Why you askin'?'

'Looking to move from Dawar District.'

'Mm. Rough district.'

'Want to know if here is better. Anything been going on?'

'Not much to say, gladly. Just talk of some spat between the tor who lives in that tower over there and some old noble wench from another district.'

'Oh?'

'Nothing worrisome. Whole bunch of her soldiers came through here yesterday afternoon. Single half-life with them. Was here cleanin' up when I saw them come past. Went to the door, delivered the shade and left again. No clashin' or fightin'. Peace offerin', methinks.'

Heles found a sappy palm-pear she liked the look of and flicked the merchant half a silver. 'And which old wench would this be? Not from Dawar, is she?'

'Too many bloody nobles to count these days. Big soldier had a seal on him.' The merchant poked at a blackened tooth with his tongue. 'Three hanging corpses. That were it. Came right past me.'

Heles turned her gaze to Jym, watching him trying to match up a name. He was clueless, staring at the azure sky for help.

'Mm,' she hummed. 'Well, I'll hopefully be seeing you around, friend,' she said.

The merchant nodded absently as he bit the silver and winced sorely.

'Who's three corpses hanging?' Jym asked as they moved back into the throngs of people.

'Widow Horix, Proctor Jym. One of the oldest tals in the city. Quiet woman. Quite the mystery. Been a noble for fifteen years or so, I believe, since some husband of hers died. Extremely fond of her privacy. Doesn't like to meddle. That's why it's unlike her to be sending her house-guards out into the city at night. Especially here, amongst lower nobles.'

She could almost hear the proctor's mind churning, as if it were full of ratchets and cogs instead of grey mush. 'So...' he said, groping to make sense. He wasn't alone. Horix's involvement complicated matters. Heles spoke her thoughts aloud. She always found that helped to untangle them.

'So, Proctor Jym, Horix may be involved or she may not. It is strange Miss Jexebel should make an appearance, I admit, but all we've discovered is that more questions need to be asked. And though that may be irritating, is it not our job? To ask questions? To find answers? Remind me of the Chamber's creed, Proctor.'

'Crime is falsehood. Justice is truth.'

Heles grunted. 'You're learning, Proctor. Slowly, but you're learning.'

'What do we do now, then?'

'I think we'll pay Tor Temsa and Widow Horix a visit.'

'Now?' Jym looked far too eager for her liking.

'Not now.' Heles was firm. 'But soon. Now, we report to Chamberlain Rebene. If he doesn't get some news soon, I think he might rupture something.'

It wasn't that she cared for the chamberlain's health. All she cared for was justice, but bureaucracy was still a game to be played, and she couldn't do her job with Rebene breathing down her neck.

'Here,' said Heles, tossing the remaining half of the palm-pear to Jym. 'Eat something. Keep up your strength. You'll need it.'

CHAPTER 14
HERE BE MONSTERS

Ma'at was originally a minor goddess, one
of truth, balance and justice. It is her feather,
her symbol, that we see on today's shades,
or ba'at, as they are still called amongst
Duneplain tribes. The concept of ma'at was
rather significant in the legal systems of those
that came before the age of shades. It allowed
every citizen, with the exception of slaves, to
be viewed as equals under the law regardless
of wealth or social position. And with the law,
what went around came around, so to speak.
Like Ma'at herself, it was fair and balanced.
Sadly, it is a concept that has retreated to the
sands with the desert-folk.

FROM 'A REACH HISTORY' BY GAERVIN JUBB

THE MOON MADE A DARK rift of the river. The Ashti was now some distance away, and the land had become uneven and rocky. Dunes and stretches of sand curved in strange, gigantic whorls. Some looked like gurning faces, twisted by hate or horror. Others were like whirlpools waiting to swallow an unwary traveller. The moon painted everything a silvery grey. No colour had survived the day, only the faint glow of the golden city lights in the far distance, and several campfires burning amidst the wastes.

Brazen as any bandit party armed to the teeth and running on revenge, the Ghouls had set three fires to light their camp that night, gathered around a small outcrop of rocks and skinny dunes.

Nilith shaded her eyes, blocking out the glare of the huge moon. It was almost full tonight, like a bone saucer. Nilith stared only at the camp, trying to gauge numbers, patterns, or weaknesses. Occasionally, the night breeze would bring her a cackle or a scream, cowing the noises of desert creatures.

'You can't be serious,' Ghyrab said again, his mantra for the evening. 'You, against all of them?'

'Deadly serious. Farazar could be down there, prime for the binding at the next town. I can't let that happen. Besides,' she said, patting her neck, 'that Krona bitch stole a copper coin from me. I want it back.'

'You're mad. You're just one person. You won't catch me 'elping you.'

'You're no help to me anyway, old man. Not in your condition.'

It was true: the bargeman was of little use. His wounds were keeping him from anything but a shambling waddle. His back was as bent as a fishhook. He was currently propped up against a rock, halfway through eating a gritapple he had found in the oasis.

Anoish was sprightly at least. His days on the barge had clearly made him miss the desert sand, and even though plenty had passed under him since losing Farazar, he seemed eager for more. It was a shame the bright moonlight made him so easy to see coming.

Nilith laid out her plan for Ghyrab, to see if that would shut him up. 'I'll wait until they've drunk themselves into a stupor, as they did in the crater. Then I'll use the dunes to sneak in and quietly take down the lookouts. I'll fetch Farazar if he's there, then slit Krona's throat, torch the camp, and send the rest packing off into the night.'

'You're still just you.'

'Just me will have to be good enough.' She patted the golden scimitar she'd taken from the dead Ghoul. 'Won't it, horse?'

Anoish cocked his head and drummed his hooves. The horse was brighter than a sunray; he knew what was going on. She wasn't surprised when he stood up with her.

'Not tonight, Anoish, but I'll be back. Then we'll ride all night, I promise. For now, you stay with this old coin-purse.'

'Less of the "old", Majesty,' grumbled the bargeman.

'Look after my horse.'

Without waiting for his reply, encouraging, doubtful or otherwise, Nilith stepped over the lip of the ridge, and slid down onto the swirling duneplain.

The spiralling banks of sand made her path weave back and forth. It made the going slow, and if she measured the stars right, it took an hour to make it to the outskirts of the Ghouls' camp. Every step was measured, every breath controlled. She barely blinked, constantly looking out for shadows, or the dreaded purple glow of a dunewyrm's dangling lure. The Duneplains were full of the fearsome creatures.

Nilith settled down behind a dune shaped like a goatherd's crook.

In its curve, a watchman sat rubbing his shoulders against the cold. The noises of laughter and revelry that had led her across the plain had died away to a muttered conversation.

She crept along the crook, keeping herself low and her sword down lest it shine. As her free hand plunged into the sand, she felt a ridge beneath her, like an armoured plate. The lip that poked into the air was black against the grey sand. Nilith paused to trace its jagged edges, rough like a beetle's hide, though it was too big for even the largest of riding insects. It must have been a sunken boulder. She ignored it and moved on, honing in on the heavy snuffling of the Ghoul watchman.

Nilith desperately longed for a cloud or two. The moon cast her a clear shadow, though one that fortunately fell away from the direction of the camp. She pressed herself against the lip of the dune, barely a lunge from the guard, and stilled her heart. Peeking over the sand, she studied the fires of the camp. Four tents squatted at the edges of their glow. Between them was a crag of rock with a wide basin of blackened stone at its base.

Her heart forewent a beat.

A Nyxwell.

She cursed beneath her breath, reaching up to tug at her hair. These wild, untended springs were rare. If Farazar had been captured, they could have already bound him, and that ruined everything she had fought for. Nilith refused to let that possibility distract her. She tucked her knees into her chest, ready to pounce.

Pounce she did. With a move akin to a starving panther, she jumped straight over the lip of the dune and down onto the man. He turned in his last moment, gawping, but her scimitar had speared his windpipe. Not a gurgle came from his lips. The blade had cut into his spine, and his carcass sagged to the ground.

Nilith crouched to take his long knife, the kind made for throwing.

She ripped a length of fabric from his dirty shirt and pulled out the pouch from around her neck. It had dried out since her dousing in the river, and made a good stand-in for her coin until now.

With much care, she poured out a hefty pinch of Old Fen's black powder. Maybe a third of it went into the strip before she bagged it up and slid it into her pocket. She kept the pouch around her neck, hidden under her tunic.

When she was ready, she pushed out along the edge of the camp, towards the next Ghoul: a yawning woman holding a triggerbow, barely wider than the span of her hand. Nilith slit her throat before she knew she had company. She caught the bow as the woman fell dead. One bolt was all it held, but it still meant an easily-made corpse, and that was worth it.

With half the camp unguarded, Nilith crept closer to the fires, where handfuls of Ghouls lay about, like flies on a cold windowsill. Half of them snored, the other half lolled about like fattened hogs, still swigging determinedly from flagons or skins, mumbling the occasional wisecrack or nugget of drunken wisdom. No ghosts could be seen amongst them. No Farazar.

The tent listed at a violent angle. A slight scratching noise was coming from within. Nilith used the sword to poke aside its fabric, and inside she found a half-naked man, his back slick with sweat, gyrating away against another half-stripped body, face down in the sand. Whoever they were, they were not putting up much of a fight. Another limp form lay in the corner, blond hair painted orange with blood and grit. Nilith pulled away, but not before the Ghoul spoke.

'In a bit! Leave a man to fuck in peace!'

Something in his tone reminded Nilith of a rat-faced man and groping hands. Without a second thought, she pushed into the tent and drove her sword under the Ghoul's armpit. Coughing blood, he wriggled off the blade and crumpled by the side of his victim, a young man with pale skin. Nilith brandished the triggerbow while she tugged at the young man's arm, trying to wake him. The skin was colder than it ought to have been, limp as a clubbed fish. He was already dead.

Horrified, Nilith shrank away, only to come back swinging at the foul man lying blubbering and bleeding in the sand. She drove the sword deep into his groin, and with a twist, she spilled his insides. Such creatures didn't deserve to die swiftly.

The outside air tasted sweet after the vileness of the tent, and with a dizzy head Nilith crept on to the next. This one contained something just as loathsome, though this one was fast asleep, lying on her back while her chest lazily rose and fell. Krona still wore her patchwork mail even while she slept.

Though it was a struggle to tear herself away, Nilith let her sleep, slipping away to check on the last tent and the Nyxwell before wetting her sword once more. Farazar wasn't there, and the dead emperor was more important than her revenge, as sweet as it might be.

She ducked under the next flap to find two sleeping Ghouls, naked as babes but filthy with dust and blood. An empty wineskin lay between them. Still no Farazar.

Nilith dispensed with all creeping as she rushed to the well. She heard no trickle of water. The Nyxwell had no shimmer of moonlight to it. When she pressed her fingers to its stone pan, she found it drier than desert bones. It seemed the rich men of the White Hell had been right: there was a Nyxwater drought. Despite how unusual that was, the relief sent her sprawling. Nilith refused to believe Krona would have sent a sellable soul to the void in spite. *Not even to get to me.* She whispered that to herself as she snuck back to the bitch's tent.

Nilith took a stance by Krona's neck, scimitar and knife hovering ready as she stared down at the twisted scarring of the woman's face.

The eye was gone, now just a white smear bleeding into the crisscross of char-marks and raw flesh. A portion of the wound had healed since Abatwe, perhaps through Nyxwater and a ghost's touch. The rest looked far uglier: rot had spread into the veins around the wound, web-like and the colour of coal. There was a musty smell around the Ghoul, and not from lack of washing. Nilith wondered how long it would be before the decay claimed her. Nilith gritted her teeth. Even one more day alive would have been much more than Krona deserved.

Beside the Ghoul's head, half-buried in the sand, was a copper coin on a leather string. Eyes wide, Nilith grabbed it, holding it tight against the handle of her knife and feeling the cold metal dig into her palm. It was a relief to reclaim it, and she quickly looped it around her neck, letting it hang next to the powder. Though it was just a simple copper coin, it was worth more than that to Nilith. After the long weeks in the desert, it had become the symbol of her struggle. The embodiment of her goal. It was the would-be half-coin that would change her life.

Taking a deep breath, Nilith raised her blades for the kill. As she did so, a drip of Ghoul's blood escaped the sword's tip, landing on the good side of Krona's cheek. The bitch's eyes snapped open, and seeing the resolute face hanging above her, she flung herself sideways.

Nilith stabbed down as fast as she could, nicking the side of Krona's unprotected neck before she could escape from her bedroll. In the monochrome of night, a spurt of blood stained the sand a dark grey. Again and again Nilith stabbed, but her blades met only sand and air. Before Nilith could catch her, Krona was up and ripping aside the tent flap so she could fight in the open, where she was at her most dangerous.

Nilith ducked under the canvas and dashed for the nearest fire. Krona came barrelling after her, one hand clamped to her neck and the other clenched in a fist. Her wordless, enraged screeching began to rouse the camp, but not fast enough. Many were still mid-yawn or blinking goggle-eyed as Nilith's blade slashed their throats. She sprinted past the drunkards and their fire, tossing the bundle of Old Fen's powder into the flames as she did so.

Despite flinging herself to the sand like a mouldy sack of flour, nothing happened. She threw a wild look behind her, seeing no pop. No fizzle. Only Krona's grinning face, smeared in blood.

Just as Nilith was about to curse Fen for being nothing but a trickster, the powder caught.

CRACKOOOM!

The campfire exploded in a mushroom-shaped cloud of white and yellow flame. Screams and a piercing ringing filled the night air. Pale smoke billowed upwards as the fire died away.

Half-blinded by falling cinders but grinning all the same, Nilith took a stand halfway up the nearest dune and raised a fist for Old Fen.

The force had knocked Krona to her knees, but only momentarily. Though her hair and armour smoked, she kept on coming, tree-trunk legs pummelling the sand. Bloody spittle flew with each raging grunt. Nilith raised her triggerbow, and the bolt struck Krona in the shoulder. It barely made her stumble. The woman snapped the shaft from her skin and contemptuously tossed it to the sand.

'You came to me in the end, eh?' she called up the dune, as she put bare feet to its slope. Her words were as malformed as her lips. Behind her, the remaining Ghouls were hauling themselves up and forming a pack. 'Thought you might, somehow. You knew I wouldn't stop, see? So you had to come finish it for yourself. And here you are, eh? Well, that proved fuckin' successful, didn't it? Ready to die, eh?'

Nilith was on the cusp of threatening to ruin the other side of Krona's face when the sand beneath her began to quiver. With a lurch of her stomach, she felt the dune shift to the side. The grains around her boots danced away to reveal the ridges of a thick black carapace.

Nilith dropped to her knees, hugging the edges of the shell as Krona tumbled from its side with a curse. Two whip-like antennae rose from the sand, each sporting a glowing purple tip. A low clicking began to rise, like clockwork being wound.

Up went the frenzied cry of 'Dunewyrm!' from the campfires. In the desert, few words had the power to chill a person. That just so happened to be one of them.

Eyes so wide they hurt her cheeks, Nilith watched the many legs unfolding, and the sand scattering from the creature's sides in clouds. Five, ten, twenty, thirty feet of carapace was revealed, black as sin and solid as stone. The plates clanked noisily as ripples ran through its hide. A hissing joined the hum, as if it were some machine of steam. The wyrm's head emerged from the sand. Black spines ringed its face; a horrifying crown to the gnashing, violet mandibles. Its antennae shivered as it let loose a deafening, burbling roar.

Nilith knew then it was too late to run. Instead, she wedged her sword's hilt under the dunewyrm's armour and hung on for all she was worth – not a moment too soon. The monster lurched forwards, travelling in one effortless surge. No canter or gallop, just speed and hungry intent. The rumble of its claws striking the sand drowned out the cries. Nilith had thought these creatures close to myth two moments ago. Now she was riding one.

The wyrm reared up over the nearest Ghoul. Noxious dribble spewed into the man's eyes, and he managed only a short scream before the beast's disjointed jaws enveloped him. The man's armour split under three quick bites, and then he was swallowed whole. Nilith pressed herself close to the carapace, feeling the undulations pass beneath her as the creature's gullet went to work.

A spear smashed into the wyrm's carapace a yard from her hand. It barely punctured the shell, and its owner stared for a moment, confused and disheartened, before the dunewyrm's spiked tail spread him across the sand like jam across grey toast.

Nilith could do nothing but cling on and pray to any god who was listening that the creature would be full by the time she was shaken free. For the moment, at least, she could view the carnage from a relatively safe – if not bizarre – position. The wyrm had no care for the Ghouls, batting aside, crushing or swatting aside anybody who dared to come close or couldn't run fast enough. That meant pretty much the entire band.

Nilith watched as the brutal vengeance was doled out: for her, for the bodies in the tent, and for however many others these bandits had wronged. It didn't matter that the revenge wasn't being delivered by her hands; just that the Ghouls received it. After all, her hands couldn't rip people in two.

As the wyrm paused briefly to look around for something else to gobble, a sword came swinging towards Nilith. She moved her leg just in time to avoid having it hacked off. The blade dug deep between the carapace instead, with Krona snarling on the other end of it. The dunewyrm screeched, thrashing its tail. Nilith hung on dearly as Krona was knocked flat.

Though it cut deep into her palms, Nilith grabbed the throwing knife and hurled it at the vile woman. To her delight, it skewered Krona through the bicep, and the Ghoul leader wailed as she realised she was momentarily pinned to the sand.

Krona gave Nilith a stare so full of hate, the empress felt her skin prickle. But Krona's cries had attracted the attention of the dunewyrm. The creature turned on her, jaws gnashing, eager to finish the job Nilith had started.

'No!' Krona's scream was cut short as everything above her chest was turned to mush with fierce snaps of razored mandibles.

Nilith was considering sliding off the beast and running for the nearest dune when another screech stopped her dead. Another monstrous shape surged out of the darkness, antennae aglow, jaws splayed and quivering. Nilith immediately realised what was happening; she had seen wolves fight over a deer carcass many times before. Her fear increased to mortal dread.

The newcomer wyrm charged straight for the first. Nilith tensed every muscle as they collided with ear-splitting screeches. Banks of legs clawed and clawed until they were entangled, and their mouths and front legs grappled. Their antennae whipped back and forth, cutting red stripes on Nilith's forearms.

Noticing its opponent had a morsel clinging to its back, the second dunewyrm reared up to snap at Nilith. It was time to let go, she decided. It was either that or lose an arm. As the wyrm's jaws opened up, looking like the ugliest orchid imaginable, Nilith wrenched the scimitar from the carapace and tumbled. Hot, stinking breath was all that caught her. The jaws snapped mere inches from her face, spraying her with foul green dribble.

A feverish glance over her shoulder told her the two wyrms were entangled in a writhing knot. Their armoured forms crashed about the camp, flattening anything that wasn't already dead.

Nilith ran as fast as her tired legs would carry her. She wasn't about to hang around to watch the monsters fight. Krona was dead, and that was half of what she had wanted from the evening. A small corner of the desert had been cleaned of its filth tonight. A very small corner, but it was something.

Nilith looked down at her hands and found them slick with snot-green wyrm saliva. She could feel it burning, as if the sun shone on it. She quickly wiped her face with her tunic, leaving red, patchy skin behind. She ignored the pain, clenched her fists and continued to flee.

With every turn, Nilith dreaded seeing purple lights rising into the night to lure her in. She expected every dune to explode in a shower of sand, and snapping jaws to come crashing down. The fear kept her insides tight as a triggerbow string, and her feet moving.

Perhaps her luck was strong that night, or maybe the commotion of the fight in the camp was a good distraction. In either case, not one dune moved during her mad dash back to the ridge. Still, she didn't stop until she had climbed it.

Nilith flopped to the dirt like a gutted fish onto a cutting board. She stared up at the speckled sky with its saucer moon, and chased her breath. She clutched the copper coin to her bosom.

Ghyrab came into view between the stars. 'You hurt?'

'Somewhat.'

'That bitch dead?'

'Very.'

'And the rest?'

'Probably all the same by now.'

'We heard a bang, and screams...'

Nilith rolled to pat Anoish on the rump. The horse was pretending to sleep. She saw the slits of his black eyes.

'Dunewyrms. Two of them. Somehow, I think they saved me.'

'This is why I stick to the river. Ain't no bloody centipede dragons in the river.' Ghyrab snorted, going back to his curled-up state against the black stone. 'And your ghost?'

'Gone. Still on the river, maybe,' Nilith muttered, knowing the bargeman was already asleep. She could give him an hour, at least.

Nilith positioned herself so she could watch the lights die on the duneplain. The dying fires quivered as large shapes moved across them. One by one, the flames surrendered to the cold, and left the job of il-lumination to the moon and stars. Not a single smudge of blue could be seen; just lingering purple lights, roaming to and fro.

Nilith sighed to herself. 'We'll find him. I have no choice.'

———————◆———————

NO EMPEROR SHOULD HAVE TO drag any body across a desert, never mind his own. It was an outrage. An injustice of the highest level. A foul crime against the glory of the Arctian royalty.

It was the toil of it, more than anything. The only manual labour Farazar Talin Renala the Eighteenth had done in the last few years was raising wine to his lips and rutting with Belish concubines. He'd outdone a decade in a mere day of pulling his remains across the ever-undulating Duneplains. There was no sweat, of course, no strained muscles, not even a breath to gasp for. It was purely a mental strain. Though his hands did the gripping, his arms the hauling, it was his head that hurt from the constant tensing.

The river had failed him earlier that day, as had the barge, which had got something stuck around its steering pole and nosed into the shallows. Even if Farazar hadn't been lacking in naval skills, the river had begun to widen and wallow, curving eastward for Araxes' farther-flung districts. Farazar was left with no choice but to strike out toward the city on foot.

He spared a moment to stare at her again, blazing bright in the morning sun. White and yellow spires caught the daylight on their metal caps, spurs and crystal panes. A haze clung to the city, and in the desert heat, it seemed an anaemic brown hue. Farazar did not blame it on the pervasive dust, nor the spewing stacks of the docks and factory districts, but the morning mist from the Troublesome Sea.

Sea.

How he longed to see a sprawl of blue instead of puke-yellow and shit-brown rock. There was a reason his mighty city hugged the coast, and that was to be as far away from this sweltering, dusty arsehole of a landscape as possible. If he could have, Farazar would have ripped the whole city up and moved it to tropical Ede, or the Scatter Isles, where green things ruled over the land instead of the sun.

Even as he inwardly cursed it, the desert appeared to hear him. Sand scattered from the lip of a dune, showering the emperor and his body. He watched the grains fall through his glowing hands, slowing only momentarily, like pennies tumbling into a pool.

Farazar struck on, leaning against the weight of his baggage and the hot wind coming from the north. His borrowed, tattered smock helped somewhat, but he still felt hollow and nonexistent as the sand and air rushed through him.

His corpse seemed to gather weight with every mile. Perhaps it was the sand clinging to it, or the growing strain, but it slowed him to a crawl. The landscape did not help: the dunes had risen up in taller peaks and longer valleys, and their fine, wind-carved sands shifted even under his ghostly feet. On the steeper slopes, to go one step Farazar had to take three. At the very least, his body could slide down the other side and give him some rest. It wrinkled his lip to watch it, but the more time he spent as a shade, the more he saw the body more as meat rather than person. *My person.* Like every Arctian, he knew there was no way back from binding, but that didn't stop him longing for one. Such was the desperation of loss.

With the sun overhead and no shade in the gaps between dunes, Farazar baked. He was somewhat used to it – perhaps something residual from his life and his breeding – but with the added work, he felt thinner than gossamer. He felt as if his vapours were evaporating.

Onwards, he trudged, until the sun was halfway closer to the horizon and Araxes blushed a deep gold. He used it as a lure to keep his legs moving. Whenever he crested a high dune, he stared out to Araxes and traced the wandering lines of paths escaping from the Outsprawls.

Farazar stared north for some time, blue eyes sliding between the wash of white and yellow buildings and the glimmering city, wondering which held more hope for him. After the Duneplains, there was a hundred miles of crowded city before he reached the Cloudpiercer. The question was, how would he walk those miles? Would it be dragging a body behind him, or as a free shade? *The first dead emperor in history.*

If there was anything an Araxes royal had a deep affection for, it was to be the first to do something. A thousand years of stabbing others in the back meant an ever-churning royal line. A lot of firsts had already been claimed. Even names were unlikely to be original. Yet here Farazar was, with his murderer lost behind him and his body at his side; a position coveted by any slain ruler of the Arc. He looked to the Outsprawls once more, blue tongue emerging from blue lips. If a Nyxwell could be found there, he had a chance to do what no royal had yet managed: to rule from beyond the grave. And, even more deliciously, Nilith's plans would be foiled. All he had to do was bind himself before he was claimed, and make it back to the safety of the Core Districts. Then he would reign for a hundred years. Perhaps a thousand. He would crush Nilith's precious Krass, and claim the whole Reaches as his.

With a grin, Farazar leaned to spit on his promise, but was swiftly reminded of his inability to do so. Instead, he just made a strange, vaguely determined noise.

The noise had an echo. Then a puff of sand drew his eyes. Two sharp and twisted spikes rose above a dune to his left, each the length of an arm. Farazar fell protectively over his body as a black, shiny head with wiggling antennae and beady eyes emerged. Two simple legs, hooked at the end, flopped over the ridge and hauled the creature's body forwards. More dark carapace followed, huge jointed shoulders, and then an abdomen that dragged a rut in the sand.

The beetle burbled again, louder and more effusive. It seemed interested in the body under Farazar. However, it did not charge or muscle forwards as he expected, but sat upright, rearing at least eight feet tall, and tasted the air with the wiggling bits in its ugly face. There must have been a stench to the creature, but not one Farazar could smell.

'Away, beast! Not for you!' he yelled, finding his voice.

It warbled, but didn't move. Insects, unlike horses and other beasts, were not spooked by shades. Farazar recalled that after spending several minutes waggling his hands, trying to shoo it away. Even when he got close enough to punch it in the nose, or the beetle equivalent, it didn't rear or gnash at him. Instead it just warbled away until he was forced to assume the insect was mentally impeded, and left it alone.

Buoyed by purpose and with the outpost fixed in his mind, Farazar pulled his corpse down the slope of the dune. To his annoyance, the beetle followed, kicking sand at him with its spindly legs. Farazar wished he had something to poke its eyes with. He doubted his vaporous fingers would do a good job.

There was a moment when the creature looked close to tumbling on top of him, but it scrabbled to a halt disturbingly close to Farazar and immediately plopped itself down in the sand again. It seemed almost… apologetic. It was then that an idea came to him, but he shoved it away.

Kings did not ride beetles. Stallions or carriages, yes, but not beetles. Beetles were the steeds of desert scroungers and Outsprawlers, lowly traders and others who couldn't afford or steal good horseflesh. Insects were also unpredictable creatures, with an intelligence far below that of a horse, and a blank coldness only a fish could mimic.

This one looked docile enough, and irritatingly dutiful; the beetle followed like a hound no matter which direction Farazar walked in. Only once did it make a move on his corpse, but it just tripped instead.

Farazar saw then the strange bend in one of its legs. It had been lamed in the past.

'Go away! Back to your master! Or family! Or nest, or what have you!'

No amount of shouting seemed to dissuade the beetle. When Farazar resorted to kicking sand back at it, it would retreat a little, but then come clomping back. He tried some running, using the slope to his advantage. When he finally stopped at the base of the next dune, the beetle was right there behind him, and Farazar the weaker for it.

'Fucking insect,' he cursed, looking to the blue above for patience. Then, with a sigh, he gave in to his idea.

Dragging the body in a wide arc around to the beetle's rump, Farazar slung the rope of his corpse around a horn-like protrusion on the creature's back. His clumsy fingers worked a knot that would have made a sailor weep. All the while, the beetle stayed put. Whether that was because it was dumb or well trained, Farazar didn't know. It muttered away happily through its ugly jaws.

Farazar kept the tail of the rope in his hands, and he flicked it like a whip against the gleaming carapace. The beetle jerked forwards, much to his satisfaction. Walking on beside it, he tugged on the rope, and lo and behold, the creature followed dutifully.

He could have laughed at the joke of it all. It certainly sounded like a joke: an emperor, a corpse and a beetle walking across the Dune-plains. Yet no smile curled his lips. No chuckle came from his throat. For it was he who was the joke. He was the punchline. Here he was, Emperor Farazar Talin Renala the Eighteenth, dragging his own body across a desert.

His growling filled the silence.

CHAPTER 15
DAMNED FATES

Beer is the murderer of all good intentions.

WORDS OF THE PHILOSOPHER THEMETH

I FELT WRETCHED. MORE DRAINED THAN I had ever been in life. I felt hollower than any cloud of vapour should. It was small comfort that I had come to my senses, and realised the error of my self-indulgence.

Four times I had tried to vacate my spot, only to stagger so much I decided the attention wouldn't be worth it, and went back to 'rest' in my hollow.

The first and second attempts were feeble efforts that took me halfway down the alley and back.

The third time, a blind old woman had come out to offer me tea, not realising I was a ghost. The tea had looked more like whale-oil to me, so I declined, and she went back to banging and crashing about her tiny hovel.

On the fifth attempt, with Pointy offering meagre encouragement, I finally made it to the street. I say encouragement. It was more mockery than anything. He still preferred to sulk, and so did I. It was all I felt good for that day.

Speaking of days, one had already passed me by. The second was gradually slipping into evening. I would soon be stuck in the night once more.

I aimed high, managing to climb a zig-zag of steps onto a flat roof so I could look above the endless warehouses. My eyes roved over the fanged horizon, full of towers large and small, curved and twisting. Some were needle sharp, pillars for the sky, others fat and bulging with questionable renovations.

I looked for one as sleek as Horix's. It was a sight I had first fixed in my mind while traipsing home from Vex's shopping challenge. It was like finding a needle in a pile of needles, and it must have taken me an hour to spot it. When I did, I stumbled over the rooftops like a bow-legged street urchin, aiming for the nearest washing line. After absconding with a set of trews tied with rope and a tunic I could charcoal a black feather onto, I went back to the boardwalk and set my feet to a new path. *West.*

'Back to the Widow we go,' I muttered.

'You've come to your senses then, I see,' Pointy replied some dozen busy streets later. His voice echoed around my head, even though I had no skull. I looked down at his obsidian pommel, finding his carved face a flat line of discontent. I held my hand over it, as if to hide from his disapproval, and saw my vapours swirling, as if trying to reach his grip. I quickly withdrew.

'And you've found your voice at last,' I said.

'Your foolishness made me doubt your sanity, never mind your senses. I've hung from the hips of madmen before, and I refuse to do so again.'

Pointy had clearly been working on those words for some time, so I gave him his due. Grudgingly, of course. 'I'm not mad. Just desperate. There is but a fraction of a line between them.'

'Hmm. And what happened to your dreams of a glorious final few weeks? Of taking another body for a ride until the widow decides to melt your half-coin?'

'Choices, sword. I have few.' The realisation had come to me like a headache after a night of hard drinking. As always in Araxes, it came down to who held my half-coin. 'Running won't solve anything. Horix may be my master, hold my coin, and be as untrustworthy as every other beating heart in this city, but she's the closest thing I have to freedom. At least she doesn't keep me in a cupboard or make me fight, and no matter what that old bitch has planned for me, I have my freedom in writing, hidden away in an alcove in her tower. And if not, then now I have the power to take my coin from her. I'll take my chances.'

'What about your would-be employer, this Etane and the empress-in-waiting?'

'No. A dead end, pardon the pun. What is it they say? Better the daemon you know. The empress-in-waiting would destroy me when she was done with me.'

'And what about the Cult you were so interested in?'

The thought had crossed my mind after learning they preached about the betterment of ghosts, but Araxes' hatred against them was far too prevalent to be just a misunderstanding. I had no trust in them, either. The call of the dead gods crossed my mind again, rearing like an errant cobra as always. I stamped it out, unwilling to face the guilt of doing nothing.

'If Horix found out I'd gone to the Cult, she'd melt my coin quicker than a goose can shit,' I asserted. Until I had my half-coin in my hand, that was all that mattered. I could haunt the fuck out of the Cult then, if I fancied it. 'Why are you so interested in running all of a sudden?'

Pointy sighed. *'It came to me this morning. The seventh Tenet. Shades keep no property. The widow won't let you have a sword.'*

I growled, drawing a look from a fellow ghost in the street. 'All you have for me are problems, sword. Besides, I'm counting on Horix to owe me a favour.'

Pointy's voice trembled, though from what, I didn't know. *'Would you gamble your own soul in such a way?'*

'Yes.' It was a half-lie. I could have argued I was doing the same thing, but I had the power of haunting, and the fact that Horix needed me. I wagered she had little use for a talking sword that would no doubt irritate her to the point of smelting within a week.

'I don't believe you.'

'And that's your choice,' I reminded him. Feeling a new kind of wretched, I added, 'We can say you're a gift from Busk's household. I'd recommend maybe not talking, however.'

'I doubt I'll have much more to say to her than I do to you.'

I shrugged, tugging his hilt further around my backside. 'Fine,' I said. 'Be the inanimate, unfeeling object you are. You wanted to come along, not I.'

The sword said no more, and left me to my journey.

I wound my way on a diagonal path through the central districts and into the main core of Araxes, where the daylight became scant between the long and crowded shadows of towers. I kept my eyes fixed on Horix's spire, to the southern edge of Araxes' centre.

My pace quickened with every flagstone I put beneath me. I watched the lights of the widow's home twinkle as though I were a ship and she was a port. Though no storm chased me, I moved like there was, like a child running home across the steppes, with rain lashing their back. I was eager for the safety of a tower, and to hold my writ of freedom in my glowing hands.

Horix would no doubt be suspicious of my escape, and so I started to work up a story in my mind. So wrapped up in fiction was I that I failed to see there was indeed a storm on my heel: one in the form of a very large ghost clad in polished steel plate.

It was not until I stepped into the road to avoid the crowds of a bazaar and saw my path blocked by a sweating Ani Jexebel that I realised. She was staring directly at me. I turned away, and spotted Danib behind me, standing still amongst the crowds like a rock in the centre of a rushing river.

I could have torn my stolen clothes from my vapours. I was not three streets from the widow's tower, and here I was, yet again the object of somebody's greed. And twice now it had been Temsa's.

'I don't believe it!' I yelled at them, throwing my hands to the sky. 'Is he here? Come to fetch me himself? Or has he sent you two idiots to do his dirty work for him?'

Nobody in the street paid any attention to my cries. One or two ghosts gave me glances as they quickly shimmied past. Others did their best to ignore me. I strangled the air. *This fucking city!*

I itched to run, looking to a side street that ran off between two blocks of whitewashed buildings. Maybe I could have haunted a passerby and melted into the crowds. I still felt drained by my last attempt, but I had to try.

But as my feet started moving, I saw him. Tor Temsa stood in my path beneath the shade of an umbrella, wearing a leopard-skin coat trimmed with feathers, smiling his gold-specked smile and wagging a cautionary finger.

What else is there to do but smile? I asked myself, and found no answer. So I smiled; at him, at Jexebel, at his big fucker of a ghost, at the whole fucking mess of a situation.

If Temsa was confused by my boldness, he didn't show it. His guards swarmed around us until they formed a ring about their master and me. I felt Danib's hand alight on my shoulder, his giant gauntlet warm compared to my vapour. I met his eyes, shining from the gap in his barbute helmet, as he laid claim to my sword. I heard Pointy's disappointed hissing in the back of my head.

'My, my. Caltro Basalt. Or Jerub, wasn't it? It's a pleasure to see you once more,' said Temsa, eyeing my slashed throat.

'And what do you want with me?' I asked, wondering how he knew my real name. It didn't bode well.

The stunted gargoyle of a man chuckled. 'Why, *you*, of course. I've learned a great many things about you since I sold you at market.' He produced a familiar piece of wax from his pocket. A black seal of daggers and desert roses. *My invitation.*

The puzzle pieces slid into place. 'You came to Busk's for me that day, didn't you? He told you all about me.'

'Astute, for a half-life,' said Temsa. 'Seeing as you'd escaped, I thought the old crone already had you back in her tower. Luckily for me, you're apparently a dawdler, but it makes life much easier for me.'

'I should have kept you waiting longer.'

Temsa bowed his head. 'Patience leads to profit, or so the Chamber of Trade's motto goes.'

I growled. 'I'll give that limp cock a piece of my mind if I ever see him again.'

'Busk?' Temsa looked around, chuckling. 'Oh, Busk is dead, Caltro. Ani here saw to that. I wouldn't worry yourself.'

The big woman beside me leered, and I shook my head at her.

'No surprise there. You can go fuck yourself if you think I'm thanking you, Temsa.'

'No thanks necessary, Caltro. You just have to come along quietly.'

Although I hated them all at that moment, I also pitied them. They didn't know what they were bringing into their fold, what I could do with a moment alone with them. It was poor consolation, but it was the only reason I was able to smile and open my arms wide.

Temsa winked as Jexebel looped a copper-thread rope about my neck. 'Oh, it's *Tor* Temsa now. And no thanks needed, Caltro. You'll repay me very soon.'

'Allow me to guess: it has something to do with locks and doors.'

'Astute indeed. This city seems to have given you an edge since last we met. Found yourself a sword too, I see.'

Pointy sighed in my head. '*Wonderful.*'

I let Danib and Jexebel push me away in the opposite direction of the widow's tower. I longed to fly at the nearest un-coppered body and haunt my way to freedom again. I doubted I could have achieved it, though, not with copper looped around my wounded neck. And so I held myself back. Instead, I met Temsa's curious gaze and returned his wink.

'A lot has happened since you sold me, Temsa. A lot indeed.'

———————◆———————

A NIGHT AND A DAY, and I'd yet to see anything but burlap. Despite my repeated requests, curses, and eventual attempts to remove it myself, the sack encasing my head had stayed on. I was left to mutter to myself, pondering which glorious moron it was that had started the trend of leaving prisoners to stew like old legs of mutton.

When the door to my room finally swung open, hands plucked me from my chair, hustled me a short distance, and placed me down in another chair. I had no idea where. Through the sack, the only details I could discern were that this room had more light in it and thicker, cloying air. It was irritating how perceptive you became of changes to the air when you were pretty much comprised of the stuff.

The hands withdrew, and I was left to look around at the shadows and shapes between the crisscross sacking. I felt eyes upon me. Somebody sighed in my head, like wind moaning behind a thick windowpane. Pointy was here.

A fellow who finds his head wrapped in sacking must rely on methods other than facial expressions to communicate his emotions. No amount of scowling conveyed my displeasure and outrage accurately enough. I tried speaking, but the thick burlap muffled me. I had to resort to crossing and recrossing my arms, drumming my fingers, and a good deal of fist-clenching.

It was some time before my display had any effect. A familiar smoke-aged voice cut through the silence.

'De-sack the shade, will you?'

The burlap was lifted from my head, and I blinked in the hazy shafts of light penetrating the shutters. Sitting behind an expansive desk, wreathed in wobbly halos of smoke, was Temsa. He was dressed in emerald silks from head to toe. His fingers were so encrusted with rings he could have been wearing gold and gem gauntlets. At my side stood the ubiquitous Jexebel. I noticed the blue glow about my feet and felt the cold of the monstrous shade behind me. No others stood in the dingy office. If I strained my ears, I could catch the clink of bottles and tankards below us. We were in Temsa's tavern.

'Been too busy to tend to your guests, have you? I've been waiting some time,' I muttered. All the smart words and insults I'd rehearsed in the privacy of countless nights faded now that I sat in front of him.

'I have, in fact. My third Weighing, if you must know. Tor Busk had many a half-coin stashed away, and our years of business dealings mean that in his death, he owes everything to me,' the man gloated.

'Convenient, that.'

Jexebel whacked me around the back of the head with the copper haft of her axe.

'Now, now.' Temsa held up his hands. One held a smouldering pipe. 'As Caltro said, he is our guest, not our prisoner.'

I nodded to the discarded sack. 'I think we disagree on the definition of "prisoner," Temsa.'

He cut straight to the point. 'I've met many like you in my time, Caltro Basalt. You think a smart mouth is a shield, and you hide behind it. The problem with men – half-lives – like you is that you don't know when to stop hiding. Take a peek, Caltro. Put down the shield. You might find you can profit if only you play along for a change.'

'Profit? According to the Tenets, a bound ghost can't earn any profit.'

'What are rules, if not just words scratched on papyrus by those seeking to feel better about themselves?'

Lately, I'd had enough of windbags spewing reasons and stories to justify their evils. I crossed my arms once more and waited patiently for the point.

'I imagine you want your freedom, hm?' Temsa asked.

'How ever did you guess? I must be the only ghost in the city who wants such a thing.' He stared at me with the eyes of a dead toad. My anger began to rise. 'I want back the life that *you* stole from me!'

Temsa juggled his hands like the pans of a scale, as nonchalant as if he were testing the ripeness of fruit at a bazaar. 'Some things that are taken can't be returned. Short of forcing the sun to move backwards, freedom sounds a bit more achievable, doesn't it? I hear indenturement is tough. Especially under an old prune like Widow Horix, or Busk.'

'Tough is one way to describe it.'

Temsa rubbed his goatee, playing the magnanimous noble. 'Well, Caltro, I can provide you such freedom.'

'No, you can't. You don't have my half-coin.'

Temsa winked. 'But I shall. And soon.'

For a short man, the fetid twat had set his sights high. I couldn't decide whether that worried or impressed me. I watched him reach for a pipe and light it with a taper. 'You'd take on the widow, just for the half-coin of a humble locksmith?'

The seal I'd found on my doorstep all those months ago slid across the desk towards me. 'You're too modest, Caltro. Your reputation crosses seas, man! You and I both know you were summoned by the empress-in-waiting herself. Such a man must be a worthy locksmith indeed. Busk hadn't a clue, and yet he saw fit to tussle with the widow for you. She hasn't broken your coin yet, so she must see some worth in you. Besides, I have been busy, Caltro. As of this morning Weighing, I am a tor of some substantial wealth. An equal rival to Horix, perhaps. You haven't been the only one working hard.' He paused, and I could see his words brought him satisfaction. He entwined his ring-covered fingers to hide his grin. 'But in all honesty, I would be knocking on her door even if you had never set foot in Araxes. That old bitch and her tower full of half-coins have been in my thoughts for weeks now.'

I waited for him to go on, wondering why I felt a measure of anger at his plans to murder the widow. Allegiance had always been a stranger to me, and yet here I was, extending a hand towards it.

'I see you've learned the value of silence since you were last in the Slab. You shouted from the cells for days, if I remember rightly. I see now you're a plain man, so I'll speak plainly. You open what I tell you to open, do a good job, and when I take Horix, you shall have your half-coin and your freedom. After that, you may choose to work with me as a free shade. Earn some profit, perhaps. Turn this trip into something other than a complete loss.'

He had me there. My ears were well and truly pricked. 'Work *with* you, or *for* you?'

Temsa leaned forwards, digging elbows into the desk. The pipe-bowl glowed as he puffed. 'That would be up to you.'

I sighed, knowing the next question was a pointless one, but habit drove me to speak. 'And if I refuse?'

'You can go back into that sack until you change your mind.'

'That's it? No threats? No beatings?'

Temsa looked between Jexebel and Danib, the inklings of a grin on his face. 'Would you prefer that?'

'No. I've simply grown accustomed to a certain way of doing business in Araxes,' I said with an exhale. 'But if you think I will be a lackey for the man who murdered and enslaved me then you are sorely mistaken, Boran Temsa, or mad from the sun.'

'Very well. The sack it is.' There came a grunt from the big shade behind me as Temsa arose. 'Your choice, Caltro. In any case, I'll be taking your half-coin from Horix. Shame. I would have let you take it from her yourself, too, if only to see the look on that old cunt's face.'

He paused at my side and pulled several pieces of metal and two springs from his pocket. *The rest of my tools.* Even the pieces Busk had were there.

'These change your mind?' he asked.

The strange loyalty to Horix gripped me again. I wondered if it was some magic of the binding spell and the half-coin, and her ownership of me. Or was it more than that? A sense of honour? I could have laughed. I decided it was less: the only allegiance I held was to myself. Horix was just the better option. I bared my blue teeth.

'You're a soultrader. No stranger to the markets, right? Here's an offer for you. Give me the sword you took,' I bartered, 'and then I'll help you.'

'*Caltro...*' said Pointy's voice, faint between my thoughts.

'Those are not the terms.'

'Well, I'm changing them.'

Temsa managed to squeeze words between his chuckles. Jexebel was baring an ugly row of teeth. 'Ridiculous! I'm not giving a bound shade a sword. As it was Busk's, it now belongs to me.'

'No deal, then,' I told him.

'Counter offer.' Temsa bent closer to me, lighting his face up with my cold glow. 'When you have your half-coin, you can have that sword. As a gift for your hard work.'

I couldn't help but push him. 'You going to wrap it for me?'

'Take some time to think about it, Caltro,' he replied with a tut.

Danib hauled me up with no more effort than it cost Temsa to lift his pipe. His thick vapours and steel plate pinned my arms and pointed me at the door.

'I shall call for you shortly,' Temsa shouted after me.

The ghost muscled me downstairs and into a large room I hadn't seen before. It was sparse, holding nothing more than a writing desk, chair and cot, but it was better than a sack or wardrobe. Danib shoved me inwards and promptly locked the door. I pressed against it, but the copper in its metal nipped my hands.

I looked around my meagre surroundings and abruptly realised this was the first room I had been given since my murder. No alcove or storage for me this time. Whether it was a bribe or an insult in that I had no use for the cot, I found myself prodding at its straw-stuffed bedding.

A clatter drew my eyes to the small, barred window set into one wall. If I stood on the desk, I could stare into the street at ground level and admire the passing feet of the crowds, or the armoured cartwheels, or the hooves of horses and spines of insectile legs. I pressed myself closer, then yelped as the copper bars stung my nose.

By angling my head, I could see into the junction that the Rusty Slab occupied a thick chunk of. With one eye shut, I could stare along the flank of the tavern to its entrance. The press of bodies was thick, but between its ebb and flow, I spied the great lump of Jexebel standing guard in the sun. She held a hand over her eyes, beckoning to somebody. I pressed my face against the bars once more, ignoring the hiss against my vapours.

I caught a streak of red in the crowds: a figure with a hood pulled low, head bowed and walking straight for Jexebel. Before I saw them enter, a large shape stole them from view.

I heard a scrape of hooves and turned to find a plump and piebald cow sidling up to my window. Her breath was laboured, her eyes crossed and her knees shaking. Flies had already begun to gather about her foaming nostrils, as if sensing an end. I saw the great load on her back: wooden chests and blanket rolls piled high, all cocooned in rope. The knotted fibres had chafed the beast's belly to blood. The owner was berating her in some dialect I didn't understand. His switch scourged her black and white flanks.

With a great moan, the cow sought the comfort of the earth. As she collapsed with a thud, I was sprayed with sand and rank spittle. Fortunately, most of it passed right through me, though I couldn't say the same for the desk below.

I looked into her bulging chestnut eyes, buried beneath great swirling horns now wedged against the sandstone and the street. I saw a panic in them over the fight to get up or lie down. She stared at me through the bars, and I at her.

Several pairs of feet gathered around the cow's head, and some sort of argument ensued between the drovers. A honey-coloured boot jabbed her in one leg. A finger hooked inside her foaming mouth. The eyeball I stared at was opened wider by a dirty thumb.

The cow's breathing quickened in a last rally of life. She made a struggle to get up, but it finished her. A great, hot wheeze ruffled my vapours and her head thumped into the sand for the last time. She blinked at me, resigned now, as I heard the harsh sigh of a blade being drawn. It plunged into the back of the cow's skull, right behind the horns, and twisted with a crackle of bone. The beast twitched once before her tongue lolled out. Her stare had wandered, looking past me and into a void I knew all too well.

I recoiled as the cow's dark blood began to pool around my windowsill. One adventurous drip slipped over the wall and drew a straight line down the brick. I edged over to watch the men go on to argue over the luggage that was now strapped to a corpse.

The cow's body jiggled as they saw to the ropes, making her gasp in death with leftover wind. I wrinkled my lip.

'Caltro.'

I looked to the door at first, and then, as I realised, rolled my eyes back to the cow.

'Of course,' I said. Another visit was well overdue. 'Who are you this time?'

The beast's dead gaze swivelled to me. The rubbery lips barely moved as it talked. The tongue flicked around in the dust. Her breath was hot and laboured.

'Basht said she had doubts. And you have proven her right, dear.' The voice had the texture of the cow-blood: liquid, oleaginous, seeping into my ears.

'And you are?'

'If you must know, dear, I am Haphor, and you are wasting our time.'

'If you haven't noticed,' I said, gesturing to my new cell, 'time is all I have at the moment.'

'Even an immortal knows time is finite, Caltro. One shouldn't presume to know the universe when one hasn't seen more than a grain of it.'

There I was, being chastised by a dead cow. The corpse bucked again as the drovers cut its load free. The bulging eye blinked at me, waiting.

In recent days, I'd learned that there is a recalcitrant child we all keep hidden within ourselves, even into our elder years. The years never truly change us, nor evolve us. They merely wrap another skin around us and tell us the lie that we've grown.

'It's not my damn fault! You haven't told me anything meaningful about this flood I'm meant to stop. Or the Cult you and the rest of this city dislike so much. All you've done is give me some strange power and told me to get on with it. With what?! I'm just one ghost, and all recent events considered, a pretty shit one at that. What makes me so special that you continue to plague me?'

The cow sighed. Its breath was now colder than me. 'Sense is hard to make across such distance, such dimensions… through flesh. Even now, I am most likely confusing you.'

'Yes, but you're doing better than the cat.'

'I am stronger than my sister and more patient than all my brethren. Yet you are still wasting time.'

'So you said.'

'You had a chance and squandered it. The Cult are still working towards their goal, seeking to ruin what we built.'

'Why? How?'

'The why?' Haphor took a moment as the men pushed her bovine body further against the wall. Her white horns clanged against my bars. 'For our brother.'

'Sesh.'

'That's him, dear. The how… is difficult. The river you call Nyx is souring. It will flood the world. Turn it upside down. Life will become death. Only death. We gods are not dead, but we starve, Caltro. That is why we gave you the power, as you call it. Our gift. It is so you can fight for us.'

'What do you mean, "starve"?'

She took so long in answering, I thought the goddess had departed. When she did respond, her foaming lips managed to wobble slightly. The sandy tongue flicked at me. 'For every soul that passes the gates into *duat*, we live on, the same as you. The gates were closed the… how do you say… *day* Sesh killed the boatman and reversed the Nyx. The day we imprisoned him. So it has been since. It has choked us. Choked *duat*.'

Pointy's stories, spilled from the mouth of a dying cow. I felt Haphor's panic in my chest, and through some connection, the concentrated fear of her brethren beyond, in a place I couldn't begin to fathom. I thought of the crowded space standing before five faded stars, and finally understood its vastness.

Perhaps the Cult did seek to flip the world. Perhaps I had been called upon to finish some celestial battle, but as much as that awed me, it did not change Haphor's words.

'You *use* us?'

'Time is wasting, Caltro.'

I thought of the millions denied heaven, waiting and screaming in the dark, and why the gods wanted them. Not for the continuation of their creations' existence, but for their own survival. They, like the rest of us, had been sold a lie.

'We are nothing but fuel to you, are we? Sustenance.'

'Not fuel. Symbiotes.'

I had never heard such a word, but I doubted its definition would have satisfied me. I felt cheated somehow.

'Am I just a tool to you, as I am to all the rest?'

'As Horush would say, all men are tools in war.'

'Then why me? Why is this my fucking responsibility?'

Haphor twitched her head, making the nearby men yell in surprise. The one with the sword was already priming himself for another stab.

'Would you like me to say you're special, dear? That you're our chosen hero, destined to save this world?'

It would be nice.

She wheezed as the men came to prod at her again. 'I cannot. There are no heroes; only those who do their duty no matter the price. You aren't special; you simply died at the right time. A locksmith in a land of locks and doors sounded perfect. Even so, I knew you were a bad choice, and dear, so far you've proven me right. We gave you a gift, and you took it to the nearest tavern. Be selfish if you want. Drink and whore in borrowed bodies until the skies turn black and the sun bleeds. We have no more power to give to another. We cannot stop you, but you will suffer with the rest of us.'

In came the knife again, into a spot beside her jaw. Her words came as a faint whisper.

'Or you can believe our words, and do the duty we ask of you. You have no love for your common man? Fine. Seek to save yourself, at least. Maybe in the process you'll save the world you're part of.'

Ichor trickled from her nose, and that was the last I heard from the dead goddess Haphor.

I recoiled from my window as the sand turned scarlet. Retreating to the cot, I sat in the shadow of the cow's corpse and watched her blood paint the wall, line by line. I felt like a boy again, bade to sit on the step in silence, meditating on the sting of a belt across my arse cheeks.

Duty. Duty was a sharp word for a man who'd lived a life working for himself, taking whatever he pleased. It was why indenturement held such a sourness for me. I had become the opposite of myself: alive to dead, master to servant, thief to lackey.

I had wrestled over which path to take towards freedom, and now I had three to choose from: Temsa, Horix, or the dead gods. A soulstealer, a promise, or fending off some sort of apocalypse. The potential of freedom lay with all of them, and it caused a battle to rage in my head. Loyalty duelled with selfishness. Pride with moral fortitude. Trust with fear.

The hours that followed were torturous.

———◆———

TEMSA WATCHED ON AS SISTER Liria paced along the bars without expression, watching the naked shades crowd each other. There must have been a hundred to each cell. The weaker ones were pressed in so hard they almost merged with their neighbours. Their glowing eyes wandered between the sister's face and the white feather on her robe. Whispers followed in her wake. Blue light flooded the cellar.

'Silence!' Temsa struck the bars with his cane. 'Never had so many in these cells before,' he said to Liria. 'And there is a warehouse that has a key with the Cult's name on it.'

'Is it as full as these cages?'

'It's as full as your seventeen percent, that's for damn sure. All spoils from the names you gave me.'

Liria turned, face glowing brightly. He could almost see the wrinkles her skin had worn before her death, however many centuries ago that had been. 'And the other names we did not give you?'

Temsa took a wide stance and crossed his arms. 'I'll have you know, Enlightened Sister, that what I do in my own time is none of the Cult's business.'

'Church.'

'Excuse me?'

'We are a church, not a cult.'

Ani, ensconced in a corner like a thug in an alley, scoffed. 'You are no church,' she said.

Liria approached in slow, measured steps, hands clasped inside her vacuous sleeves. 'If you can be a tor, we can be a church. The Church of Sesh.'

Temsa shook his head irritably. It was an insulting comparison. 'The shades we agreed on are yours. Have we any further business? Any more names for me?'

'We may have, once the list is completed *in order*. That is most important.'

He waved his hand. 'Yes, yes, your sister has told me that already, and it is still none of your business if I seek opportunities elsewhere.'

'It is the elsewhere part that concerns us most. Habish. Merlec. Urma. Kanus. Ghoor. Horix. Finel. Boon. That is the order that must be followed.'

'Why?'

'Dominoes fall in sequence, not randomly. These names must fall in the same way.' She sighed softly. 'Why Tor Busk, might I ask? Why such a minor noble?'

'He had something I wanted.'

'What?'

'A new locksmith. He refused to give him to me.'

'A locksmith.'

'Yes, if you must know. One of the best in the R—city.'

The sister nodded slowly. 'Interesting.'

Temsa realised he'd said too much and swiftly diverted the subject. 'How are you transporting these half-lives?'

Liria watched as an extremely young shade, standing barely as tall as her hip, pawed through the bars for her red cloth. She did not move away, but she ignored his fawning touch. 'We had hoped you might have the means to do so.'

Ani threw up her hands. 'Oh, you'd hoped, had you?'

'Miss Jexebel, calm yourself, m'dear,' said Temsa, a smile growing. 'We can arrange it. At the cost of one percent, of course.'

Liria was good at keeping a straight face, but not perfect. He saw the swirl in the vapours of her cheek. He had spent years dealing with shades. He could read them like he could flesh.

'That is fair,' she said, though he couldn't see her believing it. 'To-morrow evening?'

'And the following two. I'm not stupid enough to transport that many shades in one go. They'll light up a whole street like a beacon.'

'Acceptable. And they are in good condition? The warehouse shades?'

A few in the cages groaned in disagreement.

Temsa yanked a long and toothy key from his breast pocket. 'Care to check for yourself?'

Liria dwelled on that for a moment, eyeing the key dangling before her. 'No. I have many other duties to attend to.'

'The busy life of a cultist, eh?' Temsa winked and gestured towards the stairs. 'Tomorrow night, then. You will have your first shipment.'

Her sapphire stare became piercing. 'Trust is being provided in great quantities, Tor Temsa. You wouldn't seek to betray us or otherwise let us down now, would you?'

Temsa stood his ground as she floated past. 'I'm insulted you even asked the question, Sister Liria.'

'Remember, Tor. The list. In order.' Liria paused to produce an envelope from her pocket, one sealed with blue wax and what looked to be a smudge of lip-paint. 'You will need this for Ghoor.'

He held her stare until the curve of the stairwell took her, Ani bristling behind him.

CHAPTER 16
REPARATIONS

Secrets, holds the deserts plenty,
full to brim but seeming empty.
And though the sand might look like naught,
trust you not to paths unwrought.
Friend or foe or lost to nether,
many ways to fade forever.
Older times still walk the sand,
and ancient ones still claim the land.
Better here, 'neath city lights,
than twixt the dunes on fearful nights.

NURSERY RHYME FROM THE OUTSPRAWLS

NILITH'S BODY JOLTED AWAKE, BUT her eyes remained closed. She felt the grit at her fingertips, felt the weakness of the campfire. The night breeze had stolen its heat. The soft wall at her back gently rose and fell. Anoish was dead to the world.

She heard the shuffle of sand and cracked an eye open. Only embers remained of the fire, but their faint ruby glow still lit the crags of a face sitting opposite her. For a moment, she thought it was Ghyrab, and then noticed the long, lank hair, and a hunch far too crooked to be the bargeman.

Slowly propping herself onto her elbow, Nilith's other hand slid to the dagger on her thigh. She'd taken it from the wrecked Ghoul camp under the light of morning, once the dunewyrms had eaten their fill. The scimitar was embedded in the sand near her head. She had also taken another triggerbow from a dead soldier, with three bolts stuck in it.

Nilith met the woman's eyes. They looked like spheres of grey wool hiding diamonds in their centres. There was something familiar about them, and about her clothes, if a bundle of rags could be called clothing.

'Beldam,' Nilith whispered. Her hand stayed on her blade. There were more lines in the woman's face and deeper bags under her eyes than last time she had seen her. There was a quiver in her chapped lips.

'Aye,' she croaked.

'How did you get here?'

'With better fuckin' luck than you did. Got into some trouble, I see?' The woman raised a shaky hand to point at the bruises still spread over Nilith's face like a faded map.

'Have you been following me?'

'I 'ave.'

The beldam must have been short on customers to trail one this far, Nilith thought. 'I can't pay you for any—' She was interrupted by a short gasp.

'Healin'. Is that what you want?' Quivering hands dug deep into pockets, and a pinch of dust was thrown to the fire. The embers sputtered, turning green.

Nilith pulled the dagger from its sheath as the beldam began to shuffle around the fire towards her. The old woman halted at the glint of the blade as it caught the sickly glow.

'What's wrong, witch?' Nilith challenged her, whispering lest she wake the others.

Black teeth came to gnaw at flaked lips. 'I took too much.'

'What?'

'From you. I took too fuckin' much and now the balance is skewed.'

'I—'

The beldam scratched at her head furiously, as if a horde of lice had made camp in her ragged hair. 'Winds're changing. Sands shifting. The Nyx sours…' She faltered, looking north. The lights of the distant city were like the coals of countless dozy fires, scattered across the horizon and blurry in the haze. 'Life is not what it was for a woman of the old ways. When I saw your gems, your belief, I took too much. *Ma'at* dictates I make amends.'

The beldam's hands clawed at the sand, as if the imbalance she had spoken of had needles that pierced her skin. Nilith's eyes were growing heavy in the green light. Something about the thick smoke wafting from it made her head loll.

'You stay away!' she mumbled, watching the witch shuffle closer. 'I need to get back to the city.' Nilith waved her dagger in one last feeble arc before her head met the earth. 'Farazar…'

'Then luck you'll need,' came the whisper. 'Bones and skin will mend themselves, but balance must be given or taken.' Nilith felt the woman's breath in her ear. It sounded strained, sad. Lost.

———————◆———————

NILITH WOKE WITH A START, narrowly avoiding stabbing Ghyrab as she reared up onto her knees, dagger still in hand and waggling.

'Mercy!' he said, skipping away as fast as his old bones would let him. Anoish whinnied nearby disapprovingly.

Nilith caught herself and her breath along with it, and sat down to rub the sleep from her eyes.

Ghyrab sat nearby, resting tentatively on his heels. He too had taken a knife from the bandit camp, and it protruded from his boot. 'No sign of that falcon or the ghost. We thought we'd let you sleep on. Well, I did. Horse 'ad nothing to do with it. Needed the healin'. Some good it's done you, by the looks of it.'

The bargeman pointed a finger and Nilith probed herself, feeling the smaller lumps and scabbed-over cuts, now clean and greasy with the dab of oils.

'The sand-witch...'

'Witch?'

'A beldam.'

Ghyrab shook his head. 'Probably bad dreams, Yer Majesty. Desert gives 'em to you, the nomads say. That's why I stick to the riv—'

'No,' Nilith cut him off, getting to her feet. 'She was here.'

She cast around for tracks other than theirs, which the breeze had turned to faint pockmarks. There were no others; no foot or hoofprints for a dozen yards around their camp.

'What's got into you?'

'A woman came here last night. The beldam I met in the Long Sands. She was babbling something about balance.'

Ghyrab picked at his fingernails. 'The nomads also say never trust a beldam, and if you do, then never cheat a beldam.'

'And just who are these all-knowing nomads, if you please? I cheated nobody!' Nilith snapped, looking to the horse instead. Anoish skipped away from her, as grumpy as she was. Perhaps they had all slept through strange dreams. 'I'm sorry,' she said, pinching the bridge of her nose. 'She wanted something. For her, not for me. Something about balance and *ma'at*.' She kneaded her brow, trying to recall. All she saw in her mind was green fire.

There was silence as Ghyrab pondered. 'Sounds like a dream, if'n you ask me.'

Nilith conceded with a huff. 'Maybe you're right.'

With no further talk of witches, she and Ghyrab mounted the horse and began their gallop north. Nilith pressed Anoish harder than she would have liked. Farazar had no need for sleep, and had likely travelled through the night just to spite her. Who knew how many miles he had put between them while she had dreamed of old crones and green flames?

Nilith explored her body between the movements of the horse. Her legs no longer felt sore. Nor did her backside, now accustomed to Anoish's spine. Her jaw had ceased its clicking, and her breathing came easier instead of setting her ribs alight. Perhaps it was all down to a deep and deserved sleep, she thought, and yet she couldn't shake the dream from behind her eyes. Whenever she grew distracted from watching the dunes, she found the beldam's words echoing in her mind. She tried to piece them together, knit them into sense.

The winds are changing. The Nyx sours.

Ma'at Nilith understood better than most. It was what had set her on this path in the first place. But what it had to do with the Nyx, she had no clue.

A change in the landscape managed to distract her. Wide streaks of colour began to paint the plain ochre sand. Anoish's hooves met reds, bronze greens, greys and even a faint blue. As the streaks began to stretch and elongate, so did the dunes. Like the swell of the ocean meeting a shore, they became regular and evenly spaced instead of the half-hearted mazes they seemed to enjoy so much. Their peaks flattened, as if the wind had eaten away at their height, and the going became easier.

The desert knew no true kindness, and what mercies it gave were always countered by another form of hardship. Though the terrain became gentler, fierce winds had carved great troughs between the dunes. No wonder, when they stretched so evenly east to west. The wind had no challenge here, and it raced along the strange channels as if it relished the opportunity. The only respite seemed to come on the dunes' flat peaks, where they could listen to the howl below them, and wipe the sand from their eyes.

Nilith gave her head a few thumps to shake the grit out of one ear. After ducking into three of the channels, she had taken to wrapping her borrowed cloak around her head and trusting the horse to guide them. 'What new evils are these?' she called out. She had not seen these in her journey south.

Ghyrab, who had barely spoken a word all morning and most of the afternoon, muttered something in Arctian she did not understand.

'What?'

'The Race Ruts!'

'And what are they?'

'Roads, of sorts.'

Nilith teased another answer from him, like a stubborn splinter from a fingertip. 'For what?'

'You don't know? Nomads, mostly. Though they're few these days. Thousands of years old, their tribes are. The Windchasers, or Jubub in Arctian. Or the Akanzi, the Whorltreaders. There's the Meernabi too, though I don't know what it means in Common.'

'Who makes these channels?'

'Nobody. The wind does,' he said moodily. 'Just as the river made my canyon.'

Their stilted conversation was paused as they descended into another of the Ruts. The wind battered them, threatening to steal their clothes as well as their breath. Nilith breathed as slowly as she could through the cloth of the cloak, and still she crunched grit between her teeth.

When Anoish had slogged his way to the top of the next dune, she decided to give him a rest. She slid from the horse's back and shook the sand from her body. It fell from her in a cloud.

'How many more of these?'

Ghyrab shrugged.

'If I've offended you, I apologise again.'

The bargeman's eyes met hers briefly and he nodded, though his face remained firmly downturned. 'Better be a nice barge, this replacement you promised.'

Nilith cracked a smile, feeling her scabbed lips split anew. 'The nicest,' she said around the taste of blood. 'You'll be back sailing the Ashti in no time.'

As it turned out, there were four more Ruts, or so her squinting scrutiny of the striped landscape told her. She saw the sand blowing up from the rim of the next one in great swirls, and huffed to herself while Ghyrab fetched the waterskins. The bits of the Ghouls' camp that had survived the dunewyrms had furnished them with enough supplies to reach the city. They had clothing, food, water, weapons, and yet she was still travelling one ghost and one body short.

Nilith stared out at the Race Ruts, privately simmering, and wondered how Farazar had fared with them. Part of her hoped they would find him curled up with arms crossed in the next channel, refusing to go on. The other part knew his stubbornness all too well to flirt with such fancy.

'Come on,' she said, waving to the horse and the bargeman. 'Let's clear these ruts before the sun sets.'

No doubt missing his tiller, Ghyrab took up Anoish's reins and led him on, leaving Nilith to walk behind them and stew. Her eyes scoured the dunes for a flash of blue, but she was disappointed. Before she was blinded by the rushing wind of the next rut, she threw up her cloak and trudged on.

This channel was wider than the others, and although the gale was lesser here, it had more time to harry them over the larger stretch. By the time they reached the peak, they were desperate for another rest.

'Three more,' she sighed.

On the edges of the next rut sat a curious collection of stones. Boulders had once lain hidden in the sand, but the wind had uncovered them like thieves in a grain hoard, and taught them a lesson in time and erosion. Most of them were pillar-shaped: tall and skinny, yet whittled into odd shapes by the harsh winds. They too were striped like the desert around them. Where one layer was more mulish than the next, it had resisted the carving, becoming flat and saucer-shaped. Nilith noticed others where the reverse had happened; where holes had appeared in the stone. They were completely natural, and yet Nilith's mind tried its hardest to find chisel grooves or sculptor's marks.

She felt an urge to run her hands over the smooth surface of the pillars, but before she got halfway, an even more curious sight appeared beyond them.

'Erm...'

A donkey bearing an enormous and oddly-shaped pack on its back rose above the rut. Nilith would have unsheathed her sword, thinking another traveller had snuck up on her, but the beast kept rising. And rising… Straight up, and with no jolt to its gait.

Its legs came into sight above the sand, then its hooves, and Nilith saw there was nothing beneath them but air. Like the rest of the donkey, they hung limply from the great pack. A single rope was fastened about its neck. It was taut, its other end disappearing into the rut.

'Ghyrab?' she hissed, too confused to put volume to her words. She stared at the canvas-and-wicker contraption on the donkey's back, examining how it shook and squeaked with every gust of wind. The donkey wriggled in mid-air, heehawing mournfully, and as the pack swayed, Nilith saw how wide it was, like the spread wings of a bird.

Hearing the braying over the gusts, Ghyrab turned. Concerned shouts rose up from below. There came a ring as Nilith drew her scimitar. She hurried to the edge of the dune, keeping one eye on the donkey hovering above her head. In Krass, there was a saying concerning a correlation between the occurrence of impossible events and pigs achieving flight. She wondered whether there was a flying donkey equivalent in the Arc.

'Nomads!' Ghyrab called out, hurrying after her. 'Windchasers.'

Below in the rut, a whole caravan of donkeys had come to a halt. Nilith saw similar sets of wicker wings below, and from above she saw they were a squashed triangular shape. A score of men in sky-blue robes stood around the gap in the caravan where the intrepid donkey had floated free. Nilith would have called it a daring escape had the beast not still been whinnying woefully.

Several men had hold of its rope, and were struggling to keep it from climbing further into the bruised sky. Others were pointing at the ridge, where they had spotted Nilith with her sword. Triggerbows were raised. The shouts became frenzied.

Nilith waved her arms and thrust the sword into the sand for all to see. With a sharp whistle, Anoish was at her side, and together they sidled down the dune into the windy rut. The robed men approached cautiously, wearing goggles fashioned of crystal and brass. Nilith immediately envied them; her cloak was still flapping maniacally about her head.

Thick ribbons of blue fabric wrapped their faces. Short horns, rounded at the tips, poked out from their foreheads. Bushes and strands of beards and moustaches protruded through every available gap. They chattered at her in a strange language. It was unlike any dialect Nilith had heard during all her years in the Arc. She was clueless, and instead relied on the common solution to every language barrier: a great deal of pointing.

She jabbed her finger at Anoish, at the rope, and then to the donkey still dangling aloft. Twice more, she repeated the dance before they understood her, and began to wrap the rope around the horse's muscled shoulders. Somehow, they found time to admire his stout flanks and bright eyes, as if he were a product for sale.

Anoish heaved forwards as nomad after nomad leapt to pull the rope down with their weight. Their movements hinted of practise; as if this was not the first of their donkeys to develop a taste for flying.

Within a few minutes, the donkey was hovering several feet off the sand. Its legs cantered as if it were already on solid ground. One heave later and it landed, promptly beginning to kick at any nomad who came near. They seemed accustomed to this, too, and with the power of numbers the nomads gently wrestled the beast into calm.

Ghyrab hobbled down the dune, conveniently late to the party. He held his hands up, intertwined in some greeting. The nomads recognised it and returned the gesture. Nilith did her best to copy it, and broad smiles broke out between their blue wrappings and wiry beards.

'Only the Windchaser men use that greeting. You use this one,' Ghyrab told her, joining his fingers together like an urchin.

'Ah.' Nilith performed the new movement, and a cheer went up from the small crowd. They gathered around her, touching her shoulders respectfully. Nilith flinched at first, but at the bargeman's scowl, she allowed it. Her hand gradually left the hilt of her knife.

'You speak their language?' she asked, having to yell over the wind.

Ghyrab shrugged. 'Some, not much. We've crossed paths before, where the Race Ruts meet a westward bend in the Ashti. Traded a bit, but like I said, they're a rare sight. More now than ever.'

'Why?'

'Your precious city is why! Soulstealers don't have any qualms about hunting them. No respect.'

The nomads were watching them swap their foreign words like a ball being batted back and forth.

'Ask them if any speak Commontongue!' ordered Nilith.

'*Shesua sikri Arctiri?*'

They mumbled between themselves until one clicked his fingers and ran up the line of the caravan. Shielding her face against the wind, Nilith watched him reach a large wagon, also sporting its own wings, and bow to its door. It was flung open and a figure in inordinately long robes jumped to the sand. Nilith waited while they came closer, watching their tendrils of blue fabric flail wildly like streamers in a sandstorm. The man walked behind, being repeatedly slapped by the errant clothing. Fashion and necessity had never been the closest of allies.

Nilith made the sea urchin gesture when the figure stood before her, closer than comfort, eyes and face hidden behind wrappings and goggles. The gesture was returned, and a female voice emanated from the blue cloth. A long pair of horns sprouted from her temples, sharp and curled.

'Travellers?' she asked, turning her back to the wind so she could talk instead of shout. Nilith copied her.

'Yes.'

'Traders?'

'No, sorry.'

There was a collective groan from the group as the woman translated.

'Where headed?'

'Araxes.'

This did not need translating. Nilith thought she heard hissing on the wind. Several men slid away to tend the donkeys.

'Always city. Never deserts. They are drier for it.'

Nilith didn't bother to justify her direction, but she understood their annoyance. Araxes was like a lantern, drawing moths from far and wide. Except in this case, the moths were people, trade, and prosperity. It left little lifeblood for the deserts and Duneplains.

'Where are you headed?'

'Hebus. We have spices and stones to sell.' The nomad held up a hand, showing a stone of red carnelian embedded in her palm, bound with matching silk.

Hebus was as far east as a person could get without falling off the Arc into the sea. It was an expedition that made Nilith's look like a trundle around a courtyard. 'That's a long way.'

'The Race Ruts will lead us there. Jubub have travelled them for...' The woman paused to think. 'Thirty generations. I do not know the number in your years, but we have spent them walking.'

Nilith had to say it: 'Or flying, it seems. Do your donkeys often fly away?'

The woman spoke louder, seizing an opportunity to admonish the other nomads. 'Only when wrong packs are put on wrong donkeys,

Rerenzi.' A man with a patchy beard shuffled away, head bowed. 'Wings meant for heavier donkey.'

Nilith bowed her head. 'I see.'

The woman saw she did not, and waggled the wing of a nearby pack. It seemed so flimsy, and yet when the wind blew, they were as rigid as iron. 'Journey very long, hard with east winds. Ancestors see birds follow caravan, year after year, floating on winds. Ancestors have idea. They build wings like birds, keep donkey light, sometimes float. That way, donkey don't die on journey, and neither do we.'

'Ingenious,' Nilith said, meaning it. She had already lodged these rare people in her mind. *Another facet of the Arc that Farazar and his ancestors have let wither and die.* Her fists were clenched as she bowed and backed away. While she untethered Anoish and waved to Ghyrab, the nomad woman stared Nilith up and down.

'I wish you luck with your journey,' Nilith told her.

'No. You stay.'

Nilith's fingers automatically twitched for her knife, but the nomad parted her wraps, revealing a dark-skinned face and a wide, milky smile.

'Our camp not far. Evening come fast!' She waved her hand towards the sky, which was already darkening at its eastern edges.

Nilith squinted at the far edge of the channel, chancing the flying grit. *Three more.* She yearned to be after Farazar, to catch him before he found the next Nyxwell; a well that was wetter than the last one they'd encountered. She bit her lip, torn, until the Windchaser put a gentle hand on her shoulder, and pointed her towards the hazy lump that was their wagon.

It too had wings. Two sets, one above the other, stunted and pinned to its sides over a curtained doorway. At its narrow head was a team of three donkeys: the plain, ground-dwelling type. The stretched skin and wicker of the wagon's frame had been dyed blue and was covered in glyphs that swirled and interconnected, the like of which Nilith had never studied before.

'Spells,' said the woman nonchalantly, as if magic were as common as souls. In the Reaches, magic was deader than the gods who'd once fashioned it. 'Keep the winds straight.'

Nilith nodded as if she understood. She did not. 'What's your name?' she asked as the curtain was pulled aside for her. The stink of perfumes and a smoking brazier met her like a fist.

'Mizi.'

'Emp—Nilith.'

Mizi touched her horns with three fingers and then gestured inside as shouts came rolling down the caravan. It seemed the intrepid donkey's wings had been trimmed, and the Jubub were ready to chase the wind again.

'What about Ghyrab?'

'Men walk.'

'And the women?'

Mizi gestured again, impatiently. Nilith started to like the sound of this tribe.

A half-circle of women, a spectrum of different ages, watched her as she climbed into the wagon and out of the wind. They were draped in multicoloured cloth, and apparently the older the woman, the more clothing she was required to wear. The youngest sat bare-chested with a skirt of threads, two nubs of horns on her brow. The oldest looked like a small, pointy hill of white hair swaddled in a knitted rainbow. She had the look of a ram, with grey horns that curled in spirals around her ears. Every face was uncovered, blank as a new scroll, eyes staring hard. Each of them must have been related in some way to the next; their features were too similar, even down to the spread of freckles across their noses and cheeks. As Nilith looked around the half-circle, it was like watching time perform its awful dance, from elfin girl to wizened great-grandmother.

A pillow was thrust towards her, and Nilith tested it with her backside. It was a lot softer than Anoish's backbone. Mizi joined her, shutting the wind out with the curtain and a toggle to tie it fast.

Silence reigned in the wagon, brooding under its low ceiling, thick like its smoggy air. Nilith was glad when the vehicle jolted forwards; the rattling wheels and howling of the wind took away the silence's edge. The moment she felt the wheels spin freely and the wagon rise slightly, the oldest of the women spoke up.

'*Zeratim, bal am kitish. Fareni kazim Jubub leera.*'

All of the circle besides Nilith laughed. 'What did she say?'

Mizi covered her mouth. 'She say you have pretty face. Could almost pass for Windchaser.'

Nilith cracked a smile, and the old woman replied with a grin, showing off a row of teeth that looked like a burned fence.

'*Zerimir herin lesim?*'

'She ask if you are hungry?' Mizi translated.

Nilith's stomach replied for her, rumbling away.

'*Zerimir asta?*'

'Do you like wine?'

Silence fell as the wagon lifted and bounced along the sand three times. The Windchasers leaned in to hear Nilith's answer. A sudden and terrible thirst had come over her grit-speckled tongue. Though she felt a twang of angst over halting her pursuit of Farazar, she could push Anoish all the harder on the morrow. She had not seen such charity since Eber and Ole Fen. It seemed her luck had changed, and she was not about to spurn its gifts.

'Does an Arctian like half-coins?' she said to another round of chuckles.

CHAPTER 17
CELLARS

Who said religion and the gods were dead? I
see religion all over! How about the church
of half-coins? Is the Code not a doctrine? Or
the Consortium and their cult of silver! King
Neper's Bazaar makes a fine cathedral. Or
what about those who gaze up, enraptured,
at lofty towers? I see them praising on every
street corner. And what of the worshippers of
beer, wine and fucking? What are we, if not
devoted to our gods? We are at church this
very moment! Lift your tankard!

OVERHEARD IN AN ARAXES TAVERN

I STARED AT THE COW BLOOD decorating my plain wall for most of the day. It had dried brown in half-formed, macabre puddles. All the while, two words had stuck in my head.

A gift.

Haphor and Basht's words, not mine. It jarred somewhat with their talk of duty. It was like calling a broom a gift and then asking me to sweep the streets of Araxes.

'A gift.' I said it aloud to taste the madness of it. Somehow it was bitter in my mouth, and set a stir in my vaporous stomach. If what the cow had said was true, the dead gods were merely trying to help themselves. *Feed themselves, more like.* They were no friends of mine, and I wanted no part in their duty.

My problem was I had no real idea how to use my so-called gift to my advantage. Last time, I had killed a man. I dearly hoped that my haunting didn't require murder to work. If so, it was no gift at all, and the gods could go fuck themselves all the more.

I had weighed murder against all the benefits of escaping, and then against all the downsides to staying in Temsa's clutches. I had realised one thing was certain: I couldn't stay here for long. I had even less trust for Temsa than I did for the Cult. Whatever other choices I explored, the widow was still my best path out of this mess. Horix was my mistress, whether I liked it or not.

My jaw set and grim, I strode towards the door. What was another step towards darkness, as long as it set me free? My redemption, if I was owed any, could wait until after that.

I pressed my head to the iron door once again. There was just one guard out in the corridor. I had heard him coughing for most of the day, and no guard stands with company for so long without a bit of chat. After spending most of my life avoiding them, I knew a thing or two about hired swords. The other truth about them is they're never that smart. It was as if the worldwide prerequisite to be a guard was a subpar intellect and outstanding gullibility.

There was a wide hatch in the door's face for plates or bowls, in case Temsa wanted to hold a living prisoner in this cell, and keep them alive with water and vittles. My blue fingers pried at its cold, rusty steel, but found no budge in it. It had been opened only once, when a shade had come to gaze at me for a time. I thought it had been Danib at first, but the face was smaller, without a helmet, and more intrigued than grumpy. The guard had shooed him away, and I had thought no more of it.

Years of battling locks had taught me many things, first and foremost that a lock definitely wouldn't open if you didn't try to crack it. Baring my teeth, I crouched down, concentrated, and rammed my fist against the door three times.

'Oi!' I cried for good measure.

There came a sigh, and then the thud of a more solid fist on the other side. 'Shut it.'

'It's important!'

A grunt, and the hatch squealed as it slid back on rusted runners. I pressed myself to the door, watching as a nose poked into view, eyes somewhere behind it, scouring the cell. It took an age for the clank of a bolt to come. I could have sung.

'No tricks, shade!' ordered the guard as the door swung inwards. Its hinges complained even more than the hatch. Temsa's tavern was in serious need of grease, I pondered, as I scuttled along with the swing of the door.

This guard was smarter than the usual sort. At the very least, he had been duped by a similar trick in the past. He thrust a hand behind the door, skimming my head. Before his eyes could swivel down to my glowing form, curled like a spring, I pounced.

He fell awkwardly, arms flailing at my face. I felt the sting of copper and saw he had rings around each finger. I winced as a fist caught my eye socket. My vapours turned solid where the rings struck me, pain lancing across my face and neck in white veins of light.

I sought the guard's throat, somehow wrapping myself around him as he squirmed from under me. He seemed too horrified and outraged to yell for help. Instead, he made strangled grunts of revulsion as my cold limbs encircled his neck.

'Get… off!' he panted. 'Bloody… shade!'

I pushed my forehead into the back of his skull, trying to ignore the blood-gorged louse nestled there among flakes of skin like spring blossom. *Think of nothing*, I thought, internally yelling at myself to ignore the stupidity of such a statement. I clamped my eyes shut and pressed, squeezing with my arms. I prayed I would not have to strangle him.

Nothing. Nothing. Nothing.

As before, I felt something slip, like the pop of an aching joint. At first I thought his neck had failed him. Immediately I felt a force rail against me as my cold met a wall of warm flesh. This man's soul was stronger than my last victim's, and fought hard for its body. It battered against me, forcing me out for a brief moment before I drove my concentration into the man's skull like a forge-hot knife.

Within a moment, I lay sprawled on the floor, clutching at empty space around my aching neck. All was silent in the cell save for the trundle of cartwheels and idle scuffing beyond the barred window. I smelled my own stink first; a tang of unwashed armpits and nethers. If I hadn't known better, I'd have said the man was already dead, and three days rotted. For a moment, I feared I had killed him, but the beat of a stolen heart said otherwise. As did my lungs. No pipe-lover, this man. He had the lungs of a forgotten childhood, when I had run for endless miles through meadows, never without breath. That had been before city soot, dusty workshops, smog-filled taverns, and the general ravaging of age.

Straining to hold on to the body, I remembered those simpler times, and coveted them. All children are blank canvases, waiting to have life's brushstrokes and splatters spread across them. Some they paint themselves, others are painted for them, some dark, some light, and more come every year, until our self-portraits are one day finished.

Perhaps that was why all souls echoed their deaths; unfinished canvases stolen before they were complete.

When the man's muscles had slackened under my hold and no longer fought me, I tested my limbs and found them sturdier than his care for hygiene would have suggested. This guard was strong. I wondered whether it was because this one hadn't used a club for a headrest.

I put his strength to good use, dusting off my borrowed clothes and getting to my feet. I slid the hatch shut on the second try, once I'd gotten used to my fingers, and the door quickly after. I remembered the bolt before I shuffled down the corridor.

Despite the wax that clogged my ears, I heard the rumble of the Slab above me, busy in the hotter midday hours. I shoved the guard's feet towards the first set of stairs I came across: a spiral case that led me up several levels. At the uppermost step, a guard clacked a spear-butt and my head snapped up. I heard a crack in my neck as an old but unfamiliar wound dogged me.

'Spiss. What are you doing up 'ere?'

I grunted, clearing my throat, and said, 'Need to find the boss. Gh—shade's acting up.'

'*Tor*, you mean. He put a knife through Olageph's throat t'other day for callin' him boss.'

'I'll remember,' I said. I tried to peer past him to see if Pointy lay on the desk, or hung from the wall. No such luck. 'So… is he in there?'

'Nah, down in the cellars.'

I nodded my thanks, but another knock from the spear caught me before I left.

'Oi, you remember what I told you?'

I turned slowly, my face torn between a raised eyebrow and a knowing smile.

'You idiot. Too much ale is your trouble. She had twins.' The man beamed. 'Two healthy twins.'

I was about to congratulate his new fatherhood when the guard tucked his spear into his armpit and grabbed at imaginary – and rather huge – breasts. 'Two very healthy twins, if you know what I mean. Could barely walk after a night with h—'

'Good for you,' I cut him off as I turned away. Cheated of his celebration, he grunted and went back to his guarding. His muttering followed me down the stairs.

'Suit your fucking self.'

I figured the cellars must be where I'd been locked up on my first visit to the Rusty Slab. The weeks since then had stretched into what felt like a year. I chose down instead of up, and wandered into the dark of the tavern's cellars and tunnels. I felt my bare skin prickle in the cool air, hairs dancing. I shivered at the sensation. It was marvellously diverting.

The warren of underground cellars and warehouses Temsa had dug beneath his tavern were winding, and they led me a merry pattern past the cages of the dead. I looked at them and their woeful expressions, the same as I'd once worn. I spied the high-born amongst them, with their proud cheekbones and marks of torture. One was burned to a sapphire husk.

The cages were full to bursting in places, the ghosts twitching as their comrades pressed them up against the copper bars. Temsa had been busy indeed. I had spent three weeks wallowing in indenturement. He had spent them becoming a tor, and being a tor in this town meant owning a lot of souls. Temsa had collected thousands in these cellars. I dreaded to think how many more levels he had stuffed with ghosts.

I saw at least one more down another set of curling stairs, where vats of Nyxwater sat between the cages. The floor was freshly spattered with its inky waters.

Ghostly hands pawed at me, their owners managing faint murmurs as I brushed through a narrow section and out into a wide dome of a room. My borrowed heart skipped a beat, my own feelings leaking into the body as I saw Temsa standing with Ani Jexebel and a group of her guards. They were busy overseeing the construction of more cages. A gang of ghosts in drab loincloths were supervising the hammering and bolting. They wore leather on their hands, saving them from the copper.

'Faster!' Temsa was yelling, stamping his eagle's foot. I noticed with a stiffening of my lip that he had Pointy in a scabbard hanging from his round hip. 'I need this finished by tonight, you hear?'

'Yes, Tor!' came the awkward chorus, some voices hoarse and new, others barely formed.

'There you are,' said the sword's voice in my head, somehow knowing it was me. *'Is this one alive, or did you kill him too?'* I nodded to the soulblade and ducked into an alcove, pretending to stand guard. I poked at a nearby cage of innocents for good measure.

Temsa was grumbling. 'I tell you again, Ani, the Slab's getting tight. New accommodations are required, methinks.'

'Hmph,' was all the big lump of Jexebel had to say.

'Did you hear me?'

'I did.'

'Again with your doubt, m'dear! You'd better start trusting me again, or put a fucking cork in your complaining. One or the other.' He wagged a finger menacingly. I watched from the corners of my eyes, which had begun to sting from the effort it took to keep them under my control. The man was desperately trying to wink.

'Magistrate Ghoor's tower might be just to my liking, and more fitting of my new station once I wash his stink from it. I have grown bored of Bes District. I shall have myself Weighed again tomorrow, to seal the claim.'

'A Chamber of the Code magistrate, though… Tor. Some might say it's too bold. Starsson said he's had the whiff of a scrutiniser sittin' in the bar, combing for clues, and after that oaf Omat killed one of 'em…'

Jexebel backed off as Temsa gave her a venomous look. 'We have our princess to cover that. Sisine will keep them off our trail,' he said.

That raised my eyebrow.

Jexebel changed the subject. 'What's the plan?'

'Tonight at midnight, we pose as guests for Ghoor's party. Enlightened Sister Liria was kind enough to give us several invitations. The Cult continues to impress, despite irritating the fuck out of me.'

My eyebrows were well and truly raised now. The cultist in the streets started to make more sense.

'Is there an invite for me?' asked Jexebel

'Naturally. And Danib, too.'

'I've got a few men in mind.'

'We'll take Caltro, too.'

I flinched at my name.

'Surely he can wait—'

'We take him,' Temsa replied firmly. 'I don't trust that fucking widow. She's a crotchety old bag, or so the tongues wag. Might decide enough is enough and cut her losses with his half-coin. Better I get as much use out of him while I can, just in case.'

Another grunt from Jexebel. She proceeded to kick a ghost with the copper toe of her boot; it sent the woman sprawling, her near-severed limbs flailing.

'Faster, he said!' Jexebel bellowed, before returning to Temsa's side.

'Keeping the sword, then?' Jexebel asked.

'I am. Seems a fitting blade for a tor. And besides, it's inordinately sharp.' Temsa looked as though he would pull it forth with a flourish, but his hand shied away from its hilt. I noticed the bandage on his thumb.

He tried to sharpen me. I cut the whetstone in half.

'Sounds like a soulblade to me.'

'Nonsense, Ani. Old fairy tales.'

'Grandfather had an axe like it. Soulaxe, I s'pose… Hey! You! I told you to watch the shade's cell!'

It took me a moment to realise Jexebel was speaking to me. Her giant frame striding towards me, finger raised, was my first clue. *Why in the Reaches do they have to breed them so big in the Arc?* I thought.

'I—' My body twitched, once again trying to signal her in some way and betray me. I clenched harder. This haunting was more difficult than the last.

Jexebel brought her burst-veined nose close to mine, bending down so she could snort in my face. 'Well?'

'Hekal's down there. Wanted to swap.' *Why did I choose such a Krass name?*

'Swap? And who the fuck is Hekal? Don't remember such a man.' She prodded me hard in the sternum and I choked on the other man's soul.

'Hekal, er… Half-Tongue? New man. Doesn't like the door shift.' I prattled off some more fiction.

'Very nice,' Pointy quietly congratulated me.

I saw Temsa clanking his way over, curiosity piqued, and I grappled for an excuse to escape Jexebel's shadow. 'I—I'm sorry, I'll get back up there right away.'

My body convulsed again, but I turned it into a swift lunge towards the doorway. I winced my way into the corridor, expecting a rough hand to land on my shoulder at any moment. But none came, and I proceeded back the way I'd come. Jexebel's curse of 'Fucking amateur' was the only thing that chased me, as well as Pointy's voice, faint with distance.

'I'll wait, then, shall I?'

I exhaled only when I was alone, save for the crowded pens of ghosts. They looked on at me, confused and uncaring. They had their own deaths to deal with.

My encounter with Jexebel had been far too close for comfort, but her conversation with Temsa had been a mine of information.

Firstly, the infamous Cult were aiding Temsa. Secondly, he was going after the Chamber, the only pillar of justice I knew of in this godsforsaken city. A bold move indeed for a soulstealer, never mind that he had murdered his way to nobility. And lastly, he had a princess in his pocket.

There was only one princess – and Sisine – I knew of, and that was the empress-in-waiting. I wondered whether she knew I was here, locked in Temsa's cellars. No doubt she still had need of me, unless she had gone to that bitch Evalon Everass instead. Even though I would have likely found a knife in my back at the end of it, the missed opportunity to work for the royal family of the Arc stung me. At least if Everass did get the job, it would remove my competition.

I heard a scuff on the stairs, and looked up to see Danib standing tall at the end of the corridor. His armour was minimal, for once. I tried to keep my eyes away from the gaping wound encircling his skull as I cleared my throat, straightened and walked towards him. I even chanced a nod as I passed. He looked at me with his glowing white eyes and scowled, as if sensing my wrongness. Perhaps I bulged to him; two souls crammed into one body. The guard wrapped around my vapours ached to scream and shout, but I bit my borrowed tongue until I could taste blood, and carried on up the stairs. Danib watched me until I disappeared from sight.

I decided I would bide my time, lull Temsa into a false sense of security while I picked locks, and pray Horix wasn't too hasty with my half-coin before I managed to escape with the damn sword. It wasn't the first time I had entrusted my future to my skills, and I hoped it wouldn't be the last.

There was a more immediate issue that lay before me: I had no idea what a live body would do once I hauled myself from it. Half of me thought the guard would be a raving lunatic by the time I exited him. The other half imagined him running off, yelling to Temsa of what I had done. Even though there was only a slim chance the soulstealer would believe him and think him sane, it wasn't worth the risk.

As a locksmith, I was useful enough. As a pet circus ghost, I was worth untold amounts.

I put my hands to my head and scratched at my dirty scalp, racking my brains. I swore they were mushier than when I had been alive. The guard's less than adequate mind was no help, too wrapped up in trying to cast me out. He was managing it, slowly but surely. I felt myself squeezed, pushed up against his skin. Time was short.

I found the stairwell up, and heard the roar of the tavern again. An idea mercifully struck. *Sane.* I needed the opposite. I need insane.

Fighting to move my legs, as if the guard had read my thoughts, I jogged up the stairs and hovered at the heavy curtain separating me from the busy tavern hall. I looked out over the greasy dockworkers swilling their thick beer; the painted entertainers dressed in ostrich feathers and not much else; the scrapings of the dusty streets wetting their whistles; and the guards staring sleepy-eyed out over the writhing masses. A dirge was being howled from one corner.

I set my fingers to my leather jerkin and yanked at the toggles. My hands fought back, wrenching away, and it took some wrestling to shrug the garment off. Next came the shirt, and with more fighting, his trews. I left him his boots, primarily because I couldn't be bothered with the laces, but his loincloth I ripped away and tossed down the stairs.

Pausing, I stared down somewhat wistfully at the parts my ghostly self now lacked, but then a grin appeared. Mischief always won over the morose.

Thinking of feathers and a painted body, I tore myself from the man's flesh, falling from his naked back. The sensation dizzied me, but I remembered to kick out with all I had. My foot caught him square in the back and sent him sprawling into the crowd before his eyes could stop spinning.

The last I saw of him, before I tumbled down the stairwell, was him naked and spread-eagled across a table, drenched in beer, arms flailing like an upturned tortoise, yelling something about a ghost under his skin.

The laughter followed me down the stairs, and I landed in a heap with a smile. Uncurling myself, I scuttled back to my cell, hauling the door shut with a bang. The bolt I could do nothing about, but lies I could. With any luck, the guard would be out on his backside within the hour. Alive, at least, and that was what counted.

I was no murderer.

DUST. IT WAS A PANDEMIC in the cavern beneath the widow's tower. Like a greedy mould, no surface had escaped its attention. On some of the higher rafters it gathered like carpet. Pale piles of it sat in banks by the walkways and ramps. The finer particles refused to sink, hanging in the stuffy air like a stubborn smog. The lanterns caught the motes in their light and painted them yellow.

The shades were caked in it. It clung to their naked frames or robes like a false skin; like the fashions of free shades of old, caking themselves in powder to appear alive. It had never worked then, and it didn't work now. The workers just looked paler and more ghoulish.

Widow Horix stared at the beams crisscrossing the walls, keeping the dirt and rock at bay. She sought patience – calm, perhaps – in between the seams and iron spikes. Her eyes betrayed her, slipping instead to the mound of earth that had swallowed a portion of what her shades had built for her. Her great creation listed to one side under its weight. In the hazy gloom of the cavern, figures could be spied, glowing a faint blue as they hurried to clear the cave-in.

'That one,' she said, pointing to one of the kneeling half-lives before her.

The shade winced before the copper whip had even touched him. He cried out, eyes flashing white as the whip lanced across his shoulders.

'And that one.'

Another pointing finger creeping from her sleeve. Another snap of sinew and copper twine. Another screech.

Kalid kept his whip at the ready, but Horix held her tongue. She paced along their line, skirts swishing angrily as she watched them cower. Five of the sad bastards, and one or more of them were responsible for this delay. They were lucky their mistake had only set them back a few days, and not caused worse damage.

If she hadn't already sealed her tower so tightly, Horix would have assumed foul play, a spy of Temsa's in her midst. As it was, she had only mere stupidity to deal with.

'I'll ask again. Who didn't ask for the wall to be shored up?'

Silence, save for snivelling and the scratching of blue fingers in the dark dirt. Horix took up her crook-like walking cane and prodded each of them in the foreheads. 'Who?'

At last, a shaking hand arose from the group. It belonged to the Skol woman.

'Your name?'

'Bela, Madam.'

'You were the one responsible for this delay?'

'No, Madam. He was.' A glowing finger shot out. The shades in the line each ducked to avoid its damning direction, until one alone was left upright: the crippled shade, bent almost double. He had been cheap, Horix remembered that about him. He blinked owlishly at her.

'You! Your name?'

'Kon, Madam. Son of Karabi.'

'Did you cause this damage, Kon, son of Karabi?'

He took his time to think, then snapped his fingers. 'All I did was mention that I once was an acolyte for the Chamber of the Grand Builder.'

'And were you?'

'I was. I told Bela that, and she put me in charge.'

'What did you do for the Grand Builder?'

'I carried scrolls and fetched tea.' The half-life almost looked proud.

'I see,' said Horix, nodding. She folded her arms behind her back as she paced once more. 'Her, Kalid. The accuser. She hid behind the stupidity of others when she clearly knew better.'

The colonel wrapped the whip around Bela's neck, forcing her face into the dirt. 'Shall we put her in the sarcophagus, Mistress?'

Horix watched the shade struggle and claw furrows in the dark earth. 'Let's go for something simpler, shall we? One of these new Outsprawler punishments I've heard so much about.'

Bela began to gasp. Her vapours undulated through an entire spectrum of blues as the copper collar continued to burn her.

'Water or fire. Or both. You choose, Colonel.'

'Aye.' Kalid said nothing more as he dragged the shade off on her leash, as a noble might walk one of their fancy miniature beetles.

Horix whirled on the line of shades. 'Do any of you have knowledge of building, digging, or the like?' she hissed. Kon flinched away.

She turned her face up to the rafters of the cavern, up to the hundreds of shades that scampered up ladders, down ropes, and dangled from buckets. Glowing ants, swarming over her vision, her creation. Horix took a moment to admire its growing angles before a shriek tore from her lungs. Its hoarse echoes died along with their frantic digging. They stared down at her, eyes wide and fearful, like chickens hearing the boots of the farmer.

It had been a week since Yamak had promised her it would be finished. It was in no such state, and now this cave-in had no doubt cost another week. Yet another setback, when the sand in the hourglass was running thin.

Horix let her voice bounce around the darkness. 'Don't any of you useless creatures know how to fucking build anything?'

There was a rustle of whispering from a wooden gantry overhead. A shade was pushed forwards and a head popped into view. He was a young man with an axe-head for a face, with Skol cheeks and tiny eyes. He looked fearful enough to be truthful, at least. The kiss of a whip was always good for breeding loyalty.

'I… er…' His voice was tremulous. 'I also worked for the Chamber of the Grand Builder, Mistress,' he said.

'And did you also carry scrolls and fetch tea, half-life?'

'No. I… I *drew* the scrolls, Mistress. Cranes, docks, high-roads. I drew them all.'

'Your name?'

'Poldrew.'

Horix gestured to the great lump of wood and canvas sat between her and a roof that was lost in the dusty haze. 'Can this be finished in a week's time, Poldrew?'

She saw the twitch in his cheek.

'No,' he said.

'No? How long, then?'

'I never built anything like... like *this*.' His eyes wandered off for a moment, seeking courage. 'I wouldn't want to lie, Tal, but maybe two weeks would be more accurate.'

Horix levelled a grey bone of a finger at him. 'It had better be,' she warned, hearing the heavy stomp of Colonel Kalid returning. 'Because you're in charge now, understand? Two weeks. Not a day more!'

Poldrew's nodding was so vigorous he almost shook himself from the gantry.

'I thought Yamak was in charge of building,' Kalid grunted.

'That man is a shade driver, not a builder. Whereas this man...' She let the colonel follow her pointing finger. 'This man *is* a builder, and he has given me his word he can finish within two weeks. You will watch him like a hawk.'

'Are you sure, Mistress?'

'I never gamble when the stakes are so high, Colonel. I thought you were a man who liked his card-dens.'

Kalid cleared his throat. 'I used to be. There's a sickness hidden in cards, and I found it. But if I could interrupt, you have a visitor.'

Horix's eyes flashed angrily. 'I said no visitors.'

'Apart from this one, Widow.'

'Ah, good.' Horix adjusted her skirts before giving Poldrew one last look. 'It's on you, shade. Get this done, otherwise Kalid here will have another soul to play with.'

The widow and the colonel left, disappearing into the poorly-lit haze, leaving Poldrew to stare out into the darkness and meet the countless blue eyes staring back at him. His gulp echoed through the dusty silence.

———————◆————

HORIX WAS WANDERING HER SPARSE garden when Kalid brought her the spook. The cold of the cellars had put a shiver in her old bones, and she wanted to feel the sweltering day on her face. Good for the wrinkles, she'd heard, not that she gave a damn. Age was how wisdom was measured, not in looks.

Meleber Crale strode confidently towards her as if his performance so far had been naught but exemplary. Horix put a sour curve on her lips and stared him down into a shuffle. By the time he reached her, his hands were stuffed into the pockets of his robe, and his eyes had fallen to the sand.

'I don't see why you appear so happy with yourself, spook. You have not delivered what I asked for.'

'No, Tal Horix, I have not. But I have located your locksmith.'

'Where is he?'

'In the cellars beneath Tor Boran Temsa's tavern,' Crale said proudly.

'Are you sure?'

'As sure as I stand here.'

Stalking along the beds of plants, the widow regarded the waxy green stems waving at her. She traced her hand across a few before snapping one's neck. She held its bulbous head up to the shade and crushed it, letting its black seeds trickle through her fingers. 'And why have you wasted time coming to tell me?'

'Temsa's a wily man, Tal Horix. He employs no shades outside the confines of his bar, or his warehouses, or factories. The only shades beneath the Rusty Slab are behind bars, ready for market.'

'And yet you managed to find Caltro?'

'I saw him in his own cell, and it almost ruined me trying to get that far. Breaking him out will be infinitely more difficult.'

Horix clicked her tongue sharply. It seemed this was a day of disappointments. 'I am a frugal woman, spook. I sow my silver only where I know it will grow and blossom. Currently, I don't see anything sprouting from our arrangement but let-down and delay.' She strolled a circuit around the shade, staring at the flecks of dust on his cream robes. 'His own cell, you say?'

Crale gave her an avid nod.

'Temsa knows Caltro's worth and history,' mused Horix. 'And I'd wager that if the tor is the one behind these murders, then he's not done yet. That means he'll keep him safe. If we push him, Temsa may decide to destroy Caltro just to spite me, and at any time that pleases him.'

'If the locksmith's worth what you think, and Temsa's that greedy, I doubt that.'

'Leave the doubting to me, Master Crale, and busy yourself with doing your job.' Horix stared at the black seeds clinging to her craggy palm. 'Get me Caltro back by any means necessary. I don't care what it takes. Fail me, and you'll think death is a summer breeze compared to what I will do to you.'

Crale looked as if he were going to say something, which, judging by the worried curl to his mouth, was most likely an alteration to his price. His finger hovered in mid-air and his mouth hung agape, but Horix's glare kept him speechless. All he did was nod, and let Kalid show him the way out.

When the colonel returned, Horix was busy staring into the sky, at the spike of the Cloudpiercer, just visible between two towers. A pair of thin spectacles, stained a dark grey, balanced on her nose so the sunlight wouldn't offend her.

'Is he gone?' she croaked.

'Yes, Widow.'

'Temsa is far more ambitious than I thought.'

'If you'll pardon my boldness, Mistress, I don't know why you won't let me take ten-score of my best men and go knock on Temsa's door.'

'The same reason he hasn't come to claim Caltro's half-coin in the same way, Kalid. A battle in the streets is worth nobody's time and everybody's attention. And with these recent deaths, the Chamber of the Code is currently out for blood. Never mind the Cloud Court and the emperor.' She scuffed at the cracked earth and sand at her feet, feeling the ridges of stout wood beneath. 'It would jeopardise our plan.'

Kalid took a while to muster the question. Perhaps he sensed the serrated edge to her mood. 'Do we continue without Caltro?' he asked.

'My plan was in motion before he came onto the scene. We are simply back to brute strength and surprise, Colonel.' At the sound of Kalid's growling, she whacked him with her cane. 'We have two weeks. Until then, we trust in the spook, and see what he delivers us. If not…'

Kalid cocked his head as he waited for her sharp mind to carve a plan out of this mess. Horix threw him a grin, showing off grey teeth.

'If not, Colonel, then you will have your battle after all.'

CHAPTER 18
MAGISTRATE GHOOR

They say you can find anything in Araxes, even
things you didn't know you wanted. Trinkets?
Craftsmen? Silks? Spices? Furniture? Sellswords?
Weapons? King Neper's Bazaar has five thousand
stalls teeming with delights from every edge
of the Far Reaches. Soulmarkets sit on every
corner. Stranger fancies? Pleasures of the flesh?
Young boy or girl, perhaps? Snefer and Mankare
Districts have towers of brothels and cathouses
offering all manner of delights. Fight-pits abound
in Dawar. Gambling and card dens in the High
Docks, where the beasts coming off the ships are
otherwordly and, yes, for sale. Whatever you
desire can be yours in the City of Countless Souls.

FROM 'THE CITY OF COUNTLESS SOULS –
A KEEN-EYED GUIDE'

TEMSA CAME FOR ME AT night, just as he'd promised.

The unlatched door from my previous excursion had been discovered by another guard. As was to be expected, suspicion was rife on the tor's face as he swaggered into my cell. He hadn't interrogated me yet, but the number of men watching me had tripled. He seemed to have trouble buying my nonchalant pose: arms crossed and lounging at the back of the stone room.

Temsa certainly had taken to his part as tor. Some Arctian royals would have had trouble dressing so garishly. The grey had been dyed from his goatee and his receding hair shone with oil. His attire was a layered affair of golden silk, velvet, embroidery, and a few agate pendants thrown in, just in case he wasn't glamorous enough. The rich threads shimmered as he hobbled, playing games with the light. Pointy was hidden beneath those distracting folds, I was sure of it. Somehow, I felt his presence in the room, but he had no words for me.

'Been up to mischief, have you, Caltro?' Temsa challenged me.

I was the paragon of innocence. 'I think you'd better start watching who you employ as guards. You have a madman loose in your establishment. He came in here raving about the evilness of shades, knocked me around a bit, then left me to it. Bollock naked, he was.'

Temsa walked closer to me, looked up into my eyes and took some time measuring my lies. In the end they proved weighty enough to pass his inspection.

'And what of your verdict?' he asked me. 'Will you continue to stare at these four walls, or will you do what's best for your vapours and work with me? I have need of a locksmith tonight.'

'Based on the late hour, I'd say you have nothing legal in mind,' I replied.

'If it's not legal, it's no fun, my father always said. Bless his soul.'

'Sounds like a fine upstanding gentleman. Shame he had to go and conceive you.'

Temsa's talons dug into my uncovered foot, grinding against the stone beneath. My vapours refused to come free, as if he had impaled real flesh. There must have been copper in those gold claws. As he withdrew them, I hissed at the pain bounding up my leg.

'Yes or no, shade? The hour is late indeed. Some of us still have lives to lead.'

I played reluctant. At the very least, I'd get to stretch my lockpicking fingers. It had been too long since the lockboxes in the widow's tower. 'Fine. Yes.'

Temsa blinked away the surprise as quickly as it had appeared on his face. Perhaps he had been expecting more of a battle. I shrugged. 'No point fighting what I can't fight, is there? I've had enough of that. Might as well do what I'm best at.' At the very least, I could crack some locks while I waited for Temsa to drop his guard.

'Smart shade.'

I clapped my hands together soundlessly. The blue vapour of my fingers intermingled. 'So, what have you got in mind?'

Temsa bared a gold tooth. 'An orgy.'

'Excuse me?'

He took to circling me. 'No event of mine, Caltro. Magistrate Ghoor's. The good magistrate has a penchant for holding grand parties in the safety of his own home. Word has it they are very popular with the tors and tals. It's a perfect opportunity to catch him unawares and claim a few extra spoils while I'm at it.'

'Clever,' I said, pandering to his scheming. 'Who gave you the tip?'

Temsa snorted. 'I have my eyes and ears, living and dead.'

I knew he meant the latter. *The Cult.* 'Well, since you're so flush with information, Tor, what are we talking? A vault? A safe?'

'Vault. Like the others I've recently paid visits to, Magistrate Ghoor is old-fashioned. Has no belief in the security of our fine banks.'

'Such a pity.'

Temsa smirked. 'You're catching on.'

'Thieves think alike.'

I saw displeasure curl his lip. '*I* am a tor, Caltro. You're the thief. And it is time to do your thieving.'

'I don't suppose I get any of the spoils?'

Temsa looked about my room like a decorator given up on life. 'A proper room, perhaps. Maybe one with a decent window. How's that?'

'I—'

Before I could get further, he clicked his fingers and the guards grabbed me by the arms and muscled me along after him. Even though it would be temporary before my escape, I'd take a room over a cell or a wardrobe any day.

Ani Jexebel was waiting for us in a small warehouse adjoining the tavern's pyramid. The slanting walls were lined with figures in black armour. Each bristled with various degrees of sharp implements. Nearby, covered wagons waited with mules and horses lashed to them. Jexebel was standing beside the monster ghost, Danib. Both were wrapped in silk gowns that covered them head to toe, barely hiding the full suits of armour beneath. They looked like wardrobes with heads. As I was marched along, I idly wondered how quickly my manhood would have wilted after seeing those two arrive at an orgy.

Temsa headed towards a carriage that was at odds with the rest of the gathering. It was a square box with gilded edges, with classic Arctian swirls and glyphs painted down its flanks. Two horses had the privilege of pulling it, and each wore a gigantic purple plume on their heads. How the driver could see over them, I had no idea.

Before I was prodded into the coach by Jexebel's gauntlet, another ghost draped a silk robe around me, one with silver thread spread like a ladder down its front.

Inside, I was the paltry filling between a sandwich of Danib and Jexebel. Temsa sat opposite with far too much space to himself. He draped his hands over his ornate cane and stared at the three of us, a smile resting on his face. An uncomfortable grimace hovered on mine. I concentrated on ignoring the solid press of the armour-bound hulks either side of me.

The carriage lurched onwards, and I listened to the sounds of myriad streets and their milling people roll by. Araxes never truly slept, but something about its air tonight seemed subdued, as if a fog had settled on the streets. I saw no such mist in the brief snatches of city I glimpsed through the shutters; just the hooded lanterns of closed shops, and the fleeting shine of blue as shades went about their business. I saw more of them as we swerved onto a high-road and rattled over flagstones built upon squat roofs. The going was faster with fewer peasants in the way. I could see why the rich had built their raised thoroughfares.

The high-road led us deep into the city. As it turned out, Magistrate Ghoor lived near the Core Districts, far from Temsa's lowly tavern. To attack a noble so brazenly in Araxes' centre made him bolder than I'd thought him, and within me a poisonous weed took root: a hope that he would pull it off. The thief in me respected the challenge, but far too much for my liking. I cleared my throat, scrubbing that weed away. I received a sharp nudge from Jexebel in return.

'Keep still,' she growled.

'Something to say, Caltro?' asked Temsa.

I groped for some words, an excuse to try and weaken his wariness some more. Thief's banter.

'This Magistrate Ghoor. What's he done to deserve a visit from the likes of us?' *Us.* No lines drawn between him and me. He raised an eyebrow.

'His name was on the wrong list.'

'Whose list? Yours?'

Pointy interjected, making me flinch. *'The Cult's and the princess'. I heard him talk of both.'* As always, only I heard his voice.

'You're far too curious, Caltro,' Temsa was saying.

'I want to know this is not a dead-end job, pardon the pun.' Now, puns need no pardoning, but I was playing a different Caltro tonight. I heard Pointy chuckling at the tor's hip.

'Impress me tonight, shade, and I will have more use for you.'

I pushed him again. 'When are you going after Widow Horix?'

Temsa's face became stormy. 'Leave the widow to me.'

'She still has my half-coin—'

'You think too much of yourself, Caltro. You are not the glowing light at the centre of my plans. You are a cog in a machine much bigger than you know. Your freedom will come at my leisure. I told you, I will get your coin.'

That nettled me, though I kept my tongue polite. 'You don't need to lecture me on cogs, Tor Temsa.'

Temsa sighed. 'Perhaps I should have opted for a less talkative locksmith. I cut the last one's tongue out, you know.'

'Harder to threaten a ghost with that.' I stuck out my blue tongue. Impish, I know, but I was proving a point.

Danib moved faster than thought, pincering my tongue with one hand and producing a copper blade with the other. The blade sizzled against my vapours, and I squirmed.

Temsa was sniggering to himself. 'Is it now? I've been a soulstealer for twenty-five years, Caltro. I know how to threaten men, dead or alive.'

'Oo wom ime a memer ogthmeh,' I gurgled, like a nursing infant grappling with my first words.

'A better locksmith? What about that Evalon Everass? I hear she's the best in the Reaches.'

'I'm eh begth!'

'Release him, Danib.'

I rubbed my mouth, eyeing the big glowing lump with a sour face. 'She wouldn't work with the likes of you.' At Temsa's scowl, I added, 'Whereas I am happy to.'

'Happiness is for the living, Caltro, not for half-lives like you.'

That put a cork in my unsuccessful attempt to lower his guard. I decided to distract him with my skills instead. I flexed my fingers as the carriage began to slow. An old habit, as I had no sinew to stretch, but it immediately brought a smile to my cheeks. I was there to pick a lock. A vault, no less. I could almost feel my old self again. Temsa was wrong; happiness could come to the dead, too.

'We're here,' murmured Temsa as we jolted to a stop. The driver hauled open the door, showing us a square courtyard washed orange by two torches. They framed a wide door: a half-circle built of layered, varnished wood and black iron. I recognised it immediately: a Maxir door. Named after a doorsmith history had mostly forgotten, Maxirs were eye-wateringly expensive, designed to grow sturdier the more they were attacked. The harder the door was jolted, the tighter the springs held their bolts, the more the pins rattled down their channels into the frame. I hadn't seen one in half a decade. Besides me, the only way through a Maxir door was to have a key, a battering ram the size of a house, or a polite invitation.

We had the latter.

Temsa swaggered assertively from the carriage, making us wait inside. House-guards loomed from the glare behind the torches. No questions, just lowered lances and a statement of, 'Invitation, or leave!'

The tor did not break pace, his foot, cane and talons making an interesting song on the courtyard's sand and stone. He produced four envelopes and fanned them for one of the house-guards to examine. I watched the man's eyes scan the lettering more than once. After a pause far too long for comfort, he waved a hand, and the other guards formed a channel towards the entrance. Jexebel and Danib plucked me from the carriage and practically carried me to the door. I let them, too busy admiring the Maxir design to care.

A small hatch was embedded in the layers of wood and iron. It snapped open, and the house-guard thrust the invitations through the gap. We were rewarded with a clank and the ringing of greased cogs. The door cracked open, its jagged seam spilling lamplight across the courtyard, and we were ushered in.

The starkness of the courtyard seemed to have sneaked into the atrium, and the two levels above that. Plain marble walls and carpetless steps led us upwards. Only half the oil lamps had been lit. I could see Temsa's wary eyes shifting to Danib and Jexebel. They kept their hands straight by their sides, surreptitiously grabbing at weapons beneath their silk gowns. I just looked about, enjoying a change of scenery. Drab though it might have been, it was far more interesting than my cell.

Pointy's voice strode into my head. *'Are you really going to help him?'*

'All part of the plan,' I breathed, and the matter was left there. It wasn't trust that kept the sword silent, I knew that.

It seemed Magistrate Ghoor had a penchant for theatre. Our small party was left alone at the top of the stairs in front of an overwhelmingly plain iron door. The house-guards swiftly clattered down the stairs, ready to greet the next guest. Jexebel growled like a bear with a thorn in its paw.

'Feels like a trap.'

Temsa poked the door with his cane. There were no handles, no locks, no features of any kind. 'Surely the good sisters couldn't have made a mistake, m'dear.'

Danib had already grown tired of the discussion and set his giant hands to the door. It was a simple riddle: with a mighty push, we were bathed in light and merry, cacophonous noise.

A sprawling den of revelry and iniquity lay beyond the doors. My eyes, narrow in the glare of the shining braziers, torches and fire-breathers, flitted about, attempting to take it all in.

Gossamer curtains hung at random from the domed ceiling, obscuring the true size of the hall and painting the various lewd scenes sapphire, emerald or copper. Draped in silks that left little to the imagination, crowds of guests swirled between the veils. They were either festooned in jewels and feathers, or daubed head to toe with coloured dyes and sparkling dust. Some wore masks decorated with antelope and beetle horns, others the patchwork pelts of desert cats. The guests danced and capered wildly between braziers and couches, whooping along to the battling melodies of a hundred harps, flutes and moans from about the hall. Miniature beetles, each as big as a wolf or desert hound, were led about on velvet leashes. I saw a brace of monkeys using the curtains as tree branches. Somewhere in the depths of the hall, behind the haze of pipe smoke, I swore I heard a cow lowing.

Kegs of wine and beer sat on every surface not taken up by food or fornication. People lay beneath the kegs while others turned spouts above. Others looked on, cackling as the drunkards choked.. Golden platters clattered to the marble every now and again, sending fountains of grapes, gritapples and roast shrews into the air. Laughter and cheers would follow as the strange rain pelted the crowds. I watched a wobbly pudding fly across the hall like a jellyfish plucked from the ocean. It collided with a curtain and slid onto a writhing mass of painted bodies. It barely halted the proceedings. Disturbingly, there were a few glowing figures in that tangle.

I was proud to say that this was not my first orgy – I had once stumbled upon one during a heist, and spared a few moments with a very forceful lady lest she sounded the alarm – but it had not looked like this. This hive of lewdness was bedazzling, dizzying. It looked as if these people knew an apocalypse was coming on the morrow, and wanted to cram a whole life into one night. It was the distillation of all Araxes' love for sin and debauchery, poured into one hall. There was no envy in me, no longing to have blood pumping through me so I could dive in. It was closer to horrifying than exciting. The complete abandonment of rules and civilisation wrinkled my lip. Had I been in the possession of a stomach I didn't doubt it would have been turned.

Temsa looked on with a bored look, as if this was an average night for him. He prodded me with his cane. 'They say whatever your thirst, Araxes can slake it.'

I stepped backwards as two naked men, barely older than boys and covered in grease, sped past us snorting with laughter. A man – who to call obese would have been putting it kindly – came shuffling after them, completely devoid of breath. He grinned at us with wine-stained lips and hurried on. I tried to keep my eyes from his bare midriff.

'Let's find our magistrate,' ordered Temsa.

We waded inwards, picking a weaving path between the rainbow drapes and the moaning piles. Several naked figures clung to Temsa, cooing at his eagle's claw. He did not thrust them away, and instead allowed them to whisper saucy things in his ears. I heard some of the offers and they did not sound appealing, even to one such as me, whose sexual interactions were beyond scarce and usually expensive. The more I watched Temsa, the more I could see him enjoying the attention.

'The perks of tordom are many, Caltro,' he opined, seeing my side-ways glances. 'It's almost a pity to ruin this party.'

I caught the roll of Jexebel's eyes and pondered whether there was a crack forming in her loyalty.

Pointy grumbled privately. *I've seen some parties in my centuries, but never like this.*'

Temsa's naked partygoers were distracted by two men bathing in large marble seashells filled with pink wine. We continued our tour.

After much wandering, we found a small ring of men and women in a secluded alcove, propped up on massive burgundy cushions. The group was a spectrum of inebriation. Three lovers were mid-fuck, yet each was so drunk they kept forgetting what needed to be put in where. One man had fallen asleep between the buxom breasts of an enormous lady, naked but for a silk shawl. I wondered if he had suffocated. There were worse ways to die. *Trust me.*

'Emperor and Code bless you!' announced Temsa as he strode into the circle. I was held back by Danib and Jexebel. I felt the latter's breath on my shoulder, disturbing my vapours. A few heads rose from their goblets, eyes rolling about drunkenly. 'I am Tor Boran Temsa. Who might you be, Tals, Tors, or Sereks?'

'Drunk!' yelled a woman with a ponytail protruding from the side of her shaved head. Raucous laughter came from her fellows.

'I hearda you. Heard the rumoursh,' another slurred, a large man utterly covered in wine stains and crumbs. His bushy blond beard had been dyed purple, and his foot was resting on the back of a naked ghost. She was frozen in shape, eyes shut.

'Me?' Temsa beamed.

'You're the... the...' He paused to belch explosively. 'Quick rysher, ain't you? Wash out for him, shenelmen.'

A few of the others propped themselves up on their elbows, blinking like stupefied toads, then remembered they held wine in their hands and slurped away.

Temsa spread his hands wide to the group. 'And who do I have the pleasure of addressing?'

The man looked around. He jabbed his fingers at the two immediately beside him: a woman busy trying to keep her head from lolling, and a pox-scarred raven of a man. 'She'sh Tal Berinia. He'sh a sherek. I'm a Shamber mashistrate.'

After a bow, Temsa took a seat on an empty pillow beside him. 'Magistrate…?'

The fat man took his time recalling the answer. 'Ghoor!'

Temsa took up a discarded goblet of wine and raised it as high as his crooked back would allow. 'To change!'

Ghoor needed no excuse to drink. 'To shange!' He banged his foot on the back of the ghost, and I heard her whimper. I pursed my lips. This man certainly didn't look like he deserved his rank, his tower, or his life. Neither did any of the others, by my reckoning. In a way, perhaps Temsa was doing good work, lancing these boils from the skin of Araxes. I looked behind me and saw just how many boils there were. The skin of Araxes was pustulant, and it dawned on me then that Temsa might kill them all. The game of the City of Countless Souls was a lucrative one when played without mercy or moral.

After a wink from their boss, Danib and Ani marched back through the rambunctious crowd and to the nearest doorway. Nobody noticed. The house-guards standing about the hall were busy grinning ear to ear, their eyes murky with wine. Most of them had somehow misplaced their armour.

For half an hour, Temsa kept the drunks busy with idle chatter, dancing around vague politics and city rumours. Time and time again, a murderer was mentioned by slurring tongues. Temsa seemed to be the talk of the city.

'An' there wash the fire, in Nebra'sh tower! And Rebene knowsh nothing,' murmured Ghoor, slopping wine over his legs and the ghost girl. Half of it dripped through her, the rest swirled with her blue skin, turning purple.

'Is that so?' Temsa looked pleased. That irritated me. 'Nothing, eh?'

Wine decorated the floor and the ghost. 'Shcrutinishersh are cluelesh! It's all too shushpishus!'

The tor had the gall to look sage. 'In such dangerous times, it pays to keep your wits about you.'

Through the rainbow drapes, I saw Danib and Jexebel sneak back into the hall, keeping the iron door ajar. Their faces were avid, almost thrilled, and their nods sure. Temsa had spotted them too.

'For instance,' he said, 'buying good doors and locking them tight.'

A rumble of agreement came from the drunks. I swear I heard a muffled word or two from between those great bosom.

Temsa got to his feet and tapped his way around the back of the cushion pile, refilling their wine from a crystal decanter as he went. 'Paying good silver for good house-guards.'

'Mmm!' Ghoor raised his goblet for some more wine. Temsa didn't care where he poured it, dousing the magistrate in the ruby liquid. Ghoor giggled like a child with a bug under his shirt.

'And watching who you trust enough to invite to parties...'

Magistrate Ghoor's eyes were firmly crossed. As I stared down at him, I wondered if there was some glimmer of realisation, somewhere deep within that addled mind.

'*Caltro...*' I heard Pointy's murmur, deadened as though a hand were clamped around his mouth.

With a flash of golden silks, Temsa whipped the sword from his scabbard. Razor-sharp obsidian opened the pox-scarred serek's throat, spattering Tal Berinia and Ghoor with blood. They were too drunk to make sense of it all. The magistrate was still giggling, thinking it was more wine. He even licked his fingers.

Berinia was next, her head finally escaping her shoulders. She kept her confused expression until it met the floor. I saw it all too well, seeing as I had been thrown to the stained flagstones and fallen next to it. Danib and Jexebel had cast aside their gowns and drawn their blades. They set about putting them to work. That set the screams alight.

Men in Ghoor's livery poured into the hall, and for a moment I thought Temsa's game was up, but then I saw how they attacked the useless house-guards, and realised their disguises. I watched with a clenched jaw as they went about earning their silver, painting over the kaleidoscopic scene with red. The guests were caught completely by surprise, drunk and defenceless. Temsa's soldiers had no care for which activities they interrupted. I saw a couple impaled on the same spear, and a drunkard's arm lopped off as he reached for another beer. Those who managed to scramble for the door found their way blocked by Danib and Jexebel's axes. After I saw the second man split down the middle, I had to turn away. Licentious and depraved the party might have been, I was still human – a shade of one at least. This scene was far more disgusting than its previous iteration.

The massacre lasted for some time before its horrific music faded: screams dying one by one instead of in concert, cut short with a percussive clang or a thud. Torturous minutes I waited while Temsa looked past me, watching his orders being followed to the bloody letter. I could see the carnage reflected in his eyes, and I had to turn away from them as well. I looked instead to Ghoor and shared his horror, growing deeper the more he sobered up. And he was managing it swiftly.

When the last groan was uttered, he found his words. No slurring now. Not with a keen sword at his throat. It had already cut away a great deal of purple beard.

'W—why?' he stammered.

Temsa waited until Danib rejoined them and hauled the fat magistrate to his feet with one hand. The tor stared up at Ghoor, his ardour for butchery smouldering in his eyes.

'A colleague of mine asked me that earlier, and I'll give you the same answer. Your name was on a list; nothing more. Though with you being a man of the Chamber, after seeing the kind of company you keep, and because of your sheer apathy over your guest list, Magistrate, I could think up some more reasons for you, if you'd like?'

Ghoor's chins wobbled like the concertinas of a smith's bellows. 'I… no.'

Temsa clicked his fingers, and his soldiers brought forth a well-dressed man whose face was a pale shade of green. He stepped over the entrails and lost limbs, flinching every time his polished shoes came into contact. He looked the financial type. I found they looked the same all over the Reaches. It was easy to spot them, for they liked to be known for what they were, and how much power they held. No better than royals bearing their crowns. I preferred to see their suits as prisoners' stripes; their crimes were just rewarded instead of punished.

The tor greeted him cordially, wrapping an arm around him and leading him to Ghoor. 'Ah, Mr Fenec. My trusty sigil. Are you well? You look thin. Must be all the stress of the banking world, eh? How's the family?'

The man possessed the voice of a timid mouse. 'Fine.'

'And may they continue to stay that way.'

From my spot on the marble, I could see the bile in this Fenec fellow's gullet rise and fall. I guessed him to be another cog in Temsa's machine.

'B—Tor Temsa, my father grows suspicious. I…' His voice failed him as Temsa's grip tightened.

'Perhaps I should have a word with your father directly. Especially after tonight. There'll no doubt be some careful counting to do here. Inheritances, insurances and the like. Dealings with other banks. Perhaps it's over a sigil's head. Wouldn't you say, Russun?'

Russun bowed his head solemnly, as if he had just physically thrown his father in front of an armoured carriage.

'On that note: Ghoor's papers. What will it be this time? Distant cousins? Business partners?' Temsa stuck out a hand, and Russun sighed as he produced a scroll.

'People are talking. I've had to get... inventive. It'll pass through several vaults before yours. Harder to trace.'

'Fine work! You do your kind proud.'

The sigil had no more words, it seemed. He nodded, turning greener by the moment. He kept his hand clamped over his mouth just long enough to pass over a reed before running to spew his guts up in a corner.

'Let's hope your father has a stronger stomach,' Temsa tutted.

Ghoor stared goggle-eyed at the scroll held before him. One of his hands was released and the inked reed stuffed into it.

Temsa tapped the papyrus. 'Sign.'

'What is this?' The magistrate's pickled brain struggled to make sense of the situation. I watched him squirm in Danib's grip.

'Sign it, and I might just spare you.'

'I will not sign anything!' Ghoor remembered his status, as if that could help him with a serek and a tor lying dead next to him.

'Danib?'

There came a loud crack and a squeal as the magistrate's other hand was crushed in the press of the ghost's gauntlet. Blue vapours curled from the seams of his helmet, and I imagined Danib was smiling beneath it.

Ghoor was apparently short on spine. The reed scratched across the papyrus marvellously quickly after that, albeit shakily. Temsa cracked a smile, looking between his minions.

'Well, that was simple! A man of the Code, giving up so easily? Doesn't that speak more about this city than my murdering does? There we are, Sigil!'

Russun came scurrying up, his chin decorated with vomit.

Temsa pressed his cane into the man's chest. 'Take a tally of every corpse here that banked with Fenec Coinery. I want their half-coins transferred to my vaults. Them, and any others I can claim without a ridiculous amount of suspicion; you point them out and my men'll pile them up.'

Jexebel piped up. 'And the rest?'

'Bind them. Take their trinkets. Cut their tongues. Sell them cheap at market, or to the Consortium. I hear Kal Duat's expanding.'

'Tor… My father will never—' Russun squawked.

Temsa jabbed him hard. 'Tor Fenec won't have a problem, I'm sure. Like you, he had the stupidity to breed.'

Russun's green pallor faded to white as he was forcibly embarked on a gruesome tour by two black-clad thugs. Temsa winked before turning back to Ghoor.

'Now, Magistrate. I hear your vault is hidden. Be a good boy and tell us where it is, hmm? Save us some time.'

'No.' Ghoor's wide eyes scrambled over the dead, clearly trying not to count. It is in these moments that a person has to decide what's worth dying for; what can be given up to save a skin. Ghoor proved himself a fool, thinking he had a choice. 'No, you can't have my coins!'

Temsa chuckled as he took a measured step backwards. 'What do you think you just signed? They're already mine. And see this shade? He's the best locksmith in all the Reaches. You are of no use to me.'

'I…' Realisation struck the magistrate like a cheap punch. 'The

Chamber will see you dead for this! Stoned to death at the Grand Nyxwell!'

Temsa sighed, looking to Jexebel. 'Useless threats always come once all hope is lost, don't you find, m'dear?'

Pointy was a black and copper blur. The cut was so fine that everyone present shared a look, wondering where the blood was. It chose that moment to flow down his neck and chest, pouring as if from nowhere.

'I hate my new life,' Pointy sighed.

Unnervingly, Ghoor chose to stare at me while he choked his last, as if holding me personally responsible for robbing him. I couldn't meet those bulging red eyes, and found escape in Temsa's. Ignoring my gaze, the tor reached into Ghoor's bloody collar and plucked forth a key on a chain. He threw it at me.

'Get to work!' he roared.

Jexebel pushed me, following her boss out of the blood-slick hall and high into the upper levels. Temsa's soldiers swarmed about us, pouring down corridors at every level, hammering walls and tearing apart cupboards. They seemed far too used to this sort of work. I heard the clash of more fighting far below. There were still house-guards to be dealt with.

Temsa guessed as I would have, and found the vault in the magistrate's bedchambers. Some noble folk couldn't help but keep their fortunes close by. It was why many of them never dallied with banks; they couldn't believe they were rich unless they could see and touch their wealth. I once burgled a house where the vault was under the bed, so the man could sleep on his spoils.

Once again, the men went to work. Velvet curtains were dragged aside. The fake wall was wrenched away. In a short space of time, the gleam of gold and steel lit the room.

Temsa whispered encouragement in my ear. 'Your turn, Caltro. Don't fuck it up.'

I was shoved forwards, despite the fact I was already rubbing my hands together. A small pouch landed next to me with a clink, and I knew it contained my tools. I clutched them to my side as I measured up my challenge.

The vault was pretty, for a monster. Its face was a rectangle of polished metal, chiselled with all sorts of Arctian history in which I had no interest. A squat door sat in its middle between two thick golden columns. An array of locking mechanisms protruded from it: overlapping plates hiding the clockwork guts of the door. They were fashioned after the heavens, shaped like stars or moons, studded with amethysts, carnelian, and ivory.

'Hello, dear,' I whispered to the vault, my gaze roaming over its jewellery.

Temsa rammed his cane into the marble. 'Well? What are you waiting for?'

'I'm thinking,' I snapped.

'Having second thoughts, are y—'

'This vault was built by Fenris and Daughters. Poured stone door, with steel outer layer and gold fascia. Two-key sequential mechanism, backed up by a combination lock, no doubt with false gates on the discs. Welded strike plates, drilling guards, and sealed hinges. Tough, but far from impossible. Ghoor should have spent less on his Maxir door and more on his vaults.'

My smirk was not shy. Temsa just folded his arms.

I raised the bloody key to the ceiling. The metal frosted at my touch. 'We're missing a key, but fortunately for you, Tor, Fenris and his daughters make some of the noisiest vault mechanisms known to locksmiths. Lot of slop in those locks.'

Stepping over the marble, I bent my ear to the gold near the first keyhole, inserted Ghoor's key, and listened as I turned it, once, twice, thrice. The cogs beneath the metal plates sang to me like a choir. I left it unlocked and moved to the next, tucking two picks into the guarded keyhole. It had been some time since I held my tools, and my fingers were number than usual. I blamed the hauntings, and yet the steel between my blue fingers felt more solid than anything I had known so far as a ghost. Setting my jaw, I began.

To me, it was a battle. My wits against machine and ingenuity, my tools my weapons. To everybody else, it was a ghost muttering away in front of a pretty door.

Temsa soon got bored of my tiny movements and gurning face of concentration, and left me alone with Jexebel. He and Danib wandered off, eager to explore the magistrate's tower. That was fine by me. I was busy duelling with the door.

Left one. Right three. Up and across. Left seven.

There came a click as the tumblers fell and stuck. I chuckled to myself. 'Sorry. Not tonight.'

'Tell me you aren't talkin' to the fuckin' door,' Jexebel challenged me.

In my concentration I had forgotten she was there, lurking behind me, axe resting on her shoulder. I shrugged. 'Maybe.'

'Fuckin' fool.'

I moved on to the combination lock, analysing a series of wheels protruding from a plate carved in the shape of a fiery sun. Number glyphs ran along their edges, and a column of disc-like cogs sat beneath them, trapped behind gold filigree.

'Who's the bigger fool? The fool, or the fool who follows him?' I asked her. It was some old Krass proverb that had lodged in my head since childhood. My wisdom was rewarded with a whack, and I bared my teeth at the taste of Jexebel's copper-edged gauntlets.

'What's that supposed to mean?' she hissed.

'You follow Temsa, right?'

The hand rose for another strike. 'Calling me a fool?'

'No,' I said, meeting those dark brown eyes of hers. 'I'm saying don't be led by one. Makes you a fool too.'

She struck me anyway. Once I'd peeled myself off the floor, I went back to the vault, keeping one eye closed as pain swam through me. I put my hands to the filigree. My glowing vapours trailed over the golden threads. 'This will take some time.'

'We have all night.'

I was already too engrossed to answer. Flicking any wheel set the discs in motion, winding down to some clanking resolution before they snapped back into place. I pored over every clank and twang, listening to the heartbeat of the vault.

'Why do you work for him, anyway?' I asked, once I'd found the first number. Its disc spun once with a clockwork ticking, coming to rest pointing east, if it were a broken compass.

Jexebel ignored me for some time, as if my words had fallen on deaf ears, until finally: 'Pay's good. Killing's good.'

'But why him? Why not some other tor or tal? One without all the…' I wiggled my fingers. 'Hassle.'

'I like hassle.' Jexebel spat for punctuation. 'He's smarter than most. Got more balls than any. Look how far he's come. A bloody tor now. And the more he claims, the bigger my share.'

I flashed her a sidelong look. 'Taken to tordom quite easily, hasn't he?'

The furrow in her brow was gone in an instant, but I caught it. And pressed it. 'He looks very different from the man who lectured me on death my first day as a ghost. And he wants his own tower now, I see?'

The muscular lump of a woman pretended not to hear me.

'He's got protection, I'd wager. Someone high up.' *The empress-in-waiting and the Cult.* And I highly doubted either knew about the other. Temsa must have been wedged between them.

Jexebel merely grunted.

I paused as I found the next combination, snapping my picks together into a slim file to persuade a disc into skipping a tooth. 'Promises seem to be slippery things in this city. Doesn't pay to put your trust in the wrong people.'

Jexebel gave me a dangerous look. I had plucked a nerve, but seeing her gauntlets clench for another blow, I lacked the balls to go further. I'd sparked the tinder. Now to let it smoulder.

Clank. The disc fell into line, and half of the golden plates spread across the face of the door rotated. I had shaken the heavens.

The last disc was a little bastard, tucked away behind the door's surface so that I could barely see it. I used my file to break apart some of the weaker filigree so I could follow the clockwork back to the number wheels. It took me almost an hour to figure its combinations, and it left me with one solution. I wasn't usually one for brute force, especially with so much work poured into making a vault so alluring. But I was also a thief, and severely lacking in morals. If I needed to play dirty to win a duel, I'd be knee-deep in mud before you could blink.

'I could use your axe, Miss Jexebel,' I said.

'You can fuck right off—'

'You can swing it, just right here. How accurate are you with that thing?'

'I can cut the nose from your face with it.'

'Perfect. Then cut the nose from the face of this plate, if you please.'

She took one swing for practice, and another for the damage. There was a whoosh and a clank as the axe-head took the corner off the ornate plate in a shower of sparks. In the gap Jexebel had made, I could see the last pieces of the puzzle. I set about rearranging the wheels with my picks, and seeing as I was poised for the killing blow, I celebrated by goading Jexebel some more.

'See? Temsa might have the balls, but he's got no brawn. Imagine having both. That would make a person a great tor. Or a great tal...'

I managed to duck the first fist, but the second caught me in the midriff and flattened me against the door. Had I flesh, the stars and moons would have been cutting neat patterns in my ribcage. As Jexebel loomed over me, debating another strike, I raised a finger and placed it on the nearest metal wheel.

'It's done,' I said.

With a flick of my finger, the discs began to whir. The golden heavens performed their rotating dance, and after a great groan – both from me and the vault – the door was released from its locks. I got to my feet, clasping my hands as it swung open, blazing gold and copper. This was not one of Horix's empty chests. This was a vault bursting with a hoard of half-coins. If only mine had been in there, this moment would have been all the sweeter.

'Boss! TOR!' hollered Jexebel, right in my ear. I dropped my tools, and as I bent down, she kicked my knees from beneath me and pinned me to the floor. I felt the soles of her boots sizzling against my vaporous skin.

Tap, *clang*, *tap*, *clang*, came the cane and talons down the hallway. Temsa soon appeared, eyes wide and full of greed as he gazed upon the open vault. 'Quick work, Caltro Basalt.'

'You asked me to do a job. I did it,' I said, somewhat muffled with a face full of marble.

He hobbled past me and into the vault itself. Stacks of half-coins lined tight shelves, bound in papyrus string and inked with number glyphs. He pored over his new coins. 'Quite the haul.'

I stared at the other trinkets on the mahogany shelves: a gilded helmet, a jewel-studded vase, and a crystal skull whose eyes called to mine. 'Do I get anything for my troubles?' I asked.

Temsa sneered at me. 'I don't see a white feather on your breast, shade. Do you? Ani, escort this pretender back to the carriage and back to his cell.'

I pounded my fist on the marble. 'Cell? You said a room—'

Temsa prodded me in the ear with his cane. 'Next time, talk less, Caltro.'

'You—' My hopes were further quashed when Ani Jexebel hauled me upright and sent me staggering out into the hallway.

Pointy had some words for me before I was out of earshot. *'Whatever you're up to, don't leave me with him. You owe me that much…'*

I kept my silence until Jexebel shoved me through the Maxir door, where a number of wagons and a few carriages had arrived. More men in false livery stood about, shaking their heads firmly at several enraged nobles. The guests were too busy waving envelopes in their faces to know they had narrowly escaped massacre.

I spied a flash of red in the crowds and saw the glowing, hooded face of a familiar figure: the cultist I'd seen leaving Temsa's tavern. She seemed to be smiling at me, or Jexebel, I couldn't tell. In any case, I heard my minder growl over my shoulder, and I was stowed in the nearest wagon.

Two guards joined me, sitting opposite with swords drawn. I crossed my arms in pathetic defiance. Before Jexebel could shut the door, I speared her with a glare.

'See?' I said. 'Promises are slippery in this town.'

The door slammed with a resounding finality, and the carriage lurched into the night.

CHAPTER 13
A DEBT

Beetles. You shipped us four score riding-beetles
instead of perfectly good, four-legged horses.
Damn things refuse to cross any water: rivers,
even a stream, dead gods damn it! I'm surprised
you got them on the ships. What am I supposed
to do with these creatures, you cretins?

FROM A SCROLL SENT TO THE CHAMBER OF
MILITARY MIGHT BY GENERAL HJEBE IN 998

I T WAS DAWN WHEN NILITH awoke to a soft pecking at her cheek. She felt the light beyond her eyelids but refused to open them.

'My, my,' said a small voice near her head. 'Somebody got shit-faced last night.'

Nilith had to use her fingers to pry her eyelids apart. Even the dim sun was enough to scald the inside of her skull. She felt like ants had crawled into her head and were carving up her brain, piece by piece. It felt like the little bastards were pulling her eyes into their sockets by their nerves.

She had clearly gone mad. There was a bird standing before her. A falcon. Its golden eyes pierced her. And it was talking.

'Morning, pretty face. Remember me?'

'What the—? You're back,' she managed before retching. Nothing came up. 'All I remember is a flying donkey.'

'Don't know about any flying fucking donkey. What did Her Royal-ness drink, then, hmm? Or smoke, for that matter?'

Nilith slumped back to the sand, chin on arms. She stared up at the falcon. 'I don't feel very royal.'

'Royally fucked is what you are. Now you know why these nomad types call their wine daemonjuice, don't you?'

'Where's Ghyrab?' she croaked.

'The bargeman? Over there, currently downing a whole skin of water.'

Nilith managed to angle herself to see Ghyrab standing by Anoish. He'd woken up a different man. Gone was the crooked back and the scowl he was so fond of wearing. He was shirtless, and for the first time, Nilith saw tribal tattoos curling around his ribs, like ivy around a pillar. He held a waterskin high, half of it missing his mouth and washing the sand from his neck.

He caught her stare and wandered across the sand to drip water over her. Nilith groaned.

'Morning, Majesty. Falcon.'

'Old boat person,' said the bird, dipping his head before pecking at an empty bottle.

'How are you not… like me?' Nilith asked.

Ghyrab puffed out his chest. 'Ain't the first time I drank daemon-juice. These are desert-folk. I am desert-folk.'

'And I, clearly, am not.' Nilith dug up some reserve of strength and staggered to her feet. 'I have drunk Dolkfang medea, tasted firewine from the northern tribes, even tried the black pirate rum of the Scatter Isles. But never in what precious life I have left will I let that cursed daemonjuice pass my lips again.'

She tottered towards the horse, who took one sniff of her and whinnied. 'We have to…' Nilith scratched her head, finding a lump and wondering where it had come from. She remembered dancing. Or at least trying to dance. 'What were we doing?'

'Finding Farazar.'

'Shit!' The hangover spread its anxiety through her as if her blood had turned to needles. Her poisoned gut growled as it clenched. 'He could be leagues away by now.' Nilith scrabbled around the horse, checking her supplies.

Bezel looked up from his idle preening. 'Oh, I know where he is.'

'What?'

'He can't navigate for shit, even with the city right there. Keeps wandering east and west.'

Nilith looked up, seeing the glint of marble and glass that filled the horizon.

'He's a day's solid ride ahead, nearing the Sprawls, but not moving as fast as you with all his zigzagging. Got some beetle with him. Dead gods know where he found that. Or how he charmed it into suffering him.'

'I... Thank you, Bezel,' sighed Nilith. The news didn't stop her trying to hop up onto Anoish's back. It took her several awkward attempts, but she managed it eventually. Anoish shook his mane disapprovingly.

'Ghyrab, there's no time. Come on.' Nilith shuffled forwards on the horse's spine to give him some room, but the bargeman didn't move. 'Come on!'

'I'm stayin',' he said flatly.

'That's great. Co—What?' Her neck clicked horridly as she whirled around.

The bargeman wiped the water from his grizzled chin, staring south. 'Like I said, I'm desert-folk. I can't remember a time with so much dancin' and singin'. I've been alone for too long.' His tone was wistful. 'An' I ain't made for horseback, nor chasin' after dead kings with queens, no offence. This is your battle, not mine.'

Nilith was deeply confused, and somewhat disappointed, until she saw a nearby tent flap waver, and a Windchaser woman with grey hair and curling horns staring at them through the gap. 'I see. But what about your barge?'

Ghyrab chuckled, baring yellow teeth. 'Forget the barge. Maybe I'll ride the Race Ruts instead of the Ashti for a time. Won't be long until the Consortium own the whole river, rate they're going. Maybe it's time to get back to dry land.'

Nilith manoeuvred the horse closer to the man, who held up a hand. She shook it tightly. 'I would have kept my promise, you know.'

He nodded. 'And that's why I came this far with you. Whatever it is you're fighting for, it seems a good fight, and I wish you well with it. Maybe there's change in the winds coming for the Arc. Good fortune, Empress,' he said. For the first time, he bowed deeply, with true reverence.

Nilith lowered her head to him, and after one last look around the Windchaser camp, with its skinny donkeys nibbling at forgotten plates between the blue tents, she spurred Anoish into a gallop.

The desert flew by in their eager chase, but she ignored it all, trying her best to forget the pounding of her head and focusing on keeping her stomach contents where they were. She slurped water from a skin between Anoish's strides, but that gave little comfort, and as they charged in and out of the last few Race Ruts and back into a patchwork desert of greens and reds, the sun began to bake her.

She was glad Bezel had returned. He flew beside her for a time, racing the horse, then took to the clear blue to keep his eyes on the distant Farazar. Or so Nilith hoped. She trusted the bird's eyes.

When he swooped back down again, she lent him a perch on her arm. She winced as one of his talons punctured her leather-bound sleeve.

'Sorry,' he squawked. 'That happens.'

'What did she want?'

'Who?'

'My scheming daughter.' Nilith had never heard a bird growl before, but Bezel managed it.

'Oh. *Her*. To know where you are.'

'And?'

The falcon winked. 'Your secret is safe, Empress. I muddied your trail. Kept her guessing.'

Nilith took a breath, not wanting to know the answer to her question. 'What is she up to? Do they still think Farazar is in his Sanctuary? Tell me Araxes isn't aflame.'

'Seemed normal to me, if you call a shit-heap of human effluence and withered morals normal. They still think Farazar is safe and sound, or so it looked. Though there has been one fire, now that you mention it. I saw the smouldering wreck of a tower before I left.'

That did not fill Nilith with confidence, and her gut wrenched again. She held up a finger and bent over the side of the horse to vomit.

Bezel tutted. 'Fuck me.'

'Shut your beak. I think they poisoned me.'

'You poisoned yourself.'

'Mgrph.'

A moment passed as Nilith gathered her thoughts, like herding cats into a basket. 'Throughout this whole ordeal, I have thought of her. Worried over her. I left her with my duties, hoping they would distract her long enough. Thought I could busy her with the whining of the Cloud Court.' Nilith winced, feeling dread rear its head. 'I've been away too long—' Another heave stole her words. When she was finished, she wiped her mouth. 'Who knows what she is plotting in my absence?'

'What did you expect?'

'From her?' Nilith stared at the city, gleaming like treasure on the horizon. 'I don't know. For her to surprise me, maybe. But her hate for Farazar and me runs too deep.'

'Can't that Etane shade of yours keep her in check? Isn't that why you left him behind?'

'I can only hope he's reining her in, but few things, if anything, can keep a Talin Renala in check. Especially Sisine. Not since Farazar got his claws in her. He and his parents spoiled her, poisoned her against me. It's why she's…' Nilith grimaced. 'Like she is.'

'What? Arctian?' Bezel clacked his beak, and she watched the wind pester his feathers.

'I could have done more. Fought harder for her.'

Failure. The word stung her then, as it did whenever she dared to look into the past and wonder what she could have done differently as a mother. *The past is a clear window, and yet memory stains it with its own colours.* Motherhood had been soiled with gloomy tones.

'Look, Empress, I've seen a lot of that family come and go in my time, and from what I can tell, she was always going to be her father's daughter, and follow in his bloody footprints. She ain't no child of yours, and I mean that in a good way. Like you say, the Talin Renalas had their hooks in her the moment the emperor was in you, pardon the bluntness.'

Nilith nodded. She had never felt like Sisine's true mother. Sisine had come from her womb, true, but tradition had put her in the arms of nurses and maids instead of Nilith's own, as if an empress was too busy to bother herself with a child. Nilith had tried to tear that tradition down like a moth-eaten tapestry, but Farazar, old Emperor Milizan and his wife Hirana had rallied against her, enforcing Sisine's heritage. They had even named her without Nilith's consent. Two years passed had like that, until the drama of the Cult and the murder of Milizan wrenched Sisine from the sunny plains of childhood to the sharp-toothed mountain range of life. Titles. Power. Greed. She had taken to playing with these instead of toys. Farazar had encouraged it, while at the same time becoming increasingly fond of his Sanctuary, leaving Nilith to battle with their ever more aloof daughter.

'Still with us?' The falcon's voice made her flinch.

'Aye,' Nilith said, slipping back into an older accent.

'See? Krass through and through,' he squawked. 'Which is why I'm surprised at this game you're playing.'

This was no game. 'What game?'

Bezel shrugged his wings toward Araxes. '*Their* fucking game. The Arctian game. The claiming the throne for yourself game. Husband sneaks out of his Sanctuary to go fuck southern girls. Fools everyone, including you. You find out, and decide to teach him a thing or two. I get it. Didn't want to say anything before, but an outsider? Teaching them all a lesson? Beating them with their own dirty rules? All fine by me.'

Nilith narrowed her eyes at the bird. 'That's not what this is about.'

His golden orbs matched hers. 'Oh, no?'

'No.'

'Then please, fucking enlighten me.'

They stared at each other, wordless, woman and falcon, each bobbing along to Anoish's gallop.

'Don't tell me you've got something,' he pulled a wry face, looking disgusted, '*virtuous* in mind?'

The past month hadn't felt very virtuous to Nilith. It felt a lot like pain, and sickness, and fear. The desert had taught her a thing or two about virtue, but it was far from rewarded in the wilds of the Arc. Punished, even, just like the city.

'We'll see,' Nilith grunted. 'Once this fucking nonsense is dusted off my palms and all of Araxes has heard my words. We'll see.'

'Hmm. As the new and sole Arctian empress, I take it?'

'You judge me, bird? Without knowing what I intend to do?' Nilith demanded imperiously.

'Shit. You sound just like Farazar,' he replied, looking north. 'Maybe there is a bit of Arctian in you after all. Bit of desert dust in those green Krass eyes?'

'You better watch your... beak.'

Bezel launched himself from his perch and went back to flapping alongside her. 'In all my years, I've found there's always a reward hidden in selflessness. Like a charity that gathers alms for the poor yet paints its ceilings with gold.'

'That's not what this is,' Nilith insisted. 'There will be little reward for me. If any.'

'You always this fucking cryptic?'

Nilith looked across the Duneplains, ever wary despite ridding herself of the Ghouls. There was a sandstorm billowing in the west, distant for the time being, and she hoped it would stay that way. She looked north, to where Araxes shimmered in the heat, as if it lay under the waters of a mountain stream. The sprawling edges of the city came closer with every hoofbeat, but to her eyes it seemed to stay still, forever out of reach. Sprawled before it, the rise and fall of dunes and rifts offered a dull path. A few errant roads had begun to appear and coalesce, like tributaries winding out of the desert to join a sea of adobe and sandstone. She squinted. A hundred miles to the Sprawls, she measured. Another hundred to the tower the size of a titan's spear, standing upright in the earth, and the Grand Nyxwell.

Nilith wondered whether anybody would notice if she just gave up now, went back to the Windchasers, and faded into the desert. Such thoughts had become more numerous in recent days. Louder, too. As always, she leaned to the side of the horse, and spat what saliva she could muster. 'This is a mantle I should wear myself. As it has been this entire journey. Maybe years before that.'

Bezel laughed shrilly. 'If you're not going to tell me, I can only assume it's because it's risky as shit. Or you don't trust me.'

Nilith forced a smirk. His talk had set a fresh thudding in her head. She hunkered down, holding Anoish's coarse mane tight. She stared at the falcon, wings beating the air in rapid yet calm succession, his little body arrow straight, keen eyes constantly flicking over the horizon.

'I trust you.'

His cackle was mocking. 'Trust is overrated. I don't need you to trust me. Just keep up your part of the bargain.'

'And I shall. Though I have been thinking.'

'I thought I could smell burning…'

'Why not live on, free to do what you want?'

'I have done that. I've lived two hundred years as a fucking bird. I've seen half that many emperors and empresses come and go. I've seen parts of this world your maps don't even have names for. I am fucking bored. Done.'

'And why not throw your bell into the Nyx? Reach the afterlife. *Duat.*'

'Why would I want to spend another two centuries amidst a crowd of fucking dead?'

Nilith was confused. 'Crowds? What crowds?'

Bezel looked angry, as if remembering some past hurt she'd inflicted on him. 'It's the great lie, Nilith. There is nothing beyond life but endless crowds of shades. Whining, crying, waiting, staring at nothing but dead stars. I hovered there for what felt like an age before the Nyxites dragged me back. Most souls don't linger there long enough to make sense of it, that's why it's not spoken of. I would rather be nothing than visit that place again.'

Before Nilith could reply, the falcon tore upwards into the blue so he could look around. She waited for him to come back down, a confession poised on her tongue. She had sworn not to spill her secrets until she was standing over the Grand Nyxwell, but the bird had bared his soul, and Nilith felt the need to do the same. She knew all too well how sharing words could share their weight, and she was already withering under her burden as it was.

But she never got the chance. Bezel announced his return with a screech. 'There's a man coming this way.'

Nilith buried her face in Anoish's mane, feeling exhaustion paw at her. 'Dangerous looking?'

'Can't tell. Looks the travelling sort. Coming from the north and west. He's riding easy on a wagon. Two horses. If we keep going this way, we'll pass him before sunset.'

'Just one man?'

'Unless he's hiding somebody else under that mound of silks and jewellery he's wearing. Or on the wagon. Got a sheet over some box.'

'Silks and jewellery…' Nilith trailed off, her thoughts turning inwards. She thought of pompous vapid men, standing over Ghyrab's barge, speaking of tolls, and yelling threats. 'Keep an eye on him. And where's my gods-damned husband?'

'Maybe ten miles ahead, going slower now.'

'Well, come on!' Nilith yelled, making her headache flare. 'Let's deal with one idiot at a time.' She kicked the horse with her heels, and Anoish put more speed into his gallop, throwing up a column of orange dust behind them.

———◆———

'BLASTED BEETLE!'

The confounded insect had decided it needed a rest. Though it might have trotted about like a faithful steed, it certainly did not follow the rules of day and night.

The day before, it had resolved to take a break for two hours just because it saw a rock it didn't like. Now it was hunkered down and chattering at a distant sandstorm splayed across the western horizon like a smear of orange dung. Farazar regarded the storm with the same distaste, a hint of fear tugging at his lips.

His last encounter with a sandstorm had been far from pleasant. He spread his hands over his naked frame and remembered the hissing of the sand passing through him, of copper dust stinging him. It was occurrences such as those that reminded Farazar he was dead. Dead as a doorstep. Just another half-life that made up the glowing masses of the Arc.

He snarled and kicked sand at the beetle.

'Come along, I say!' He tried again to lead it away, walking a short distance to a cairn of rocks between the dunes and clapping his hands together. They made a soft *whump* noise, which was altogether disappointing.

'You dull-witted bastard! I haven't the time to waste.'

The beetle stared at him with black, soulless eyes, and then back to the storm, clicking its mandibles disconcertingly. Its forked toes dug at the sand, once, twice, thrice, and yet it did not move.

'Fine!' Farazar stomped to his body and laid a hand to the rope. It was hard to grip at first, but he had learned to channel his thoughts into his fingers, and soon he was hauling the corpse in foot-long increments through the sand. The beetle watched him impassively, wiggling its horns.

Farazar made it halfway up a dune before he collapsed to his knees, his concentration evaporating. 'Ugh!' he yelled. He kicked at his own body in anger. There came a ripping sound, and one of its – *his* – arms lolled out of the stained, half-shredded sacking. The limb was dried grey and wrinkled, like a prune left under a couch. Where the flesh had escaped the dry heat, it had begun to putrefy, turning black and gelatinous as oil. The plump rice grains of intrepid maggots squirmed here and there. A dark mould filled the veins where blood used to flow, and the nails were bile-yellow shards poking from shrunken fingers.

Farazar's hand hovered over the cloth. A blue tongue ran across his cold lips as he debated looking at the rest of his body. He held the cloth, lifting it gingerly and unhurriedly. Sunlight showed him a gaunt, grey-brown chest, sunken and slimy, then his neck, where Nilith's knife had cut him to the spine.

As he revealed black, rotten lips and the crenellations of white teeth grinning at him, Farazar lost his nerve. He dropped the cloth and scrambled to move the arm out of sight. As he grabbed it, he felt its looseness, and immediately plunged it back into the sack with a squelch. It flopped out again, and it took three attempts to wrap it back up. He was glad he had no sense of smell in death. Nor a stomach to empty. Instead, he just gulped with a throat that would never again know saliva.

With a glower, Farazar stared south, looking for a galloping blotch in pursuit of him. His eyes had always been poor, and they were worse in death. With the heat haze, there was nothing but wobbly strips of red, yellow and white, and spikes of salt gathered like misplaced stalagmites.

In the west, the sandstorm was gaining on him. The barrage of sand had reared into the sky, curled like an orange wave poised to come crashing down. It tore across the dunes with all the speed of the gales that drove it. Sand roiled like river rapids at its base, devouring anything in its path. Time was short.

With a curse, Farazar wrenched himself to the top of the dune to look at the city beyond. The miles stretched between him and his shining home, and yet if he squinted he just about pick out the spires of this tal or tor, that bank or chamber. And the Cloudpiercer, three towers thick even at its peak. Its marble flanks shone with the golden light of the afternoon sun, dwarfing every structure for districts around. The Outsprawls were so close he could see the adobe pimples of buildings, domes, minarets, the odd tower, and most importantly, the scratches of roads escaping Araxes.

His gaze followed one road in particular, losing it here and there amongst the dune peaks until it joined up with a blotch lying in a broken crater at the edge of the Sprawls. Farazar shielded his weak eyes, leaning forwards. The structure shone with the brightness of polished metal, yet it looked to be made of black stone. There was a faint haze about it, and that was enough to give him hope. It was a Nyxwell, by the looks of it. Farazar began to grin. Unlike the wild peasant wells, no Nyxwell in Araxes or her Sprawls had ever run dry.

The sand stirred at the peak of the dune, blowing in Farazar's face, and he looked away, wincing. It was then that he saw the traveller.

A man, a wagon, and a horse for each, all travelling south. He must have been half a mile away, parallel to Farazar's path. He trotted at no great speed, yet did not dawdle. On the wagon sat a large box, covered in a green tarpaulin. A coat of arms Farazar couldn't make out was emblazoned on its side, and no doubt also on the man's flowing white silk trappings and wide-brimmed hat. As he bobbed up and down, Farazar caught the glint of gold on his chest and arms. He was either brave or a dullard, to wear such trinkets whilst wandering the wilds. There were far more bandits and soulstealers in the Duneplains and Long Sands than the Ghouls. However, there was something in the man's demeanour that spoke confidence, and it perturbed the dead emperor. Farazar was glad his course wouldn't cross the man's

Keeping his face close to the sand, he let the man make his way out of sight, lost between the dunes. It was then that Farazar felt the wind growing. The sand around his glowing fingers began to eddy and swirl.

He half skidded, half tumbled down the dune's side and kicked sand in the beetle's face as he came to a violent halt. 'Up, beetle! Come on, you bastard!'

But the beetle would not be moved, and instead folded its legs close to its thick shell, sucking its head into its neck. Farazar stared up at his body, then back to the cursed creature, and then threw up his hands.

By the time he reached his body and dragged it back down the slope, the sandstorm was poised to strike. Farazar barely made it into the beetle's shadow before the wind slammed into them. The sudden roar was deafening, and as wave after wave of sand buffeted them, he gritted his teeth, sparkling white as the metal in the rushing storm bit into him.

'Fuck this desert!' he howled to the winds.

———————◆———————

THE BEAUTY OF HANGOVERS LAY in the fact they were wonderful excuses to sleep. All they demanded of the body was to sit, be still and endure. Though the sitting still part was proving difficult on the back of a galloping, slavering horse, somehow Nilith managed it: slumped and crooked as a crone, with her chin bouncing against her chest. It was a broken sleep, but sleep nonetheless, and the healing sort, good for ill stomachs and churning minds.

As such, the chase had been one of pieced-together moments. A jolt would wrench her eyes open for a brief time, just long enough to see the limbs of the sandstorm curling across the sky; or Bezel, a black kite against the endless blue; or a pillar of gathered salt, tall like a termite mound and stained with purples and pinks. Once she saw a herd of long-faced sandrabbits, scattering before Anoish's whinnying. The sun hopped from one place to the next along its arc. When Nilith finally managed to drag herself from drowsiness, it was wallowing in the west, half hidden by the storm.

'Where is he?' she croaked, throat clogged with sand. Nobody answered. Bezel was still above her, wheeling in spirals to keep an eye on both their prey and their tracker.

Nilith waved for him, whistling as loudly as her dry lips would allow, and he fell from the sky with all the force of a marble block. He took a rest on Anoish's head, much to the horse's grumbling, and kept his yellow talons curled.

'Where is Farazar?'

'Closer. Seems to be trying to veer away from the storm.'

'He didn't like the last one.'

The falcon eyed the angry orange storm, now spread from northwest to southwest. 'That makes two of us. It'll catch us soon.'

'He'll try to hide, or run for shelter. We'll find him.'

Nilith tugged the reins, spurring Anoish on once more. With a cooler wind on her face, she felt the best she had all day, which, by any other day's standards, was just past half dead. Her head still throbbed with every hoofbeat, and the anxiety still clung on, but she was gaining on the ghost and that was all that mattered.

'How long have you got?' asked Bezel, taking to the air again. His pinions twitched in the growing breeze.

'I've lost count of the days,' Nilith said in a small voice. 'Maybe a dozen left?'

'You're cutting it fine.'

'I am painfully aware, Bezel.' Every day since slitting Farazar's throat, the spell of binding had loomed over her like a second shadow. And each day that passed, it grew larger and darker, not unlike the sandstorm churning along the horizon.

There was no arguing with the problem. No solution but to move faster. Though the Tenets of the Bound Dead may have been written by man, they were gods-given. Unfortunately for Nilith, the third Tenet concerning the window of binding was unflinchingly clear. If she failed, Farazar's ghost would fade into the air, and his body would be worth less than the meat it was made of. No binding. No claim.

It may have been the manifestation of her hopes, but Nilith swore she could see the glowing lump of Farazar appearing now and again as he mounted a dune. She wondered sourly how he had gotten hold of an insect to ride. More so, how in the Reaches a creature had tolerated him this long without bucking him and striding off into the Duneplains.

Nilith thanked the dead gods for the fact she could see no shadows of towns or settlements between her and the Outsprawls. No dark rifts spread across these plains. No lurking bandits. No Nyxwell in sight. That calmed her, though she could not drag her eyes from the edges of Araxes. Those warrens of dust and desperate people were more fickle than the desert. Farazar could lose himself in a moment's work.

Even without the weight of Ghyrab, Anoish was tiring rapidly. Nilith felt his gait slow as the dust clouds began to fill her view. Half the sky had been claimed by the storm. She looked up at its lofty red tendrils, reaching across the Duneplains as they swirled on the air currents.

Bezel spiralled down to take up residence on the horse's back. He hid his face from the grit with his wings. Wrapping cloth around her neck and face, Nilith hunkered over the falcon and Anoish's neck as the wall of sand came racing across the dunes to meet them. It almost knocked her to the earth, but she clung on with aching thighs as the bright sunlight was swallowed by a thick orange haze.

As the storm howled around her, she kept her eyes up and open as wide as she could bear. Narrowed against the lashing grit, they desperately searched for a flash of blue, or the spindly shape of a beetle fighting its way through the howling murk.

And how it howled. This sandstorm was worse than the previous one, as if it knew Nilith's time in the desert was short and was intent on making a lasting impression. As well as the battering from the curtains of sand, spheres of barbed thorns cartwheeled through the gloom. One slammed into her calf and ripped a bloody hole as a brief greeting. Anoish cried out as another lacerated his flank. Nilith felt the sticky warmth spread across her leg. Baring teeth, she patted his side and he slowed to a trot, then a determined walk. Lightning fizzled in the high reaches of the storm. The bursts of yellow and white momentarily lit the rushing clouds of sand. To Nilith, it looked as though malformed creatures stooped over them, waiting.

For the most part, they trusted completely in forward momentum and pressed on blindly. Nilith spared quick glances through her make-shift wrappings to make sure the ghost hadn't slipped by. They walked only a small channel of visibility. He could easily have wandered east or west. The more time they spent in the belly of the sandstorm, the greater her anxiety grew.

An hour in the murk felt like a day. By the time Nilith felt its gusts weakening and saw spears of light breaking through the shadows, she had half a mind to swing her legs from the horse and sprint ahead herself.

'Bezel? Can you find him?'

'The storm's not fucking over—'

'Please!'

The falcon irritably shrugged off his cloth trappings and held out his wings. The storm snatched him away, and she heard his keening shriek mix with the howl of the wind.

He was gone some time. So much, in fact, that Nilith began to give ear to her doubts and fear the worst. Knowing to stay put, she withdrew from Anoish's back and paced back and forth. It was only as the storm was dying around them, blowing its way south, that she heard the thud of talons meeting sand. The sand still filled the air, hovering on the trailing breeze, and she had to squint to spy Bezel's waddling shape.

'I can't see him. Storm's not passed yet. I—'

'Good afternoon!' hollered a voice, Arctian-lilted and clear as a brass bell.

Nilith's hand flew to the hilt of her sword. The triggerbow was strapped to Anoish, too slow and too far to reach for. A large shadow appeared in the haze, growing darker by the moment. Bezel took to

Anoish's back, and the empress stood before them both, chin raised and muscles clenched.

'State your business!' called Nilith.

There came no reply, only the rattle of something wooden and steady clip-clop of hooves. She bit her lip, fearing an arrow or bolt would fly at her any moment. Her blade inched from its scabbard as the figure materialised from the sand.

A man riding a tall black horse emerged. His flowing silks were cream-coloured, tinged with red in the wake of the sandstorm and late sun. Great gold chains bearing glyphs hung about his neck. They were so numerous and prodigious that Nilith wondered if he struggled to sit upright. His dark-skinned hands were held out by his knees, manicured, open, and empty. His nails were painted a shining cobalt. Red ink tattoos of cogs and number glyphs decorated his powdered cheeks and neck. Covering his head was a flat, wide-brimmed hat; the sort she had seen Grand Builders of the eastern districts wear. Every thread of him spoke Araxes, not Duneplains. There was something both heart-warming and yet altogether disturbing about that.

Nilith looked for weapons but saw none. She stared past the stranger, eyes following a rope between him and another horse, to which a small wagon was hitched. A dark lump of tarpaulin sat high upon it. Even in the baking heat, the hairs on her nape stood to attention.

'State your business, I said! I've had enough of chance meetings on this road.'

The man looked down past his heels to the spinning sand. 'Not much of a road, now, is it?' He smiled, showing a tooth studded with a ruby. A man this bejewelled should have had guards aplenty for a trip into the desert, perhaps a whole phalanx. Even making it through the Outsprawls alone should have been a challenge for him. Nilith's wariness grew. Behind her, she heard a deep rumble in Anoish's chest.

She flicked him a look and saw his dark gaze was fixed on the wagon.

Nilith stood to one side, casting her free hand as though she was bowing. 'In any case, it seems it was taking you south. I bid you good travels, sir. If you don't mind, I'll be on my way.'

The man did not move. He simply stared at her, eyes just a glint beneath the shade of his hat.

Nilith gestured again. 'If you're a trader, I have nothing to sell and no need to buy.'

'I am no trader, though my masters are.'

'Wonderful,' Nilith replied, stepping towards Anoish's side and putting her hands on his back. Before she could hoist herself up, the man kicked his horse forwards, and positioned the beast in front of Anoish.

Nilith's sword emerged, a ribbon of silver. She held it towards him, double-handed. 'I'd urge you to move. I don't want to hurt you.'

For a moment, the man seemed disappointed, as if he'd come out with the will to do a job, but had forgotten the heart needed to finish it. He sighed deeply and hung his head. 'I wish I could say the same.'

A triggerbow appeared between his sheets of silk, aimed directly between Anoish's eyes. Nilith involuntarily yelped, but there came no twang, no thud, no whinny of death. She held up a hand, while the other patted the horse's baggage for her own bow. She felt the tension in the horse's muscles.

'Just hold on one fucking moment! What do you want from me?'

The gaudy man held the bow without a tremble. 'Not I, madam. My masters. The Consortium, a group of traders and businessmen who are interested in anything that earns silver.'

Nilith had heard that word before, in a white hell. 'Kal Duat.'

He seemed proud. 'Though one of many quarry facilities spread across the deserts, Kal Duat does rather stand out from the crowd, wouldn't you say?'

'And what do you want with me?'

'You refused to pay the toll for passing through Kal Duat. It is now overdue, and I have been sent to fetch your payment.'

Nilith could have laughed. 'Don't be ridiculous! The only thing I refused was to accept their right to levy such a toll, and to recognise your Consortium, whatever your claims.'

'Nevertheless, the debt remains.'

Her temper realised its shortcomings. 'Are you seriously saying you've come all the way out into the Duneplains to find one person who didn't pay a horse-shit toll? Surely this Consortium of yours has more pressing matters, like digging more gaping holes in the earth!'

'The daemons are in the details, madam. Not just one miscreant…' Without breaking eye contact, the man produced a scroll with his free hand and let it fall open. 'I have here a list of four individuals, sent by hawk to Araxes from the Duat. A woman matching your description – I believe the description was "bedraggled" – an elderly bargeman, a shade, and one horse.'

Nilith gave the man a dose of royal fury. 'This is fucking laughable! What is your name, man?'

If he was shaken, he didn't show it. 'While I don't see that as pertinent to the case, you may have it. It is Jobey. Chaser Jobey, and if you pay the toll, all will be resolved. The Consortium are fair in all business dealings.'

Nilith's eyes flitted between the shining bolt poised on the triggerbow to the impassive expression of this interloper. She thought her luck had turned after sighting Farazar, and yet, even as the desert lay almost conquered behind her, she had already stumbled on the city's thorns. 'How much?' she asked. 'I have little to trade, but if you insist and it will put an end to this preposterous conversation, you can have it.'

Jobey made a show of checking, rechecking, and then triple checking the scroll. 'Your shade,' he said.

'As you might have noticed, I don't own any shades.'

'Oh, I shall find him, but I'm afraid you misunderstand me. I mean to take *your* shade, madam. Your corporal being. Your soul. Those are the terms.' He shrugged. 'As I stated, the tolls are now overdue.'

Nilith waved the sword, standing between the bolt and Anoish. 'Go fuck yourself, before I do it for you with my blade.'

Jobey sighed dramatically once more as he tugged on the rope trailing between him and his wagon. The other horse came trotting up, face as glum as an empty wine bottle. Only when the rattling of the wagon had stopped did Nilith hear the hissing.

Keeping the triggerbow aimed, Chaser Jobey got down from his horse and trundled over to the tarpaulin. He seized one of its corners but hovered there, unmoving.

'It is customary to offer you one last chance to change your mind before I proceed with the recoupment. I must warn you: I have worked as a reclaimer for the Consortium for seventeen years, three months, and nine days now,' he said. 'I am very good at my job.'

Nilith held her sword up, making the steel shine. 'And my offer still stands.'

Jobey cocked his head, and the faint smile that had been smeared there fell away. 'You are not a woman of business, are you?'

Nilith was not. Had she the time or the inclination, she would have lectured this man on precisely why she loathed the leeches who preyed on those with too little or too much silver. Consortiums. Firms. Guilds. Whatever name they slapped onto their coats of arms, they all put profit at their centres. That made them no better than the tals and tors who traded in souls. Be it the banks and their half-coins, or the Chamber of Trade and their shipping routes, greed was the same in any currency.

'I have no love for it,' was all Nilith said.

Jobey sighed again, looking to Araxes. 'That great capital was not built by shades or royalty, madam, but by enterprising, ambitious minds. It was built on success, on profit, on power, by those who understand the merits of business. And those who understand business know that a live horse is worth more than a dead woman. You, clearly, do not understand that at all.'

Thunk!

The triggerbow let fly. Only Nilith's reactions saved her. The bolt was aimed low, for her stomach, but with her dodge it dug into the sand between Anoish's legs. He reared up, hooves waving in fright and outrage.

Nilith dashed forwards, sword poised to strike. Jobey tossed out a swathe of silk to entangle her sword. In the same movement, he swept the tarpaulin from the wagon, revealing a black cage. As Nilith swivelled away, blade up and ready, she froze as she saw its contents.

'Do something!' screeched Bezel, busy flapping around Jobey's head, trying for his eyes. Ignoring the onslaught of beak and talons, the chaser was wasting no time knocking the thick bolts from the cage door.

Part worm, part insect, the whole was a hideous creature about four feet high. Slate grey and purple, it glistened with either sweat or slime. Its sinuous body was curled around itself, and at its head two spindly, carapace-bound arms reached out. At their ends, blue claws hung curled, glowing softly like the vapours of a ghost. It looked sightless; the only features of its face were a disproportionately large mouth, a pair of nostrils, and three milky-white antennae that waved like river reeds. The stench wafting from it was that of offal left in the sun, enough to make Nilith's eyes water. But it was the teeth that held her gaze. Like the claws, they glowed, translucent and ever shifting.

Despite its lack of eyes, the creature seemed wholeheartedly focused on Nilith. Blue claws seized the iron bars with a clang as it pressed its weight against them. Fear emanated from it, wafting across her like a winter draught. Behind her, Anoish whinnied fearfully and skittered away.

One.

The monster salivated in great drips as its jaws opened wide, ravenous.

Two.

Nilith swallowed her fear and closed the gap in great bounds, sword high and a cry peeling from her throat.

Three.

The last bolt slid free and Chaser Jobey cackled. 'Go to work, my dear!'

There was a burbling screech as the creature thrust itself from its confines. It flew at Nilith as her blade met Jobey's arm, slicing a notch from it. She heard his cry before the wriggling body knocked her flat.

She pushed it free with a roar, slathering herself in slime as she thrashed about with the sword. The creature's monstrous hunger battled her craving to remain alive. It darted and weaved like a cobra before a beggar's flute. Over and over the creature pressed her, sand hissing beneath its sinuous body. Its claws snapped each time they reached for her. Its jaws were open so wide Nilith thought its head had split in half. Two rows of glowing teeth gnashed at the air. All the while, it screamed like a cat being burned alive.

Its ferocity was exhausting. Fear added weight to Nilith's swings and a tremble to her legs. As she stabbed for it, her feet tripped over themselves and Nilith fell to the sand. Her legs were immediately pinned by the creature's slimy weight. Frigid claws pressed against her chest, keeping her sword at bay. Over Anoish's fierce whinnying, the falcon's screeching, and the pain-filled shouts of Chaser Jobey, she heard her own pathetic wail as the foul creature closed its jaws around her hand. Teeth like icicles met her skin.

'NO!'

CHAPTER 20
A CHAMBERLAIN'S DAY

Of the estimated one million people that
visited our grand city last year, almost half
that number were reported as missing or
murdered, supposedly fed into the soultrade.
Out of that number, Chamber scrutinisers and
proctors managed to recover three thousand
and ten wrongfully indentured souls. Forty-one
soulstealers were stoned to death.

REPORT FROM THE CHAMBER OF THE CODE
TO EMPEROR FARAZAR, YEAR 1002

A MAGISTRATE! A BLOODY MAGISTRATE! ONE OF OUR OWN!'

Chamberlain Rebene waited for his howls to descend from the rafters before continuing. The scribe standing beside his desk scribbled furiously with her reed.

'This is inexcusable. A damn shame and a terrible loss for the city.' That was debatable, considering the calibre of the scores of nobles who had so far been reported missing. Rebene cared only for the loss of Ghoor. The man was a pompous, indulgent fool, but his death was more than a murder. It was an insult. It didn't matter that Rebene had an empress-in-waiting breathing down his neck; this was a personal prod at the Chamber. Not in Rebene's history, nor in twenty of his predecessors', had a soulstealer been so bold as to attack the Code itself.

'Where are the answers? The arrests? The justice? Damn it all!'

'Do you want the cursing included, Chamberlain, sir?'

Rebene shot a look at his scribe. 'Yes, I want the fucking cursing included! *Verbatim*, I said!

'Yessir, Chamberlain, sir.'

'What of the scrutinisers' and proctors' investigations? Has nobody heard a rumour? A tavern bragging? Did no shade escape? Are you telling me a Chamber magistrate can be murdered in his own home by ruthless thugs, and nobody can give me more than a nervous fart in the way of explanation?'

He saw the scribe's hand pause over the scroll.

'VERBATIM!'

'Yessir!'

'I want results. I want justice. I want this uppity soulstealer's head on a plate, delivered to the Chamber forthwith! Otherwise it will be my head being served to the empress-in-waiting!' Rebene snapped his fingers. 'Change that to "your heads". Otherwise it will be *your heads* on a plate.'

'Of course, Chamberlain.' The scribe looked up from her scroll when silence fell. Rebene was still pacing, white knuckles pressed to red lips, thinking. 'Will that be… all, sir?' she ventured

'Have a copy of that scroll sent to every magistrate and scrutiniser's post in the Core Districts. Every proctor. Every guardhouse! And while you're at it, find me that damned Heles!'

'Yes, Chamberlain,' said the scribe, seizing her chance to scuttle from the room.

In an attempt to steady his heart, Rebene performed several angry circuits of his expansive office. It hadn't known calm since the disappearances and murders had started. He put a hand to his chest, feeling an ache behind his ribs, and shook his head. The more he clenched, the more he noticed the fear hiding beneath his outrage.

'Calm yourself, Rebene, old fool. You're not next,' he whispered to the silence.

Ghoor had been a lavish man. Unlike the rest of the city, rank in the Chamber was decided by length of servitude, and scrutinisers were paid in silver, not shades. Ghoor had fancied himself a tor instead, and built up quite the hoard. Once, he'd even petitioned for a change of title: "Noble Consultant", of all things.

Rebene was not so fond of such opulence. The only shades he owned were house-shades, and a few hundred at most. His title as head of the Chamber of the Code was the only treasure he feared losing. He had no family. No lovers. Few friends besides colleagues. Fewer now

Ghoor was gone. Rebene prodded irritably at his temples, trying on his old scrutiniser mind.

'A fool has no enemies,' went the saying. Over the years, time and time again, the Chamber had been made to look like a fool, and yet it was beset on all sides. Fighting the continuous criminality that pervaded Araxes' streets and upper echelons was impossible. A toothless wolf, somebody had once called Rebene's Chamber. That person had always stuck in his mind: a cheat he caught swindling a card-den. A pudgy young man, all vim and fire, and missing a leg below his knee. *Words like that are splinters. If they are not plucked out, they worm inwards, and become as much a part of the body as a fingernail.*

Rebene heard the creak of his oak doors. A timid whisper followed. 'Chamberlain?'

He roared as he turned. 'I've told you a dozen times—!' He was about to remind the scribe about the importance of knocking when he noticed a streak of blue standing beside her. The lump in Rebene's throat grew.

Etane Talin stood in the doorway, dressed in a silk suit of green. He stared idly up at the vaulted ceiling and long tapestries that told the thousand-year history of the Code. Despite the Chamber's rules, the shade was armed with a ridiculously large broadsword. The gold feather on his breast gleamed mockingly at Rebene.

The chamberlain waved the scribe away and Etane to a chair with a single annoyed gesture.

'I shall not be here long,' commented the shade.

Rebene pasted a polite smile onto his face as he took his own chair. He steepled his fingers to keep them from shaking.

'Am I to assume—'

Etane sighed dramatically. Though he was the voice of the empress-in-waiting, he did not look like he wanted to be in that office any more than Rebene did.

'To assume is to admit a lack of facts, Chamberlain. As you do not have the facts, allow me to lay them out for you. Fact the first: after the greatest massacre this city has known in a decade, a magistrate is dead, along with a large number of tors, tals, minor nobles, and Serek Berinia. Let us not forget Hashya the Voice, either. Priceless bard, that one. Fact the second: as far as the Piercer has been made aware, no culprit has yet been arrested for the aforementioned slaughter. And fact the third: Her Majesty Sisine Talin Renala the Thirty-Seventh is not best pleased with either fact one or two. Nor is her father, your emperor.'

'Not... best pleased?' Rebene shuffled in his chair, trying his best to retain his smile.

Etane shrugged. 'To put it gently, considering all the silver she has invested in you. Not to mention all those soldier shades.'

'I see.' Rebene kept his hands in front of his face, hoping it would hide the glow he felt in his cheeks. 'I would like to assure Her Majesty I am doing everything in my power—'

'Suspects.'

'Pardon?'

'Suspects. Culprits. Lawbreakers. Malefactors. Do you have any?'

Rebene cursed his shaking hands as they reached for several scrolls, scattered about his desk during an earlier angst. He gathered them up and peeled them open, reading names from scrutinisers spread across the city's core and inner districts; scrutinisers he held in the highest regard, and yet now inwardly cursed for not doing better. Especially Heles, having the cheek to ask for autonomy, then failing to deliver no more than a suspicion.

'A gentleman named Farassi has recently claimed tordom, supposedly after a lucrative trade with a Scatter pirate. Pendrago, a Skol man who is a known soulstealer in, er... the Dawar District. There's a Berrix the Pale, known thug and soultrader of Quara. Some of my scrutinisers have even suggested the Consortium – that group of merchants who run the desert mines – might be behind it, making a power grab.'

Etane's face hadn't twitched. He looked on, still waiting. Rebene snagged another few scrolls.

'Er... we have an Astarti of the Whitewash Beaches. And Boran Temsa. Bes District. From tavern-owner to tor just a week or two ago, though nobody's sure why or how. Definite soultrader. Suspected soulstealer. The notes are from Scrutiniser Heles. She's one of my best. And that's all.'

'That's all,' echoed Etane. Not a question.

The shade took on a ponderous look and leaned over the desk to look at the scrolls for himself. Rebene shrank back into his chair, feeling swallowed by its grand back, and tried to hide his lip-biting.

Etane hummed. 'Overall, not very impressive.'

Rebene waved his hands at the scrolls, insulted at being brought to task by a house-shade, even if he did belong to the princess. 'I am doing my best!'

Etane raised a doubtful eyebrow. 'Allow me to help you. This Boran Temsa, he's a dead lead. Your man—'

'Woman.'

'—*Woman* Heles is wrong.'

'She's rarely wrong. If ever.'

The shade shook his head. 'Temsa is a distant relation of the Renala line. A far, far cousin, but is known to the Piercer nonetheless. He is a soultrader, not a stealer. Ignore him. Pour your resources into a more useful avenue, like this Astarti, or Berrix.'

'I trust Heles—'

'The empress-in-waiting does not, and frankly, she is displeased with your lack of progress, despite her donation of silver and shades.

You'd better redouble your efforts, and catch this ambitious fucker before they pluck the courage to come for your head.'

Rebene felt cold seep into his cheeks as the colour drained from them like bathwater down a drain. 'Her words? Or yours, shade?'

'Hers. *Verbatim.*' Etane winked then, rapped his knuckles on the desktop, and left.

The chamberlain sagged as the door slammed, wondering what witch or beldam had cursed him this day. He rested his forehead in his hands, and the sweat rolled down his wrists.

———————◆———————

ETANE STROLLED FROM THE CHAMBER and into the corridor with idle steps. He let the dry rush of air fan his blue vapours, making them curl around the seams of his suit. He wondered, had he a nose, whether it would scent musty papyrus and ink; the odour of endless towers of files and claims.

He passed one of the domed halls on his way out, and ducked to see the peaks of the scroll piles. On the floor of this strange forest, lit by disparate sun rays, scribes and proctors beavered away, their reeds never pausing as they flitted from paper tower to paper tower. It was strangely refreshing to see no glowing blue amongst their crowded number. No half-lives worked the Chamber's halls. Only the living could be trusted to handle their matters.

Etane had reached the Chamber's vast atrium and its black-clad, tattooed proctors when he heard an all too familiar voice.

'Etane Talin. As I die and glow.'

He came to a stuttering halt. 'Enlightened Sister Liria. And Sister Yaridin, too, I wager?' He turned with a sigh, finding two shades loitering behind him. They were hooded and cloaked, and they had foregone their usual scarlet attire for a rusty brown colour.

'How did you get in here?' he demanded. 'No cultist is allowed in the Core Districts.'

Liria smiled, showing no teeth. 'It seems the Core Guards, the Chamber, and even the new soldiers of Sisine's have no interest in us any more. Not while this murderer is afoot.'

Etane crossed his arms, avoiding the sisters' glowing eyes. He looked to the vast queues instead, weaving around in tight geometric formations between the doorways and a seawall of ivory and marble. The desks were manned by people with sage expressions. Most of them seemed to have nothing to do but shake their heads.

How did these two circumvent the queues?

'Who let you in?' he asked.

'You know better than most that we have our sympathisers,' replied Liria.

Etane hadn't bothered to give it thought. There was currently enough nonsense going on in Araxes to occupy his mind. 'And what could you possibly want in the Chamber? Sneaking back into favour, are we? I should have a proctor drag you from the halls, if only to see the looks on your faces.'

'And yet,' Liria said in hushed tones, like scales sliding across sand, 'you promised us loyalty, in return for our information.'

'I did no such...' Etane went to bite his lip. *Still. After so many years.* He remembered their conversation in the shadow of the banks. The deal he'd made. The deal he'd utterly forgotten about. 'What are you doing here?'

Liria stepped around him, eyeing Etane as if she were planning how to climb him. 'We have an appointment.'

Yaridin piped up. 'A claim. We have not gone untouched by this chaos. Several of our free brothers have been stolen by miscreants taking advantage of the panic.'

Etane cackled. 'What a shame. I'm surprised the Cult isn't taking matters into its own hands.'

'*Church,*' Yaridin corrected him. 'And we bow to the authority of the Code as deeply as we do to Sesh. These are new times, Etane. Unlike you, we move with them.'

'Do you, now?'

Liria spoke up again. 'That gold feather never suited you, brother.'

'Freedom would.' Yaridin raised a blue eyebrow.

Etane lifted his chin. 'At the cost of wearing your crimson robes? Tried that. I am loyal, but not to you. Just you try and change it.' He patted the hilt of his broadsword. 'Freedom? Pah. I don't see you trying to prise my half-coin from the royal vaults.'

Liria wagged a finger. 'Hmm. Alas, our business awaits. As I'm sure Sisine awaits you.'

Yaridin chipped in again. 'All these murders must be keeping her busy. We bid you a good day.'

They swept away from him, heading for the warren of corridors that led off from the atrium. Etane watched them until they were swallowed by the masonry and crowds. It was at times like this he wished he had spittle to decorate the ground with.

Striding out into a morning choked with the haze of a passing sandstorm, Etane walked west, towards the dark shadow of the Cloudpiercer. He could see its shining pinnacle above the murk, where yellow and orange bled into clear blue. He found himself rolling his eyes at it.

He took the next turn and approached a tar-black, iron-plated carriage waiting in the road. Two concentric circles of armoured men stood around it, spears tucked into the cobbles and bristling outwards like a sea urchin.

Etane gestured for them to move, and a narrow corridor parted, leading him to the carriage's door. He opened it a fraction, enough to see Sisine's face wreathed in a golden veil. Her eyes were narrowed and questioning.

'Our good chamberlain suspects Temsa, but I made sure he won't pursue him. Some slick scrutiniser sniffed him out. Rebene will steer clear and focus on some other miscreant instead.'

'Good.'

'I know you gave Temsa a slack leash besides those you named, but six tors, nine tals, a serek, a magistrate, and a dozen nobles? The man's rabid. What are we—'

Sisine cut him off. 'Is there anything else?'

Etane looked back to the bastion walls of the Chamber of the Code, rising high above the surrounding buildings, as though they had fallen prostrate before it. He thought of two crimson-cloaked shades worming their way through it.

'No. Nothing. Apart from the fact that Rebene looks fit to pop. I hope putting all this pressure on him doesn't come back to bite you – or the dog you've let loose on this city.'

Sisine scowled. 'I'll replace them both once I'm sat on that throne.'

'Of course you will, Your Regalness.' Etane barely managed to hide his impatience. Had he a brain, he swore it would have ached from all her insidious scheming. 'Of course you will.'

He pulled the door wider to climb up, but she thrust out a foot bound in silver laces, blocking him.

'Feel free to walk home,' she said.

Etane forced a smile as he pushed the door shut. He heard the thump of her fist against the wood, and the carriage moved off slowly with the soldiers jogging alongside it, armour clanking long after they'd faded from sight.

'Feel free,' he whispered, with a curl of his lip.

Spending a hundred years indentured did not curb the yearning for freedom. It stoked it like the sun of the desert stoked the Duneplains, day after day, until life itself bent before the heat.

———————◆———————

REBENE HAD JUST ABOUT FINISHED sweating when there came another knock at his door.

'What is it *now*?' he yelled, his voice hoarse from all the terse chiding of himself, the city, and all things royal.

The scribe poked her head around the door again.

'Your next appointment.'

'Why don't I ever get to review these appointments?'

The scribe pushed the door open, revealing two skinny brush-strokes of rusty brown.

The chamberlain sat straighter in his chair. He scowled deeply. 'What are *they* doing here?'

'Enlightened Sisters Liria and Yaridin—'

'I know who they are! I asked what they are doing *here*, in the Core! Fetch me the proctors!'

'It will only take a moment, Chamberlain Rebene,' interjected Liria, her voice floating effortlessly across the expanse of marble.

The scribe looked to the visitors, then to her employer, and shrugged. With a whimper, she retreated behind the door as the chamberlain roared after her.

'I want to see my diary, woman!'

Silence answered. Rebene yelled once more.

'Proctors! Scrutinisers!'

He did not try again. With a weary sigh and a pinch of his brows, he gestured for the shades to approach. They did so without a sound, gliding to the edge of his desk.

Rebene jabbed a finger at both of them. 'You have moments before I have the proctors turf you out! Emperor Farazar's orders still discourage your being here. Or twenty streets from here!'

The two sisters spoke in turn.

'We come here with benevolent intentions.'

'No meddling to be done.'

'What has passed is the past.'

'We wish no ill will on the city, Emperor Farazar, his family, or this Chamber.'

'Or you, Chamberlain.'

'Unlike some.'

'Stop!' Rebene yelped, holding up his palms. 'Speak plain, Sisters. I haven't the patience for riddles today.'

Yaridin put her hands on his desk. Rebene saw the polished wood fog at the touch of her cold skin. 'You have a tumour in this city. A soulstealer bolder than any other you've ever seen. A murderer of wealthy tors, tals, sereks, and… magistrates.'

'Slaughtering them in their own towers and bringing panic to the streets. We have heard the rumours and the worried whispers,' added Liria. 'The city treads on glass shards.'

'Do you think I don't know this? Have you come here to torture me?'

'We want to help,' Liria said.

Rebene thumbed his nose. 'Why? Why would you want to help?'

'Our Church—' Liria paused to let the chamberlain snort. 'Our Church is committed to helping restore Araxes to its former glory. To its namesake. It is why we have recently opened our doors to the living as well as the dead. In doing so, crime could be washed from our streets.'

'Instead of our streets being washed with blood.'

Rebene raised his hands to his vaulted ceiling. Part of him wished it would come crashing down, and end this troublesome day. First Ghoor's murder, then the prick Etane, now these melancholy outcasts.

'Wouldn't that be wonderful. A pretty dream for any city! Tell me your great secret, then. What is this magical solution that's escaped chamberlains and scrutinisers for thirty generations? And mark my words, if it involves the throne in any way, I'll have your ghostly arses tossed to the flagstones!'

Yaridin smiled. 'Allow us to assist you in guarding the streets.'

'We have many shades who've earned their freedom from the Chamber of Military Might.'

'They already help keep some of the Outsprawl districts safe.'

That was news to the chamberlain. Uncomfortable news. 'Ridiculous…' he croaked. 'The emperor would never stand for it.'

Liria shook her head. 'We have no intention of interfering.'

'We will follow your every order.'

'Our resources will be at your – and the emperor's – disposal.'

Rebene held up his hands for quiet. His temples throbbed with the beginnings of a headache. 'I…' He looked at the scrolls still spread across his desk, their inked names dark against the white papyrus. Plain to see. He saw Yaridin's eyes follow his, and read them.

'We are aware of several of these men and women. Berrix. Astarti. Farassi,' she said. 'We have watched them for some time.'

Rebene's hand paused in mid-air, undecided between snatching the scrolls back to his side of the desk, or dashing them to the floor. 'Why? What business is it of yours?'

'We have always dealt in information.'

'For the city's welfare, Chamberlain.'

'The city's welfare,' Rebene echoed, and yet, shamefully, he could not think of anyone's but his own.

Yaridin leaned closer. 'It is a shame what happened to Ghoor. But in a way, perhaps his murder can provide opportunities for more than just his murderer.'

'The seed of change.'

The chamberlain pressed his fingers to his aching forehead, thinking, balancing, trying to trace the threads of consequence as he had done as a young scrutiniser. He stayed like that for some time until the silence became heavy and uncomfortable. Until the cold of the sisters spread across his desk.

When Rebene looked up, his mouth was a thin line. 'How many shades can you offer?'

The sisters smiled.

———————◆——————

AN HOUR HAD PASSED SINCE the departure of the so-called Enlightened Sisters, and Rebene had yet to push himself up from his desk.

A pact. He had made a pact with the Cult of fucking Sesh. And with zero input from Emperor Farazar or the empress-in-waiting. Not even a magistrate had been consulted. The words had left his mouth like vomit after one beer too many. It was a good deal, by all accounts, seeing as it cost Araxes nothing yet bought thousands of shades. Information, too. And yet it hadn't stopped the silence damning him for the past hour.

Shaky and slick with sweat, Rebene finally managed to reach his feet. The knocking on the door sent him straight back down again.

'WHAT?!' he shrieked. 'I said no more!'

The door burst open, letting loose a stormy-faced Scrutiniser Heles into the room. There was lightning in her eyes and a glower on her face. If it were possible, even the tattoos swirling over her neck and through her shorn hair looked darker. Behind her, the scribe hopped from one foot to the other, utterly useless.

Rebene pressed himself into his chair, already hiding behind a hand.

'Chamberlain Rebene!' Heles barked, banging her palms on his desk. She poked at the gathered scrolls. 'Why haven't I heard anything about my report?'

At her cheek, he almost summoned the energy to give her the dressing-down of her career. Almost. Instead, he adopted a withering tone. 'And what report is that, Scrutiniser Heles?'

'The one on Boran Temsa. *Tor* Boran Temsa, if I can stomach to say it. I need men to move on him, and quickly too. You know better than anyone that I wasn't Ghoor's biggest fan, but he was one of our own. I believe Temsa's the one behind it. Perhaps in league with old Tal Horix, too.'

Rebene spent an awkward moment brushing the creases out of his robe. He felt pinched, like the arms of his chair were the jaws of a vice – the Cult and the Crown – and now Heles was slowly winding them inwards.

'No,' he whispered.

Heles' eyes became saucers. 'What do you m—'

'I said no, Heles!' he yelled. 'Temsa is not the man. You're wrong. Look elsewhere.'

The scrutiniser took her time measuring her words. Rebene stewed in the meantime, trying not to bend under her avid, damning stare.

'Twelve years,' she said. 'Twelve years, and when have you known me to be wrong?'

'Once or twi—'

'When?'

'Fine. Never. But there's a first time for everything.' Rebene started to gather the scrolls together. 'I'm sorry, Scrutiniser Heles, but that's an order.'

Heles leaned so far over the desk Rebene felt the heat of her breath.

It was no more pleasant than the cold waft of the sisters.

'Autonomy. You promised me, Chamberlain. Now is the wrong time to try and fuck me.'

Rebene stood. 'Times are changing, Scrutiniser. It's time you changed with them, as I intend to.'

Heles laughed then, and he had never heard a more mirthless laugh. It was the harsh and sudden crack of a whip, and he flinched.

'Fine,' she seethed. 'Look elsewhere, eh? So I shall.'

With an animalistic snarl, Heles swept from the desk and barrelled towards the door. The handle popped clear as she slammed it behind her, most likely locking Rebene in his office.

With a groan, he sank back into his chair, fingers reaching up into his hair, grabbing a handful, and pulling until he roared.

CHAPTER 21
SPOOKS & ZEALOTS

A thousand years is time enough for fables to evolve, and unsurprisingly, most Arctian fables involve ghosts. There are tales told in the desert quarries of phantoms of the dunes; great ghostly dunewyrms and giant antelope. Tales of ghosts changing shape into wolves or bat-like creatures, or screeching so loudly they can shatter glass. There are even stories of ghosts reaching through walls – or worse, reaching into a living body. Though the Tenets are absolute, there must be fear deep down in the populace over the fact the dead walk among them. It cannot help but bleed into their mythos.

FROM 'SHADOWS AROUND THE CAMPFIRE', A HISTORICAL STUDY ON FOLKLORE BY JIM JIMIN

I N MY ARMPIT OF A cell, I felt like some ape confined in a zoo for paying customers to gawp and laugh at. Except my visitors weren't laughing, and I had no shit to hurl at them.

Curse my vaporous body.

Four visits I'd had that day. One from Temsa, checking his prize was still where his people told him it was. Two from Danib, flat-faced and dull as ever. And one again from another ghost, who was promptly told to scarper to the sound of a crashing tray.

The dust showed the work of my prowling, a fine figure of eight surrounded by a circle of scuffing. I lingered now by my pathetic excuse for a window, my face pressed to the bars, and stared out across the dust of the busy street.

The passersby afforded me some entertainment, at least. I mouthed along to the shouting of the nearest grocer, bellowing out his dubious claims and complicated deals. I knew all his shouts by now.

'Four oranges or a bugfruit for a deben, or six and a gritapple for two! Get your lemons! Best lemons this side of the Scatter! Nobody serves pomejuice by the hekat in this district!'

Then there was the farrier, and his penchant for beating the hot iron in a galloping rhythm between his quenchings. I heard another hiss of glowing horseshoe from across the road. I had even begun to recognise the wagons of various couriers and traders. Some of the ghosts, rushing by on repetitive errands, had begun to lock eyes with me.

The wagons had been streaming in and out of the Rusty Slab all day long. Mostly out, to the banking district and to the soulmarkets, I wagered. Even by what little I knew of Araxes standards, Temsa had bagged quite the haul, as my old master Doben would have said.

Blue feet encased in gold thread stomped by, flicking sand and a chunk of dung in my face.

Her again.

A ghost had been performing circuits of the busy junction all day, and part of her route passed my bars. She was dressed all in white powder and moth-bitten silks. She tossed her glowing hair at any man with flesh and blood and the silver to afford her. I hadn't seen her get any luck yet, and now her circuits were becoming quicker, her smile tighter, eyes more frantic.

I had no sympathy for her. It was not distaste for her profession; we all had to make money somehow. I just hated her because she was outside and I was not.

As the hours dragged by and the shadows began to stretch, I saw the masses of the streets change. Those with homes or taverns to occupy – mostly the living – hurried to them. The dead dragged their heels, drawing out the minutes before they went back to their masters. I saw one ghost, naked save for a loincloth, pushing a cart full of broken reed birdcages. It must have had no weight, even to a fresh half-life, and yet I had to squint to see if the wheels turned.

The pointy shadow of a nearby building had almost swallowed my window when the hatch slid back with a snap. It was clearly viewing time once more. I silently placed a bet as I turned, and lost it immediately when I saw a furrowed brow and beady eyes.

'Good evening, Temsa,' I greeted him, crossing my arms.

He didn't bother to open the cell door. His words came muffled by metal. 'You're being moved on the morrow.'

I wandered closer, mostly to show him my indifference. 'To your new abode?'

'If that's the Krass term for tower, then yes, Caltro.'

'I knew this tavern couldn't hold an ego the size of yours for long, no matter how far down you dug.'

Temsa narrowed his eyes at me. 'Seeing as that cell can barely hold yours, I would agree.'

'Did you come down here purely for an exchange of wits, or...?'

The black and silver blade of Pointy slammed up against the slot.

'Hello, Caltro.' His voice was clear in my head, as metallic as usual.

'This sword. Where did you get it?'

'I stole it from Busk.'

'And where did he get it?'

'How am I supposed to know?'

'The man liked to brag, long and loudly.' Temsa spat. 'What do you know of it?'

I made a show of thinking. 'That it's bloody sharp.'

'I've taught him that a few times now,' Pointy interjected.

'Anything else? Did Busk mention a curse? Anything about a soulblade?'

'Curse?'

'Like a charm or a spell on it?' he replied irritably.

I pulled a face. 'What have you been doing with him?' I asked this more of the sword than Temsa.

Temsa seemed flustered. Specks of spittle darkened the sand at my feet as he snapped at me. 'What a stupid question! It's a sword, damn it! Not a him.'

'I've been whispering to him at night. Like this.'

Temsa viciously waggled a finger in his ear. 'Bloody thing has a curse on it, I say! If you know anything, you'll tell me!'

'Busk didn't say a thing about it. Honest.' I held up empty hands.

'Poetry, for the most part. A few insults every now and again. I get bored.'

I could have hugged the sword.

'Bah!' The tor slammed the grate. I listened to his angry footsteps recede down the corridor with a smile on my face. I almost laughed aloud when I heard a thwack and a guard's yelp. Instead, I returned to my bars to watch the sky bruise and blacken, like a fist-fighter's eyes.

Sunset pounced quickly in the desert lands. No sooner had the sun receded behind the peaks of steel and brick and glass than the heat died. When its fiery glow had faded, leaving a wake of dark red and purple, the city began to sparkle with lamps and torches. Ghosts in cowls moved around the outside of the Slab, lighting the tavern's lights as they went, and filling my street with their liquid gold. I felt their heat on my reaching arms, but they gave me no warmth. One of the guards accompanying the ghosts was nice enough to kick my hand back inside the cell. For the second time that day, I found myself wishing for faeces to throw. Half of Temsa's men would be bespattered by now.

I took once more to pacing about my cell. Even though my muscles couldn't appreciate the effort, my mind could. My scuffing gave me a beat to which I could drum out my irritable thoughts. It helped to drown out the doubt and impatience that were gnawing holes in my plan to wait for Temsa to grow complacent.

I had to give it to Pointy. The sword was a marvellous irritation to more than just me. It could have been the day of boredom, the silence, or his mischief, but I found myself briefly missing my cellmate.

He did have a spell on him, and I found myself wondering what other magics the Nyxites had once weaved with soul and metal, or animal flesh, all for the fashions of the Arc. Before they'd been banned from doing so, that was.

I'd heard of an hourglass that could shout the time. I'd listened to stories of statues coming to life with the souls of ghosts. I'd once even stolen a spear that almost always hit an enemy when thrown. How many souls had been dead or strangebound just to amuse the living? It felt as if there was a locked door before this subject, and ever the thief, I wanted through it. If only for curiosity's sake.

It was nightfall when my final visitor announced himself with a scuffle.

When the moon had sandwiched itself between two lofty spires I could crane my neck at, the guard changed. It did so with some muffled conversation; talk of certain tavern girls, an irritable Temsa and the like. I listened to the footsteps leaving while the squeak of stool legs told me this guard was a tired guard. I heard him muttering to himself, complaining to an empty corridor. This went on for some time, until he made a game of throwing nutshells – or that's what it sounded like to me – against the wall.

Then came the thud, shortly followed by another. The first came from down the hallway. The second came from outside my door. I hugged the corner, wary as ever.

The waiting made the shadows grow, and every noise from outside a clattering. Keys momentarily chimed, then a hand silenced them. They rattled in my door before it swung open. There was a faint blue tinge to the light that spilled inwards.

'Caltro. Caltro Basalt?' hissed a voice I had never heard before.

I'd been waiting until he peeked past the door until I answered, but the spiked tip of a club preceded him, and I held my tongue. It was a ghost, willowy of build, bearded, wearing some dark leather garb and wrapped in a black cape. He was barefoot.

'Here,' I said, curious enough to speak. 'Who's asking?'

White eyes turned on me. 'Widow Horix.'

I understood, but the situation called for some cheek. It was how I dealt with surprises and their usually spiky edges. A blanket of humour always dulled them. 'Horix? You've gained weight, found some manhood, and died since I last saw you.'

He strode towards me impatiently. '*I* am Meleber Crale, and if you want to get out of here then I'd advise you to shut your face and come with me. Widow Horix has sent me.'

Temsa wasn't the man to dabble in idle tricks. This was no game. I recognised the glint in Crale's eye as one of impatience. He had as much to risk as I did, and judging by the white feather dangling around his neck from a chain, perhaps more. I wasn't about to complain. In fact, I may even have grinned as I followed him eagerly out of the door. *At last!* I'd been right in trusting the old bat. My solution had come to me after all. *Fuck Temsa. Fuck the dead gods.*

I stumbled over the prostrate form of a guard, face-down, lying in a pool of his own blood. 'What are you?' I asked my rescuer as I followed on the tails of his cape.

'I'm a spook.'

'A what?'

'Don't have us in Krass? Maybe I should move there. Make a killing, so to speak,' he hissed over his shoulder. 'We're hired by people who need things done. Things only a dead man can get away with.'

He held me back at a corner, peeking ahead. I could hear the rumble of voices and feet above us, and the clanging of cage doors below us.

'If you're good at something—'

Crale finished my sentence off. 'Never do it for free.'

I grabbed at his shoulder. 'Wait. I need my sword.'

'What sword?'

'It's a… special sword. Family heirloom. I promised it… *myself* I would take it with me.'

Confusion twisted his lip. 'Where is it?' he snapped.

'On… Temsa's belt.' I felt that thing they called guilt tug at me. It was still a new experience. I had broken so many promises I couldn't remember the definition of keeping one, and yet here I was, about to break another, and nibbling my nails like a tardy schoolchild over it.

'Impossible. I'm not even sure I can get you out. You'll have to come back.'

'No, I have to take him now.'

Crale bared his teeth at me. 'Tough. It's my vapours on the line here too. If I don't come back with you, Horix will take a copper blade to my throat. I don't care if it's the emperor's sword. We leave now.'

'No.'

He shoved me back the way we'd come, his palms thumping against the vapours of my chest. 'All right, back to your cell it is!'

'No... wait.' He stared at me long and hard with burning eyes, daring me to disagree. 'Fine,' I growled, consoling the guilt with the fact I'd at least tried.

We stared down a corridor, empty save for the two black-clad men lounging at the end of it. 'Any other way out?' I asked.

'Few, and each of them worse than this. Temsa is apparently at war with the city. He's not stupid. Now!'

Holding his cape out in front of us and sticking to the shadows, we pelted it halfway along the corridor, our bare, ghostly feet making hardly any noise on the flagstones. Say one thing for being dead, if you like sneaking around, it's the perfect state to be in.

Crale produced a coin of iron and threw it past the guards, down into a stairwell leading to the Slab's bowels.

'What the fuck?' came the combined grunt of the guards. As they wandered over to investigate, Crale tugged me past them and up another stairwell.

The cape did us no favours this time, and one of the guards spied the flash of blue.

'Did I just—Oi!'

'Run, Caltro!' hissed Crale, thrusting me forwards. He paused briefly to deal the man a wallop around the head with his club, spattering skin and brains on the wall. With a kick, the body tumbled backwards into his colleague.

Within three paces the spook was back at my side, leaving me to wonder if being free meant being more alive. I resolved to find out one day as my feet thrashed the flagstones in an attempt to keep up.

'Left!' Crale cried as another figure came around a corner. 'Right and up!'

More stairs flew by beneath us. I imagined I could taste the night air ahead. A door to the tavern passed us, momentarily dousing us in light and blaring noise. I could hear the clank of armour and thud of feet in hot pursuit. Crale could hear it too. He moved ahead of me, pulling me along as we weaved through more passages.

He spied the archway before I did, and barged me in its direction. Its glowing frame was lit by twin braziers from the street. A lone guard stood in its glow, and two more in between him and us. Crale raised his club, and I heard him utter 'Shit' beneath his breath.

As Crale dashed the first man to the floor, I felt my brief hope come crashing down into a pit of anger. I leapt over the flailing body, somehow having time to admire the crater Crale's club had left in his skull. Shouts filled the narrow gap of stone and steel, squeezing the glowing door tighter. I reached out for it as I ran, face contorting in a noiseless shout.

Hands groped for my shoulders, but without copper their fingers couldn't grip me, and I barrelled on, Crale the spook close behind. One of the guards snagged his cape, and the ghost let him have it with a flourish that dragged the man to the ground and knocked him senseless.

'Almost to the street!' he yelled, sounding almost breathless. Perhaps it was the worry I recognised in his wide eyes. He didn't look the sort who was used to failure, and this corridor of blood and yelling bodies screamed failure.

The shouting had summoned the attention of the guards outside. I could see one poking his head around the archway, blocking my way. I launched myself at him as he ran inside, spear at the ready. Crale's club knocked the weapon aside as I dove into him.

I don't know whether it was my desperation to be free, or an accident, but by into him, I wholeheartedly mean *into him*.

In an instant, I felt the warmth of a body envelop my coldness, and yet I was still falling, facing backwards now. A wall struck me, and I felt a dull pain lance through my back. I tried to draw breath, but I could not. Something was stinging my skin, as if my chainmail was fresh out the forge.

My chainmail?

All too late I realised where I was, and the haunting broke, snapping like a frayed rope. I burst free of the guard's body, staying upright just long enough to catch Crale's shocked expression, frozen just like the rest of his body, club still raised over a cowering guard.

The spook's hesitation cost him his legs.

As I collided with the wall, a broadsword swung out from my peripheries. There came twin bursts of white light as the blade passed through Crale's thighs, and reduced everything below to blue smoke. He crumpled, splayed and whimpering on the floor. A blue shine washed over me as Danib Ironjaw emerged from an alcove like a troll from his cave. He wore no armour tonight, just a bare torso that looked like a mountain range covered in scars. A kilt of mail hung from his waist, and a horned helmet encased his head.

Without a word, he rested the tip of his humongous sword on the stone next to my head.

'I—' was all I managed. The guard I'd briefly inhabited was coming to, twitching as if spiders infested his clothes and mail. His words were condensed into one stream of panicked screeching.

'Whatthefuck! Whatthefuck!'

I winced as the sword arced from the floor, grazing my cheek before lopping half the chest from the guard. Steel bit through iron links and sternum with a horrific crunch, and the man sailed into the street.

The corridor quickly filled with guards. They came upon the scene with horrified, confused looks. Sword still raised, Danib greeted them with a growl. He pointed to the half ghost, and then upstairs.

'Come on, lads,' said a self-appointed spokesperson. Gloved hands set to the spook and Crale Crale was hauled away through pools of blood, leaving a faint smear behind him. He had few glances to offer me. They were mostly reserved for his missing legs. But when I did meet his eyes, all he had for me was hatred.

I lay there waiting under Danib's glow while the rest of the bodies were hauled away. I had no words or taunts for once, but plenty of inner cursing to be done. *I should have known better. I should have taken my chance. I shouldn't have hesitated.* All manner of self-made accusations rained down.

They say there is a beauty in hindsight, but I say it is an ugly creature. Almost as ugly as its daughter, regret. Life is made of many paths. The cruel joke is you can only choose one, and move only forwards along it. Regret is the bitch that follows behind you and paves the paths you didn't take with gold and glitter.

Danib saved me from my thoughts by grabbing me by the throat and lifting me upright. The ease with which he did it was frankly unfair for a dead man. Once I was on my feet, I began to brush myself down. The only noises were armour scraping down stairs, and the clamour of the tavern several walls away from us. A small crowd had gathered in the street, stopping to look at tonight's entertainment: the broken corpse of a guard bleeding all over the sand.

I was about to make a pun about tough working environments when Danib pushed me ahead of him. He practically carried me down the corridor. Had I any less shame, I could have let my feet dangle and been held aloft solely by his grip on my neck. Even to my cold vapour, his fingers felt like ice.

Out, he took me. Not down. Not up. Not to Temsa or the cellars. Out. I watched the corridors grow narrower until we came to a dark space with a thin square of light etched into it.

'What are we—'

Danib pushed me forwards with a grunt, pressing me up against a door.

'M'kay,' I garbled, my face against the rough iron panels.

Light blinded me as his keys turned, three altogether. A brazier shone to my left, lighting a thin street bordered by two warehouses, stocky and windows dead but for a faint blue glow. I still heard the clanging of work within their walls. That, and the rumble of drinking and singing from the building behind us.

Danib guided me around the borders of the tavern and then across the sand and wagon-ruts to an alley heading north. At least, that's what the moon told me. I'd spent enough bored nights watching her passage to know her movements as well as the sun's.

The ghost still pushed me before him, but at least he had released my neck. I rubbed away the cold echo of his grip as I idly stared up at the canyon walls of sandstone and window ledges and guttering. The sky was a speckled strip above me, and I followed its path more than the alley's.

Danib spared as many glances behind him as he did for me and the road ahead. The noise of the tavern and the warehouses had died, but the streets ahead were brightly lit, and offered their own clamour.

We switched from darkness to light once again, and I negotiated the busy traffic of shabbily dressed people and masses of ghosts. Between impatient shoves from Danib like a battering ram to my spine, I caught sight of bazaar stalls glowing with candles and blue light. Ghosts stood behind their wares, both free and bound. They offered little in the way of food or drink, but plenty of trinkets, costumes, scrolls and books. Mountains of books.

I supposed when you had immortality to waste, spending it on books wasn't such a bad idea. I saw the sense in it. Books – at least the good sort – were doors into worlds beyond our miserable own. Perhaps I'd pay this night bazaar a visit when I had my own time to waste. That was, if Danib wasn't escorting me to a chopping block.

'Temsa won't be pleased,' I warned him, trying to avert any permanent fate he might have planned for me. 'Whisking his locksmith into the night.'

Another shove was my only reply, and together we took another alleyway. This one wound about the busy areas, taking a curving route to the edge of the city's core. We walked in stilted and one-sided conversation. I probed him about his previous life, whether his armour chafed, and how heavy his sword was. Every time I got either a grunt or another knock from those ham-like fists.

I was about to ask him what it was like working for a maniac when I felt his fingers around my neck again, and he brought me to a halt.

Blue, knotted knuckles met the wood of a nearby door three times, and Danib stared at me through the holes of his helm while he waited. I avoided those blank white canvases. A man could have drawn any emotion on them. Perhaps that was Danib's secret to surviving so long in the proximity of men like Temsa. That and being the size of a cottage.

I stared at the door instead, finding it unremarkable save for its crimson colour, freshly painted, its brass bars and the lack of a handle.

The building it belonged to was a featureless wall of stone, reaching high into the night—

Crimson.

I flinched in the ghost's grip, a fraction before the door creaked open to reveal two women clad in red robes. They must have been sisters, for they were practically identical, both of shaven head, hooded, and sharing the same impassive expression as my captor.

I didn't know whether to smirk or frown. This city was choked with treachery, and yet still I was shocked. 'My, my, Danib. Fuck me. You're not Temsa's at all, are you?' I asked.

Without a sound, he slammed me against the doorjamb. There was no pain, just a sheer crushing weight as he pressed. I waved my hand, his giant fingers covering my mouth. I waited while Danib bent low to whisper between the sisters. After some time, one of them pointed at me.

'Brother, please. Release him.'

Danib released me, and I spent a moment with my palms on my knees, wincing the vision back into my eye. A softer, smaller hand alighted on my shoulder, but I shrugged it away.

'As I die and glow. Caltro Basalt, I presume?' asked one of the women, bowing shallowly.

I stretched to my full yet modest height and tried to suck in my gut. I even bared my neck wound, seeing as I naked of my usual scarf. That had gone into the Troublesome Sea with Foor. 'You presume correctly. And I would wager you're from the Cult of Sesh.'

'Incorrect. We are from the *Church* of Sesh,' the other told me.

I thought for a moment. I felt a tension in my chest that, in a past life, would have been my heart racing. Was I nervous? Naturally, as one was when being marched to shady places with shady people. Curious? Absolutely, seeing as the Cult had come to me, not I to them. As usual, I retreated behind my shield of impudence. 'Calling a dead goat a live one doesn't change the fact it's rotting.'

The two smiled and retreated into the gloom beyond the doorway. 'Won't you come in?'

Danib didn't hear that as a question. He picked me up and hurled me inside. The door slammed behind me as I picked myself up, brushing imaginary dust from my naked arms and thighs. I wished Temsa had dressed me better, rather than gifting me with only a loincloth and a frayed linen waistcoat. My belly couldn't be covered.

The sisters had already taken a seat behind a circular table with some sort of spinning device at its centre. Holes marked with coloured glyphs pockmarked its wide bowl. I noticed the gilding of silver and gold around the table's edge and was drawn forwards, as powerless as a magpie. Other tables sat at the edges of the wide, low-ceilinged room. In the thick gloom, I saw a half-finished game of ballast still standing upright, the precariously balanced sticks still waiting to tumble. I knew this type of place, and it seemed fitting for my first meeting with the elusive Cult to be in a card den. A place of lies. A place of taking risks.

'I am Enlightened Sister Liria,' said the left one.

'And I am Enlightened Sister Yaridin,' said the right. 'You already know our brother here.'

'Intimately,' I replied, hearing the growl close behind me.

'And who are you, Caltro Basalt?' Liria asked.

'Well, it seems you already know—'

'Where did you come from?'

'How did you come to be entangled in this mess?'

I traced my hands across the velvet tablecloth, noting the dried blood spatter, and gave the wheel a slight push to make it spin. A musical clinking played briefly. 'I'm originally from Taymar, in Krass. Ran away to Saraka in my twelfth year. Was orphaned in my thirteenth. Healer parents died of swelterflux in winter on the barren steppes. Got pretty cut up over it. Ran back to Saraka. Studied with a master until I got real good at breaking locks. Then I got even better. Plundered vaults and lockboxes all over the place. Some have called me the best in the Far Reaches. Hence why I came here. Turns out I got the wrong ship. Somebody had paid off the captain or the port guards, and I wound up dead, throat slashed and my blood carpeting an alleyway. Since then, it's been a barrel of laughs going from the care of one lunatic to the next. Then I discover this strange ability I didn't ask for, and all of a sudden I'm here, chatting to two ghosts I couldn't tell apart if you paid me. How about you?'

Liria held up a sphere of what looked to be ruby. She placed it in one of the holes bored in the wheel and gestured for me to push it again. I did so, harder, and the jewel skittered around the bowl along to the metallic melody. As the music and the spinning slowed together, the ruby fell into a hole and stuck there.

'You win,' said Liria.

'Win what?'

Yaridin spoke for her, like a double act. 'Our kinship, Mr Basalt. And, more importantly, our protection.'

'What have you heard of the Church?'

Seeing as we were in a place of gambling, I held some cards tight to my chest. I wasn't about to tell them I'd had visits from the sworn enemies of their god, but I could be honest about the rest. All the rest. 'A great deal, and none of it good, I'm afraid. From what I've heard, the city sees your order as a bunch of self-serving traitors after you tried converting some old emperor. Not only that, but you worship a very old, very dead, and by all rights, very calamitous god of chaos. That rings several alarm bells immediately, but then there's the fact you can't enter the Core Districts without being arrested. I know Horix hates you. I imagine the emperor and his daughter hate you. And Temsa has a distaste for anything that glows, so he probably hates you too, despite working with you.'

The sisters traded knowing looks, and Liria smiled. It was not a thing of warmth. 'A common occurrence in this city. We are very much misunderstood.'

It was not the response I'd expected to such a deluge of truth. I'd found people were not fond like the truth. I crossed my arms. 'Misunderstood? I can't see why, especially when you deal with soulstealers and murderers.'

'And that is why we thought it was time to introduce ourselves, and show you otherwise.' Yaridin stood, plucking the ruby. She rolled it around her glowing hands, turning it purple. I watched as the ball wandered around her fingers, defying gravity and sense. 'For centuries we have worked to help and protect our fellow shades. To do that, we must play the great game of power, just like everyone else in Araxes. The emperor plays. The Widow Horix plays. Tor Temsa plays, albeit a most violent version. Even you play it, Caltro, though you find yourself playing unwillingly. It is the goal of the game that matters most; what each competitor strives for.'

There was nothing unwilling about my desire to be free. 'But you're working with Temsa. You're involved in these murders, same as him. Surely your goals align with his.'

Liria spoke up, still seated and smiling, but her eyes now pools of proud, bright light. 'Ha! Oh my, no, Caltro. We do not work with Temsa. He works for us. He is but a tool for our motives. He is our wild dog, the rabid wolf Araxes needs to push it to the edge. We chose him, provided him with the excuses he needed to fulfil his desires, and let him loose. We gave him names, like rungs on the ladder to his bloody success. We even found him a princess to protect him. Yes, we pointed them at each other purposefully. And yet do our goals align with his?

Scarcely. His sights are set far below ours. Like most players, he seeks to pry the emperor from his Sanctuary and claim his crown and throne. We are using Temsa to achieve something altogether grander.'

Dead gods. The Cult was behind it all. I had thought Temsa the orchestrator of the mayhem in Araxes. The great risk-taker. The man who had conned both a cult and a princess into his pocket. But no. These ghosts – these sisters who looked as though they would struggle to count sixty years between them – were the masterminds.

I glanced at Danib, who was staring resolutely at the ceiling, as if he was pretending not to listen; as if this was too much betrayal for him.

'And that is?' I asked with a croak.

'Peace. Justice. Freedom,' Liria shot back. 'For both the living and the dead. For years, the Church of Sesh have stayed on the sidelines, helping what few shades we could while watching Araxes slip further and further into the gutter. Change is desperately needed. Especially for shades like you, who had their lives taken away through murder and greed. Wouldn't you agree?'

I hushed the traitorous voice inside me, though I had to agree. *Finally, somebody in this city with some sense.* How strange that it would be the bunch of widely-loathed outcasts.

Yaridin spoke up. 'We confess, though we trade in information, we have only watched you for so long. You were quite the surprise when Danib told us Temsa had claimed one of the Reaches' best locksmiths.'

'*The* best.'

Yaridin cocked her head. 'Saying that, we feel confident wagering that you long for your freedom, Caltro?'

'Sister, it's all I've wanted since the moment I rose from the Nyx. But you can't help me. Unless you have my half-coin stashed in those threads, you're no better a chance at freedom than Temsa is. I'll take my chances with the widow.'

'You would trust Horix?' asked Liria.

I spread my hands across the desk, fixing her with a stare. My tone was sharp as flint. 'She's a means to an end. As I keep trying to tell everyone, I do what I want, how I want. I always have. I trust in myself. Nobody else.'

That cold smile returned to the ghost's face, and a clawing hand reached to spin the wheel. 'And how has that worked out for you so far?' she challenged me, above the rattling of music.

I had no answer, and so she spoke for me. Her eyes drilled into me all the while, as if picking through my thoughts and memories to furnish her argument.

Liria stood now, and came closer. 'We know what it is to be indentured, Caltro. We are kin. Brothers and sisters. You think you're the only one who has fallen foul of a blade, that nobody can understand your pain and loss, and so you have trusted yourself. You've thrown yourself at every cage door, but all it has achieved is another master, another mistress. You've been beaten, kidnapped, passed about like furniture instead of a human soul. You've seen animals treated better than being branded a half-life.'

The complaints were far too familiar for my liking. I had spent my life telling myself that nobody understood me. It had kept me mysterious. Now in death, these sisters seemed to know every inch of me. Liria had stoked some curious fire in me, but I stayed silent and dumb, in case my speaking would shatter the moment of wisdom I felt coming.

It was Yaridin who answered, stepping the other way around the table. 'Caltro. Do you know why the living hate the dead? Truly?'

'Because we are less than them?'

'No, brother. We are *more*. Think. We shades are immortal. We are impervious to all but copper. We are innumerable. We are in their towers. We run their lives, guard their doors, even fight their wars, and yet they believe themselves our lords and masters through the power of a few laws and a half-coin.'

Yaridin's voice had become louder and harsher with every word. I felt the sister's cold wash over me, deeper than a winter's breath. I saw anger in the whiteness of her eyes, one I recognised very well. I felt my fists clench, my chin rise.

Liria whispered in my ear now. 'They fear us because they know the fragility of their grand system! Neither the Tenets nor the Code can truly control us. They are rules drawn up by the first kings of the Arc in order to profit from Sesh's sacrifice. Our Church knows better. We know our true power.'

'You know something of true power, do you not, Caltro?' asked Yaridin.

And there, like the red crescent of a new dawn's sun breaking over the horizon, I felt the purpose of my visit emerging. Once again, I looked over my shoulder at Danib, thinking of how he had killed the guard. I saw it in a different light now. He had not punished the man; he had silenced him. Danib had seen my haunting and covered my tracks for me. And now I was here, within an hour, standing in front of the Cult.

'I imagine there's no point lying,' I told them, laying some of my metaphorical cards down on the table, but not all. 'So I can haunt. I don't know how, or why, but apparently I can. Question is, why do you care? You spin a good yarn, Sisters. Best I've heard since I've arrived in Araxes, to be honest. But I've heard a lot of similar conversations during my time here, and they always end up with me doing something for somebody. Normally, it's picking a lock, and normally, it's against my will, but I get the idea that's not your style. Instead, given the hour and the swiftness with which Danib marched me here after our little corridor debacle, I would wager it's something to do with my ability to haunt. You call me kin, so don't waste any more of my immortality with further lies. Spit it out, please. What can I do for you, Sisters?'

Both ghosts scrutinised me with narrowed eyes. Liria spoke first, after a lengthy pause. 'Nothing.'

'Horseshit.'

'We merely want to help you, Caltro, as we have helped so many others like you.'

'Others with gifts.'

That knocked the vapour out of me. 'What do you mean, "others"? I'm not the only one?'

'Others with gods-given gifts.' I flinched as Liria stole the phrase from my memory. 'It is rare, but not unheard of,' she said.

If that was true, then Haphor had been right. I was not special, it seemed. Perhaps I was one of a long line of failed experiments the dead gods had sent back to save themselves. I found myself clenching my fists. 'I don't fucking believe it...' I hissed.

'You will see, soon enough.'

'But why?' I snapped. 'Nobody helps anybody in this city. Not unless it helps them.'

'And perhaps that is the problem,' sighed Yaridin.

'We will help you gain your freedom and justice, Caltro Basalt. You will see.'

Although I had my doubts about the Cult, numerous and sharp-edged, it was the first time I had been made a promise in Araxes and not wanted to laugh in the face of its deliverer. Somehow, the sisters' words felt as tangible as the writ of freedom waiting for me in the widow's tower. They certainly didn't seem like the world-killers the gods had described. Then again, when had any of my dead visitors been truly honest with me? They certainly hadn't ever offered me freedom.

Liria extended a hand, a simple and innocuous gesture for all the weight it carried. This was a pact in the forging. A pact with the servants of the god of chaos, no less. The puppet masters behind Araxes' panic. The true power in the city.

The sisters whispered in turn.

'Are you with the Church?'

'Are you with your dead brothers and sisters?'

I realised I had lifted my hand, fingers twitching to straighten. *What am I doing?* My vapours flowed in spirals across the back of my wrist, agitated. The air grew brittle and polar as I continued to reach out. In the darkness, I saw the eyes of a dead cow, a dead cat, and a dead man. They had extended me no such promises of kinship. Only duty.

Liria and I touched as tangibly as two passing storms. Finger to finger, our blue mists intermingled briefly before I snatched my hand back. 'I'll say so when I see my half-coin in my hand.'

Liria smiled that frigid, withered little smile once more. 'And so you shall. But for now, you must return to Temsa.'

My mouth fell open. Whatever hope had been kindled was crushed. 'What the fuck? Why? I thought this was my escape?'

Liria tutted. I wondered how with a lack of tongue. I had tried many times, and failed with a useless hiss. 'Appearances must be maintained,' she said flatly. 'You are too useful to Temsa. He sees you as his secret weapon.'

'We still need Temsa to succeed for the greater good.'

'You must continue picking locks for the time being.'

The flattery was welcome, but it changed little about my indignation. 'Then what about my half-coin?' I spluttered. 'What if she melts my—'

'Widow Horix is a curious player indeed. Cunning. Sharp.' Liria swapped a look with her sister, like parents rolling their eyes over a misbehaving child. 'For some reason, she holds you in high regard, but like all the rest on our list, she will be removed from the board. Your half-coin will be reclaimed, Caltro. Fear not.'

It was poor comfort. I had plenty to fear.

Yaridin hummed to me. I could feel her hand in the small of my back, guiding me towards the door. I wanted to shrug away, but Danib's hand was also on me. It felt like an anvil had alighted on my shoulder. My back was turned on the dusty games and velvet card tables. I wasn't sure if I'd lost or won tonight. Currently, it felt as though I had been robbed. And I was the thief.

'You're just going to send me back?'

'You should leave the game to other players for now, Caltro. When the time is right, we will come for you. With our help, you shall have your freedom,' whispered the sisters in unison. 'Be patient.'

I was growing tired of being patient. I wanted to call them both a pair of useless cunts, but I held my tongue tightly and allowed Danib to grab my arms and steer me into the night. Not that I could have stopped him.

'Stay useful, Caltro Basalt,' the sisters chorused, before the door slammed behind me.

Once again I was marched through the streets, though this time with a head full of words and half-promises. As I trod the sandy flag-stones, I pondered the offer of freedom and kinship the Cult had ex-tended. Although the offer had come from the mouths of Araxes' grand-est schemers and I was still undecided on how genuine it was, to know I was not alone was somewhat warming to my cold soul. The weight I carried had lifted somewhat, as though I had shrugged off leaden boots.

Once I'd spied the point of the Rusty Slab above a rooftop, I de-cided to break the silence. I turned to the scarred monolith by my side, my tone cheerily conversational. 'I suppose you wouldn't like it if I told Temsa about this? About your friends in red?' I asked.

Danib's fist struck me in the nose, sending me ricocheting from a wall. Blue and white lights swam before my eyes until I was thrown into the cool of a stone corridor.

'I guess not, then.' My voice was somewhat muffled by my hands, and yet behind them, I smiled. Leverage, however small, was always a gift for those with the necessary lack of scruples to use it. Whether I trusted the sisters' words or not, they had inspired me. Not in the way they'd have liked, I wagered, but I was grateful for their mistake. They had shown me that the Cult's promises, the gods' begging, Horix's writ of freedom, and Temsa's offer were all worth less than horseshit. I saw now that the price of their freedom made me nothing but a pawn. I refused to be a pawn any longer. I was done being patient, done doubting myself. I had power. Value. I had spent enough time in Araxes awash, floating about on the scant mercy and loose promises of others. I could feel that changing now. I would play the great game of Araxes, and I would win my coin. Gods, cults, widows and soulstealers be damned.

At last, my tide was turning. I was coming ashore.

CHAPTER 22
EVERYBODY'S GOT DEAD

Law creates crime. Crime creates law. Like
shadow and lamplight, one cannot exist
without the other to define it.

FROM 'A REACH HISTORY' BY GAERVIN JUBB

NOISES WERE PLENTY IN THE fight-pits. The pulsating cheering of the onlookers, stacked like the layers of a tall cake, reaching up to the skylight far above. The cackle of winners. The cursing of losers. The wet smack of sweaty palms and beer-soaked gums. The tinkle of silver flicking from hand, to purse, to bucket, to ever grubbier hand. The harsh spatter of the occasional patron pissing against the plain sandstone wall.

But for all the various sounds, there was one kind that held Scrutiniser Heles' ears: the noises coming from the pits. The straining. The grunting. The dying.

Spread in a triangle under the dusty shaft of orange light were three holes. Each was the depth of three men and about twenty wide. Their walls were sheer and plain, hewn earth. Antelope and bull horns had been drilled into their higher reaches, pointing downwards like teeth, as if the pits were the throats of some colossal dunewyrm. At their edges the crowds stood, leaning as far as their daring – and the railings – would allow. It wasn't uncommon at the fight-pits for an overly zealous soul to fall in and become part of the fight.

Hooded and dressed in smart silks, Heles was squeezed against the railing, watching the fight from the front row. It was a long way down to the sandy floor, strewn with palm fronds and blood spatter. This was where the noises emanated from, where the unlucky, the criminal, and the insane tried to survive whatever games the pit-masters had thought up. Tonight it was gangs of naked shades against one living. The shades got a rock each. The man or woman got as much armour as they could stagger about in and a copper spoon.

The man in Heles' fight-pit – a skinny pickpocket, from what the announcer had bawled – had already succumbed, and was currently having his face smashed in. The crowd around the black iron railings were going wild. A miniature fight broke out nearby between two women; somebody had clearly taken offence to losing. Musclebound shades moved in to break it up. They were perhaps the only half-lives in the crowds. Torturing the dead was a sport reserved for the living.

Judging by the squeals and shouts, it sounded as if the living in the other two pits had also fallen to raging blue vapour. The cheers and bawls of outrage drowned out the sounds of rock finding skull. More shades emerged from hatches to drag the bodies away. The announcer appeared upon his lofty pedestal so quickly there was barely a pause between the loser's last breath and his first.

It wasn't his shining baldness, nor the ponytail sticking from the side of his head, nor his heavily painted face that made Heles hate him. No, it was the fact he was draped in a suit of yellow canary feathers.

'Well, fight fans!' he bellowed through a cone of cheetah hide. 'Get ready to place your bets, for now we give our survivors one last chance to win their freedom!'

The grimy hall began to throb with the stamping of feet. Heles looked down at the remaining shades in her pit: four of them, all pale Scatterfolk shades, probably prisoners of war shipped in for cheap sale and back-alley soulmarkets. The saying was that being sold to the pits was better than being sold to the desert mines like Kal Duat; shades survived at least a week longer in the pits.

'Last shades standing get their coins! Double or nothing for losers. Extra silver in it for streaks! A'here we go!'

With the snap of a hatch door, a cage was pushed out across the sand and palms. The hungry snarling was immediately drowned out by the hubbub of fierce gambling. Bet-takers struggled to keep up, screeching terms as silver rained down on them. Heles ignored the riot, watching the cage and the shades cowering from it. They hugged the earthen walls.

It was an enormous ram, pitch-black of fleece and apparently enormously short in temperament. Three pairs of wild milky eyes studded a face that was bared to the bone. Horns curled like gnarled tree branches. They had also been dipped in molten copper, and wreathed in spiked rings. Sparks flew as the ram hurled itself at the cage's bars. As it half-baaed, half-roared, Heles saw the multitude of fangs crammed into its mouth. The hooves that raked the floor of the cage were claw-like, like the talons of a bear. No peaceful grazer, this ram.

The announcer waved a palm frond across the mouth of the pit. 'All bets are now… FINAL!'

Heles had to brace herself as the press swung from the betting tables back to the railings. She winced as an extremely rotund woman leaned close and bellowed, 'Go oooon, sheep!' in her ear.

'Will we see freedom here tonight, fight fans?' came the announcer's call.

A resounding thunder-roll of laughter shook the hall. Chants of, 'Baphmet! Baphmet! Baphmet!' filled the air. In the pit, Heles saw one of the shades crumple to her knees and close her eyes.

'It's up to you!' yelled the announcer, waving a hand and grinning at the naked, quivering shades. Chains hauled at the cage's door, cranking it open. 'Well, then! LET'S! RELEASE! THE BEAST!'

With a bellow that momentarily conquered the noise of the fight-pits, the ram burst forth from its cage. Scrutiniser Heles watched one shade torn limb from limb in a cloud of sapphire smoke before she decided that was enough. Elbowing herself clear, she turned away from the fight, if this slaughter could be called such a thing.

She was seething with anger when she reached the wooden plank they called a bar. A slam of a fist brought her a clay pot of beer, and she choked it down to keep from screaming.

A hand alighted on her forearm. Heles almost twisted it off before its owner yelped a familiar name.

'It's Jym!'

'Fucking dead gods, Proctor. I almost broke your arm.'

It took a moment for him to squeeze the pain from his hand. He blinked at her, watery-eyed and puffing. The skin under his tattoos was flushed. 'You're telling me! Ahhhh.'

'I told you not to sneak up on me,' she hissed. 'Progress report?'

'Farassi doesn't seem to be here. I think it was a false rumour. And if you don't mind me saying, why ain't we investigating Temsa? It's strange the Chamberlain wants us to follow Farassi, especially after our report...'

Heles surveyed the balconies one last time. 'It *is* strange, isn't it? You're correct for once. You're learning, Proctor Jym.' She saw him swell even out of her peripheral vision. It should have brought some warmth to her heart, to see a young proctor so proud of doing such a grimy, thankless job. Instead, it made her snarl.

'What's wrong, Scrutiniser?' Jym asked.

She briefly contemplated dismissing him with a wave and a curse, but he needed to hear the truth. 'A pointless fucking night is what's wrong, Proctor. You might be new, but you better get used to failure. You'll see a lot of it in this job. Job. Hah. More of a curse. Because just when you see a glimmer of success, progress of any kind, somebody above shits on you. Like you don't already have enough mess to deal with while you're down here, in gutters like these.'

Jym's silence was cold and awkward. At last he found some words. 'I thought you never failed.'

'I don't. This is out of my hands,' Heles snapped, slamming a fist on the bar. Another beer quickly appeared after a shifty look from the barkeep. The scrutiniser narrowed her eyes. 'Temsa gets to keep on rampaging, going unpunished, and we get to stand by and watch. How fucking rewarding. He must have powerful friends to get Rebene on his side. And that's all it takes to ignore the Code. Power. What use are laws if they don't apply to everyone, Proctor? What is the point?'

Even in the face of her heresy, Jym's optimism refused to be crushed. It was deeply infuriating. 'It's much easier to fail when there's some-body else to blame, ain't it? Like me leaving the locks open the night the soulstealers tried our family's door. I blamed them. It's easier, for a time, but it doesn't last.'

Despite the fact he was right, Heles shook her head resolutely. 'Stick to the Code, Proctor. You're a shit philosopher. And I told you, everybody's got dead. I know all about blame, like lighting fires in cellars only to see two families burn alive. How's that for you, Jym? I'm not angry because I think I failed, or because of blame. I'm fucking angry because others have failed me. There's an infinite difference, and that is why you will stay here. Stick around in this shit-hole and make sure Farassi isn't just late.'

The proctor licked his lips. 'And if he does appear?'

'Do what you're supposed to do. Fucking scrutinise.' Heles thrust her hands into the pockets of her cloak and stood straight, like a watchman over a stormy sea. Jym retreated slowly, as though wondering whether he should press her for more, but he wisely refrained. The proctor melted into the crowds and left her be.

Escaping from the stuffy air, Heles returned to the streets. An hour she spent standing in a doorway, several down from the musclebound shades guarding the fight-pits, until the sun moved overhead to scorch her face. She let it, for a time, before striding west for the rim of the Core Districts.

Heles had calculated. She'd measured. She'd weighed. It was what she had done for a decade and it was what made her feet move now, despite all the risks and orders that stood against her. Fine, she couldn't go after Temsa, but Rebene had said nothing about his conspirators. *Conspirators like the Widow Horix.*

With cloak-tails swishing behind her, and a stride that paused for no bumbling pedestrian, Heles weaved through the crowds like an eel through a forest of kelp.

The walk from the outer district was long, and sunset was falling by the time the scrutiniser found herself in fancier surroundings. She hovered by a cart full of steaming pastries, and decided to quiet her growling stomach. Eating was such an inconvenience; she wished there was a magic draught she could quaff and never have to eat again. The streets would be better for it.

There she waited, until the half-eaten pastry in her hand grew cold, and the stall-owner started to give her leering looks. She gave him a withering glance and chose another spot to linger, one that sold spring water instead. The salt and spice of the – frankly foul – pastry had given her a thirst.

Horix's tower began to sparkle as the lamps were lit. It seemed the widow was being scant with her whale-oil; barely a dozen windows glowed across the entire tower.

'Lying low, are we, Horix?'

Something beneath Heles' feet trembled for a moment. She looked around for any dropped barrels or passing carts, but the street was still. Busy with people and shades, yes, but no more than usual.

Heles crouched to lay a hand on the stone, but felt nothing but sand, clinging to the grease on her hands.

When the darkness had reached an appropriate level for her duties, Heles stepped out into the thin flow of people and edged her way past Horix's tower. Two laps, she did, before spying a garden through a narrow alley. A wall blocked the way, spiked and tall, but she could still see the fronds of palms and the open space of a courtyard. She'd contemplated the front door, showing Horix's men her Chamber seal, but that usually just meant long waits, lies, and heavily abridged tours of dark and overly legal buildings. Back doors were always better.

Heles ducked into the small gap and crept along it. Brick and sheer adobe brushed against her fingertips. When she reached the wall, she found no door or hinges, just sandstone and crumbling mortar. Her fingers could touch the top at a jump, but there was nothing to grasp but spikes and chiselled stone.

Pressing her feet against one wall of the alley, and her back to the other, Heles tensed herself and began to climb, shuffle by shuffle, step by step. When she'd shimmied above the spikes, she saw a sparse garden hemmed in by walls and the flanks of the tower. Two guards and a shade stood watch at a door a good stone's throw from the last of the plant rows. The foliage below Heles was far out of the reach of their lamplight.

It was her last moment to think, and she used it sparingly. The Chamber believed in evidence over suspicion, but evidence was hard to find when nobles hid behind their locked doors and lofty games. Evidence had to be rooted out, hunted down, and a scrutiniser couldn't do that by standing on street corners.

'Fuck it.'

Heles' hands found the edges of the wall, and she yanked herself towards them, falling down into a bush below. Fortunately for her, it was the fruity sort, not the thorny. Even so, she felt the cold of something squashed bleeding into her thigh. She stayed put, watching for moving shadows, but none came.

The plant rows gave her darkness, and from it she watched the guards to measure their movements. They were turning out to be pretty stationary until a shout called them inside, and the heavy door was locked with what sounded like six bolts. The widow was playing cautious, too.

Even though the twin lamps stayed burning, this side of the tower lacked windows – for security, of course. Heles grew bold enough to creep beyond the foliage and onto the dry scrub separating her and the building. She could have marched more than a score of steps and not reached the sandstone. By the door, she noticed a pole stuck in the ground, with a thin rope coiled about it. It looked like something fit for a hound.

Heles' foot knocked something solid and metallic. She looked down at a divot in the dust and saw what looked to be the head of a bolt. Heles, painfully conscious that she was visible in the lamplight, bent down to pick it up.

The thing didn't budge. Clearing the sand, she got a good grip, but all it gave her was a squeak. Scraping with her nails, Heles dug deeper until she found its base. A seam of cold iron met her fingers, and…

'Wood,' she muttered as she watched some of the sand grains fidgeting.

Heles knelt, pressing her ear to the ground. She heard a low rumbling, something akin to chiselling or hammering. It was constant, yet ever changing. At one point she swore she even heard a shout.

Heles' mind was already scrambling over possibilities like a recruit over an assault course, desperate to survive until the end: the solution. She felt stuck at the base of a ten-foot wall.

There. She heard it: a shout. More like an order, yelled by a foreman. 'What in the Reach—'

Six sharp bangs sounded as bolts were dragged back. A man swollen with muscle and two lesser creatures burst into the garden with purpose in their eyes.

Heles drew herself to her full height and reached for the seal in her pocket. 'Scrutiniser Heles of the Chamber of the C—'

The big man's fist came swinging. Heles threw up an arm to fend it off, but his fist kept coming, clobbering her in the shoulder.

'I'm here on official business!' she yelled, before knuckles caught her under her chin and sent her spread-eagled to the sand.

As boots began to pummel her ribs and chest, she swore she heard the familiar crash of something landing in a bush. 'No!' she cried out.

She'd received beatings before. Every scrutiniser who did their job right had at one point. She knew the difference between a beating and a death sentence. She was getting the former.

Heles lashed at, bit at and scratched at any leg that came near her. She took one guard to the ground, but before her nails could get to his windpipe, strong hands ripped her free. Heles was thrown like a grain-sack, the grit grazing her cheek as she landed and rolled. Her long knife came out of her pocket.

'Stay back! I am a scrutiniser of the Chamber!'

They said nothing. That was the most chilling aspect of the fear that tried to claim her. Usually there was a brag, or a cold threat, even just a snarl of emotion. These men went about their duties as though the sooner they finished with her, the sooner they could get back to their suppers.

'I said stay back! Desist! In the name of the emperor and the Code!' Heles' knife darted back and forth, but splitting the blade between three meant one could pin her. So he did, and the knife was thrown to the dust.

The fists worked her stomach, then her face. Once she'd slumped to a heap, the boots came back with a vengeance, breaking what was left of her. Her head was knocked about like a street boy's bladderball.

Heles was left in dizzying darkness, with just a slit of light to see by. Even that was quickly fading. She fought and she fought, but it was determined to take her. As sound followed the light, she heard a faint cry over the silence of boots shuffling.

'In the name of the emperor and the Code!'

Bravery was a fool's armour, they said, and in Araxes, it never failed to kill a man. Or a boy.

Damn it, Jym.

CHAPTER 23
TRESPASSER'S FOLLY

To truly know evil, one must first look
into the eyes of evil. Even if that requires
looking into a mirror.

OLD SCATTER ISLE SAYING

S AY ONE THING FOR THE spook, Meleber Crale was a re-
silient one.

A day and a night he'd suffered the pokes and prods of copper, the slicing and the cutting. He had endured it all with lips pursed
tighter than a banker's coin-purse, only grunting occasionally as the
pieces were taken from him.

Tor Temsa stood back to assess his work, eyes roving like his fingers
had while the shade swung gently from the chains hooked under his
armpits, a foul glare on his face. His cobalt glow filled the dark, earth-
walled room, making it seem cold.

All the fingers from one hand.

An ear.

His nose.

A section of his belly.

All of that, and all he had given Temsa was his name in return.

'My, my, Mr Crale. You're not quite the shade you were when you
came in, are you?'

Another grunt came, Crale's nostrils flaring like those of a spooked
horse. His eyes had a white fire in them, just like the ragged edges of
his injuries.

Temsa's copper knife waved again, wandering from shoulder to groin,
as if torn between what to work on next. He was running out of options
besides snuffing out the half-life altogether like a sputtering candle.

A sigh came from behind him, and Temsa turned to regard Ani
Jexebel with a raised eyebrow, challenging her. She avoided his gaze
but spoke all the same.

'This is a waste of time. You know who the spook works for. That cunt Horix, is who,' she said.

'I want him to *say* it, Ani!' Temsa bellowed, thrusting the knife at her. Several feet of empty air stood between its quivering point and her breastplate, but still she growled at him, her eyes now narrowed and fearsome. Temsa felt sweat navigating his forehead as they stared at each other. He whirled on Meleber Crale instead, the knife lancing a white scar across his collarbone. 'Do you hear me, spook? I want you to say it, and then you can go free!'

Crale snorted, quiet words creeping from between his thin lips. 'I'm already free. You can only make me freer.'

'I remember now,' Temsa whispered in his ear, feeling the shade's cold vapour trail across his lips. 'You spooks hide your coins, isn't that right? You can't be owned, only sent to the void.'

Crale clung to silence once more. Temsa brought his face close, staring at the dark pit where the shade's hook of a nose had been. 'Most of the spooks I've worked with use the banks. They're the clever ones, right?'

The spook's eyes strayed to Ani, now looming over Temsa's shoulder, but the tor slapped him with the flat of the knife.

'Which bank is it? Hmm? Who do you keep your half-coin with?'

There. The flicker of uncertainty every torturer hunted for. It needed to be prised out and shown to the light before it could be bled. Temsa placed the knifepoint on Crale's chin, hearing the soft sizzle of copper against blue mist. He hunted now.

'Akhenaten's Vaults? Neben? Belepan Trust? Flimzi Consolidated? Which is it?'

'B—Tor, the other spooks won't look too kindly on this,' warned Ani, stepping closer.

Temsa ignored her. 'Harkuf's? Bank of Araxes? Tor's Choice? Setmose? Fenec Coinery?'

The spook was a good liar, but not that good. Whether it was the modest widening of an eye, or the betraying tremble of a lip, everybody had a tell. Crale's was a gentle crinkle in his brow. Temsa caught it easily. The spook hissed as the knife cut a slice of vapour from his cheek.

'Your luck is poor, my good half-life! I happen to have quite the relationship with Tor Fenec and his son. Your freedom? Forget it. I'll leave you here to dangle and pay a visit to Oshirim district right away! I'll have your coin in my hand by tomorrow.'

The dead were no different from the living when broken. Even the stoic ones all turned to spit and spite. 'You're a fool, Temsa! I have connections. Importance!' Crale screeched.

Temsa crooked a finger to the soldiers standing by. They hauled the maimed shade from his chains and muscled him down the dark corridor. His shouts fell away to echoes, and then to silence. All save for Ani's heavy breathing.

'That was a mistake,' she said.

Temsa snarled as he moved to light a lantern with flint and taper, replacing Crale's cold glow with a warmer orange light. 'Fuck the spooks and their guild! They won't give a shit when I tell them how stupid their associate was taking on a job like *me*!' He flung the dagger, striking sparks on the sandstone wall. 'It's this fucking tavern! Too many people in and out. We should have moved sooner.'

More grumbling from Ani, but given Temsa's fiery mood, she wisely pretended she hadn't heard.

'Bah! Who does this Horix think she is?'

Again, Ani feigned deafness, and tapped her ear.

'Who even is she?!' Temsa yelled up at her, stamping his talons. He had done business with Horix, sure, but all he knew of the old crone was her scrawl and her seal.

'Neither the men nor the spies have heard anythin' more about her,' said Ani. 'She's seen occasionally at the soulmarkets and Neper's Bazaar, and that's it. No guests. No parties. No gossip. Horix don't act like a normal noble. She's a hermit, and that means she's dangerous.'

'How so?'

'Ever heard that old saying about corners and wild animals?'

Temsa threw his hands to the ceiling, wishing it would come crashing down to save him from the bothers of being rich. It was a fleeting desire, quickly replaced with injustice and outrage. 'She's a piss-stained old bag! Fuck her! Naught but a hunched widow with rheum in her eyes and barely a decade left in her. How dare she think she can meddle in my affairs? Send spooks to my door? She's a fool.'

Once again, Ani had no reply. Temsa didn't need one.

'That bitch's time is up, m'dear, I tell you that! I can't afford to risk her destroying Caltro's coin now that her spook is smoke. After we hit Finel's tonight, she's next. The Cult will have to deal with me deviating from the order of their precious list.'

He watched the frown deepen across Ani's scarred and tattooed face. 'Finel's? Why not hit Horix first? Avoid pissing off the Cult?'

'I need Caltro for Serek Finel. If we attack Horix too soon, she'll snuff Caltro out before we can take on Finel and Boon.'

'The sisters were pretty fuckin' specific, Boss…'

Temsa's hand rested gently upon the hilt of Caltro's blade, still strapped to his waist. Ani's incertitude had become too bold, too vocal. Her doubt was feeding his, like spraying whale-oil onto a fireplace, and he did not appreciate it.

'That's enough, Miss Jexebel!' he yelled. 'In all the years you've worked for me, you've never once shied away from a bit of knife-work. Now, at the height of my success, when you could be richer than ever before, you fret like a schoolchild, blubbering that I'm moving too quickly. That the Cult will be upset, for dead gods' sake. We have a princess in our pocket, woman! You don't hear Danib complaining, do you? Maybe you should follow his example and learn to hold that fucking tongue of yours. I don't pay you for your advice. I pay you to kill things and keep order, not bitch like a fresh-bound shade.'

Temsa watched Ani's bulging eyes flicking between each of his. The breath heaved in and out of her nostrils. He could see the muscles tensing in her thick arms, the cord-like tendons in her thick neck twitching. He could almost hear the cogs whirring as she calculated her response.

After a tense moment, Ani's fists unclenched and she nodded curtly. 'I wonder how much Sisine will protect us when she finds out you have her locksmith,' she said before striding angrily from the room. Temsa felt the impact of her heavy steps reverberating up through his metal talons.

He waited there in empty silence, distracting himself with the dimples and gouges in the earthen walls, the dark stains in the sandy flagstone, the way a gutter tucked into a corner dribbled something foul and green, the copper dagger lying forgotten behind a stool.

It kept the doubt at bay for a time, but silence was an unlocked door for cynicism, and in a mood like his, his thoughts were nothing but derisive. Inner voices berated him for his brazenness, and for taking great and callous leaps. He met every false claim with a curse until one stood out from the crowd. One that sounded like an enemy whispering in his ear.

'Fucking failure.'

'Shut up, damn it!' Temsa yelled, pulling at his greasy hair. His fingers scrabbled for the sword's handle, tearing it loose from the scabbard so he could glower at its obsidian face. 'SHUT UP!'

With a grunt, Temsa slammed it into the floor, driving it halfway into the stone before he was deprived of his balance and pitched onto his face. Caked in dust and grit, Temsa lay there, breathing heavily, staring at the pommel stone of the sword and its accursed, smirking face.

———————◆———————

OVER FOAMING TANKARDS AND SMOKE-STAINED lips, I have heard people opine that prison does not work. That it is not a fitting punishment for crime. Before my death, I would have agreed, primarily because I knew no prison in the Reaches was capable of holding me for longer than a week. But now, I knew differently, and I would have raised my tankard heartily and cursed those old tongue-waggers if I could have.

Linger long enough in a prison, and it becomes more than a construction of stout stone and iron bars. It becomes a construction of the mind. The sense of prevailing entrapment, the overbearing order, the complete lack of control – they all conspire to make the passage of time a grinding, maddening thing. There is some escape in sleep, but then you wake each morning, and in those few blissful moments of transiting from sleep to open eyes, you forget where you are. Just for a moment, you believe you could be somewhere and something else. That's when the bleak reality comes crashing down, and you remember your sentence. In the end, it is the prisoners who deliver their own punishment. The prison simply provides the venue.

Indenturement was worse. I had no sleep besides the strange state of complete boredom I had perfected. But even that wasn't enough to make me forget where I was and who I was. Just long enough to make me scowl when I saw the walls before me, and my glowing fingers clenching in anger.

I blamed my mood on Temsa taking away my window. I had hoped Magistrate Ghoor's tower would offer something nicer in the way of accommodation; perhaps a room with a sea view. But old dead Ghoor had been a perverted prick, and had built himself his own cells for dead gods knew what. Temsa had rubbed his hands at that discovery.

Disturbingly, the cells were not in the bowels of a tower, as tradition would suggest, but near the bedchambers, which occupied the whole top third of his abode. Judging by the peepholes in the door, and the holes in the strangely thin walls between the cells, they had been designed more for pleasure than for punishment. I was perhaps the first prisoner who had entered these cells unwillingly.

Suffice to say I jumped to my feet when the keys came to jiggle in the locks. Indigo light spilled into my cell, followed by the looming bulk of Danib, armoured to the gills and sporting a helmet with a single horn at its brow. His gaze bored into me, warning me silently before Temsa and Miss Jexebel entered.

'Eager tonight, are we?' asked Temsa, tossing me a black smock. It couldn't have been more at odds with Temsa's gaudy outfit of purple silk and leopard pelt. 'Here. Clothe yourself.'

I shuffled the rough smock over my loincloth and waistcoat, dimming my glow. 'It's night?'

Temsa postured with a new copper cane bearing an eagle's head. He had polished and coiffed himself for his murderous evening. 'Daylight is for pickpockets and the foolish, Caltro, you should know that,' he replied with a tut.

'Or the exceptionally skilled,' I replied, staring flatly at Temsa as I held out my hands for Danib to bind with copper-core rope.

Temsa had a sourness in his eyes that suggested his mood might be fouler than mine. His clenched knuckles were pale even through his tanned skin. He spoke as if he had swallowed a spoonful of sand. I was also surprised and somewhat concerned to see Pointy absent from his belt. His only weapons were his foot and his sharp cane, made of twisted oryx horn and copper leaf.

'*Over here,*' said a familiar voice, leading my eyes to Danib's waist, where two swords hung from his belt. I recognised Pointy's black and silver scabbard instantly.

'He doesn't like me any more.'

I inwardly smiled as Temsa waved a ringed finger in my face, disturbing my vapours. 'No more attempts to escape, Caltro. My patience has all but evaporated.'

I was shoved from the room and into an opulent bedchamber that was predominately bed. *Stay useful*, the Enlightened Sisters had told me, and for now, that's what I intended to do. 'Like I told you before, it was a ghost-napping. I was taken against my will.'

'Mhm,' came the growl, and I stayed quiet. In truth, I was glad to be out of my cell, even if it meant playing along to Temsa's bloody will. At least it gave me a chance to carry on driving a thick wedge between Temsa and his cronies. It was a gambit that needed to be played in small increments, the same as picking a lock. Tiny rebellions – and plenty of them – were what built revolts. Therein lay my escape.

Amongst the clank of armour and boots, I looked to Jexebel. She was striding ahead of Temsa and altogether separate from him. She also seemed irritated. I could recognise the aftermath of a spat when I saw one.

Danib was staring down at me, my rope bindings seized in one huge hand. His gaze was heavy and cold, full of threat. I smiled up at him as sweetly as I could and then yelped as he backhanded me with his gauntlet. Temsa glared at me over his shoulder, and then at the soulblade bouncing on Danib's hip.

I followed his eyes to the pommel stone. Pointy's face seemed fixed on me.

'Did you try to escape without me?'

I slyly shook my head.

'You fucking did, didn't you? Just when I thought you might have a heart, but it looks like it died with your body.'

My eyes wide and jaw thrust out, I gave Pointy my best and most earnest look, willing him to trust me. If his silence meant trust, then I got it. When I blinked, the face had turned away from me, eyes narrow. I knuckled my eyes as I was pushed into the silk interior of an armoured carriage, covered in spikes and emblazoned with a black-painted seal.

Over the next hour, the carriage took us on a winding route to the High Docks and then west along the coast, until crowded ships and warehouses transformed into regal towers and narrow strips of beach. Coiled nets and lobster pots filled tightly-packed streets of cobble and yellow plaster. Beyond them, the Troublesome Sea looked like rumpled black velvet scattered with diamonds. A white disc of moon presided over the waves. I saw a raft of fishing boats huddled around their buoys. They were skinny, spindly things with lateen sails.

The buildings here seemed older. They shouldered up against each other, leaning in the way of old buildings built far too high far too long ago. Their bricks were rounded at the edges, eaten away by salt and sand. I saw wood beams, tarred black, lining adobe and pebbledash walls. Dried palm fronds formed most of the awnings and roofs. If I peered closely enough, I could still see the shanty town this district had been a thousand years before, when Araxes had been just an itch in a builder's hand.

Unfortunately, history was not a precious commodity to a city unless it was profitable. The tors and tals had spread here too, hunting for sea views and relative privacy. Every now and again, a huge edifice rose from between the dishevelled buildings. Pale, sheer sandstone stood next to flaking mortar; or black marble, dark even against the night. I examined each of them as our caravan of carriages and wagons rattled past, wondering which one would be Temsa's prey tonight.

Almost an hour later, we lurched to a halt at a sawn-off stump of a building encircled by a low set of concentric walls. It looked more like a Chamber building, and for a moment Temsa had me wondering just how bold he was. Curiouser, we were sandwiched in a tight back street, nowhere near an entrance.

'Out,' ordered Temsa. I was already stumbling across the cobbles.

I stared up at the walls behind me, noting their wavy rows of black spikes. There was no gate, just flat grey granite drawn into neat squares by silver mortar. Plaques bore warnings of, "No Climbing!" or, "Trespass At Risk of Death!" in bold Arctian glyphs. There were even translations for the Scatterfolk and us eastern fellows. It reminded me of a place in Aerenna, an unwiped anus of a town in eastern Skol. A job had taken me there, much as I had been drawn to Araxes. There was a hollow in the mountainside there, with a great semicircle of stone wall around its mouth. The Aerenna Ark, they'd called it, full of all creatures feathered, scaled and furred. I had walked those walls many a time but never entered. I'd only listened to the gossip of the nearby taverns, and the tales of what wonders it held.

I turned to Temsa, who was busy directing his mercenaries into groups. 'It's a—'

'A zoo. Yes. Well done,' he replied, cutting me off.

'What do you want a zoo for?'

The tor cackled, showing the cracks in his mood. 'I don't want the zoo, Caltro, I want who *owns* the zoo. Some eccentric bastard named Finel. A serek.'

'A serek. Look at you, taking on the big marks,' I said, folding my arms. I slung a sideways glance at Jexebel. 'How very ambitious.'

Temsa prodded me with his cane, and the copper tip made my shoulder flash. 'Haven't you noticed? This is Menkare District. We're practically in the Outsprawls. The Chamber of the Code is even weaker here than it is in the city, and Sisine's soldiers are all stationed in the Core Districts. Now move. Time to work, locksmith.'

'The clue in that sentence is "lock", Temsa,' I said as Danib hauled me to the granite wall. 'I don't work with stone.' I jabbed my foot at a block of stone, barely eliciting a thud. At that moment I heard the echoing growl of something on the other side, something altogether not human. 'You sure you're not losing it?'

With a snarl, Temsa pounced on me, trapping one of my legs with his talons and shoving me up against the wall. His cane pressed to my throat. I gulped habitually, but all I felt was pressure and the sizzle of copper. Danib loomed over us, watching carefully. He needn't have worried: Temsa occupied all my gaze. The vicious little man was close to frothing at the mouth. His eyes were wide and bloodshot, their whites like milky granite veined with rusted iron. He was not a sweater, and yet beads hovered on his quivering forehead.

Knowing my worth, I waited patiently for the threat, but it never came. He simply released me and began to moodily trace the circumference of the wall. Danib made sure I followed, a scowl visible behind the cross-shaped gap in his helmet. Jexebel lurked behind us, cursing any man or woman that didn't hug the wall closely enough. I shook my head, but I grinned as well. Temsa's wasn't the only temper fraying. *Fuck small increments*, I thought. I reckoned I could have them all in tatters within the hour. I wondered what the Enlightened Sisters might say if I sent their rabid wolf to madness.

It was then that Temsa held up his cane. His small army came to a halt, bunching up behind Jexebel and Danib.

'Useless bunch of pricks. What have Yaridin and Liria got for us, Tor?' Jexebel hissed, and I smiled as she swaggered past me.

Temsa pulled a strip of papyrus from his pocket and thrust it at her, avoiding her eyes. Jexebel snatched it away and my smile grew. I heard another roar from behind the walls. I wondered who was wilder, those encaged inside the zoo or those poised outside it.

Jexebel shrugged, her great pauldrons clanking. 'Fuck all apart from a few back entrances, it seems.'

Temsa jabbed his finger at the papyrus. 'Guard numbers. Patrol schedules. A smaller gate. Not the best, I'll admit, but we'll have even less information when we tackle Horix, so you'd better get used to it, m'dear,' Temsa snapped. There was no affection in that epithet now. I was dead, and even I felt its coldness.

'And when will the next patrol be?' I interjected.

Temsa ran me through with a look. 'Imminently.'

I stuck to Temsa's side as we followed the men to a skinny gate. Light from braziers pooled on the cobbles and leaked out into the street.

'All-out assault, then, Temsa?' I whispered.

Temsa cackled, and I heard the feverishness in his tone. 'Finel believes in using walls and his strange collection of creatures to deter the curious. And like I said, Caltro, this is practically the Sprawls. If nobody gives a shit in the Core, who do you think would give a shit here?'

A distant ringing of a bell spurred a few scuffles of boots, a cough, and murmured words from the other side of the gate. I heard the rustle of chain and plate mail. I instinctively stiffened, my glow fading.

'Triggermen,' hissed Jexebel, and four hooded soldiers with quivers at their sides came forward obediently, pausing at the edge of the shadows. They heaved up their heavy triggerbows: stocky constructions the length of a man's leg, with two bows crossed in the shape of an X. A bolt the thickness of my thumb and fletched with black feathers rested at their intersection.

There came a series of thuds as the gate's bolts were drawn back. Dark shapes moved across the orange light. At Jexebel's nod, two of Temsa's soldiers sprinted into the light and blasted bolts into the breastplates of a pair of guards emerging from the gate. The remaining two followed suit, catching another guard with a cry as he ran up to investigate the noises. As he died, gurgling blood, he managed to pull the gate closed, spring-bolts locking it firmly.

Jexebel slammed her fists on the bars of the gate. Everybody present held their breath. I listened hard. No shouts came. No alarms. The soldiers around us murmured their relief.

Temsa signalled to his monstrous shade. 'Danib.' It barely sounded like a command.

After the tor produced a copper knife and held it to my already scarred neck, the ghost released me and strode towards the gate with the heavy clanking of steel plate. The soldiers began to chant softly, swarming in Danib's wake. The monstrous ghost drew both his blades with a harmonic ring. One was a huge longsword that would have taken two men to lift. The other was Pointy. He held both weapons low at his sides, stretched out like scythes. I heard Pointy's cry, plaintive and distant in my head.

'I think I preferred Temsa!'

As Danib neared the stout bars, he pivoted on his heel, bringing both swords together at the crossguards as he spun. His blue glow flared brightly between the gaps in his dun armour, like a star wrapped in steel.

The blades met the gate with a horrendous clang. Sparks fountained, scattering over Danib's horned helmet and shoulders. As he followed the momentum into another blow, I saw the great notch on the broadsword. There wasn't a mark on the soulblade.

There was another rending crash, and a thick section of gate fell outwards. Danib threw it aside, crushing one of his own men in the process, and strode into Finel's zoo.

'Effective,' Temsa muttered, prodding me onwards with the knife.

'What? Your monster of a ghost, or my sword?'

'Both.' He paused to sneer. 'Though judging by *my* sword, you're becoming rather redundant, Caltro.'

'I'd like to see it face a vault door that's three feet thick,' I retorted with a scoff. In truth, I really did want to see what Pointy could do.

The soulblade was keener than a winter wind across the Krass steppes. He certainly would have made lockpicking far easier.

With soldiers now spiralling around us, their swords facing outwards like the teeth of a vicious cog, we followed a short path into what appeared to be a maze of cages. Great and small, they filled the trench between the outer wall and the next, which was taller and spikier than the first.

The silence was soon shattered. It seemed we had found the feathered creature section. Every cage was filled with squawking, flapping things. That was a fine alarm if I had ever heard one. Feathers and down drifted through the fine bars like a strange and unexpected snow. Lanterns hung from poles every ten paces, and they lit the wonder around us. Like the soldiers around me, I stared at each and every cage with wonder, all thoughts of murder and burglary momentarily forgotten.

In one cage, I saw two birds both taller than a man. They had hooked beaks and long, scaly necks like snakes. They raked their sickle claws against their cage doors while screeching at the top of their lungs. I saw a sign at the foot of their cage. It said, "Sicklestritch".

In another enclosure, two brightly coloured yet tiny gazelles hid in a corner. They were covered in iridescent feathers that switched between a spectrum of colours. Red, blue, gold, white, back to red… I couldn't keep up.

The next cage held a pink featherless thing with two heads. It was hanging upside down from the iron bars like a skinned pig waiting to be butchered. Each head bickered feverishly with the other, brandishing copper beaks not too dissimilar to lances. At the creature's wingtips, hooked claws flashed as it took a break from its internal arguing to spit at us.

'Shut these beasts up!' Temsa barked.

His triggermen went to work with ardour, sliding bolts into their bows and starting with the loudest bird. I flinched with every snap of their strings, and then again with each matching thud as the bolt met a different feathered beast. The night grew a little quieter with each one, and my grimace a little grimmer. Though I might not have been fond of my fellow man, I knew the value of beasts. Animals had purer, more ancient souls than we humans did, and for most of my life, I had privately held onto the notion that if animals ever learned to speak, they would melt our minds to shit with all the wisdom we've forgotten. All apart from sheep. They're dumb fucks.

'This is useless, Temsa,' I blurted, watching a doleful ball of feathers get a bolt to the face and disappear in a puff of down. 'You can't shut them all up. Just move on!'

His blade was at my throat before I'd finished my sentence. 'Presuming to give me orders, half-life?'

I met his gaze. 'Recommendations. Seeing as you won't take them from anyone else, I thought I'd give it a go.'

My words nettled him in more ways than one, but chiefly because he knew how right I was. Now that we stood on a path following the curve of the walls, he could see how the cages stretched into the darkness, north and south. The ruckus was spreading from cage to cage. Perhaps it was the death-squawks of their feathered kin, or the smell of blood on the air. It didn't sour my nostrils, but I imagined it was there.

'Ani! Up the pace. Onto the next gate!' Temsa waved his scrap of papyrus at her as she and the soldiers jogged forwards. A dozen stayed with us, sticking to Temsa's hobbling, clanging pace.

The clamour of the cages masked the screams at first. We soon realised the difference as we rounded a huge enclosure holding what looked to be a thousand finches. They tore about their cage in a great blurring swarm, like a furious, cheeping tornado.

We found chaos waiting for us at the next gate. Serek Finel's guards were worth their coin. They had barricaded the iron bars with benches and fence-posts. Danib was there alongside Jexebel, hacking at anybody who dared to come near enough to skewer or hack. Temsa's soldiers clamoured either side of them. Every other moment, I heard the *thunk* of triggerbows over the melee.

Temsa put two fingers between his teeth and a piercing shriek came forth. Even to my numbed senses, it was loud. I wiggled my fingers in my ear, and half my skull in the process.

The two hulking figures extricated themselves from the clash of steel and came loping over. Temsa had his hands on his hips.

'The *next* fucking gate! Didn't you look at the map, Ani?' He didn't wait for her answer, and instead pointed back through the cages. 'You two alone. Go!'

The tor waited patiently while his soldiers feigned a siege. Meanwhile, I stared at an owl that had one singular eye. It sat in a cage nearby, totally aloof from the fighting. The eye was far too big for its body, taking up half its face. The big orb fixed on me as if I was a mouse. It was a pool of oil with golden edges. The metallic flecks began to revolve around their black pit, swirling like molten gold escaping down a plughole. I felt myself falling into its centre, feeling just as liquid, glimpsing stars in the darkness. A whole night sky beckoned to me, filled with ribbons of blue and red and gold, and in their great clouds, mindless in their scale, stars exploded to be reborn in ashes. I swam in a vastness not even a god could have—

'Caltro!' Temsa's shout wrenched me back.

I snapped from the spell as if I had been shot by one of the triggerbows. 'Fuck! What?!'

I found the cage bars in front of my face. The owl stood disturbingly close on the other side. I saw the size of the claws that gripped its tree branch, and I flinched away. Though I was eager to escape the tricksome beast, I had a hard time not staring back at it.

'Fuck! Wh—who… How did it… I think I saw the whole world in those eyes. Fuck!'

'Stop being dramatic. It's just an owl.'

'Some strange fucking owl.' I stared back at it, looking for signs it was not a god in disguise, half-expecting it to drop dead from its perch any moment. All it did was croak at me, and shuffle back into the shadow. I stared at its sign. 'A hexowl. Hmph.'

With a shudder, I rejoined Temsa and the soldiers as we waited patiently for Ani and Danib to go to work on the other gate. We didn't have to wait long. Crashes and screams flooded the air. The barricade was torn aside by a great-axe, and Jexebel appeared through a cloud of splinters. She had the gate open within moments. A man wearing a conical helmet – or rather, the torso of a man wearing a conical helmet – flew out of the gateway mid-scream, showering the soldiers with gore. They cared little, too busy rushing through the wall like invaders on the tail of a victorious battering ram.

We trailed the soldiers, picking our way through pools of blood and lopped limbs. A score of bodies lay around us. Those who had fallen close to the cages were being pawed at by their inhabitants. A great cat, spotted black and white, had got rather lucky with a corpse slumped against its bars, and was already nibbling on the man's shoulder.

The pace of the evening quickened as we hurried after the soldiers. Temsa's tapping became an awkward canter. *Clang. Tap. Clang. Tap.* And repeat. This felt like a battle, not a burglary.

As the sound of fighting began to compete with the growing roar of the zoo, it became clear that it would be a fight all the way to Finel's chambers. I didn't know whether to be pleased or fearful for my vapours. I was on the soulstealing side, after all. Rooting for Temsa felt like a betrayal to myself, and so I watched and waited.

The next gate was under siege. Danib was using Pointy to break the bars one by one. Arrows and bolts ricocheted from the ghost's breastplate and greaves, but he did not care. Temsa's soldiers were already squirming through the holes he'd hacked. A bloody pile of bodies was growing beyond the gate.

'The fucker's putting up quite the fight,' I commented idly.

Simple as twiddling a reed, Temsa spun his knife and jabbed me in the thigh. I saw the white light leaking from the hole in my smock. I hissed through clenched teeth. Hobbling a few paces away, I turned back to the cages and let Finel's collection waste my time.

Here, the torches had been hooded with coloured glass, casting strange hues upon the zoo creatures. Palms grew over them, casting shade and hiding the stars.

Another great cat was encaged nearby. It paced and yowled at the ruckus, baring two great fangs that reached beyond its jaw. Its spine was ridged with rattling spikes and its tail came to a devilish point.

A trio of white wolves sat beyond, painted green by the unsettling lanterns. They licked their lips at the blood making streams of the cobbles.

In one great cage behind our circle of blades, I glimpsed an enormous shape, like an upturned fishing boat with thick legs and hooves. It was scratching at the ground and lowing like a cow, and an extremely disgruntled one at that. In the flashes of fire, I saw plates of armour on its back and spikes on its snout, which it was thudding against its bars. The iron was already starting to bend.

It was then that a new noise rang out above the din. A shrill horn, first from over the wall, and then a reply from somewhere in the streets behind us. I knew what it was before Temsa could summon the words.

'Shit!' Temsa cursed. 'They've got reinforcements. Get moving, you ingrates!'

'They're bloody in, Tor!' came a yell as we pushed through into the next set of walls.

I was expecting more cages, but instead the soldiers found wild grass and bushland under their boots. A bowshot away from us, a herd of armoured scarabs clipped at bushes and trilled between themselves. Beyond them, a long-legged creature strode sedately between palms, its three snakelike heads waving about as they nibbled at flowers.

As my gaze traced the stretch of wall encircling the grassland it soon became apparent this was not Finel's garden, but a giant cage in itself. At its centre was a squat tower, black of brick and sporting a bulbous crown. It all looked a bit phallic to me. Lights studded it, but they were obscured by the mass of torches at its base, where a copse of sharp spears waited for us. I rolled my eyes with exasperation. I refused to die all over again because Temsa had bitten off more serek than he could chew.

Jexebel came striding up. She was bespattered with gore and yet somehow her expression was still more gruesome. 'Fucking mess, this is. And now we're trapped!' she raged.

That word had a knack of striking worry into the heart of anyone. I had no heart, but it still struck something in my chest. I had wanted Temsa in tatters, and I would have settled for bloody strips, but I hadn't wanted to be anywhere near him when it happened. A safe distance and a spyglass to watch the justice would have been perfect. I bit my lip and looked for gaps in the lines of soldiers around me

Temsa was busy eyeing up the phalanxes of guards clustered around the tower. A horn sounded once again. 'I don't disagree, m'dear. Trapped, maybe, but not hopeless.' He clapped his hands. 'Get back to the cages! Find something fearsome, let it loose, and herd it straight at *them*!'

Ani Jexebel's jaw didn't know whether to rise or fall. She crooked a hand to her ear. 'Let it loose…?'

'You heard me! Let it loose!'

'Then what? A siege? How long will that last? I say we cut our losses and leave.'

Personally, I agreed with Jexebel. I was about to interject and stir up their desperation, but Temsa beat me to it. Sparking mutiny was proving a lot easier than I thought.

'You coward!' he screeched at Jexebel, his knife waggling furiously in her face. She said nothing, spending the moment wiping the blood from her battleaxe, but the heat in her eyes spoke volumes.

Temsa snarled. 'Danib! You lot! Get one of those cages open. Make it two!'

The men Temsa had pointed to visibly gulped, but did not move.

'Go! Curse you!' Temsa yelled, and with that, the soldiers trailed slowly after Danib, their eyes fixed on the knife in the tor's hand.

As we and the remaining soldiers – almost two-score of us lucky buggers – tucked ourselves behind the shattered gate, I heard the ring of an impossibly sharp blade shearing through metal bars. A roar followed, the roar of something extremely upset and hungry.

I heard a fresh round of shouting. The rhythmic beat of swords striking shields rose, and then a scream as a soldier came scrabbling back through the gateway. Two wiry creatures made of black hair pounced upon him and promptly ripped the spine from his back with paws the size of dinner plates. The man's screams were hideous, but paled in comparison to the faces that turned to us afterwards, full of white burning eyes, bare of fur and made of bone instead. Their grins were full of sharp teeth and their many eyes shone like the windows of a city. The creatures seemed to be part-bear, part-wolf, part-daemon, and they howled at the taste of fresh blood. Danib appeared behind them, beating his metal chest to drive the creatures on. When they didn't move, too busy snarling and flicking their long tongues, he wrenched the arm from a dead soldier and hurled it towards the tower.

It was a gruesome trick, but it worked. The arm sailed through the air with the bear-wolf things snapping their jaws beneath it. They had almost caught it when they noticed the spearpoints ahead, and realised a buffet was better than one sole arm. They leapt the weapons with ease and became a whirlwind of claws and black, matted hair. I wondered if they had longed to do such a thing while they toured their bars every day, watching their captors and guards and wondering what they tasted like. I was glad they had got their chance.

'What fine animals! See, Ani? Our situation is far from hopeless,' remarked Temsa. He marched towards the tower, leading the final charge. His soldiers and Jexebel swarmed with him.

I looked to Danib, who was already back at Temsa's side. I realised the panic over being trapped had made them forget me. My wrists were still bound, but I was practically ignored. I felt the opportunity seize me, tight and sharp as pincers.

I threw a look over my shoulder at the broken gate and all the escape it promised me. I couldn't help myself. Finel's guards lay behind me, but so did freedom. This was my moment. *At last.* It was clear to me now. I could not wait on the loose promises of the Cult to set me free, or for a madman to send me to the void. I was tired of playing patient. This may have been a half-life, but it was mine.

Feeling a shiver of cold run through me, I tentatively watched the gap widen between me and the soldiers. Nobody noticed my absence, and so I ran.

I was not a natural runner. My frame was wide and my gut had a tendency to jiggle. But in death, with no weight to me but mist and a desperate intent powering my legs, I streaked across the wild grass. A cloud of pollen and winged seeds chased me as I pelted towards the gate. My feet met its broken iron bars when I heard Temsa's shout.

'CALTRO!'

I turned to find Danib racing after me. Strength overpowering weight, he charged at me like a glowing catapult rock tearing through ranks. I swore I could hear the pounding of his armour over the cacophonous roar of the zoo around us. I heard Pointy's angry yells too.

'You bastard! You're doing it again!'

'You're following, aren't you?' I yelled to the night, inexplicable to all but me and the sword.

Leaping through the gateway, I skidded on a cobble and introduced my head to it seconds after. It was in moments like that I was thankful I was a ghost; that I could get up and keep running instead of wallowing in a pool of my own blood.

I could hear another noise building, like floodwaters rushing down a gully. It was distant but racing towards me. I knew I was running to meet it, but I had little choice. Danib was closing fast. For a big lump, the bastard was quick on his feet.

As I weaved between the cages, avoiding clawed swipes and flying spittle, I saw Finel's reinforcement guards pouring around the next gate, They lifted their voices with war cries, raising their spears and torches. Their black and gold armour looked fluid in the light, like the eyes of the hexowl.

'The cages.'

I skidded to a halt, running to the nearest cage, where a mopey lion walked tight circles. He soon came to life as I tackled the gate, baring teeth at me and snapping at my hands. It was a simple pin-lock, and with the barb of my ropes' copper core poking from the fabric, I managed to jimmy it open in moments.

I leapt to the side as the lion sprang free, ignoring my deadness and dashing for the roaring men instead. I had already moved on to the next cage, which held some giant baggy-skinned lizard. Its eyes were deader than all the ghosts in Araxes, like black stones pinned to its face. At least they kept its jagged fangs company. It hissed at me, and I swear it said my name.

Another snap of a lock and it too was loose, running in an awkward side-to-side manner, but at least in the right direction. I heard the shouts as the lion and the lizard collided with the ranks, and the guards' charge momentarily stalled.

Danib's had not. He was barrelling through the inner gateway now, a stone's throw away, my own sword raised against me. I had no more time for picking locks.

'Run, Caltro!' cried Pointy.

I did, straight for the guards who were busy fending off two rather disgruntled and hungry beasts. The commotion had infuriated one creature in particular: the great horned fellow in the tiny cage. The bars were now bent almost to bursting. As I watched, the thing uttered a trumpeting bellow and threw itself against its door. I ran to help it, planning on a last-ditch distraction, but it had no need of me. The scream of steel drowned out the cries from the guards standing between the beast and me.

A few whimpering orders rang out. A handful of guards dug in their heels and spearbutts. The rest parted like crabs scuttling before a cartwheel. I glimpsed the beast in the light of their torches. It was like a huge armoured cow, over ten feet tall and just as wide. At first I thought it was part beetle, the kind the Arc was so fond of, but this thing wore no carapace. Its was an armour of leather, inches thick, striped grey and black and wrinkled like an old purse. Its face was an axehead of bone and armoured plates. From its forehead and snout sprouted two almighty tusks each as tall as me, and each curved to a barbarous point.

I gulped. Needlessly, of course, but old habits die hard, especially in the face of such a monster. I watched, almost stunned to stumbling as the beast broke the guards' ranks with a roar. Men flew aside like trees under an avalanche, broken before they touched the ground. Their screams superseded the roaring. I even saw the big lizard cartwheeling into the night, coming to an abrupt halt against a wall.

It was then that I realised I was next. The beast had chosen its course, and I lay in its path, as did Danib. I glanced over my shoulder and saw the ghost had not slowed. He was rushing to close the gap between us before the beast could. The fucking bastard was driven, I'd give him that.

'I'll tell Temsa! I will!' I yelled, giving him pause, but only for a moment. It was all I needed to bound forwards, rip the smock from my shoulders and fill the path with my glow.

It was a strange moment, running naked towards a charging monster, my extremities flailing wildly. They say avoiding death makes a man do desperate things, but I tell you, it's only when you're dead and bound that you know the true meaning of desperation.

'Come on!' I yelled, mainly to steel myself as the ground shook under my feet. I saw the intent in the beast's tiny brown eyes, and to my surprise, it was not for me. It was for Danib, clanking away behind me. It was his armour. It looked precisely like the beast's. He even had a horn on his helmet.

I turned back to the creature with a grin, and gritted my teeth as I met its charge with my shoulder.

If I'd had a spine, it would have snapped under the speed at which I changed direction. I had expected to be thrown over a wall. Instead I reversed the way I came, and at a gallop far beyond the speed my legs could carry me. I opened my eyes to see Danib waving his arms, trying to slow his momentum. I yelled in what may have been delight, surprise, or even terror, but in any case I felt a roar in my barrel-like chest.

I was inside the fucking thing!

I felt rage. I felt hunger. I felt a driving urge to break something, everything. I let the beast's feelings swirl with my own as I lowered my head, feeling the weight of the horns as I aimed for Danib.

With a crash akin to a banquet table being hurled down a staircase, I collided with the ghost. The impact was stunning, but it barely even slowed me. When I looked up, I saw Danib impaled on my largest horn, a gaping, shining hole in his breastplate. He was wriggling like a daemon, but he was stuck fast. His hands were empty, clenched into fists, and busy trying to wrestle himself free.

My cackle came out as a growl at a first, and then a more human sound as I ripped myself from the beast's body, tumbling out of its enormous backside. It sped on unfazed, barging through a cage of fanged rodents, too preoccupied with the thrashing ghost stuck to its face.

I shook my head, feeling the animal rage still running through me. I felt uncoordinated, foreign to my own vapours. It was Temsa's shout that awoke me.

'CALTRO, YOU BASTARD!'

My short gallop had taken me back to the gateway, and now Temsa and Miss Jexebel were on my tail. I burst into a sprint. Finel's guards had picked themselves up and remembered their previous duties. The fight still raged around the serek's tower; I could hear the clash of armour and the echo of inhuman screeching behind me.

'*Caltro!*'

My name again, but this time in my head. I looked around, remembering Danib's empty hands, and saw something blacker than shadows lying in the dirt. Scooping Pointy up as I ran, I flashed his pommel stone a cocky look.

'See? All part of the plan!'

His voice emanated from the blade now, with a metallic edge. 'You're an idiot. But a damnable lucky one.'

'Story of my afterlife,' I yelled, cutting my bindings with ease.

'I didn't know you could haunt animals.'

'Neither did I! Oh, and I'm sorry.'

'What for?'

'This.'

I swung him downwards, chopping the lock from another cage, and another, releasing anything and everything into the night. It was part distraction, part moral high ground. I had felt the giant beast's frustration melting under a glee born of freedom. It was not too dissimilar from what I was currently feeling. If I needed to be free, so did these creatures. *Fuck Finel and his collection.*

A spotted wolf. A huge hedgehog with quills the size of knives. A cow with curled horns. Even a crocodile with a sail like a ship. I set them all free with showers of sparks and drove them at the guards as I ran.

Within a hundred paces and a dozen cages, I had incited pandemonium. Beast fought man, tooth against blade and claw against steel. For the time being, nobody noticed the shade darting through the clamour, naked and glowing as dimly as possible.

Twice, I had to flip back on myself as more reinforcements joined the fray. On the second time, I stumbled over a hairy and limp body lying crumpled and face-down against a cage. From its frame, I guessed a wild dog, perhaps a small wolf. As I picked myself up, poised to dash on, I heard its spine snap as it turned to look at me.

Its head swivelled all the way around, and as its bloody tongue lolled out of its mouth, I saw its white eyes turn black, like ink fouling water. Pink lips curled into a smile, baring rows of crimson and broken fangs. I saw the chunks of teeth still swilling around its mouth, along with ragged strips of flesh I doubted were its own.

I should have been accustomed to visits from the gods, but there was something beyond the timing that disturbed me. This god had no words for me. No urgings of floods and duty. Just a black, haunting stare. It was not life seeping into this corpse, but death, and a deeper sort than had already taken this creature. I heard my name whispered by bloody lips.

'Caltro...'

My vapours prickled and I pulled myself backwards, having leaned in unknowingly. As I shuffled away from the haunting sight, I heard another crack of bone as the creature died once more. I swiftly put it behind me in a spurt of dust.

'What in the Reaches was that?' Pointy yelled in my hand.

'Something I don't want to meet again!'

I spared no more time for talking and put the sword to work again, filling the air with screeching flocks of birds. Some eagerly disappeared into the dark sky. The others shared the same thirst for vengeance as their many-legged brethren, and descended on the nearest guards in blizzards of claws and beaks. I smiled to myself, even though they swarmed me as well. They couldn't harm me, and they were finally having their vengeance, like rioting slaves.

I followed the river of fur, wings and teeth between the walls and to a large gate. I felt my face drop as I saw the ranks of spears that filled my exit. A flurry of arrows drummed against the earth and bars around me, and I threw myself against the nearest cage. I heard the gut-wrenching yowl of a big cat, and the thunk of birds meeting the earth.

'Can't a ghost catch a break in this city?' I cursed. 'Fuck!'

'Can't you use your haunting?'

'And lose you somewhere in the process? I can't hold o—'

I was knocked flat as a silver eagle landed on top of me, an arrow sticking from its breast. It gasped for air, massive wings rising and falling as if it were gliding on thermals, not sprawled in the dirt.

'This is it!' I said, pressing my hands to its feathered breast. It held no fear for me. I snapped the arrow shaft as gently as possible.

'What?'

'A way out.'

'But he's dying!'

'Yeah, and we've done that before, haven't we? This is how we escape, and I'm not leaving you behind.'

'What's gotten into you?'

'I don't know about you, Pointy, but I'm quite fed up of Temsa's company.'

'But...'

There was no time for the sword's hesitation. I saw the spotted wolf run past me, fleeing in the opposite direction. I closed my eyes and drove my mind into the eagle. It battled me even in death, uttering a piercing wail. I closed its beak for it, suddenly feeling a wash of pain in my stomach. It almost broke the haunting, but I clung on, pushing myself into its pinions and golden feet.

With the bird's nonsensical panic railing against my mind, I rolled onto my side and tested my wings, seeing my vision cloud as the pain washed over me again. I almost relished it. It was sensation, after all. I felt alive.

Clutching Pointy in my bloodstained claws, I flapped hard. I had seen birds do it plenty of times. There seemed to be no magic to it, and yet I did not move. More beasts flooded past my hiding place. Spears and bolts pursued them.

'Caltro!' cried the sword.

'I'm trying!' The answer escaped me as a screech.

I bent my knees, trying to spring into it, and I managed a moment of hovering. Again, the pain dragged me back down, along with Pointy's weight.

'Fucking bird! Fucking sword!' I screeched again. Keeping promises was a treacherous business, but I was determined.

I tried one more burst of flight. This time, I reached the lip of the nearby cage. I grasped it with my free talons and hurled myself into the air in pure hope. My wings beat the air frantically and I felt it like liquid under me. Letting the wings guide me, I pressed against it, and as an arrow whistled past my pinions, I wheeled for the spiked edges of the wall.

'Up! Up!' the sword yelled.

Clang! His obsidian blade sheared one of the spikes from its rack and sent it spinning to the cobbles below. I watched the walls pass beneath me and raised my head to see the city sprawling ahead.

For a moment, I felt the possibility: the freedom only a creature with wings and wind under them could feel. A freedom to go anywhere, away from all this strife and pain, to where only the sky mattered. The breeze buoyed me up and I felt a powerful urge to keep flapping, to get as far away from—

Thump! The arrow struck me square in the ribs, sending me rolling through the air. The sword met the earth before I did, and as I crash-landed in a barrel of mouldy food scraps, I burst from the eagle's body and rolled into a blue heap in the gutter.

Dead gods only knew how many kinds of effluence I dragged my face out of. I was thankful for my lack of a sense of smell, but I still came away thrashing. Shit was shit, after all. My arms beat the air like wings for a moment before I remembered myself.

Pointy was embedded in a doorstep a short distance away, and it took me far too much heaving and hauling to free him.

'I don't like flying,' he admitted, as I used him as a walking cane. There was no injury, just a punishing dizziness and exhaustion. The bird's dying moments were still washing through me. I flinched at an echoing clash of steel, still feeling its fear. I spared a glance for the eagle, bundled up in the barrel. It was an ignoble end for such a glorious beast, but I had no time for a proper burial. I could already hear whistles in the surrounding streets, barely audible over the cackling flocks of birds escaping from Serek Finel's zoo. Even at night, their strange colours shone. I saw one bird gliding sedately and alone towards the desert. It was the golden owl, glittering in the fires from below. Before it was lost to sight, it turned its eye on me, and somehow it found me there, naked and crouched between two buildings.

'Caltro?' whispered Pointy. 'The guards are coming.'

I nodded to the sword, but made no answer.

'What do we do now?' he asked of me.

At the end of it all, there was only one choice. 'Correct me if I'm wrong, but I think it's time we got our freedom. Don't you?'

Before he could answer, I broke into a run, heading for the glittering core of the city.

The story concludes in

Book Three of the
CHASING GRAVES TRILOGY

For all of my books, fantasy worlds, social media,
Patreon and Discord, wander over to:

www.linktr.ee/bengalley

ABOUT THE AUTHOR

Ben Galley is a British author of dark and epic fantasy books who currently loiters in Vancouver, Canada. Since publishing his debut Emaneska Series, Ben has released the award-winning weird western Scarlet Star Trilogy, *The Heart of Stone*, the critically-acclaimed Chasing Graves Trilogy, and the Scalussen Chronicles.

When he isn't conjuring up strange new stories or arguing the finer points of magic systems and dragon anatomy, Ben explores the Canadian wilds, sips Scotch single malts, and snowboards very, very badly. One day he hopes to haunt an epic treehouse in the mountains.

SUGGESTED LISTENING

Below you'll find a Spotify playlist that is a tribute to the various songs that inspired, fuelled, and otherwise invigorated me during the writing of the *Chasing Graves Trilogy*. I hope you enjoy it.

Matter	*Drift*
ARCANE ROOTS	HANDS LIKE HOUSES
In Cold Blood	*Silence*
ALT-J	OUR LAST NIGHT
Everlong	*Monstrous Things*
FOO FIGHTERS	PICTURESQUE
Cold Cold Cold	*Back To Me*
CAGE THE ELEPHANT	OF MICE & MEN
Pardon Me	*A Light In A Darkened World*
INCUBUS	KILLSWITCH ENGAGE
Lost On You – Elk Road Remix	*That's Just Life*
LP, ELK ROAD	MEMPHIS MAY FIRE
Saturnz Barz (feat. Popcaan)	*Cycling Trivialities*
GORILLAS, POPCAAN	JOSÉ GONZÁLEZ
Broken People	*Set Free*
LOGIC, RAG'N'BONE MAN	KATIE GRAY
King of Wishful Thinking	*Hurt*
GO WEST	JOHNNY CASH
Ocean View	*Chalkboard*
ONE DAY AS A LION	JÓHANN JÓHANNSSON

Ingram Content Group UK Ltd.
Milton Keynes UK
UKHW041543180723
425314UK00033B/240/J